FLAME AND SPARROW

A COURT OF THE MARR NOVEL

S.M. GAITHER

A COURT OF THE MARR NOVEL

FLAME & SPARROW

S. M. GAITHER

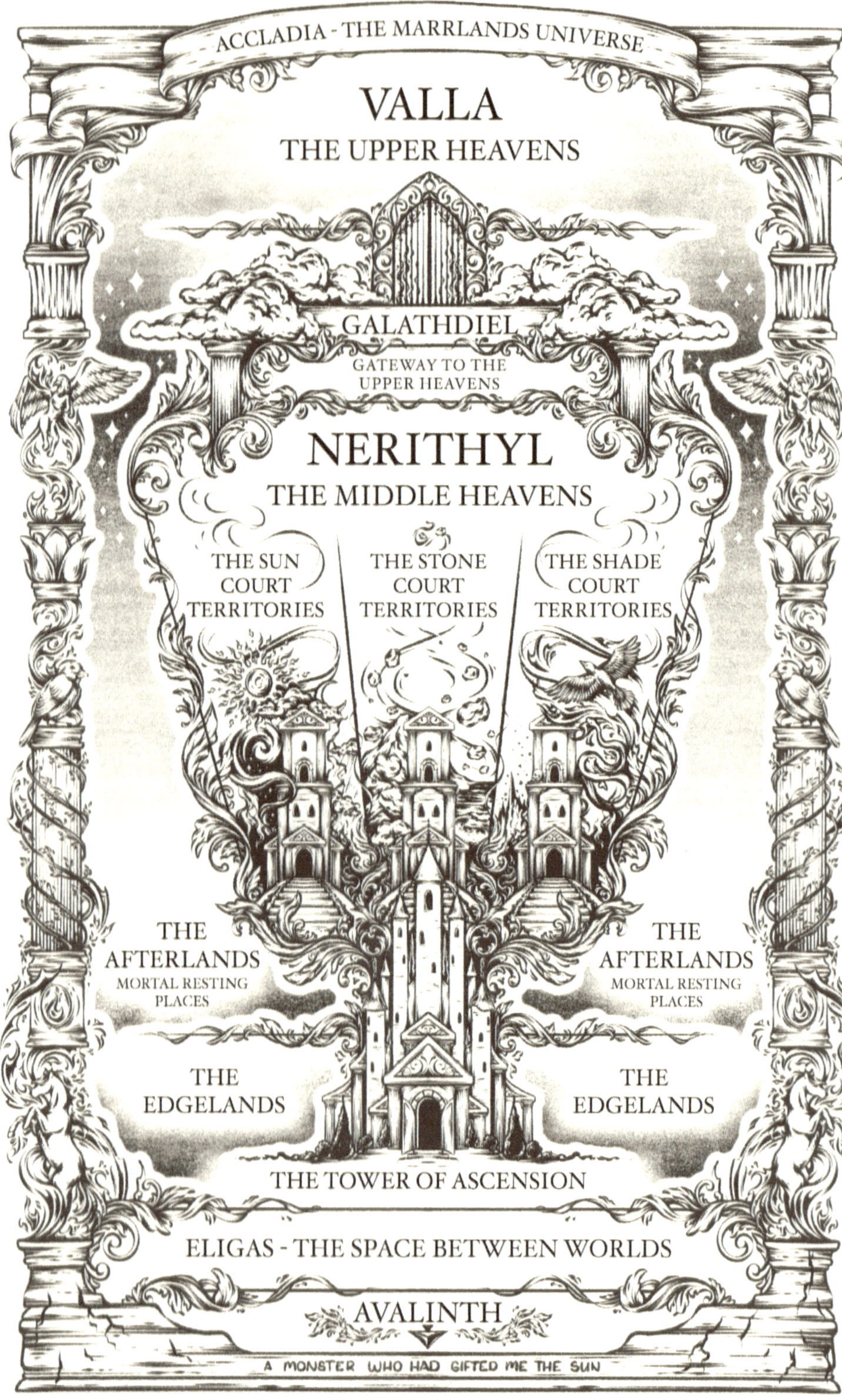

ACCLADIA - THE MARRLANDS UNIVERSE
VALLA
THE UPPER HEAVENS
GALATHDIEL
GATEWAY TO THE UPPER HEAVENS
NERITHYL
THE MIDDLE HEAVENS
THE SUN COURT TERRITORIES
THE STONE COURT TERRITORIES
THE SHADE COURT TERRITORIES
THE AFTERLANDS
MORTAL RESTING PLACES
THE AFTERLANDS
MORTAL RESTING PLACES
THE EDGELANDS
THE EDGELANDS
THE TOWER OF ASCENSION
ELIGAS - THE SPACE BETWEEN WORLDS
AVALINTH
A MONSTER WHO HAD GIFTED ME THE SUN

ACCLADIA - THE MARRLANDS UNIVERSE
NERITHYL
ELIGAS - THE SPACE BETWEEN WORLDS
AVALINTH
THE MORTAL REALM
MORTAL HELLS
MERKTH
BETHORAS
NYLTH
WE WERE LIVING LEGENDS TO SOME

THE DIVINE COURTS

AUTHOR'S NOTE

Please be aware that this is an adult/new adult fantasy book that contains explicit sexual content, violence, and adult language. It also contains depictions of death, emotional abuse/manipulation, and trauma that may be upsetting for some readers. Read and enjoy at your own risk!

For everyone who's ever been told they're 'too much'—

Go ahead and burn as brightly as you want to.

PROLOGUE

Once, when I was a child, I accidentally set fire to a god.

I recalled the flames now as I stared at my sister's empty, blood-soaked bed. The way their heat had licked at my body was remarkably similar to the scorch I currently felt creeping over my skin. The way my vision tunneled, unable to focus on anything but the bright and burning spots of red...it was the same. As was the sick twist in my gut telling me I was in trouble.

The difference was that now my sister was not here to get me out of trouble as she had that fiery day—as she *always* had.

"Karys!"

The sound of my name shocked me into moving, sending me tripping backwards, stumbling out of my sister's tiny room and into the hallway.

A hand landed on my arm, strong and unyielding. Steadying me. I finally managed to pry my gaze away from Savna's bloodied bed, and I turned to face the person standing behind me.

Andrel's bright hazel eyes met mine for a fraction of a moment before they caught on the horror inside the room at my back. His lips parted slightly. His breath caught briefly. The tiniest glimpses of emotion—most would have missed them, but I knew Andrel. I knew when he was rattled, when he was afraid. It didn't happen often.

There were voices rising outside. A fierce wind swirling stronger, creaking the trees and rattling the thatched roof of the house. The air felt strange, prickling against my skin, leaving an acrid taste in my mouth if I dared to inhale too deeply.

An unspoken understanding passed between Andrel and me.

This place is not safe.

I didn't know what was happening. What sort of darkness was falling upon my home, or when—*if*—I'd be able to return to it. So I pulled free of Andrel and took what I could of my sister, sweeping things off her desk into a bag, grabbing items from the trunk by her bed and tossing them in with no real method or reasoning. I didn't even look at what was inside before cinching the bag shut.

I just knew I couldn't leave all of her behind.

Hoisting the bag onto my shoulder, I turned and raced down the hallway, through the back door, and past the marks that had been clawed into the frame. My gaze snagged on the deepest of those marks.

A shiver skipped down my spine.

I shook it off and ran faster.

Andrel followed closely behind. We didn't stop until we were deep within the woods that stretched for miles behind my family's tiny farm. We approached a steep, rock-strewn hill— too steep for anyone to easily descend on us from above—and settled in with our backs against it, scanning the area before us for threats. The trees were thick here, wrapped in the puffy white flowers and timid green leaves of early spring. The weaving of their branches seemed almost unnatural, as though they had reached out and worked together to tangle up as tightly as possible.

The softest of footfalls snapped our attention back in the direction we'd come from.

Our heightened elven senses confirmed we were being followed, but also helped us relax soon after; we recognized the scent on the air. Earth and a tang of something fruity.

A familiar face appeared in the darkness. Deep-set green eyes, the slightly crooked nose he'd broken as a child, sharp cheekbones framed by waves of pale golden hair—Cillian. He was my sister's closest friend, and had probably been paying one of his regular late night visits to her, only to stumble on to a scene of...

What?

I still didn't know, still couldn't think clearly enough to make sense of what we'd just fled from.

I only hoped, for Cillian's sake, that he hadn't gone into the house.

If he had, he said nothing of the blood, or the strange voices, or the odd airs that had swallowed up my home— nothing at all for a very long time, until his breath caught, nearly choking him before he cleared his throat and said, "There were beasts prowling around your house."

My heart sank like a stone into the pit of my stomach. "Beasts?"

"Divine ones."

We'd been right to run.

But where were those beasts now?

Cillian choked on another breath. "And Savna..."

Andrel's expression was grim as he finished the sentence himself. "...Can handle whatever danger we're dealing with better than most. She might have escaped. She might be hiding somewhere safe and sound; no point in worrying yet."

As if to challenge that lack of worry, a rush of wind roared between us, strong enough to lift pebbles from the hillside and pelt us with them.

Cillian's usually stoic form broke a little. A soft gasp slipped from his mouth. He knelt and braced a hand on the rocky ground, tucking his head toward his chest as if fighting the urge to vomit.

I stayed on my feet, though I shared the same fight to keep my stomach in check—because it wasn't a natural wind caressing my cheek and making it tingle. Not a normal breeze lifting my hair, curling the dark, normally straight strands this way and that...

It was wind caused by magic, just as it had been at my house.

And not the cursed and earthbound type that some of the elven-kind, like myself, still possessed—this magic was stronger. Deadlier. *Divine.* It made my eyes sting and my bones tremble before leaving a terrible taste of salt and metal on my tongue.

"It's the same as the other week," breathed Cillian, shaking his bowed head. He wore his fear openly now. It was written in the creases of his forehead—the only part of his face I could see —and lifting bumps along his skin, making the pale hairs on his arms stand on end. "They're getting bolder."

The middle-gods, he meant. The Marr. The ones who had taken our kind's place at the righthand of the three Moraki, our Creators.

The Moraki were the three most powerful beings in all the

realms, but it was the damnable Marr flooding *this* particular realm with magic, rallying humans against us, trying to choke out what remained of our kind. It was a war that had raged for generations between us, turning particularly violent in the past decade or so.

Tonight the raging violence felt closer than ever.

"It *is* the same as before, isn't it?" Cillian asked, shockingly green eyes wide as he finally lifted his head again. "I'm not going mad, am I? The stench of the magic, the feel of it...We *all* felt it coming close the other week, didn't we? We should have heeded the warning and laid low. They were targeting us. That much is clear now."

Andrel ran a hand through his hair, black as fresh ink and darker even than mine. "You're not going mad." A humorless smile tugged up one corner of his full lips. "No more mad than the rest of us, at least."

"It was an omen. An *omen*. And we ignored it—"

Andrel clicked his tongue and began to pace, while I tried —unsuccessfully—to shove the memories of that omen from my mind.

Exactly two weeks ago, in the dead of night, a divine...*beast* had shown up on the doorstep of my house, its side shredded and bloody, its massive antlers broken and dangling from its head, a trail of magic following in its wake and leaching the life and color from everything it touched.

It had died on our threshold, its claws sinking into the doorframe as though desperately trying to hold on to Avalinth, this mortal realm that I—and the rest of the elven-kind—had been relegated to.

Andrel persuaded my sister to burn its body. I'd watched from the window of my room as they dragged it into the wheat fields and dealt with it. There had been no incense, no blessed water, no prayers. No rituals at all, just fire curling bright and wicked in the dark and a cloud of smoke rising, settling over our house and land.

For three days that cloud had hung there with seemingly no intention of moving.

Even after it finally dispersed, the salt and metal taste in the air lingered.

Word had spread of the incident, and the human villages we sometimes frequented had shunned us even more than usual because of it.

Disrespectful heathens, they hissed, while refusing to buy or trade with us. *Inviting curses. Did they kill the creature? Did they do it on purpose? They show no remorse, and now the curses follow. It serves them right.*

My sister had been quick to snap back at them. *What do a few more curses matter to us, given the hell we already endure in this kingdom?*

I sucked in a sharp breath at the memory of her words, wishing more than anything that I could hear her voice. I fell back against a thick tree, grateful for its strength, as mine seemed to be failing me more and more with each passing second.

Andrel finished pacing the edge of our circle and moved back to me. He placed a hand on each of my shoulders, his intense gaze forcing me from my thoughts. "We'll find her. I swear it."

I managed a nod.

The heat was back on my skin, creeping up to my scalp, making my face flush. I fought the urge to pick at the burn scars that covered much of the left side of my face. It used to be a bad habit.

Used to be.

I'd stopped years ago, burying the tendency as deeply as I'd buried the memory of what had caused the scars in the first place.

It had been an accident. A slip of my hand that sent my lantern tumbling to the ground, igniting the maps shoved underneath a table—a table holding wooden carvings of upper-gods I was meant to be praying to.

The maps should not have been there.

They were pretend charts to pretend treasures, remnants of a game Savna and I had played the day before. I'd stuffed them under the shrine table, determined to keep my sister from finding them, knowing that any place with ties to the divine would be the last place she'd look for anything.

One of the maps had been drenched in ceremonial oil spilled from somewhere above, Mother had decided afterward. It was the only explanation for how quickly things had ignited —so quickly that the flames had leapt from the table and statues, setting fire to my clothing and hair before I could escape.

My sister—the one who had finally managed to put out the flames—swore it was magic. That the statues were cursed, as were all things dealing with the damnable gods. Cursed and just waiting for a chance to burn their fallen, disobedient *mistakes.*

I'd dreamt about the same thing for weeks afterward. The upper-god of the Shade glaring down at me, making me feel small and insignificant and *wrong*...And then fire catching on his wings, wrapping up his body that turned out to be made of nothing more than wood.

But the statues never truly burned in my dreams. The gods were always still there when the smoke and flames cleared. Always glaring back at me with their cruel, carved smiles.

"Karys." My eyes blinked open at the sound of Andrel's

tired, hoarse voice. I didn't remember closing them. Didn't remember slumping down against the tree, or drifting off, but apparently I had—the first hints of daylight were filtering through the tangled trees. Birds were chirping. A rooster crowed somewhere in the distance.

Loud.

It was all so terribly loud. Like I didn't belong here, and every noise threatened to announce me, to give my presence away.

Andrel offered me a hand. I let him pull me to my feet. My knees buckled and my stomach churned more violently than ever, but I stayed upright. He began to walk, and I followed without bothering to ask where we were going.

As we walked, my hands twitched and fumbled for solid things to hold. I pulled my bag around to my chest and pawed through its pockets, my fingers eventually closing around something I couldn't resist pulling out.

A thin but strong cord of leather came first, and then the carved wooden charm that hung heavily from its center. A sparrow-shaped charm. A gift from our father to Savna—he'd given me a matching one, but I'd lost it just a few months later. I'd been devastated.

This was not how I'd wanted to replace it.

I stopped walking, my thumb tracing the wing curled around the bird's body. It was well-made, fluid and alive-looking, as if it might unfurl those wings at any moment and take off despite being made of thick wood.

Andrel slowed, glancing back at me, frowning.

I tried to speak. Failed.

"We'll find her," he said again.

My heart felt as if it might crack in two. But I trusted Andrel nearly as much as I trusted my sister. He had a way of making impossible things seem not only *possible*, but probable —not just to me, but to everyone who spent more than a few moments in his presence.

I clutched the tiny sparrow tight in my palm, and I didn't argue with him.

Weeks passed.

We didn't find her.

Months passed.

Nothing still.

The days rose and fell like violent waves against this jagged and rocky stretch of my life, and soon I came to more fully understand what Savna had known from a much younger age —that the gods took whatever they wanted and did not give back.

I saw the devastating pattern of it all so clearly now.

The Marr were the ones who had taken our identities, after all. Called us the unworthy ones. The mistakes. The Fallen. They had tried to erase us, crush us, made the humans hate us, turned us all against one another so that they could distract from whatever atrocities they wanted to commit in order to further take over this realm.

Taking, taking, *taking.*

My mother had been among those who gave willingly. But my father had rebelled, and he'd died when I was thirteen—an accident, we'd been told.

I no longer believed that.

Mother had withdrawn into herself after his death, spending her days drifting like dandelion fluff in the wind, her only outings to the shrines popping up at a relentless pace across our kingdom, her only words coming in the form of prayers and one-sided conversations with the statues in those shrines. She'd been a follower of the gods before; now it became her entire identity.

I'd tried to take on the same identity, for a time. I hadn't wanted her to be taken from me, too, so I'd knelt and prayed side-by-side with her for nearly five years—until one dreary spring morning when she packed up and disappeared, off on a pilgrimage to prove her devotion to the new gods of our world.

Good riddance, my sister had said. We'd managed on our own ever since, with Savna becoming more and more like our father every day—a rebel with her sights set on destroying the divine.

Now she was gone, too.

All of them were gone, and I realized that every major hurt or loss I'd suffered could be traced back to the gods.

Every. Single. One.

And those gods...oh, how I started to truly *hate* them.

Soon I could no longer remember a time before the hate. Before the burning. I forgot the statues, the prayers, the sacraments my mother had so fervently insisted upon throughout my childhood—it all left me so *quickly*, like a tree without any roots, a ship caught in a storm without its anchors.

Such fragile, useless, unsteady things.

Which was why sometimes I wondered if my childhood memory was faulty, and if setting fire to that smiling god had really been an accident at all.

CHAPTER I

Five Years Later

IF I DIE IN THIS TEMPLE TONIGHT, AT LEAST MY death will fan the flames of our rebellion.

This was what I told myself over and over—an affirmation that kept my muscles loose as I scaled the walls, a vow that cleared my mind as I pulled myself onto the sloped roof of the temple's second story.

The incline here was steeper than I'd anticipated. I felt heavier the higher I climbed, my bottom half dragging as though someone had filled my boots with rocks. But I kept my balance.

Somehow, I kept my balance.

Gritting my teeth, I felt my way along the roof, grappling for a better hold, ignoring the burning in my arms as I pulled myself upward. I was breathtakingly high at this point, enough that much of the city of Cauldra—with all its cramped and colorful, ramshackle houses and trash-lined streets—had started to spin and blur beneath me.

I was not particularly fond of heights.

Andrel had only chuckled when I'd reminded him of this fear earlier. He knew I wouldn't argue with his plan, fear or no fear. None of us ever did. And—to his credit, I suppose—all of us had survived every plan he'd ever come up with.

So far.

I took a deep, bracing breath. I was here, now, and I would have no room for fear in my mind as long as I stayed focused on my plan and purpose.

After shifting my feet into a more solid stance, I let my claws extend from my fingertips and dug them into a crease between the stone slab tiles of the roof. Now more tightly secured, I fully gathered my balance before resuming the climb upward, eventually coming to rest in a nearly horizontal position with my fingers curled around the lip of a recessed skylight.

I peered down through the glass, watching for movement in the room beneath me, scarcely daring to breathe.

When I was certain no threats waited below, I carefully rose into a crouched position and contemplated my next move.

In the dark glass of the skylight, I watched my reflection tucking a strand of raven-black hair behind my ear. My chest tightened at the sight of my still-extended claws. My eyes averted out of habit, but I swallowed my distaste and kept the claws out. No one was up here to see them; why not make use of them? So what if—

Enough, I inwardly chastised myself.

There was no time to waste thinking about these things.

I took a small, sharp knife from the thick pouch attached to my belt and carefully tested it on a corner of the glass. It sliced straight through, pinching off a neat, sharp little triangle that *tink tink tinked* its way over the stone roof.

I held the blade more carefully after this, even as my forearm tingled and burned from the effort of keeping it steady. It was sharp enough to sever a finger with little effort, Cillian had warned, and I should have known better than to doubt him; he was the expert on weapons.

Meanwhile, I was the one responsible for diagrams and details, while Andrel was usually the face of our operations—the one most likely to talk us out of trouble...and to appear on wanted posters afterward. He often joked that his goal was to collect enough of them to line the walls of his bedroom, and he was well on his way to achieving this.

We had more who regularly joined our cause, but the three of us were the constants. All the others had refused to join us tonight, calling it too risky, claiming that too many eyes were fixed on this newly-constructed temple.

That's the point, Andrel had informed them, heatedly. *Let as many people as possible see that not everyone wants the new gods in our world. Then maybe those people will be brave enough to step forward and declare the same thing.*

But even he hadn't been able to rally our usual support.

I also suspected that usual support was too wary of the god the humans were dedicating this temple to, and that fear about his retaliation was the *real* reason no one had shown up tonight.

I continued to slice the glass of said temple away, carefully and methodically, until I had opened a space wide enough to slide my body through; it didn't require a very large opening.

Lithe and elegant, like a swan, my father had always insisted.

Tall and gangly, like an awkward stork, was usually my reply.

However people described me, I'd always been skinny, and the years spent without my sister and parents had made me even thinner. In more ways than one, really.

My shoulder still caught a rough strip of the severed glass as I dropped down to the room below, and although the coat I wore—my sister's coat—was thick enough to keep the edge from cutting into my skin, the rip of the fabric was painfully loud. Little tears like these already covered the coat, and my heart clenched as I wondered how much more it could take before ripping completely apart. I was getting better with a needle and thread, but patching the torn places didn't feel the same as simply keeping it in one piece to begin with.

I pulled the garment more tightly around my body as I oriented myself in the dark room I'd landed in.

Mosaic tiles crisscrossed the floor in bright patterns. Elegant swaths of gold and crimson were draped along the walls, the fabric so thin and delicate it stirred with my movements, creating the appearance of softly dancing flames. The air felt thick, heavy, and smelled of various spices and lingering candle smoke.

I darted from one room to the next, soundless as a cat, my senses honed for any possible threats. With each new room, I paused just long enough to observe and memorize things. Beauty and opulence oozed from every corner, but I refused to let it distract me; I only cared about the layout of the space and any objects that might get in Cillian's way.

Once I had a clear idea of every room on the second floor, I slipped to the first floor and took similar mental notes. Then I found a tucked-away alcove to hide in, reached for the scrap of parchment and my drawing stick, and I made a quick diagram of all these spaces—a simple, concise map.

As I put the finishing touches on it and folded the scrap of parchment up, I caught the scent of fresh, damp earth. Just a small clump of it...likely carried in on a pair of boots.

Footsteps confirmed my fears a moment later: There were *two* sets of boots clomping through an adjacent hallway, drawing steadily closer to where I hid.

I pressed deeper into the alcove, attempting to fold up small enough for the shadows to fully engulf me.

The nearby window was covered in an ornamental curtain made up of more strips of delicate crimson fabric, dividing up the moonlight falling into the room. I closed my eyes to stop myself from imagining movement; the longer I stared at the columns of moonlight, the more they seemed like claws raking outward and trying to expose me.

My hand went to the dagger sheathed against my back. I had a small pouch of kastor-blossom poison on my belt, too. Just a handful of that powder would easily rise and rapidly engulf my approaching company, and—if they were weak little humans, as I suspected—it would be enough to render them unconscious for hours.

Which, given the plans we had for this temple, would ulti-mately mean their deaths.

The floorboards groaned. Whispers reached my ears, but any individual words were impossible to pick out. I could sort out scents beyond the mud now, however—the saltiness hovering beneath sweat, the certain dry earthiness that enveloped them even when they didn't wear dirty boots...definitely humans.

I held my breath as a door creaked. The sound of someone shuffling through linens and the clunking of ceremonial receptacles being sorted through followed soon after. I tensed further at the thought of these humans spending hours in the nearby rooms, setting up and practicing whatever foolish rituals they had planned for the upcoming temple dedication.

Luckily, they kept moving after a moment, their footsteps fading into the distance.

I hadn't heard the door shut, which made me think they would be back for more supplies. I crept quickly from my hiding place. Rather than risk an encounter, I opted to go back the way I'd come from and exit through a second-floor window.

As I hoisted myself out onto a narrow stretch of roof, a sudden chorus of barking dogs startled me. My foot slipped, and if not for my claws hooking into the gutter, I would have suffered a very unpleasant landing on the cobblestones below.

Another reason to be glad you have those claws.

I again swallowed down the complicated feelings I had toward them and kept moving.

I knew I was lucky compared to some—other family lines had been cursed with far more beastly features than claws, and not everyone could retract those features and hide them the way I could.

They still bothered me. Because my ancestors had never had such...*things*. No elves had until after the Fall, when the three Creators had stripped us of our divine magic. Our scholars often argued about whether or not these mutated features were another intentional punishment, or just an unexpected side-effect of having most of our magic ripped away.

Some of my kind even pretended these things were parting *gifts* rather than curses. Usually, these pretenders were the same ones who claimed the Creator gods would take us back if only we prayed enough. Begged enough.

Myself, I'd fully lost my appetite for praying and begging some time ago.

Five years ago, to be precise—since the day after my twentieth birthday, when I'd found the blood in my sister's bed.

I would never pray to them again.

Instead, I was going to help destroy them and all of their servants—one shrine, one statue, one temple at a time. To drive them away and reclaim this world that had once been ours. This had been my father's life goal, and then my sister's.

Now that they were gone, I'd sworn I would finish the job myself.

At night, I dreamed of the divine realms all collapsing into utter and total darkness, their magic and power reduced to nothing more than pinpricks of fading light.

My first thought upon waking was a similar darkness—a kind of hatred that grew and grew until it collapsed and folded in on itself, and the resulting implosion was violent enough to thrust me from my bed and into another day. Another chance for revenge.

Even now I was picturing the temple beneath me cracking in two, the dedicated riches inside of it tumbling down into broken, useless piles.

Destruction. Revenge. They were the only paths to closure for me. I needed them like I needed the very air I breathed, and tonight...tonight I wouldn't rest until I'd accomplished both in some capacity.

I leapt to the lower roof and then dropped lightly to the ground. A high fence of black iron rose in front of and behind me, stretching farther than I could see. I followed it to the back of the temple, where it curved and stretched around an elaborate courtyard. Each section of the yard was anchored by a different centerpiece, most of them massive statues and fountains featuring various divine beings and beasts.

So much money spent appealing to immortals who could turn on them at any moment.

Fools.

The humans had been created after my kind. As our replacements, according to most legends. Some were blessed with traces of divine magic at birth, but nothing like what we had once had; they were essentially weaker versions of elves who would pose less of a threat to their Creators. Although, when they passed these legends down to their children, they didn't call themselves weak, of course—they just called us monsters.

Most seemed unable to comprehend that they could be forsaken and cursed just as we had been, and that sometimes what was considered *monstrous* changed depending on the lighting.

A shadow moved across the path ahead, bringing me to a stop. I recognized both the scent of citrus and the familiar light and quick weight of the accompanying steps, so I was unsurprised when Cillian rounded the corner directly in front of me.

His cloak covered his pale hair and skin, its flowing fabric shifting through multiple shades of black and purple as he moved, blending perfectly with the night. But his eyes made him impossible to miss; their unsettling green glow was another example of the beastly *gifts* that some elves had. Mine did not glow as his did, but they were a similar shade of too-bright green, and we were often mistaken for siblings because of it—in spite of my much darker skin and hair.

He quickly looked me up and down, making sure I was relatively unscathed, as he approached. We said little, and we lingered mere seconds in each other's company...just long enough for me to give him the map I'd created and to warn him about the humans I'd heard inside.

"Get somewhere safe," he told me as we parted.

"Safe?" I teased. "Where is that?"

He gave me a wry smile. Then he was gone, sliding a bag from his shoulder as he went, searching through it for the first weapon he would be strategically planting.

I wasn't truly worried about him encountering the people inside; he'd faced far worse odds and emerged completely intact. We all had.

It was simply easier to avoid the humans if possible.

And tonight, we didn't want to give those humans *any* chance to meddle with our plans. The weapons Cillian had built for this target were new, so we were working with more uncertainty and less margin for error than usual.

He'd shown me those weapons and attempted to explain how they worked—*hang-fire bombs*, he'd called them. The fuses would burn slowly, silently winding their way through the cylinder-shaped casings, eventually igniting the firestone powder in the center.

Their power was modest, and he'd only managed to procure enough powder to create three of them; firestones were in short supply in this region. Still, they would be enough to bring down the walls closest to where they were placed...which was where my mapping of the building came into play. As quickly as I could diagram a building, he could pinpoint its weak spots. Places our weapons could do the most damage, igniting rippling waves of destabilizing destruction, and then...

Boom.

And we'd be far away by that point, of course.

I kept moving, and soon I encountered proof that Andrel had been busy with his part of the night's plans as well: three unconscious guards blocked my path. The air still smelled faintly of the kastor-blossom poison used to take them out.

The three men were heaped together directly underneath a polished arch. The arch stretched impressively tall and glistened beautifully in the moonlight, the runes etched on its face appearing to glow from within, but it didn't look particularly sturdy. If Cillian's bombs did their job, there was a very good chance the bodies beneath it would be buried by broken stone.

I looked toward the open field across the road, sizing up the distance. I was stronger than any human; it wouldn't be difficult to haul them to a safer location—though I'd probably only be able to manage one at a time.

"You're not thinking of protecting these three from whatever fallout Cillian causes, are you?"

I fought the urge to jump, cutting Andrel a cold, sideways glance as he approached from the shadows. "Of course not."

He continued as though I hadn't spoken. "Because you know that if your roles were reversed, they wouldn't think twice about leaving *you* to be crushed by this falling temple. Or worse." He leaned his shoulder against the inside of the arch, picking at something beneath one of his nails as he added, "In fact, they would likely move you into a better position to make certain you were completely buried."

I nodded, my gaze lingering over the unconscious men for a minute longer before searching for something else to focus on. "You missed two others, by the way," I said, nodding toward the temple.

"Did I?" He smiled without taking his eyes off his nails.

Understanding shivered through me. "You used a different poison on them?" My voice cracked a bit, my throat suddenly dry. "Wolfweed?"

He yawned. "I imagine it's started to work by this point."

Five deaths.

Wolfweed worked differently compared to the kastor-blossom's poison...more slowly. And though it fully paralyzed limbs, it usually left the brain alone. The two humans I'd heard inside the temple wouldn't be rendered unconscious the way the three guards under the arch had been. They would be awake to see their deaths falling toward them, but unable to do anything about it...except scream, perhaps.

I shook the image from my thoughts and kept moving, pacing the grounds and resisting the urge to pick at the burn scars on my face.

It seemed barbaric, but the gods we were dealing with were capable of far more brutality than anything we could dream up.

Eventually, the humans would thank us for these kinds of barbaric but necessary demonstrations, for our role in driving the gods away. This realm would be much better off if the once-powerful elven houses ruled it once more—a point our ancestors had tried to make diplomatically, only to be ignored.

My pacing came to a stop at one of the centerpieces of the immaculate grounds: a towering marble statue of a beautiful male deity. Slender hounds with fire-wrapped bodies curled around his feet. A symbol was etched into the pedestal beneath him, one shaped like a twisted burst of flame.

So this was him—the middle-god of Fire and Forging. The one this new temple was meant to be dedicated to during the upcoming Feast of the Shade celebration. *Dra' Zerachiel*, my kind called him. The humans called him *Dravyn*.

What a shame his temple would be in ruins by the time he arrived.

Maybe he would be so offended by this that he wouldn't even bother to come.

One could hope.

"Ugly brute, isn't he?" Andrel said, casting an indifferent glance toward the statue before turning his attention back to his nails.

I nodded, even though I didn't agree. In truth, it took me a long moment to stop circling the god and pry my eyes away from him. The sculptor had clearly been in love with her subject matter; it showed in the powerful lines of his muscles, in the elegant posture of his body, in the lifelike rendering of his arrogant smile.

But there was a very good chance this statue looked nothing like the actual God of Fire—and we wouldn't know, even if it did.

He was one of the Marr—the middle-gods who directly served the world's three upper-gods, the Creators—but he was still relatively young, and not one of the original deities who'd held that position. He had ascended to divine status only a short time ago, and I wasn't aware of any clear, credible sightings of him in this realm.

But like all of the Marr, he'd been mortal once.

This was partly how the upper-gods tricked humans into such blind devotion: by making them believe they were more connected to the divine than they actually were. They used the Marr as their servants in this realm to try and bridge the space between them and mortals. Those Marr even blessed some humans with trace amounts of magic, further quieting any skeptics that might arise—an act that simultaneously filled this realm with more divine magic, giving them a current of energy to feed off of, thus continuing their cycle of power and dominance.

The truth was that whatever humanity the middle-gods possessed was stripped from them the moment they ascended;

there was evidence of this everywhere, if one only bothered to look.

The chaos accompanying the Fire God's very ascension was well-documented, even—mountains roaring to life and spewing molten rock, wildfires raging across the lands, clouds of smoke blotting out the sun for weeks. Plenty of fragile humans had perished during the turmoil, and speculation about how powerful this new middle-god must have been to create such carnage still made for conversation fodder to this very day.

But they spoke of the carnage in awed tones rather than fearful ones, so eager to see themselves in the divine that they willingly overlooked the beastly parts.

Hence the statue before me being shaped as a mortal—albeit one whose beauty was arguably inhuman.

"I wonder how long it will be before that ugly face makes an appearance in this realm?" I don't know why I voiced the thought aloud. Or why I was once again staring at the stone likeness of the god, or why my mind seemed determined to try and imagine a living, breathing, more colorful version of him.

Andrel sauntered closer, sparing another glance at the massive statue before shrugging. "At the rate these temples are being built, it's only a matter of time."

This fire god was so new to the role that he didn't have divine servants chosen yet—which was, of course, a major reason behind the construction of temples like the one before us: The people of Cauldra wanted to draw him into their city in hopes that he'd choose one of them.

It was the last rung on the divine hierarchy ladder, and they hoped to climb it. The Marr served the Moraki, but the Marr had direct servants as well—the Miratar, or the lesser-spirits, as they were usually called. But they were still divine, despite being *lesser*, still powerful and able to walk in the immortal realms alongside the gods.

And so many humans believed they were just one prayer, one ritual, one temple dedication away from the honor. So many willing slaves, so eager to sell their souls and safety for a chance to more completely bind themselves to the divine...

The thought made me sick.

A cold wind whipped to life, carrying the scent of the nearby cedar forest and drawing clouds across the half-moon. Darkness overtook the garden, and I spat at the god's feet before turning and walking away, determined not to look at his face—or any likeness of it—ever again.

CHAPTER 2

"Cillian is taking a long time, isn't he?" I kept my voice calm despite the pit forming in my stomach.

Andrel didn't move from his spot. For the past five minutes he'd been leaning against a willow tree, partially concealed by its flowering branches, with his head bowed in thought.

He looked far more casual than he should have given the magnitude of our plans for the night.

But that had always been Andrel, for as long as we'd known each other—powerful certainty radiated out from him wherever he went. No matter how chaotic our adventures got, he never looked bothered or out of place.

"Let's give him a few more minutes before we start considering our backup plans," he said.

I nodded, settling down against a separate tree. We were across the street from the temple, camped out in the overgrown yard of a long-abandoned house. The juxtaposition of this rundown house and the pristine temple had not escaped my notice; I wondered vaguely what had become of the person who used to live here. They had most likely been magicless... and driven out of their home because of it.

The ones not blessed with divine magic got by well enough in this realm—better than my kind did, at least—but they were still considered a lower class, and certainly not worthy of living so close to the temple of such an important middle-god. The house would probably be torn down or repurposed soon.

More waste.

Andrel broke the quiet again only a minute later. "Your wrist," he said, stepping toward me and nodding at my left hand. "What happened to it?"

I lifted it, and only then did I notice what he had seen—a thin trail of dried blood winding out from under my sleeve.

I shrugged. "I must have nicked it when I was sliding off the roof."

"Looks pretty deep," he said, crouching before me and carefully taking my hand in his, twisting it around for a closer look. His fingertips were soft against my skin, his nails clean and smooth-edged.

Cillian always teased him about being too smart for his own good, and Andrel usually replied by informing him that the smarter you were, the less dirty you had to get your hands —a mantra befitting of the roles we would have had if not for the Fall, I supposed.

Andrel was of royal lineage. All three of us were, actually— our ancestors had belonged to separate, but equally powerful, elven houses, and they'd been among the last ones to stand against the rise of the Marr and the shifting of power in this realm. Not that it meant much now, as that...

Well, that was a long time ago.

Now we were reduced to crouching among weeds in the shadows of those gods we refused to pray to.

"It's not that deep," I mumbled, pulling my hand from Andrel's. "I didn't even notice it before now."

A pause, and then, "You could heal it easily, I bet."

"I could. But I won't."

He studied the cut a moment longer before turning away, his features relaxing into an approving smile as he did.

We'd all had magic before the Fall—some of it powerful enough to challenge the gods—but it had disappeared from most of our bloodlines at this point. Those who could still summon any power drew it, not from themselves or the gods, but from the residual energies divine magic left on the planet. *Earthbound*, was the term used by elven scholars to describe this new evolution of our magic.

I seemed to have a natural affinity for drawing healing power from the planet, and I had used this power by accident a few times when I was younger. But I was fully in control of it now, and I would bleed to death in this yard tonight before I wielded it on purpose.

No healing, no gods, no magic.

The one and only exception to my *no magic* rule was the sparrow hanging around my neck—the gift from my father to Savna, and now my most prized possession.

It was not an ordinary carving; it was infused with divine power ultimately derived from the Goddess of Control...enough magic to temporarily conceal or change small things. A brush of my fingertips over the worn wood, a bit of concentration, and even parts of my own appearance could be altered by it. I occasionally used it to round off my pointed ears and smooth the burned skin of my face.

Deep down, I hated concealing these things, and I dreamed of a day when I wouldn't feel like I needed to do it.

But for now, hiding my true self was sometimes a necessary evil.

I checked to make sure the sparrow was safe and tucked away under the layers of my clothing before taking the scrap of papyrus from my pack, along with my drawing stick, and getting back to work.

I was noticing trends in the various temples we'd visited and vandalized over the past months. Layouts that repeated themselves, rooms of predictable function, shape, and size—knowledge that could prove helpful. I was determined to recreate what I'd seen and simplify it, categorize it into useful notes that my fellow conspirators and I could make use of.

And, if nothing else, it gave me something to occupy myself with, taking my mind off Cillian.

Andrel had turned his attention back toward the temple, watching and waiting for the signal.

Cillian had a special whistle—one that emitted a sound no human would be able to hear—which he would use to let us know when he had successfully finished his task. All three of us had the same sort of instrument, and we had a simple system with them: One high-pitched note meant we needed help. Two meant to stay close, but not approach. Three meant it was time to leave.

Three short bursts of a whistle, and then this night would be over with.

I felt desperate for that sound, suddenly.

But the only sound for several minutes was the wind, along with the occasional rustle of the paper braced across my leg and the scratch of the graphite stick against it.

I tried to stay calmly focused on the paper.

I was not an artist by any means—my creations would never decorate the walls of temples or gardens like the ones at my back—but I was thorough. Exact. I liked...*lines*. Exact lines, orderly layouts, predictable things. Plans. Patterns. Patterns were everywhere if you bothered to look for them.

I sensed Andrel moving near once more, his head tilting toward my drawing for a better look. "I'm not convinced *that* isn't some kind of magic," he commented after a moment. "What normal being can recreate a place so precisely after merely walking through it? You've got a strange mind, Kare."

I glanced up, arching a brow. "Is that supposed to be a compliment?"

"Of course it is." He shrugged and flashed a smile, easy and genuine. My stomach flipped. My heart might have skipped a few times, too—a fluttering he'd undoubtedly heard. He'd heard it before, too; by this point he had to be aware of the effect that smile had on me.

Now *really* wasn't the time to be distracted by such things, however.

I put my diagramming materials away and got to my feet. My skin flushed hot as restlessness overcame me, and I wrapped my arms around myself and walked the length of the yard and back, squeezing my stomach as if I could stop all the flipping and fluttering if I just pressed tightly enough.

The feeling mercifully passed within a few moments, as it always did, like a bird with clipped wings that never truly took flight.

I forced my hands down to my sides, trying to appear perfectly composed. "I'm going to find a better vantage point," I said, "just in case something's happened and Cillian can't use our first choice of signals."

"Be careful."

I nodded and made my way to the yard's rusted iron gate, where I paused. My fingers—now clawless—tapped impatiently against the warped and peeling bars of the gate as I watched the distant temple for signs of any kind. I was so determined to stay still, watching and listening closely, that I kept holding my breath without realizing I was doing it, causing my vision to blur and a numb tingling to spread into my hands and feet.

Why was he taking so long?

He should be done by now.

No signal. No whistle, no lights, no smoke from any igniting bombs...

Unease crawling up my spine, I watched the road in both directions for a minute before cautiously crossing it and slipping once more into the temple's manicured gardens. I moved quickly and silently through the shadows, my hand resting on the knife at my belt, my skin prickling at every strange sound or scent.

I heard footsteps behind me. A female voice humming a quiet song. A clinking and rattling of what might have been jewelry—

"Are you here to pay your respects?"

I spun around and found myself face-to-face with a young woman. No—a girl. Her lightly-freckled skin was smooth, her blue eyes bright with curiosity and unclouded in the way that only eyes that hadn't seen much of the world and its horrors could be; she couldn't have been much older than fourteen.

Fourteen years old and already in this temple at this late hour of the night, a slave to whatever rituals and fidelities her fellow humans insisted on.

I didn't withdraw my knife, but I kept my hand near it just in case. Young fanatics could still be dangerous ones, in my experience.

"Well?" she prompted, placing a concerned hand on my arm. "Are you?"

"Not exactly," I replied, jerking away and trying to step past her.

She blocked my path. "Have you lost something, then?"

I didn't answer, but she looked as though I'd agreed all the same, her brows knitting together and her hands clutching a string of beads she had wrapped around her arm. I didn't have to look closely at the jewelry to know what it was composed of: three large beads to represent the Creators—the Moraki—surrounded by twelve smaller beads to represent the middle-gods—the Marr—who served them. These chains were becoming an all-too common fashion throughout the kingdoms.

"You won't find it here," she told me.

"I'm not looking for anything," I snapped. Something about her concerned, pitying expression annoyed me.

"Are you sure?"

She studied me closer. I fought the urge to shrink away from her gaze. I'd used my sister's sparrow to magic my ears and smooth away the worst of my scars while I was sitting in the yard across the street. My dark hair had also turned pale—the complete opposite of its usual raven-wing shade—in the process, so I wasn't worried about being seen. It was just...

Something about this girl made me feel wholly and fully exposed.

Keep walking, urged a quiet voice in the back of my mind.

I don't know why I didn't listen to myself.

"Never mind me," I said instead. "You should leave this place. It isn't safe tonight."

Her wide eyes stared into mine without blinking, and her hand—still clutching the beads—pressed over her heart as if unconsciously protecting it from me and my blasphemous words.

Her sleeve shifted with the movement, and I saw a crescent-shaped symbol upon her skin.

It might have passed for a birthmark if not for the way the edges of it shimmered. If she used magic, the whole of it would start to shine with a faint white glow.

Marked by the middle-goddess of the Moon—otherwise known as the Goddess of the Crossroads. The deity of directions, reflections, and lost things...those most blessed with her magic could supposedly find anything.

Which explained the girl's weird questioning; she was itching for a chance to flex her divine gifts, it seemed.

But I was not in need of her magic any more than I was in need of my own.

No magic.

No gods.

Even if I *was* missing something, the gods and their servants would be the last ones I'd ask to help me find it.

"I mean it," I told her bluntly. "You should get out of here. Now."

"The gods protect their faithful servants," she insisted. "I am safe here."

I snorted, barely resisting the urge to spit at her feet as I'd spat at the feet of the God of Fire.

Safe.

Ha.

The gods were many things. Safe was certainly not one of them. But it would be a waste of time and breath to try and convince this girl of such things. I could see it in her eyes—the blind devotion, the determined dedication. She was already too far gone.

I should have dusted her with the poison I carried to prove a point—that her gods couldn't even protect her from rebel heathens like me.

But I merely twisted my finger around the drawstring of the pouch filled with that poison, cinching it tighter, and I moved as though heading back toward the street.

The girl stared after me as I left. I could feel her gaze settling against my body like a dull knife between my shoulder blades, heavy and trying to pry me open.

Instead of crossing the street, I slipped around a tall row of hedges, crouching to make sure I was completely out of sight. Several minutes passed before I peered back toward the gardens.

She was gone.

I listened, but heard nothing. Breathed in deep, but smelled only an overwhelming variety of flowers all seemingly competing to be the most pungent. I took a few steps toward the gardens and knelt, hands pressed to the ground, thinking I might feel vibrations from the girl's movements.

Nothing.

My chest felt tight with an emotion I couldn't name. But I didn't dwell on it, as I soon heard the sound I'd been longing for: three quick bursts of a whistle.

The sound of distant footsteps moving through the temple's backyard soon followed, heading toward the forest beyond—Cillian's footsteps. Only minutes until the first bomb went off, then.

Had the Moon-kind girl gone into the temple to *pay respects*?

I loosed a long, slow breath.

"Not my problem," I muttered to a tiger-striped cat lounging in a nearby bed of bright and freshly trampled flowers. It swished its raggedy tail in reply, its black jewel eyes seeming to narrow in judgment...but *judging* was just the default expression of a cat, wasn't it?

"I told her to leave," I informed the beast.

It sneezed.

Heart in my throat, I stretched onto my toes and peered over the hedge in front of me, watching the dark windows of the temple for any sign of movement.

I saw nothing. But I *imagined* smoke the longer I stared— curls of it twisting through the windows, dark and wicked, just like the ominous smoke that had risen over our farm's fields in the weeks before my sister's disappearance...

Just my imagination.

I shook the images off and reached for the sparrow resting against my throat, partly to keep my hands from reaching for my burned face. Even though the magic of my sister's necklace had smoothed my scars away, I would have sworn I could still feel heat radiating from the ruined skin underneath.

A sudden *pop* echoed through the night, followed by a flash of bright light.

The cat hissed, leaping up and darting toward the road. I calmly followed it without looking back.

Warning flashes. Cillian had told us to expect two of them before the main explosion. *We should be well on our way to escaping before the second one lights up the night.*

Andrel was already several hundred feet away, strolling casually up the street. I caught up to him slowly, drifting to his side, not drawing any more attention than necessary.

Another *pop*—much louder this time. The ground shook. A few less-sturdy looking houses rattled. Several startled screams rang out at the second flash of light, and people began to stumble out of their houses, or hang out of their windows, searching for explanations.

Andrel was softly counting down the seconds. Cillian's weapons were proving perfect, as usual, their timing a precise and predictable work of art.

Five, four, three, two, one—

Boom.

We were already far enough away that the blast of bright heat didn't even make me flinch—though bumps did rise along my skin at the sound of splitting stone that followed soon after.

Andrel wrapped an arm around my waist. I huddled closer to him as if I was just another frightened resident of this human village, only sneaking occasional glances back at the burning temple. To any passerby, we would have looked like an innocent couple comforting each other in the wake of an unfolding tragedy.

I didn't have to look at Andrel's face to know there was a smug, triumphant smile threatening to spread across it.

Because everything was going according to plan.

CHAPTER 3

WE REACHED THE MANSION RUINS AROUND DAYBREAK —just in time for me to escape to my favorite spot to admire the sunrise.

I waited long enough to see Cillian arrive safely behind us, and then I left him and Andrel by the main doors and climbed the tallest of the mansion's winding, broken staircases of stone.

Rats scurried in and out of the splintered steps, nearly brushing my boots more than once. But I was used to them at this point—unbothered by them. I took little notice of the cobwebs, either, or of the dust gathered on the cracked windows I passed.

No matter how often I tore the webs down, or how frequently I wiped away the dirt and grime, these things always seemed to return impossibly quickly; it felt like we were locked in an endless battle, each waiting for the other to give up and relinquish their claim on what remained of the place.

I wasn't in the mood to fight after such a long night, so I just kept climbing until I came to the highest point I could reach—what had once been an attic used mainly for storage.

Most of the roof was gone, but the support rafters remained, weathered but intact enough to support my weight.

I hoisted myself onto the widest of them. Arms out at my sides, I tiptoed my way over to the small section with the most stable flooring, a section jutting out so far that I could no longer see the broken-down house around it—only the sky and the marigold fields dipping and rolling away from what had once been a mighty estate.

The world was waking up, filling with birdsong, and the hills below rippled like a lake of gold as the sun slipped through the rows of flowers.

No matter how many times I took in this view, it still sent a shiver down my spine.

The gods could never see the world the way I did.

I collapsed into a pile of pillows and blankets I'd stashed in this little hideaway of mine, taking the first deep breath I'd managed since leaving Cauldra.

Images of the burning temple appeared every time I closed my eyes. A taste of smoke and bitterness lingered on my lips. My stomach rolled in protest every time I tried to swallow these things down, but I didn't regret what we'd done last night. We hadn't started this war, after all. The gods and their human followers had.

And more proof of their savagery was all around me.

This mansion and all the land surrounding it had once belonged to Andrel's great-grandparents; he'd moved here himself as a young child. The House of Moreth that he belonged to had once been among the most influential of the old elvish houses, and this mansion, a centerpiece in that old world, its great halls a place for politics and social gatherings alike.

Its importance had unfortunately made it a target, too.

It had endured countless smaller attacks over the years, but none so terrible as what happened on *Blood Night*—the night when humans, their population soaring and their courage bolstered by the middle-gods they had embraced, laid waste to several important elvish houses through swift, calculated attacks they claimed had been guided and blessed by the gods themselves.

On that awful night, the fields of gold below me had turned crimson. One wing of the mansion—the grandest, filled with priceless art and a library full of irreplaceable books and binders full of our history—had burned beyond repair. Andrel's grandparents, his parents, several aunts and uncles...they all had perished in the battle, along with my own grandparents, who'd been visiting at the time.

When human soldiers raided the mansion during the aftermath, stealing whatever scraps of our culture remained, Andrel had hidden deep in the tunnels that crisscrossed underneath his home and the lands around it.

They'd assumed he was dead as well.

But he'd lived.

He'd stayed hidden for weeks—nearly starving to death in the process—eventually emerging to find himself alone among a bleak and broken landscape.

Rumors of hauntings started to surround the place, and Andrel had done whatever he could to encourage people to believe them. He learned to set traps and wield various weapons, defending what was left against the few people who braved the mansion's supposed ghosts.

Cillian had joined him some fifteen odd years ago—himself a refugee of distant but similar battles—and between the two of them, they managed to preserve at least some of the mansion. Cillian was several years older and wiser, and he came with connections to other powerful elves. Through these things, he'd helped Andrel turn the crumbling manor into a central hub of elven society once more.

My father had answered the call for one of the meetings being held there—meetings that soon turned to strategic gatherings of rebels plotting the downfall of the new gods and their followers.

Eventually, he'd brought my sister and me along to one such gathering, and this was how I'd met Andrel and Cillian, the two I now considered my only true friends: As a child with the bloody history of war at my back, snapping at my heels, pushing me violently toward them. I'd been twelve years old.

There were some who saw our meeting as fate. Three of the most powerful elvish bloodlines—what was left of them—brought together in such a way, uniting in the ruins of a tragedy... We had encouraged the rumor enough that it had become something of a modern day prophecy. We were living legends to some, and I went along with it because our kind needed hope—I couldn't deny that.

But it was difficult to see myself as much of a savior while sleeping amongst rats and rubble.

The sun was rising above the forest in the distance, the morning growing steadily warmer. I slipped off my sister's coat, trying to slip free of my jumbled thoughts with the motion.

I lifted my gaze to the sky, watching it brightening, igniting with a fiery show of red and orange streaks. It brought to mind erupting mountains, molten rock—all of the stories I'd heard about the God of Fire and the chaos surrounding him—and I couldn't keep my lips from curling in disgust even though I had no one but spiders to share the scowl with.

I heard someone else making their way up the stairs. A short time later, I glanced over my shoulder and saw Cillian carefully picking his way through the rafters, nodding in greeting as he reached me. He said nothing at first, his attention drawn, as mine had been, to the explosion of color above us.

Finally, he inhaled deeply and said, "Hopefully not an omen of a certain deity on his way to seek revenge, hm?"

"Let him show his ugly face here," I muttered, forcing my gaze to what was left of the walls around us. The show of color persisted even here, sunlight breaking through the gaps in the old wood like waves of fire pushing through cracked earth.

I dug my fingers into the itchy, worn blanket I sat upon and said, "If he could be bothered to grace this realm with his presence, I have no shortage of things I would like to say to him."

Cillian chuckled. "How I'd love to eavesdrop on *that* conversation." Despite the light tone of his voice, a shadow of uncertainty crossed his normally bright green eyes, dulling them. They brightened again so quickly I wondered if I'd imagined it.

I wanted to believe I'd imagined it.

But the gods were not the only things looming over us this morning; my own uncertainty was at least partly due to the humans who worshipped them, too.

I knew the wickedness and destruction they were capable of—this broken and beaten-down mansion was proof of it—but I couldn't stop thinking about that young girl with her moon-shaped mark. Her prying eyes. Her questions. Her body burning in the temple while she clutched the beads around her arm, fervently praying to gods who wouldn't answer her.

I'd warned her.

If she'd insisted on going inside anyway, it was her own fault.

And yet...

I closed my eyes and leaned back into a patch of sunlight,

letting the growing warmth of the day spread over my skin. It was comforting at first, but soon my stomach was shifting uneasily, accompanied by a nasty thought—that I didn't deserve to enjoy the sun's light after the things I'd done in the dark.

I twisted my fingers more tightly into the blanket beneath me, fighting the urge to scratch at the old burn marks on my cheek.

My sparrow's magic had worn off, so those scars were fully visible now, along with the rest of my identity. Pointed ears, hair the color of soot, eyes like my sister's—slender and sparkling with a vivid green shade that more than one person had told me was unsettling.

All of me laid bare in the breaking day.

So of course I was uneasy.

"It's getting close to breakfast time, isn't it?" Cillian commented. "You want to cook something? I'm starving—stomach's not feeling jumpy, for once."

I pretended to be surprised by this last part, even though I'd caught onto his ruse years ago; he often claimed our missions gave him an anxious stomach, and sometimes he'd go days without eating because of it. But I'd long ago noticed the pattern surrounding his supposed ailments—the way his stomach issues only seemed to come up whenever our food stores were running low.

I'd never called him out on it.

I likely never would.

I knew he would just deny things. He felt obligated to take care of me, I think, because of how close he'd been to my sister. The night she'd disappeared, the two of them were supposed to meet, but he'd been late to arrive at our house. I know he blamed himself for not being there. We still didn't truly know what had happened that night, but it was hard not to wonder about how things might have turned out differently if she hadn't been alone in her room.

The what-ifs haunted all of us.

I believed he'd sworn to take care of me in Savna's stead, even if it meant going hungry...though I liked to think we shared something deeper than a haunting obligation after all these years.

"It'll take your mind off everything from last night," he said, offering me a hand.

I let him pull me to my feet. As I was stretching and swiping the dust from my leggings, the sound of a commotion somewhere down below made us both go stiff.

"Sounds like we have guests, too," Cillian said. "Kinnara and some of her group, if I had to guess. They probably want to know how things went in Cauldra."

Kinnara Fellblade. The oldest daughter of the House of Greymane, and one of the few who regularly left their lands in the frigid northern wastelands to fraternize with outsiders. That house was not among our greatest supporters, but we still had a tentative alliance with them. Our common enemies kept us all civil at least—even if our ideas about how to deal with those enemies usually differed.

"I suppose I could prepare a royal feast for us all," I joked, my eyes on the dust particles floating around us, stirred up by our movements and shining in the golden morning light. "Dining and politics...the ghosts in this place will be happy to see the manor returned to its former, more glorious usages."

I could hear the smile in Cillian's voice as he said, "Perhaps a masquerade ball to follow while we're at it."

"Of course." I gave a little curtsy, pretending I had elaborate skirts to lift. "A full-scale, most splendid royal affair, befitting of our royal blood."

Grinning, he bowed low, sweeping his hand toward the staircase.

I made my way past him, glancing one last time at the landscape below us. A few wispy tufts of fog had drifted over the hills, settling in the lowest places. They looked like clouds of smoke.

My stomach clenched.

I hurried on, but I couldn't stop thinking about wildfires overtaking my beloved golden fields, sweeping through them as swiftly as the blood that had once watered them.

CHAPTER 4

Downstairs, I visited briefly with Kinnara and her company—just long enough to not be considered rude—and then I used the excuse of making breakfast to escape.

No elf had ever turned down the honor of being cooked for, so I went with their blessing into our cobbled-together kitchen, which was only across the hall from the sitting room where they all continued their meeting; I remained close enough that I could still make out much of what was being said if I really wanted to listen.

I didn't.

My head was already spinning with enough confusing, conflicting thoughts. I didn't want to introduce more to it—not at the moment, anyway. I would simply ask Cillian to fill me in on the details later, after I'd had food and sleep.

I flung open the pantry doors and considered the contents of its crooked and buckling shelves. Our increasing rebel activities had left little time for the odd jobs we usually took on to earn coin—yet our shelves were relatively full for once; Andrel had managed a deal with some hunters in the nearby village of

Habostad, allowing them to kill on our land without interference in exchange for several loads worth of food and supplies.

It had made him miserable to do it. The marigold fields and the Nightvale Woods beyond them were full of sacred things, from important gravesites to old shrines, and to think that humans would be tromping through them, spilling animal blood, defiling whatever they pleased...

"But we have to eat," he'd bluntly reminded us—and himself—over and over again.

And so we had. For the last month, our meals had been much more regular than usual, and I'd developed several exciting new dishes to record and file into the various recipe books I was creating.

But between the three of us and Kinnara's company, there were ten mouths to feed this morning.

I frowned at the supplies upon the shelves. They suddenly seemed more meager than they had at first glance.

No matter; I'd just have to make it work somehow. I'd faced bigger culinary challenges. And Cillian was right to assume this would take my mind off our troubles—proof that he knew me as well as anyone these days, whether because of obligation or otherwise. He knew I loved to cook.

Or, more specifically, I loved the challenge of trying to cook despite the limitations we faced.

The contents of my pantry had always consisted of random goods either stolen or bartered or haggled for, even when I still lived with my family. Always different ingredients, never predictable amounts, and I loved trying to fit the odds and ends into recipes.

I saw it as another place to look for patterns. Each ingredient had certain properties. Different amounts of them caused different outcomes—but the outcomes were predictable if you paid attention. Mix this ingredient with this one, and it yielded this result. Combine so much of this element with so much of another and you could create something altogether new and delicious...or disastrous.

I learned through trial and error, diligent note taking, and now the highest shelf in the pantry was the fullest, lined with leather binders overflowing with neatly scribbled recipes that had been painstakingly organized into categories, and then into subcategories, and then into subcategories of *those* subcategories...

Cillian and Andrel both teased me about my organizational systems, but at least I always knew where things were.

I didn't need any notes for the things I planned to make this morning, so I simply wiped down the counters, lit the oven, and got to work.

There were apples that needed using. I plucked a few from the bowl on the well-loved and worn-down table in the corner, peeling and chopping them as I hummed softly, my hands moving in a familiar, relaxing rhythm.

Loud voices briefly interrupted my flow, but I only shook my head and went back to chopping more fervently than before. Chunks of apple were tossed into a hanging pot beside the oven without hesitation while I rattled off the rest of the ingredients to myself.

Salt, sugar, lemon juice, lard, cinnamon...

I frowned as my hand fell upon the small bottle containing ground cinnamon. Not much left, and who knew when we'd manage to procure any more.

I debated only a moment before I tossed the entirety of the bottle's contents into the pot.

"Tomorrow isn't guaranteed. We should use the cinnamon," I informed the painting above the table—or rather, the lady it featured. My eyes were often drawn to her while I was in this room. To the shining swirls of her silver and blue dress, the perfectly-formed coils of her dark hair, the jewel in the center of her delicate headpiece.

She was the Lady Lorralin, one of the first elves to ever be created, and supposedly once a favorite daughter of the upper-gods.

But in this painting, she was depicted not as a devoted companion of those divine beings, but as a warrior kneeling with her sword stabbed into a circle of cracked and rust-colored earth, her palm braced beside it, symbolizing an adherence to the planet beneath her feet rather than to the gods above.

The House of Mistwilde that I descended from claimed Lorralin as their ancestor. I'm not sure if I believed it—or any of the countless legends surrounding this elven lady—but I felt oddly grounded and at peace when I looked at her. Perhaps simply because hers was one of the few paintings that had survived the fires and destruction that had befallen this house. Survival amongst flames and ruin; I could relate to that.

As I lit the wood beneath my hanging pot, the voices across the hall rose once more. I opened the nearest window, both for ventilation and in hopes that the birds and the tree limbs clacking in the breeze might drown out the heated conversation.

I tried to focus only on stirring the syrupy concoction in the pot—on its sweet and spicy scents melding together, tempting me to taste it—and then on mixing and kneading the dough for the pastries I was making.

But before I realized it was happening, my head had tilted once more toward the hallway, and my ears were twitching, straining to pick out individual words. I closed my eyes, listening, forgetting I was still working my dough until I felt it becoming tough beneath my touch; I'd nearly over-kneaded it.

Cursing, I drew my hands away and wiped them on my front—only to realize I'd forgotten to wrap my apron around myself.

"One of those mornings," I told the painted Lorralin, who stared back in what I convinced myself was solidarity.

Another loud voice—they were almost shouting now.

I took a few steps into the hallway, listening closer, fearing I might need to involve myself after all. It wouldn't be the first time I'd played mediator between this particular group.

Thankfully, they soon quieted down.

I hovered uncertainly in the hallway for a few more moments before going back to my dough, absently forming it into miniature pies that I scooped the apple mixture into.

I'd made this recipe enough that I could do the rest without much thought—crimping the dough, prepping the pan, checking the oven temperature, tending to the ash of the oven's perfectly-smoldering fire before I set my racks into place and loaded the miniature pastries onto them. The motions were automatic, so the only thing I was fully aware of for a long time was my own heartbeat pounding too loudly in my ears.

It was only after a deep inhale of warm, cinnamon-tinged air that I truly remembered I was cooking.

I threw myself more fully into putting the rest of breakfast together, and soon the space was filled with so many scents and sounds—smoke and spices, oils sizzling and popping in pans— that I was completely immersed and lost to everything else.

I didn't want to leave my warm cocoon of familiar and predictable things, but a short time later, I made myself do it all the same. With one arm wrapped around a basket of fresh pastries and the other clutching a pitcher of water, I headed toward the others.

The hall had grown silent, but after pushing the door open, I only had to glance at the sullen faces all around the room to know that the argument was far from over.

"You aren't listening." Kinnara leaned away from the table between her and Andrel, clasping her elegant fingers together in front of her, almost as if in prayer. Her teeth were bared in a smile, an attempt at civility she wasn't *quite* pulling off—partly because of the way the gesture revealed the sharp points of her canines. A cursed feature, like my own claws, that always made her appear far more feral than she actually was.

"There is *nothing left* of Merityn," Kinnara said in a low voice. "The armies of King Eldon razed it to the ground. And they've made no secret about what motivated them to do it. Bannerforge, Herst, Gatlin. The incidents there—all of your *successes*—have done us far more harm than good."

Merityn was a small village on the Kingdom of Aromand's northern border. It was one of the few cities in our kingdom that consisted almost entirely of elven-kind. Or it had been, anyway. And Bannerforge, Herst, Gatlin...those were all places where myself and my allies had recently carried out more demonstrations like the one in Cauldra.

I tightened my grip on the food I carried, my heart once again pounding a ferocious, unsteady rhythm, making it difficult to hear the rest of what was being said. I floated in and out of the conversation for a minute until Cillian's voice brought me back—a calm and good-natured, matter-of-fact tone among the rising tempers in the room.

"The humans hate us regardless of whether or not we attack their lands and temples," he said. "It was only a matter of time before they went after Merityn; Eldon has been threatening it for years. What would you have us do to stop that king and his followers from carrying out what they believe is their destiny, sanctioned by the gods themselves?"

Kinnara rose to her feet and began to pace, but otherwise didn't reply.

The silence settled, thick and uncomfortable, before Andrel's voice finally cut through it.

"She'd have us hide." He appeared to be his normal confident self, but there was an edge to his words—like a blade partially unsheathed, threatening violence. "She wants us to cower behind the walls of those prisons they've been building in the north."

I leaned against the doorframe, breathing in the comforting scent of the food I'd made.

The places he spoke of were not truly prisons, but new cities being built for the sole purpose of separating us elves from humans—cities protected by experimental magic some of our kind were developing. Each was its own world within this world, set apart from the ever-expanding human kingdoms.

Cillian and Andrel often called them *Cowardkeeps*, which was a term my sister had originally coined. They considered the ones in favor of such things even worse than the ones who wanted to beg and pray to the gods to take us back.

"The prisons you speak of are strongholds that others have labored tirelessly to create," Kinnara said coolly, "and they offer a strategic point of attack and defense—a much more intelligent strategy than anything you and your rebel friends are attempting."

There was a murmur of agreement from the ones who'd come with Kinnara, followed by an uneasy shifting as Andrel's glare swept over them.

"And you honestly believe the humans will leave these

places alone?" Andrel laughed a quiet, savage little laugh. "You underestimate their devotion to their gods. They will set fire to every city and fortress we build—and do it happily—to gain more favor from their beloved divine beings."

Another long silence followed as Kinnara's dark eyes narrowed on Andrel alone. The shifting in the room stopped.

Everything seemed to stop.

"Over three-hundred of them." Kinnara's voice was like ice cracking on an otherwise silent winter morning.

An even longer, deeper silence followed. She stepped closer to Andrel, moving into a patch of sunlight framed by faded curtains. Ribbons of gold caught on her mouth, highlighting the scars dragging away from the left corner of it. Torture marks from years ago when she'd been captured and refused to give information, I'd heard.

I wondered if there was anyone in this room who *didn't* have scars of some kind thanks to the gods and the ones who blindly served them.

"Three-hundred of our kin slaughtered in Merityn," Kinnara said. "Do you not care?"

Cillian started forward. "Of course we—"

"Heads on stakes. Bodies defiled and ripped apart. Several of those bodies were hung from the walls of the city itself. Not the first massacre we've endured this moon cycle, and doubtless the last. The numbers grow increasingly less in our favor with every passing day. The tides shift, and so too must our tactics." Another sharp smile, and she pushed out several of her next words through gritted teeth: "The old houses have fallen. *Your* houses have fallen. It's time to let the plans and beliefs of our ancestors fall away with them and fully embrace new things. New weapons."

Her eyes had never left Andrel.

The room remained perfectly still, and in the quiet stillness the sunlight filtering through the curtains seemed brighter all of a sudden, illuminating the cracked plaster walls and the chipped marble floors as though to illustrate Kinnara's point.

The old houses have fallen.

It was clear she thought the conversation finished—that there was only one response we could possibly give to her declarations.

Andrel said nothing.

Nor did Cillian.

The quiet stretched on for a painfully long time.

I could no longer stand it. I cleared my throat, stepping farther into the room with my arms wrapped more tightly than ever around the things I carried, making certain nothing and no part of me shook.

"Breakfast is ready," I said quietly.

But we hardly ate anything at all.

CHAPTER 5

LATER THAT NIGHT, I WOKE FROM A STRETCH OF fitful sleep and stumbled my way down to the kitchen for a drink.

After downing a glass of water, I went outside and found Andrel alone, sitting on the front steps of his old home with his chin resting thoughtfully on a propped-up fist.

He was beautiful in the moonlight, beige skin and dark hair shimmering with a pale blue glow. Despite the warm night, he wore a heavy cloak with bramble-wrapped daggers stitched along its hood—symbols of the House of Moreth. A reminder of his royal heritage...though whether meant for himself or our visitors, I wasn't sure.

There were piles of pebbles beside him. Rocks he'd crushed into pieces, I suspected; it was a restless habit of his whenever he was lost in thought.

He could crush them with only a gentle closing of his fist.

All elves were strong compared to humans, but his strength was different. A curse as much as an asset—like my claws or Kinnara's fangs—in his case because it came and went so unpredictably. He'd worked hard to try and wrestle some sort of control over it, but without much success. Sometimes he crushed things without meaning to. Other times, the supernatural strength abandoned him when he needed it most.

I'd often thought it a cruel metaphor for our kind as a whole—so much power coursing through our veins and our histories, yet we couldn't seem to properly harness our collective strength and put an end to all our problems.

The piles around Andrel numbered at least a couple dozen, with more intact rocks stacked at his boots.

How long had he been out here crushing them?

I cleared my throat. "You look lonely."

He tilted his face toward me and gave a crooked smile. "Why should I be lonely? Kinnara and the rest of them have decided to stay the night. Our home is overrun with more people than it has welcomed in some time...I haven't had a moment alone in hours—until now."

"Lonely and alone don't mean the same thing," I pointed out.

I glimpsed his smile inching higher before he looked back to the shadow-draped yard before us. "You're right. As usual."

I considered sweeping away the dust and sitting beside him, but something made me hesitate.

"But I'm neither of those things," he said. "Though I wouldn't say no to your company, if you're offering. You know I prefer it to most." He kept his eyes straight ahead, but I felt as if he had turned and stared directly, unabashedly at me.

I shook my head but ended up giving in and mirroring his smile as I settled down on the step in front of him, avoiding the rocky messes. I sensed his body shifting, angling toward mine. My sensitive hearing picked up the sound of his heart beating slightly faster.

Feeling a blush coming on, I busied myself with counting the crushed rocks, avoiding his gaze. Twenty-five piles of dust in total. I moved on to counting the trees, the stars, the broken spires atop the fence wrapping the yard.

Andrel and I were strictly friends—business partners, at most.

Or we *had been* until recently, at least.

I wasn't sure when the lines had first started to blur, but at some point during the last year or so we had...slipped. Somewhere between the increasingly dangerous and desperate missions, we had discovered that the touch and taste of one another was an excellent remedy to combat loneliness and other things we didn't want to talk about.

But we were nothing more serious than these occasional bits of fun, and every day I grew more certain it wouldn't become anything more—though I hadn't yet decided if this was a good or a bad thing.

We stayed beside each other, hardly talking, for the better part of the next hour.

I watched the tree limbs swaying, marveling at the patterns cast by shifting leaves and limbs over the moon-silver grass. I shivered as the night grew colder, and Andrel took off his cloak and draped it over my shoulders. I huddled under it, inhaling the comforting, familiar notes of his spice and sandalwood scent.

"Is Kinnara still angry?" I asked, finally breaking the silence and glancing over my shoulder.

He shook his head. "We had a much more productive talk this evening while you were napping. She's staying the night partly so she can help plan our follow-up to Cauldra...she just wants to be more strategic about things going forward." He gave a casual shrug.

I thought of how furious she'd looked earlier. What could he possibly have said or done to convince her to stay the night? "Your persuasiveness is frightening sometimes."

He laughed.

I chuckled as well, despite the unease curling through my stomach. I stood, wrapping his cloak more tightly around myself as I paced the path that led to what remained of the gatehouse, skipping across broken pavers and kicking the occasional loose stone aside.

"*The old houses have fallen,*" I said, repeating Kinnara's line from earlier. "Do you think she's right? I mean, we've fallen on hard times, certainly, but the way she said it just sounded so...*final.* So desperate."

"She's afraid."

"She should be, shouldn't she?"

Andrel snorted—his usual response to any mention of fear. He got to his feet alongside me, walking the same path I had, pausing at my side before turning to fully take in the house behind us.

Quietly, he said, "It looks as if it's still standing to me. As am I. Cillian still fights as well." He looked to me, head cocked to the side, a challenging little smirk flirting with his lips. "And you aren't going anywhere, are you?"

I shook my head.

No—of course I wasn't.

Where else would I go?

He stepped closer, taking hold of the cloak he'd draped over my shoulders and using it to draw me toward him. He kept one hand fisted in the cloak's heavy fabric but lifted the other to my face, cupping my chin and lifting my mouth up to meet his. My insides fluttered as his hand slid back through my hair, pulling me forward and pressing our lips more completely together.

He stayed close even after he ended the kiss, lips nearly brushing mine again as he said, "Our houses once ruled this realm. They will rule it again in due time, and the Creators will regret turning against us."

A shiver went down my spine—one that had nothing to do with how close he still was. When he spoke like this, it was hard not to believe in him, to not admire his confidence and dauntless hope.

His gaze dropped to my lips, hazel eyes shining with hunger. With invitation. Another chance to lose ourselves in one another. Every nerve in my body sparked to life at the temptation, and my skin tingled with anticipation as his fingers brushed through my hair, down my neck, across the hollow of my throat.

But then it was happening again—that uneasy shifting in my stomach.

I couldn't fully explain it...I just knew I didn't want to be lost tonight. Not even with him.

I angled my mouth away from his and said, "You've had a report about the aftermath in Cauldra by this point, I assume."

He hesitated, disappointment flashing in his expression for a fraction of a second before he composed himself and took a step back. "Yes. One of our informants stopped by with details an hour or so ago. The official reports are saying the temple is a total loss. Six lives were lost as well."

"Six?" My voice came out fainter than I'd intended.

"Yes. Six humans." His lips curled at the last word, as though it was laced with a poison he didn't want his mouth to linger on.

I counted them in my head. The two I'd heard inside. The

three unconscious guards outside. And a sixth...that Moon-kind girl I'd tried to warn?

"Were you hoping for less?"

The question made the back of my neck burn. I lifted my eyes to the stars and steeled my voice. "No. I was hoping for more."

I must not have sounded convincing; I could feel him studying me. Questioning me.

"The gods and their worshippers are violent," he said, as if I somehow wasn't aware of that fact. "They leave us little choice but to answer with violence."

"I know that."

"I wish things were different. But they're not." He heaved a sigh.

We were quiet for several moments. Not the same easy-going quiet as before; this one felt...expectant. Like I needed to fill it with something. I just couldn't decide on what that something was.

"Not losing your edge on me, are you?"

I jerked my gaze back down and found him with his hands shoved in his pockets, wearing another crooked grin. The question had sounded mostly teasing, but it still made my neck burn hotter, anger spiking in my blood and heating it—a fire directed more at myself than him.

My sister would never have been accused of losing her edge.

I had picked up her banner the day she disappeared, swearing I'd complete her goals at whatever the cost.

What was wrong with me tonight?

As if he could read my tumultuous thoughts, Andrel quietly said, "Savna believed in us, you know. In the power of our three houses, and all that's been written about us, all the promise and possibility we carry. She believed we had a chance at restoration." He let out a soft, humorless chuckle, a haunted sort of look in his eyes. "She believed in it even more than me, I think."

"I know she did. So do I."

His voice bordered on gentle as he added, "We can't let the loss of her be in vain. She would want you to keep fighting, to carry on with her cause. And so many rallied to that cause after her death—"

I flinched.

Her death.

I knew she was dead. I'd accepted it at this point.

I just hated being reminded of it.

We'd never found her body after that fateful, bloody night. But almost a year to the day after her disappearance, Andrel had stumbled across some of her blood-stained clothing and weapons in the woods, the objects ragged and rusted as though they'd been there for some time.

He'd interrogated the humans in the nearby house about them. They'd been combative, uncooperative, and had forced him to take the investigation into his own hands. A quick search of their property found a covered trio of stone slabs— the kind of ceremonial slabs used in ritual body burnings. This wasn't entirely surprising; the humans in this kingdom burned the deceased immediately after they passed—it was considered bad luck not to.

Each of the slabs featured a symbol of one of the three Creator gods in hopes of gaining their blessings, as per usual, but what had been strange about this particular set was the fourth symbol painted on the middle stone—an upside-down triangle dissected by three lines. A common ward against the elvish-kind.

So they had dealt with her body, we concluded. No human

would have bothered seeking out her family to tell them what they'd done; humans didn't care about giving us elves things like closure and peace.

Andrel had gathered up ashes and dirt from around the slabs and brought them back to me in hopes of giving me more closure. I'd been grateful for the gesture, but even then, despite all the mounting evidence against it, I'd clung to the possibility of her survival long after everyone else had given up.

Nearly a year ago, however, I'd finally agreed to a proper death ceremony for her. We'd burned her belongings and buried the ashes of them along with the dirt and ashes Andrel had collected. And I'd cried—truly cried—for the first time since the night she disappeared; up until then I'd turned mostly numb at any mention of her.

I clenched the sparrow hanging from my neck, determined not to cry now. I didn't mean to trigger the bird's sleeping magic, but I felt it happening anyway—a warm needling spreading over my scalp, tickling my ears, smoothing away their tapered ends before moving on to temporarily wash away my scars.

"I'm sorry," Andrel said, and I could tell he truly was; the regret in his eyes was obvious. "I shouldn't have said that. I didn't mean to upset—"

"It's fine. I should go, I...I was on my way back to bed earlier, anyway. I'd just wanted to say good night." I slipped out of his cloak and handed it to him, then smiled as I stepped out of his reach. "So...good night."

I hurried away before he could reply.

I DIDN'T GO BACK to my room.

I knew I wouldn't sleep if I laid down now, so instead I wandered in the opposite direction of my room and everyone else's, hoping I could make myself tired if I walked long enough and far enough.

We'd only truly restored one wing of the manor, while the rest of the house and grounds stood around it in varying states of decay. It was dangerous to navigate many of these decaying spaces...not to mention depressing, seeing the evidence of what had once been. We talked about fixing it up properly all the time. I had drawn up plans, even—detailed diagrams and notes for nearly every room, just waiting for us to implement them. All we needed was time and money.

We had neither, so most days we just avoided the broken places.

But there was one neglected space that I couldn't resist visiting often, however dangerous or depressing it might have been to wander toward it: the once grand ballroom.

It was on the complete opposite end of the grounds, nearly a half-mile from where I'd left Andrel; it might as well have been located in another world entirely. I had to walk through the ruins of the burned library to reach it, a path so decrepit and overrun with weeds and dust that it was nearly unrecogniz-able—but at least that made it easier to not think about all that had been lost in the flames.

Those thoughts didn't come until I stepped into what was left of the hall leading up to the ballroom. The path here had retained some of its splendor, its patterned tiles full of compli-cated swirls and shapes that were fragmented, yet still mesmer-izing. I studied them as I walked along, mentally filling in the missing or scratched-away designs as I made my way to the circular atrium just outside the ballroom.

There had once been two massive doors hanging here. Only one remained, but it was impressive enough on its own, its face carved full of symbols—everything from daggers, to roses, to strange, mythical creatures I couldn't readily name. There were designs along the edges and in the six distinct panels in the middle—two dedicated panels for each of the three most powerful elvish houses: Moreth, Mistwilde, and Lightwyn. The House of Mistwilde—my ancestral house—was featured along the top, with a sword surrounded in feathers on one panel and a jeweled goblet carved into the other.

I could have slipped in through the gap left by the missing door, but I always pushed the remaining one open instead, trying to imagine what it would have been like to see these doors sweeping apart to allow for dramatic entrances.

I swore sometimes I could hear music drifting over me as soon as I stepped across the threshold.

Some of the walls were still intact and glittering with a thin overlay of golden paint, though otherwise bare; the tapestries that had decorated them were long gone. The roof had collapsed some years ago, but on nights like tonight—when the sky was clear and wild with stars—it only made the room feel more vast and full of music and grand possibility.

My gaze traveled over the few unbroken stained-glass windows as I meandered toward the center of the space, turning in occasional circles, unable to stop myself from imagining I wore a gown fit for the grandeur once contained in this room.

A most splendid royal affair, I'd joked with Cillian, and I repeated the words now, whispering them to the humid air, mocking the very idea of it all.

I didn't truly care about being of royal blood. I hadn't dared to dream of such things as a child, even when my father had been around to tell us fairytales and other nonsense before bed every night. Even when he'd told me the truth when I was nine years old—that my ancestors had actually been royalty in every sense of the word—I still didn't think of it as anything more than a footnote on the yellowed and torn pages of our complicated history.

I didn't want balls or crowns or feasts, then or now. I just wanted a home not covered in dust and decaying things. I wanted my father and mother back. I wanted my sister back.

And I wanted to make the ones responsible for all this ruin pay for what they'd done. I needed that far more than a crown.

I needed it so badly that sometimes it felt like it was killing me, the desire settling so heavily in my heart that it made my chest hurt and my knees feel weak.

My foot caught on a broken floor tile and I tripped, nearly landing face-first in a pile of broken glass—remnants of a crystal chandelier that had fallen some time ago. A sliver of a broken, tear-shaped crystal sliced into my palm as I pushed back to my feet. I hissed out a string of curses, the sound echoing in the desolate space.

Clenching my fist at my side, trying to ignore the stinging and the warm blood coating my palm, I moved toward the door; I'd done enough roaming for one night.

As I started to push the door aside, I heard footsteps.

I sank toward the closest wall, listening closer. Two pairs of footsteps. At least. They were heavy, as was the breathing that accompanied them.

Humans.

I went perfectly still.

One after the other they appeared on the far side of the room, climbing through an opening in the dilapidated wall, lanterns shining. Even with the clear night sky above them, they still couldn't see what lurked in the shadows without those lanterns; sometimes I forgot how terrible their vision was compared to mine.

I continued to silently creep my way through the darkest parts of the room, heading for a door that led into a sweeping courtyard that eventually connected to another wing of the mansion.

I had nearly reached it when I accidentally stepped on a fallen pane of glass. The crack from my weight was loud—but far worse was the way the broken piece shot out from underneath me, shattering completely as it collided with the nearby wall. Between the shattering glass and my stomping as I tried to regain my balance, my cover was entirely blown.

Lantern light flickered in my direction.

A warning rang out from the two on the other side of the room, and seconds later a third man lunged through the doorway I'd been aiming for, blocking my path.

I saw a flash of steel in his hand—a knife.

He swiped for my stomach.

I twisted out of his reach, spun back around, and thrust an upturned palm into his nose. I felt the satisfying crunch of bone. He staggered back a few steps, and I swept a foot at his ankles to send him the rest of the way down.

As soon as he hit the ground, I sprinted on toward the door, veering wildly through it—

And nearly collided with the girl from the temple, who was standing calmly in the courtyard on the other side.

She'd brought more friends, too—six heavily-armed men formed a half-circle around her, blocking my escape.

I stumbled back into the ballroom.

The first two men I'd seen had made their way over. One moved to help the man I'd knocked down, while the other pushed closer to my back, drawing a short sword. The rest of the men fanned out until they had me completely surrounded.

I was still staring at the girl, trying to make sense of her as she did the same to me.

Her gaze went to the sparrow hanging from my neck. After a moment her eyes flashed with understanding, as though she'd sensed the divine magic the bird possessed. Her own magic helped her understand the situation too, most likely; I looked different from when she'd last seen me—my ears were rounded again and my scars were hidden as before, but my hair was its natural black shade—but I was the same soul her power had encountered back in Cauldra.

And nothing was ever lost or hidden to the Goddess of the Moon—or to those most blessed with her magic.

When this girl had laid hands on me back at the temple, she must have embedded a spell into my skin, and now she'd simply followed the trail of it, leading these men to me. Likely in exchange for a fat reward.

I should have poisoned her when I had the chance.

The man closest to me stepped forward, lips twisting into a nasty grin. "There are more of us outside. You're completely surrounded, so I suggest you don't cause us any trouble."

I frantically played through the potential battle in my mind.

Ten on our side if the others came in time, and if Kinnara and her group decided to fight along with us. We could handle the humans in here easily. But if the man was telling the truth about having reinforcements outside...

It was impossible to know the truth from where I stood. Too many walls were still standing, blocking my full view of the situation.

My gaze jumped back to the girl. She had led these men to

me because she knew I was involved in the temple's destruction, but she hadn't seen Andrel or Cillian last night, as far as I knew.

She didn't know who—or what—any of us truly were.

I still had the high-pitched whistle we used for communicating during our missions; it was tucked into a small ankle pouch alongside the knife sheathed at my boot.

Three quick breaths was all I needed to manage—the signal to escape. Even from a half-mile away, someone in the main house would be able to hear it; Andrel was likely still outside. He'd know what to do when he heard the sound.

I broke into a sprint, racing for an opening in the outside wall.

Surprise and speed worked in my favor, buying me enough of a head-start to make it to the ruined wall and hurdle over what remained of the frame. I rolled into the first bush I saw and reached toward my ankle, jerking the whistle free.

Three quick breaths.

Footsteps pounded behind me.

I tossed the whistle into a pile of dirt and kicked a few dead leaves over it, hiding it.

In the next instant, two strong pairs of hands grabbed each of my arms, twisting them painfully behind my back before ripping me away from the bush. I didn't put up a fight, eager for them to drag me away from the spot before they looked closely enough to see my fallen whistle.

They spun me around.

I saw and understood the full scope of my predicament, then, as I found myself facing a large group of riders. They dotted the hills surrounding the manor, stretching as far as I could see in both directions. Their dark attire made it difficult to count their exact number, but I was immediately convinced that warning my friends to escape had been the right decision.

A thick cloth slammed over my nose and lips. Its scent was terrible, too overpowering to name. My mouth watered as I fought the urge to vomit, and as the world reeled around me, my warning didn't seem like enough.

Would Andrel and the others ignore it and charge in to rescue me anyway?

No, I told myself, fiercely. *They're smarter than that.*

They would get away. And they would come after me later —but not before they had created a plan and recruited reinforcements. We'd survived as long as we had by being smart, not reckless.

I just had to stay alive until they reached me. I repeated the command over and over in my head, trying to fight against my growing dizziness.

Survive, survive, sur...

Darkness overtook my vision. My legs gave out, and I crumpled to the ground and thought of nothing else.

CHAPTER 6

As far as prisons went, the one I woke up in was not the worst I'd ever been subjected to.

It had a window at least. A barred and narrow thing high above me, letting in just enough sunlight to allow me to count the days. There was a bucket to relieve myself in. My wrists were shackled and chained to the wall behind me, but the chains were long enough to allow me to reach up and feel my face—still smooth and scarless—and touch my ears, which were still rounded like a human's.

My sister's sparrow hung from my neck, continuing to work its protective magic over me.

I couldn't believe they hadn't taken it.

I released a slow, shaky breath, running my fingers over the smooth wood, silently willing its magic to hang on a little longer. If my captors realized I was an elf rather than a human, my situation would go from bad to worse in a hurry. The fact that they hadn't realized it yet was likely the only reason I was still alive; humans usually got the benefit of a trial and a chance at redemption for their crimes, unlike my kind.

The chains attached to my ankles were long enough that I could stretch my legs. The ground was covered in dust, too, which made for unpleasant breathing but gave me a way to occupy myself—a canvas to drag the toe of my boot through, marking the days and making notes about my surroundings.

The hours dragged on, turning into days.

I tried to stay calm and focused, to watch and listen carefully for anything that might prove useful to me. I picked out different voices in distant conversations, and I strained to hear other distinguishing characteristics to pair them with—distinctive gaits, habitual things like the biting of nails or rapping of knuckles. I assigned a different symbol for each separate being I recognized. Using these symbols, I mapped out the guards' movements in the dust as they came and went, searching for patterns, learning when it was safe to relax the spell concealing me and otherwise breathe easier.

By the end of the third day I knew when to expect a changing of the guards, and I was fairly certain only four different people were in charge of my section of the prison. I continued to mark their movements alongside the counting of days.

One.

Two.

Three more days gone in a dusty, hunger-induced dizziness.

Not the longest I'd ever been in a prison, but by this point Andrel or one of the others would usually have snuck in a sign of some sort. Something to tell me they were coming, that I just needed to hold on a little longer...

The seventh day came and went, and the only sign of hope I had to cling to was the light from the window high above.

I was beginning to think it was a trick.

That I'd actually died in the ruins of the Morethian Manor,

and this was one of the three mortal hells: Every day the same, every night supernaturally long, every glimpse of the morning sun a teasing mirage conjured up to make me believe I still had a chance at light and life.

I stretched out my arms and legs, tensing my muscles and relaxing them one by one. Over and over I did this until the numb, detached feeling in them went away.

"I'm alive," I stubbornly told the damp, chill air at least a dozen times each day. "I am Karys of Mistwilde, the last royal daughter of our house, and I. Am. Still. Here." The words echoed in my bare, cavernous cell, eerie and mocking.

I suppressed my hopeless shivers.

Cups of water were brought to me occasionally, but food almost never accompanied them; I surmised that they wanted me weak, but not dead.

By the eighth day, a morbid train of thought grabbed me and would not derail—what if I refused to drink? What if I took my life before they could make me suffer further? Would it ruin whatever trial or propagandist point they were hoping to put me on display for?

It was tempting, the thought of taking control away from them.

But I could not die here.

I'd promised my sister I would bring ruin to the gods and see our reign in this realm restored. I'd made an oath over the blood staining her bed, and I'd held to it for all these years.

I wouldn't fail her now.

I singled out one guard in particular by the end of the eighth day; he sounded the youngest, and I had often heard him drifting away from his post outside of my cell, talking and laughing with people in the distance. He was also the only one who occasionally brought me scraps of food, rancid and stale though they were. Most importantly, beneath his disgusted expression I saw hints of pity—a weakness.

He became my target.

I rehearsed the things I would say, the looks I would give to turn his inklings of pity into full-blown compassion and cooperation.

But I didn't have a chance to put my plans into action.

On the tenth evening, when I was nearly delirious from lack of food, a trio of guards I didn't recognize entered my cell, hands on their weapons and sadistic gleams in their eyes. They left the door ajar, and the orange light from the hall torches flickered brightly at their backs. Their shadows stretched long and tall before them, swallowing me up well before they stood in a row before me.

They'd brought food with them. My stomach panged at the smell of it. Bread, some sort of dried meat, and maybe fruit, too—*gods*, what I would have done for a piece of fruit in that moment. I tried not to react, but my mouth salivated automatically, forcing me to swallow and lick my lips to avoid outright drooling.

The tallest of the guards—a nasty specimen of a human with oily black hair and a vertical scar dividing his lips into two even halves—stepped forward. "For every question you answer, you'll receive something to eat. Simple as that. You cooperate, you don't starve to death."

Looks like I'm going to starve to death, I started to say. But my dry throat stung and my cracked lips threatened to peel with the slightest movement, so I only settled back against the wall, silent and stoic.

The guard loomed closer. Even underneath the many layers of my own compounded filth, I could smell his pungent, unwashed, salty human scent. "You admit that you were present at the God of Fire's temple on the night of its destruction."

There didn't seem to be much point in lying about this; they already knew the truth. So I shrugged. Nodded.

He gestured, and one of his companions tossed a half-loaf of crusty bread at my feet. So at least they were following the rules of their own game.

Reflex made me reach for the bread without thinking. But I picked it up slowly, and I didn't bring it anywhere near my mouth, determined not to show how ravenous I truly was.

Scar Lips waited with one eyebrow cocked in cruel amusement.

I didn't eat. I only glared.

Finally, he spoke again. "We have reason to believe you didn't act alone on that night."

The chains around my wrists suddenly felt heavier. I shook my muscles loose and busied my hands with breaking off a small chunk of the bread and rolling it between my fingers. It felt crumbly and dry as dust, but damn it if I didn't want to inhale it anyway.

Still, I resisted, continuing to glare up at the guards from beneath my lashes.

"However," their leader continued, "we extensively searched the area where we found you and saw no sign of any others."

I fought the urge to smile or otherwise show relief. Andrel and the others had played it smart and escaped. *Good.*

"So, would you like to tell us where we might find your accomplices on a lovely day such as this?"

I coughed.

He took that—correctly—as a *no*. "Not even for more food? You look terribly hungry."

I smiled, hoping it looked as terrifyingly deranged as I felt, and then I swallowed hard. And through the pain of my peeling lips, in a voice made brittle from dehydration and disuse, I said, "Not even for all the food in all the miserable kingdoms of this realm."

He smiled back at me. "Have it your way. It's only a matter of time before we find those friends, all the same. And now you've lost your only chance at being rewarded for your cooperation." He turned and started for the heavy metal door, motioning for the others to follow.

"You won't find all of us," I growled at his retreating figure.

He stopped walking but kept his back to me. "All of you?"

I should have kept my mouth shut. I knew it was foolish not to, and I was not usually the type to run my mouth to the point of trouble.

But the lack of food in my stomach had left room for other things to fester—dark and rotten things—and it all came rising up now, the words spilling out in a heated rush. "There are more than you could ever imagine. More of us who hate your king and his devotion to the cruel gods—and striking us down only encourages more to rise. We will destroy every temple you build to those wild new gods, and when we're finished with that, we will destroy the very gods themselves. And who will your tiny brains and crooked hearts worship then?"

His head tilted slightly toward me as I spoke, so I could only just see the wicked grin stretching across his face. "Such lofty claims."

I kept my chin lifted and my defiant glare fixed on him, though my body shook from lack of nourishment, threatening to buckle underneath me.

"Lofty and *unkind*," sneered Scar Lips.

I had no shortage of unkind things to say to his sort.

Usually. But the speech I'd just given was nearly identical to one my sister had given so many times when she was alive. And now that I'd used her words up—along with what remained of my strength—I couldn't seem to think of anything else to say.

Scar Lips adjusted his gloves, pulling the buckles at the wrists and flexing the metal-studded knuckles of them in tiny but meaningful, threatening motions. "Deal with her mouth," he said with a cursory glance at the guard to his right. "If she wants to make threats, it's only fair that we help her to understand how...*delicate* her situation truly is."

The appointed guard bowed his head and kept still as the other two left. He wore the same sort of gloves as his leader, the knuckles of them adorned with barbs that flashed silver and menacing when they caught the torchlight.

There was nothing readable in his expression as he walked toward me. The sadistic gleam from earlier was gone. *Every* emotion was gone, as though he had buried them so they wouldn't get in the way of whatever he was about to do.

I forced myself to take a deep breath.

On his hip was a short sword with countless dull, dirty jewels studding its pommel. He started to draw it but decided against it, instead pulling at his gloves and flexing his fingers the way Scar Lips had moments ago.

He crouched before me, fisted a hand into the front of my grimy shirt, and lifted me as he straightened once more to his full, lanky height.

He drew his hand back.

I didn't flinch. I *wouldn't* flinch. Instead, I let the festering heat in my stomach rise up again, feeding it violent thoughts until it expanded throughout my entire body—a shield of fury and hate burning wild and hot enough to block all other sensation.

I hardly felt the guard's first strike. Didn't realize how powerful it had been until I tasted the blood welling up on my bitten tongue.

I spat to avoid choking on blood and spittle, showering the guard's pale tunic with specks of red in the process, which earned me another blow to the face. This time the metal points on his knuckles connected, scraping my chin and causing a searing pain hot enough to cut through even the thick shield of rage caging me.

Dust exploded as I hit the ground, erasing the notes, the patterns, the days I'd drawn through it. Droplets of my blood dotted the space all around me. Red, like the fire that had scarred my face. Like my sister's blood. Like the bright lights from the bombs we'd set in Cauldra. All I could see was red.

The guard didn't let up once I hit the ground. Over and over his boot connected with my side, stomped my face, unceremoniously kicked me over so he could better reach the other side of me.

At some point, he stopped.

He left.

I didn't notice him leaving, I simply fought my way back into vague awareness and realized he was gone.

I rolled onto my back, my chains clinking around me. The ceiling wheeled overhead. The sunlight in the window came and went, impossibly out of reach—but whether the changing light was from the passing of time or from my own consciousness slipping in and out, I wasn't sure.

After a few failed attempts to focus on that light, I stopped trying, closed my eyes, and drifted away with images of blood and fire swirling in my mind.

CHAPTER 7

SOMETHING TOUCHED MY CHEEK.

It startled me, and yet I didn't—*couldn't*—jump; I felt trapped in my own body. Maybe they'd used the same poison on me that Andrel had used on the temple caretakers, and now I would die as they had, unable to do anything but scream.

Maybe I deserved no less.

Maybe I deserved worse.

I closed my eyes again.

I had nearly slipped from consciousness when a deep voice said, "You can't stay asleep forever."

I wanted to recoil, but again I found myself utterly frozen. My skin felt tight, my bones brittle as twigs. I was certain that pushing through the pressure encasing me would break me into irreparable pieces.

"Yes, I can," I managed to mutter, and though the deep voice continued to speak in reply, I sank back into the darkness I'd emerged from, determined not to fully wake up to whatever horrors surrounded me.

When I finally came to my senses again, it was early morning, judging by the golden light creeping down from the window. I didn't know how many days had passed. My head was throbbing. It felt like I'd gone a week without water.

Water.

As soon as I thought of it, the need for it became all-consuming. Mercifully, I found the familiar pitcher with its chipped rim beside me, just within reach.

So they still weren't prepared to let me die just yet.

Lucky me.

My next thought was my appearance, and I frantically ran my trembling hands over my face, holding my breath until I was certain it was still smooth. My skin was sore—bruised, no doubt—and bits of crusted blood crisscrossed my chin and throat, but I didn't feel raised scars nor pointed ears.

My sister and her necklace still protected me even now.

A rush of mixed feelings overcame me. I fought the urge to curl back up on the ground, feeling battered and useless down here in the dark, and ever more certain that Savna would be handling this situation far better than I was.

Instead of curling up, I rubbed the last bits of grogginess from my eyes. They watered and stung—partly from exhaustion, but also from the acrid scent of smoke filling the air.

Was something burning outside?

I pushed myself upright and leaned against the wall, wincing from the pain in my ribs. How many times had that bastard kicked me? How many of my ribs were bruised—or worse? I tried not to think about it, focusing instead on dragging the pitcher of water to me and picking a few bugs from it. Hands still shaking, I lifted the pitcher to my lips and sipped slowly.

The bread I'd been given was still on the ground beside me as well, hard as a rock and missing tiny bites...stolen by mice, I assumed. I shuddered at the thought of them crawling over it —and me—while I was unconscious. I ripped off a few chunks and tossed them into the water, trying to soften them to something I could more easily swallow.

I was fishing one of them out when the door to my cell opened.

I pushed closer to the wall, bracing myself, trying to look sturdier than I felt.

Torchlight blazed brightly at my intruder's back, turning them into a mere silhouette, but I was fairly certain it was a man. A very large man. He lingered in the doorway a moment, his attention caught by something down the hall.

Was he one of the four guards I'd been studying?

Or one of the tormenting trio back for another round of torture?

I didn't think he belonged to either of these groups; I didn't immediately recognize anything about him. But maybe my senses were simply too beaten down and exhausted to properly gauge anything.

I tried to listen closer as he stepped into the room, but there was nothing to hear; he moved with exceptional grace and silence for a human. I tried to inhale his scent, but all I smelled was smoke—something outside was definitely on fire, more and more of the heavy odor wafting into my cell with every passing moment.

I stopped trying to smell or hear him, focusing instead on

what I could see as he came closer...and I quickly realized that this was not any guard I was familiar with.

He was a mountain of a man, tall, yet well-muscled, and despite his size, he seemed to glide rather than walk, his movements precise, confident, unhurried. I felt frail and awkwardly unbalanced in comparison—especially after over a week in this hellish cell. A hood was drawn over his head, casting shadows over most of his face. The outline of the snug-fitting hood suggested a strong jawline and a thick head of hair but revealed little else.

"What do you want?" I rasped.

He held up his hands in a gesture of peace. There were several rings of gold adorning his fingers. "I was ordered to take you upstairs when you woke, that's all."

I didn't like the idea of being *taken* anywhere.

But I was in no condition to fight him off, so I simply kept staring, wary eyes following his every movement. I scarcely blinked; if I couldn't manage formidable at the moment, then I was determined to make sure he knew I was wide awake and aware.

He stared right back at me. I still couldn't see much of his shadowed face, even with my advanced sight. Only his pale eyes stood out, and their exact color was impossible to tell. Blue? Silver? Maybe some combination of both. His gaze caught on my bloodied chin, and then my right cheek.

The bruises and cuts must have been impressive, judging by his frown—though I suspected the feeling of remorse went no deeper than his expression.

"You should have told those guards what they wanted to know." He produced a key from his pocket and removed the shackles from my ankles as he spoke. He left the ones around my wrists, but unhooked their chains from the wall and secured them in his fist instead. Somehow that fist seemed more solid than the cold wall of stone rising behind me.

"I'd die before I betrayed my allies," I informed him, still watching his every motion with as much focus as I could muster.

"How wonderfully brave of you." His tone was droll, just short of mocking.

"What good is a coward to our cause?" I snapped.

"More good than a dead woman, I'd guess."

I swallowed down my reflexive, biting response and continued to study him silently. The cloak he wore was too finely made to have spent much time in dirt-encrusted dungeons such as this one. His boots appeared recently-shined, and those rings on his fingers...yes, he was far too well-dressed for a common guard. His speech, too, was elevated enough that it wouldn't have seemed out of place in a royal court.

Who did he ultimately answer to?

Who answered to him?

And where was he going to take me?

"What do you know of betrayal and loyalty to any cause?" I continued to eye him up and down, counting the rings on his fingers. Most were relatively plain, but one on his right hand caught my attention—a band featuring several rubies that seemed to sparkle from within.

I leaned closer, drawn to the glimmer before I could help it. My vision blurred with even that slight movement, and my thoughts slurred together. I caught myself and refocused, determined to make my point despite my exhaustion and weakness. "You're most loyal to the king's coin, I suspect...not anything worth laying down your life for. So you wouldn't understand."

He huffed out a laugh. "Well, as long as we're making assumptions about one another..." He gave my chained hands a sharp tug, pulling me into step beside him. I fought the urge to jerk back, knowing it wasn't a war I could win.

"Let me guess," he continued as we made our way into the hall, "you think you serve a more noble cause than any one I possibly could?"

I didn't answer right away. I was busy blinking, trying to adjust to the new lighting, and his question felt loaded with implications that my tired mind couldn't quickly navigate.

He tossed an expectant glance my way.

Silver.

His eyes were clearly silver in the torchlight.

"Is this your attempt to draw more confessions out of me?" I asked. "Still trying to figure out who my accomplices were?"

He shrugged, a slight smile tugging up a corner of his lips. "If you're willing to tell me, it might earn me some more of the king's coin."

I turned away, keeping my eyes straight ahead and my voice devoid of emotion as I said, "You're out of luck, I'm afraid. I acted alone and served only my own purposes on the night of the temple's destruction."

Though I still didn't look his way, I could feel his gaze raking over me like claws. He clearly knew I was lying. Yet, he didn't challenge what I'd said.

We walked on in silence, climbing staircase after staircase. They seemed unending. Was this another form of torture they'd devised? Starving their prisoners and then forcing them to climb themselves to their deaths? My legs wobbled. My body swayed and lurched unsteadily about. I slipped and slammed my knees into the hard steps more than once—and my escort was neither patient nor gentle about navigating me through these things.

By the time we reached the last staircase, he was essentially dragging me.

I found my footing again once we made it to a stretch of flat floor. Every step I took made me wince from the pain in my ribs, and I felt only a tingling numbness in my right leg, but I would not be dragged any longer. I breathed slowly in and out and forced myself to march on my own two feet.

There were plenty of windows on this level. The longer I walked through the bright daylight, the warmer I felt—and the more I felt my steadiness returning. It came gradually, and I remained nowhere near my full strength, but a defiant spark of determination flared in my chest all the same.

My guard had hooked a hand around my arm while dragging me; I tested my renewed vigor by jerking away from his touch. The chains still bound me, and he held tight to those—but his actual hands no longer touched my skin.

Small victories.

With the chains pulled taut between us, his outstretched arm was partially uncovered. I saw a mark on his wrist, beneath his rolled-back sleeve: a twisted flame. Like the ruby-encrusted ring he wore, it seemed to glow from somewhere deep within.

"A godmark," I muttered, more to myself than him. That explained why he was truly here, dragging me so doggedly along—he served an even more nauseating, unforgiving master than crowns and coins. He was likely hoping for an extra blessing from the God of Fire for performing this duty.

What else did he plan to do to me to gain more of that god's favor?

I steeled myself, working up the energy to demand the answer to this, but he spoke again before I could.

"Just out of curiosity...what did you hope to accomplish by destroying the temple?"

The question caught me off guard.

"How did you think the God of Fire would respond to your crime?"

I stumbled. Caught my balance against the chains he held, composed myself, and summoned as much dissent and vitriol as I could in my sorry state.

"I spat at the feet of your god before I destroyed his temple," I said, "and I would do it again if given the chance. *That* is what I think of the God of Fire, his temples, and all who serve him—and I don't care what he does in response to these things. I don't fear him."

He slowed nearly to a stop. He seemed to be fighting to keep his gaze fixed in front of us and his posture relaxed and indifferent.

I glared at him until he finally glanced my way, silver eyes glinting as we stepped into the most well-lit room thus far. I gave him a saccharine smile, fully expecting to receive another blow to the face in response—a matching bruise for my other cheek, maybe.

But all he said before turning back to the path ahead was, "Interesting."

Which was more infuriating—and disappointing—than the argument I'd been bracing myself for. I'd been trying to goad him with that last smile, to vex him into making a careless misstep that I could take advantage of. We hadn't passed many other guards on our march, and I was feeling a little more like my usual fighting self. He was much stronger than me, but I could still be quick and slippery even if I wasn't at full strength. All I needed was a mistake I could exploit.

The guard said nothing else, however, nor did he look my way as we walked onward. His hold on my chains stayed mercilessly tight, jerking me along with increasingly agitated motions. He nearly pulled me off my feet more than once—purposefully reminding me of how easily my weakened self could trip, I suspected.

I continued to plot my escape anyway.

As we stepped into the grey, overcast daylight, more guards poured out of the prison hold as well and folded in around us, blocking any path except for the one directly forward.

I had been carried back to the city of Cauldra, as expected. I recognized the street we'd emerged onto; the temple we'd destroyed had stood at the end of this road, its red and orange stained-glass windows positioned to embrace the light of the setting sun.

A crowd was gathered in the ruins now, their voices gratingly loud after so much time in my near-silent cell. Loud and *odd*, I thought—a strange mixture of excited chatter and solemn chanting that I couldn't make sense of.

My escort indicated for me to start walking toward the noise, wearing a smile as nasty as the one I'd given him a few minutes ago. I narrowed my gaze on the distant crowd, determined not to spare another glance at him.

Slowly, the full scene at the road's end came into focus, and I saw where the horrible stench of smoke had been coming from: A newly erected platform stood in the center of what remained of the temple's foundations, and all around it were little fires, neatly spaced and deliberately set. Herbs and animal carcasses and all manner of other sacrificial things were burning, sending smoke spiraling up to the heavens—apologies for their failed temple dedication, I guessed.

Dozens upon dozens of humans were kneeling and praying around these fires, some of them chanting, some of them crying. As we approached, a man pointed in my direction—

No, not just in my direction.

Directly at me.

Several more followed the man's pointing, and then heads were turning to look my way, and a raucous cheer went up, as if they'd all been waiting in the heat and the smoke all day just to catch a glimpse of me.

There was a flurry of movement as the man who'd first pointed me out ran for the platform, vaulting onto it and grabbing a rope stretched across it. Two other men joined his efforts, and together they pulled and tied off three separate ropes, lifting and securing the wide wooden post they were attached to.

More joined in as I watched—men, women, and even children offering bundled piles of kindling and twine-tied clumps of fragrant herbs, tossing them onto the platform until it was entirely covered, save for a narrow path leading to the risen post.

My blood became ice, freezing me mid-step, as I realized what was happening.

They *had* been waiting for me. For me to be fully awake, fully conscious and able to march toward the center of the platform. Through their fresh offerings. Toward the pyre they'd erected, where their greatest offering of all would be set alight.

They no longer had a temple to give to the God of Fire.

So they were going to give him *me*.

CHAPTER 8

"Delightfully barbaric, isn't it?" asked my guard escort.

My head snapped toward him.

His smug smile remained candidly in place.

"I don't find anything about this delightful." My words came out with less bite and more fear than I'd intended.

His smile twitched the tiniest bit—as if reacting to the breath of terror in my voice—but I didn't want his pity.

I looked away, back to the crowd ahead, steeling myself. As I was marched forward, my eyes covertly darted toward alleyways and side-streets, across balconies and into windows, looking for a way out. For anything and everything I could potentially use to my advantage. For signs of my kind, my allies...

Surely they were hiding somewhere in the city, watching this unfold, just waiting for the right moment to strike.

They *had* to be.

They wouldn't leave me here to die.

A warm, smoky breeze whipped across my face, causing an

itching pain to spread across the cuts on my chin. An involuntary shudder rippled through me. My escort tightened his hold on my chains.

I didn't recall making a conscious decision to keep moving.

Yet somehow, we were at the foot of the crudely fashioned stairs leading up to the high platform, and in another blink, I was up the stairs, at the head of the path of offerings that led to the center post.

Beyond the platform and pyre, I saw a full picture of the temple's destruction for the first time. The scorch marks stretching out from the foundation, the broken ground, all the rubble that had been scraped away and stacked neatly around what remained of the destroyed building. Piles and piles of broken glass and stone, row after row of damaged furniture, sculptures, melted paintings, and other art...it must have taken hundreds of humans to organize it so quickly.

So quickly.

Would they simply rebuild it all, just as quick? Replace their fallen temple with a grander one after sprinkling my ashes over its restored foundations?

I cursed under my breath, adding fuel to the fury smoldering inside me, trying to coax my anger into rising up and pushing the waves of hopeless despair away.

Most of the crowd's chatter had given way to nervous whispers, punctuated by the occasional triumphant laugh or a loud, eager bit of prayer. The smoke and the competing smells of countless burning offerings assaulted my inhuman senses, cutting sharply up my nose and making my eyes water. Not having hands free to wipe away the tears was excruciating, and within minutes, I was effectively blind.

"One final chance to give information about your accomplices," said my escort in a low voice. "I'm sure the magistrate and the head cleric would be willing to offer you a deal, if only you'd answer their questions."

I bristled at his tone, which still danced on the edge between pity and mockery. Blinking tears away as well as I could, I looked his way and smiled another sweetly sick smile at him.

"Well?"

"Go fuck yourself."

His silver eyes flashed. His lips parted, speechless for a moment, but then they settled into his easy, arrogant grin once more. He gave a slight, mocking bow, gesturing as he straightened for the other guards who had followed us out of the prison hold.

My escort stepped back down the stairs as the other guards swarmed around me, two of them taking the chains he'd carried, several others taking a rough grip on my filthy clothing, my arms, the back of my neck. Even if I'd been at full strength, I don't think I would have been able to twist free; there were simply too many hands.

Then we reached the post erected in the platform's center, and there were too many ropes around too many parts of my body. Too many people rushing forward, setting fire to the outermost offerings upon the platform. Too many scents. Too many sounds. Too much fury and confusion and...*tightness*. I was tightly bound to the post by my arms, my legs, my stomach, and though no binding was across my chest, the tense heaviness I felt in it was nearly unbearable.

I can't die. It was all I could think, over and over. *I can't die like this. Please, not like this.*

I lowered my head, briefly closing my watering eyes, teeth gritting at the stinging pain accompanying the tears.

I heard a faint whistling sound—one too high-pitched to be noticed by humans.

Every numbed nerve I possessed tingled back to life. The tightness in my chest settled briefly, just long enough to allow a deep breath. But I tempered my hope, keeping my next inhales measured and shallow. I had imagined the whistle in my desperation, hadn't I? We'd used that instrument for years now, and I'd know the sound anywhere, but...

Could it really be them?

I kept my head lowered but lifted my eyes, still trying to blink back tears so I could scan the crowd for familiar faces. That crowd had grown loud again. Clamorous and restless, bodies jostling for position like crabs trying to fight their way out of a fisherman's bucket. The smoke atop the platform was growing thicker as embers fell from the outer offerings and set fire to the ones closer to me. Those closest to my body had not caught fire yet, but it was only a matter of minutes before they did. At most. Some of the crowd started to back away from the platform as the flames grew.

Even if Andrel and the others *were* here, I likely wouldn't be able to find them in this chaos.

And I doubted they'd be able to get to me.

I eventually *did* find a clear face through the smoke and beyond the platform's edge, but it was not one of my own kind —not an ally or savior—but the guard who had dragged me from my prison cell.

He was one of the only people standing perfectly still. His smug smile was gone, his shadowed face oddly contemplative.

I glared at him and nothing else.

As everything else steadily turned to little more than bleary, smoke-obscured blurs, he became my only tether to this realm, this lifetime. I directed every angry, desperate thought I had in his direction. All my bitterness. All my rage. The familiar hatred cocooned me as it always did, bringing safety and warmth as I sank into it, making me invincible and—

The guard looked up.

Our eyes met.

All the warmth in the world abruptly disappeared. A strange sensation reverberated through my body, pricking at my skin like needles. I couldn't readily name the feeling overcoming me, but I no longer felt wrapped in anything *safe*—I felt as if the outer layers of me had been scoured clean off, casting glaring firelight onto all of the ugliness underneath.

A sudden breeze stirred, whipping the flames around me higher and showering the offerings closest to my feet with red-hot sparks. I watched in horror as a nearby bundle of tied sage began to smoke, the edges of its silver-grey leaves glowing with heat. It caught fire with a slow, ominous crackling followed by a sudden *whoosh*. More wayward sparks flew from it onto more bundles of herbs, kindling, and loosely tied scrolls that likely contained desperate, hastily-scribbled prayers.

One after the other, the rest of these offerings ignited.

Wind and flame and smoke swirled around me. Sweat dripped from my skin, drenching my clothing. I couldn't see through the black smog. I couldn't hear anything but the crackling, the sparking, the hiss and roar of things being devoured by an increasingly violent blaze.

And I couldn't *breathe*.

It took several moments to realize that this last part was not because the fire and smoke were choking the life from my lungs.

It was only because I was holding my breath.

I exhaled slowly, disbelievingly. But the smoke I then

inhaled proved harmless, more of a refreshing mist than a choking smog.

The flames were hot, charring the platform and engulfing more and more...yet I was only sweating. My skin *felt* burned and blistered in places, but a quick glance at even the most uncomfortable spots revealed a body perfectly intact. The fire licked at my skin like spiny grass tickling it. Irritating it. Nothing more.

The entire world had gone up in flames all around me.

But somehow, I was not burning.

CHAPTER 9

Higher and higher the pyre went, lashes of fire reaching and twisting together, blocking out my view of the smoke-filled sky.

I still did not burn.

How?

Was this a new side of my magic emerging?

No, I doubted it; I had some healing power, but it had never protected me against anything—only helped piece me back together after injury.

So maybe I hadn't imagined the whistle I heard. Maybe my allies *were* here. And Cillian's brilliant mind for weapons... perhaps he'd created something that could counter fire?

I kept coming up with possibilities. My mind—so in love with neat, orderly lines and diagrams and explanations—wanted to force this chaos into a shape that made sense.

But as the tumultuous seconds ticked by, I could find no solid shape to assign to anything. It didn't help that I felt like I was floating, my mind detached from my body, the scenery spinning around me and changing every time I blinked.

So I'm dreaming, then.

It was the only explanation for the way my feet did not seem to touch the ground, no matter how far I stretched my legs. The only reasoning for the way the world kept spinning faster and faster, pulling my bindings free as it did, and for the way those bindings soon fell in pieces all around me, burning instantly to ash as they hit the ground.

The platform was gone. I stood instead on a rocky stretch of earth. My feet touched it now, but I still felt like they were only skimming the surface, like one strong breeze might whisk me into the clouds. Twisting flames still surrounded me, yet the fires here were not spreading, not wild and reaching; they were more like walls fencing me in on two sides, calmly burning as if candle flames relegated to wicks.

Directly ahead, a crowd of unruly villagers still awaited my execution. But as I watched, they too disappeared, their bodies turning into smoke before my eyes. I followed the trails of smoke as they ascended toward a sky that was suddenly perfectly clear.

Once they were out of sight, everything became strangely silent.

I couldn't take my eyes off the cerulean sky at first, trying to understand how the smog had been so quickly swept aside to reveal such a brilliant, peaceful day.

When I finally lowered my gaze, I gasped, the sound echoing in the unnatural quiet.

The most stunning man I'd ever seen stood before me. So stunning that it took me a moment to realize I'd seen him before—it was the guard from my prison. I was certain of it.

Yet, it wasn't him at all.

He'd looked imposing from the moment I'd met him in my dark and dingy cell, but in the suddenly bright, clear day, with his edges accented by the firelight walling us in, he looked...inhuman.

His hair, dark blond with hints of red, was long enough to tie into a knot—and some effort had been made to do this, but several strands had pulled loose, presumably ruffled by the hood he'd been hiding beneath. It should have looked messy, especially combined with the bit of scruff along his jawline. And perhaps it would have if that jawline had not been so strong, so sharp, and the rest of him had not looked so disgustingly...*perfect.* As if nothing about him could ever truly look disheveled.

His eyes were definitely silver, but I now saw hints of blueish-green in them as the day brightened around us, like pockets of calm water breaking up a grey and stormy sea. The cloak he'd worn had been cast aside, and beneath it he wore a finely-tailored shirt of white linen, its sleeves rolled up to reveal muscular forearms covered in strange markings—swirls of black edged in red.

Like the godmark I'd seen on his wrist earlier, these red edges seemed to glow, making me think of molten rock cracking through charred earth. With each pulse of glowing light, the walls of flames surrounding us brightened as though both the fire and markings were tied to the very beating of his heart.

"You can spit at me again if you'd like, but it won't put these fires out." His voice was low, a rumble of confidence flirting with arrogance. He waved a hand, lazily, at the walls, and the flames roared even higher, their glare bright enough to obscure the sun itself. "Only I can do that."

I shook my head. "This is a dream."

"Not exactly." He chuckled.

I was not amused. "Explain, then."

"This is *Eligas*."

The word didn't immediately make sense to my exhausted and jumbled mind, but after some effort, I recalled the mention of it in one of the few books that had survived the Morethian Manor's destruction—it was the emptiness between realms. In some stories it was said to be a place of judgment for mortal souls. In others, it was merely a neutral place filled with pathways that the divine used to more easily traverse from realm to realm. Time stood still here, and nothing within its boundaries lived or died. Not a wholly divine place in and of itself, but also not a place where mortals could tread without divine help.

And not one they could *leave* without divine guidance, either.

It took several attempts to push words out through my dry lips. "That would mean..."

His brow arched as if daring me to finish my sentence.

I said nothing.

Neither did he. He also didn't move—scarcely even breathed—but another wall of fire rose behind me, hemming me completely in. The only way out now would be charging directly through him, and then...to where?

I couldn't leave this realm on my own. My legs shook at the thought, threatening collapse. There was nothing to brace myself against. Nothing but fire and strangely cold earth and the unsettlingly beautiful man before me.

Another lazy wave of his hand sent ropes of fire twisting away from the main walls, then sectioned them further into droplets that fell like leaves loosed by a sudden breeze.

Fire should not have moved in such a way.

I flinched as the first of those firedrops landed and died against my skin...until I realized they hadn't burned anything.

I swallowed hard. "Why aren't any of these flames hurting me?"

"They very well might in just a moment, depending on how you decide to act from here."

"You're toying with me," I accused. Like a beast playing with its food before ripping it to pieces and devouring it.

"That's only part of it." He caught one of the falling fire-drops. It flared brighter in his hand, and he appraised me through the flame before looking instead at the sky, studying it as though he could still see the humans-turned-to-smoke floating through it. "I also don't want these humans thinking they control the fires of justice and vengeance or anything else in this realm. And such pitiful sacrifices are not really my taste, anyhow."

"Pitiful?" The word snapped from my mouth before I could catch it.

It was likely one of the kinder ways to describe what I looked like after more than ten days in a dungeon, but my jaw still ached from the effort of clenching back a nasty retort.

"Sorry to have offended you with my appearance," I muttered.

He accepted the apology with a graceful nod—as though I'd genuinely been asking forgiveness—and continued on as if he'd missed the sarcasm in my voice entirely. "So I decided to intervene, in hopes they might learn and do better next time."

"With a less pitiful offering?"

"Yes." He crushed the drop of flame he held, extinguishing it.

As I watched the flame go out, I could no longer doubt the conclusion I'd come to almost immediately after glimpsing his face. It had to be him. And it had to be said, even if merely *thinking* it made it hard for me to breathe.

"You really are...him." My voice came out in a whisper despite my best effort to speak normally. "The middle-god of Fire and Forging."

He regarded me with more silent appraisal, and then finally a curt nod, as if he was merely allowing me—a lowly mortal—to address him as such.

My entire body felt tense, coiled tight from years of waiting, watching, preparing for this meeting.

He'd been wrong a moment ago. This *was* a dream. My dream. I'd fantasized about this day for years, and now I was actually standing before one of the Marr. The vengeful rush of hatred and possibility that overcame me was so intense I nearly cried out in delight.

I caught myself, however, reining in my rage and keeping my thoughts level. I couldn't waste this opportunity by acting rashly. It might briefly satisfy my lust for vengeance, but I'd just been struck by a grander plan. A better idea.

A wild, mad, likely impossible idea that would require every ounce of control and cunning I possessed to pull it off.

The tides shift, and so too must our tactics. That's what Kinnara had said. She was right. And here was how we were going to shift things—how *I* was going to shift them—by destroying the gods from the inside out.

While saving myself from a fiery death in the process.

I forced my face into something resembling triumph—with a touch of reverence—and my tone into something far braver than what I currently felt. "I've succeeded, then," I said.

He canted his head slightly. Curiously.

Good.

I could manipulate curiosity easily enough.

"Succeeded in finally catching your attention," I explained, steadying my voice, "because yes, I was working with others on the night I destroyed your temple, as you so rightly assumed. But this meeting with you...it was my idea, and mine alone."

He folded his arms across his broad chest, skepticism dancing in his eyes, but he didn't interrupt.

"I was trying to attract your attention." I swallowed again to clear the dryness in my throat. "Because I want you to consider making me your divine servant."

His smile shifted from skeptical to something wild and twisted and cruel, and the dryness in my throat turned to a full desert.

But he still didn't speak, so I didn't stop talking.

"The people of Cauldra built their temple to attract your attention—to flatter you in hopes that you would find one of them worthy of walking by your side—but you must realize how empty their gold and promises are."

He snorted. "Of course I realize it. You humans are nothing if not predictably cliche when it comes to such things."

"Yes; those temple builders could never understand your true nature."

He laughed a quiet, breathy sort of laugh—one clearly tempered by the curiosity I'd managed to pique in him. "And I'm to assume that you *could*?"

"You moved mountains and set the world ablaze when you ascended. I hope to ascend in the same way. To serve in the same way."

"To serve..." Another quiet laugh. "...With fire and violence and turmoil?"

His question—and the dark glare accompanying it—felt like a challenge. A test. So I didn't let myself hesitate. "Exactly."

His stare did not soften. It pressed as a physical weight

against my body, carving in and pushing aside all the layers of me so he could better study the very soul at my center.

Neither of us moved or spoke for a long moment, leaving too much time for the reality of the situation to settle over me. I fought the urge to recoil as it did, knowing he could strike me down without breaking a sweat. That he could set me alight with a breath, leave me here in this emptiness to burn for an eternity, turn me to nothing but ashes to dance upon...

I was playing with fire in every sense of the phrase, and as the seconds crawled by, I began to think I had made a fatal mistake.

He lifted his head toward the sky, eyes narrowing, brow furrowing in thought.

I inhaled too sharply in response to his sudden movement. A muscle in his jaw twitched, he shook the tension from his left wrist, and I braced myself for the coming fire.

Then he slowly looked back at me and asked, "What is your name?"

"I...Karys. It's Karys." I managed to clamp my mouth shut then, afraid my elvish surname would give too much of me away. He'd said *human sacrifices* earlier. So for all his power and confidence, he couldn't tell what I truly was. I wondered how long I could keep up such a ruse—a problem I would have to deal with later.

"Just Karys?"

I became aware of the weight of my sister's necklace against my throat, as I often did in my most frightening, desperate moments.

"Karys Sparrow," I lied.

He hesitated.

The reminder of my necklace and its limited magic spurred me more fervently onward; I didn't have time to doubt my plan. "You've witnessed my capacity for loyalty," I pressed, motioning to my bruised and battered face.

He frowned at the injuries, just as he had back in my cell.

"You've seen how I stand within the fire," I added. "What more do you need to know about me?"

"Plenty more," he mused, but the look he regarded me with now was more conniving than cruel. "You don't truly understand what you're getting yourself into, Little Sparrow."

He was right, of course. I didn't know. His words threatened to wither my resolve, but voices pounded against my skull —Kinnara's, Andrel's, my sister's—hardening that resolve further as they reminded me of what I *did* know.

The gods were cruel without cause. Without mercy. Without regret.

They were not invincible, however—the Marr had all been human once, and if I could infiltrate their world and discover their weaknesses, I could bring them to their knees, make them answer for everything. I could do this. I could be as calculating and as ruthless as them.

I *would* do this.

I stood up straighter and said, "I am not afraid."

The god studied me for one last, long beat. "You aren't, are you?"

Before I managed a reply, he reached out and took my thin arm in a powerful grip.

His hand was so massive it was able to encircle my forearm entirely. As he squeezed, a heat just short of burning radiated from his palm, searing a path all the way up to my shoulder.

As he drew his hand away, black marks like the ones on his skin twisted along my own. He traced a finger down to my wrist, and some of the darkness sank into my body, leaving only a small blot in the shape of a twisted flame, similar to the one most of his marked humans carried—albeit darker than any I'd ever seen.

I loathed the sight of it.

My fingers itched for a chance to release my claws and rip it off. To dig out all of the darkness he'd planted in me. My entire body trembled with the effort of resisting this urge, which I hoped the god interpreted as fear. Or pain. I couldn't betray the disdain I felt toward him, or this mission would be over before it started.

"You'll need to go back to your realm for the moment, or your fellow mortals will lose their collective minds and start acting even more foolishly than usual," he said, candidly. "The mark I gave you will offer some protection until we meet again...assuming we *do* meet again, and you survive the afternoon."

I tried not to scoff at the challenge. "And after I survive it? Then what?"

"I'll send for you when I'm ready to do so."

I started to question him further, but the flames around us shifted, rising up and weaving into a complete circle around me, cutting us off.

I was alone with nowhere to go except through the fire.

Another test?

I decided it was. After gathering a few lingering scraps of my ragged and worn-out courage, I walked forward. The flames parted, but I only made it a few steps before I was jerked abruptly to a stop.

I was back in the mortal realm, bound once more to the pyre, the situation as dire as I'd left it.

No time seemed to have passed; the fires at my feet were just beginning to burn in earnest, the crowd only just starting to grow wary of the building heat and billowing smoke.

The smoke choked me, making my eyes water again to the point of blindness. The flames grew, lashing like whips against my body. Sweat drenched my hair and clothing, only to evaporate as the temperature rose around me, leaving my skin unbearably dry and tight and feeling as though it might crack and crumble away with my next wheezing breath. I strained against my bindings, head jerking this way and that, frantically searching—

The God of Fire was nowhere in sight.

And the mark he'd left on my arm, the one he'd promised would help protect me...

It was gone.

CHAPTER 10

I CAME TO A SWIFT, TERRIBLE REALIZATION: THE GOD of Fire had never been here at all. It had been a hallucination, my mind's attempt to spare me from the painful death I was seconds away from suffering.

The flames roared higher.

All of the moisture was sucked from both the air and my body alike. I felt like dust, soon to be swept away and scattered so completely by the wind that I would cease to exist. Or matter.

Then I felt myself slumping, *heavily*, and I realized I still had weight to me yet.

Down, down, and farther down—

How?

I was bound so tightly I shouldn't have been able to fall to the platform like this, yet I felt myself crumpling, sinking, colliding with the charred metal and wood beneath me.

A pair of arms wrapped around my body, lifting me up. My head lolled about. I was so dazed and dizzy from inhaling smoke that it took me a moment to realize I was moving, someone was carrying me away from the building flames—and I could control my hands and feet. They were numb, but no longer bound. A few of the binding ropes were dangling from my body, the ends of them cut and frayed.

I turned toward my carrier. I couldn't manage to lift my head and see their face, so I just pressed my cheek into the dark coat they wore and inhaled. I still smelled mostly smoke and ash, but there was also an undercurrent of something spicy and woodsy in the rough fabric I curled against. Something familiar —though my battered mind couldn't quite place who the scent belonged to.

After what might have been seconds—or minutes, or longer—more familiarity beckoned my senses back to life; I saw a flash of white out of the corner of my vision, and heard the recognizable *hiss* and *pop!* that accompanied them. Screams went up from the crowd that hadn't yet fled, and I heard muffled voices shouting warnings and evacuation directions.

The flashes of white diffused into large, puffy clouds of white smoke. I summoned every ounce of strength I had left to turn my head and study them closer. To make certain of what I was seeing. Decoys made of oil, damp wood, and a dusting of crushed limestone powder...

I'd know those smoking bombs anywhere.

Cillian's handiwork.

My friends had come for me.

It might have been another hallucination, but I didn't care. If I was going to die, I wanted to die believing they had tried to save me, their faces the last clear images in my mind before I burned away.

I closed my eyes, letting these thoughts soothe me until the world went silent and still.

I WOKE to the sight of tall trees reaching into a steel-grey sky and countless bright colors spinning around me.

Little by little I came back, testing the sensation in each of my toes and fingers before attempting larger, more coordinated movements. I seemed to be in one piece, fully functioning, even though I felt like I'd been tied to a horse and dragged down a mountainside.

A mountainside that had been on fire.

Groaning, I sat up. The forest and all its colors spun faster, but as it eventually slowed, I recognized most of the people who turned my way.

Cillian and Andrel were here, along with several of our familiar allies. Andrel stopped speaking mid-sentence to Saphiel—a longtime co-conspirator of ours who lived near Cauldra—and hurried over to me, dropping to my side and gathering me up in his arms. He held me so tightly that it instantly, painfully reminded me of the damage the prison guard had done to my ribs.

I was too weak to pull free, but eventually I managed a muffled *"Ouch,"* which sent Andrel scrambling backward and apologizing. He didn't go far, staying close enough to grab my hands when my balance swayed.

"You're okay," he kept saying, over and over.

I nodded, wincing at the pain from shifting my bruised jaw. "Thank you for saving me," I said, voice still scratchy from smoke and dehydration. "Though I have to say, your timing could have been better."

He returned the wry smile I gave him, squeezing my hands.

He started to speak several times only to press his lips back together, shaking his head. Finally, he managed another weak smile, but he still didn't sound like his normal confident self as he said, "We were much later than we meant to be, I'll grant you that."

Cillian was at our side by this point, and Andrel finally released his hold on me and allowed Cillian to step between us and pull me to my feet. His embrace was even tighter than Andrel's, though not as long. He stepped away and immediately started to explain the reasons they'd taken so long—which was what I truly craved. The facts, the details, the process of their rescue...hearing him list these things calmed me better than any touch or embrace could.

"We've had our hands full since you disappeared on us," he said. "Our base was completely overrun with soldiers we think were sent by King Eldon."

"Which suggests he and the religious order in Cauldra are even more tightly intertwined than we feared," Saphiel said, frowning as she joined us.

As recent as a decade ago, few kings in this realm would have cared about what happened at any temple dedicated to any god. But now the worship of the Marr and their Creators had become the norm rather than the exception. Demonstrations like the one we'd pulled off in Cauldra were only going to get more dangerous.

The tides shift, and so too must our tactics.

I gave my head a little shake. "So the manor..."

"No telling what will remain of it when we go back." Andrel's voice sounded distant, as if another part of him had been lost and left behind along with that manor.

"We all got away fine, thanks to your warning," said Cillian. "But they were tearing the city of Habostad apart when we left the area. Tarsis and Teshur as well...and some of the other smaller villages nearby; the soldiers were trying to bleed information out of the residents there. Kinnara and her followers stayed to run interference, along with several of our usual helpers, which is partly why it took us so long to reach you."

"But I had people here, too, watching the prison tower from the moment we tracked you to it," Saphiel put in. "We were prepared to intervene the instant things started looking deadly—whatever the cost."

Whatever the cost.

She said it to reassure me, but it only made the pit in my stomach widen. The costs of all our battles felt as though they were adding up faster than we could pay them.

Cillian glanced back toward the city we'd left behind. Several miles away from us, I guessed, but the thick haze of smoke hovering over it was obvious even from this distance. "It all went downhill faster than we expected it to."

"Luckily you lasted longer on that platform than any human would have," Andrel said.

"Longer than most *elves* would have," Cillian mused. "I knew you were tough, but I thought..." His eyes glazed over, and I suspected he was thinking of the night we lost my sister.

I fixed my gaze on some sort of creature shuffling in a nearby pile of leaves, determined not to let my mind run away with the same painful memories.

"I honestly thought we were going to be too late," Cillian finished quietly.

I still wasn't convinced they *hadn't* been too late.

Holding my breath, I glanced at my wrist. No godmark on my skin. No surprise there, really...yet I hadn't burned to a crisp.

How had I survived, if the God of Fire and his promised protection had been a mirage?

I stepped out of Cillian and Andrel's supportive reach, testing my weak, undernourished legs. I feared they might collapse right out from under me, but I couldn't make myself keep still. The rest of my rescue group gathered around and embraced me one by one, and I basked in their familiar company for several minutes as I tried to regain my composure and catch my breath.

Andrel watched me curiously as I moved among the others, maybe still trying to make sense of how I'd survived. I wished I could explain it myself; I felt like a ghost trying to convince myself and everyone else I was still alive, that I'd been here all along.

I forced a reassuring smile despite the uncertainty that overtook me as I stepped back to my companions. "I'm fine, really. You all were just in time." Eager to change the subject, I asked, "So where do we go from here?"

Andrel and Cillian exchanged loaded glances, but they clearly hadn't come to a consensus on the matter.

"You two really do fall apart when I'm not here to make decisions for you, don't you?" I teased.

Andrel smirked, averting his eyes, while Cillian gave a sheepish shrug and said, "We've been debating."

"If you've truly caught the king's eye," said Saphiel, brusquely inserting herself into the conversation as she had a tendency to do, "it would make sense to lay low for a while— perhaps somewhere like Hael? I have a cousin there who may be able to help you; she's both knowledgeable and well-equipped to hide a few fugitives."

Fugitives.

My heart sank at the word. I wanted to go back to our

home, and I could tell—by the clench of his jaw at Saphiel's suggestion—that Andrel wanted the same thing. I hated this feeling of being adrift, of fighting for a home that didn't have a foundation, running from one battle to the next without stopping to catch our breath.

It's not like it was the first time I'd been displaced, though. I would manage. I always had, and yet...

Baring my teeth, I couldn't help turning my arm over and over, still searching for the mark I knew wasn't going to be there. Had it really been a dream? It had felt so real, so tantalizingly close to a different way of fighting. A chance of breaking the exhausting cycle I'd been living for so long.

My hands clenched into fists, nails digging into my palms hard enough to sting. I felt a strange sense of abandonment. *Abandonment.* By a god I was growing more and more convinced I'd hallucinated. How stupid was I?

Even if he had been real, it was foolish to think we'd truly come to any sort of agreement, or that he'd given his word about anything. The gods didn't truly give anything. They only took whatever they wanted and did not give back.

Bastards.

"You should rest more before we head off to Hael or anywhere else," Cillian said, misreading the bitter anger and exhaustion that I'm sure was written all over my face. "I don't think you need to—"

"I nearly died at the hands of humans eager to sacrifice me to their chosen god," I interrupted quietly. "And it was a godmarked human—one with the Moon deity's power—who tracked me down and gave me away. They will not stop hunting me just because I slipped through their hands this afternoon. They wanted more than just *me,* too. They wanted the names of all of you as well." I inhaled sharply at the memory of the bloody interrogations I'd suffered.

"Karys—"

"I owe them. And I don't plan on resting until I've evened out the score between us and those damnable gods again." My voice was loud and angry enough that everyone else in our circle stopped what they were doing to look in my direction, their eyes wide and uncertain.

I started to apologize for my harsh tone, but Cillian didn't look offended when I shifted my gaze to him.

He looked...afraid.

"Karys." My name fell hesitantly from his lips, like something had latched on and tried to drag it back.

"What?" I demanded, voice still sharper than necessary.

"Your...*your arm.*"

A tingling sensation swept from my scalp down my spine. Fear followed in its wake, trying to freeze me in place, but I took a deep breath, closed my eyes, lifted my arm, opened my eyes again...

And there it was.

The god's flame-shaped mark had once more appeared on my skin, bright and burning for everyone to see.

CHAPTER 11

"OH," I SAID.

"Oh?" Andrel repeated, breathlessly. "What do you mean *oh*? What in the name of all the realms *is that*?"

A fresh silence draped like blankets of snow over the forest clearing, settling even heavier than before.

Cillian, with arms folded across his chest and green eyes narrowed in thought, finally broke the quiet as he calmly said, "It looks...like a godmark."

"I know what it *looks* like," Andrel said, "but why the hell is it appearing on Karys's skin?"

I was again struck by the instinctual urge to extend my claws and carve the mark and all its dark connections out of my body.

Saphiel stared, along with nearly everyone else who'd helped with my rescue, for several beats before taking a deep breath through her nose. "Explain yourself."

I met each of the gazes searching me in turn. The truth seemed murky at best, heretical at worst, but I didn't want to lie about what I'd done. I needed to make them understand why I'd done it—hell, I needed to make *myself* understand why. Anything else could be disastrous to the overall plans and attempts we had to unite our kind against our divine enemies.

"This is how I survived so long on the platform without sustaining so much as a burn," I said. "He was there, controlling the flames somehow."

Andrel went silent and rigid, lifting his gaze to the rain-thick clouds.

Cillian kept his gaze perfectly leveled with mine. "Who do you mean by *he*?"

"Dra' Zerachiel—the God of Fire." I'd nearly whispered the name, but I might as well have shouted, given how high Cillian's brows reached in response.

I told them every detail I could recall, then, of what had happened from the minute I woke in my prison cell to the moment I'd been paraded up to the burning platform. Andrel kept up his silent contemplation while Cillian grew increasingly restless with every word.

"I still don't understand why he gave you this mark," Cillian said, and the others crowding around us nodded and whispered, wanting to know the same thing. "Didn't he realize what you were? Who you are?"

I ran a hand through my hair, anxiously tucking and untucking it. "My ears were hidden by my necklace's magic," I explained, "and the mark...it came only after I struck a deal with him."

Gasps and whispers broke out all around me.

Cillian looked as if he might be sick.

I couldn't say I didn't deserve the skeptical and sickened, disapproving looks shot my way—particularly after the risks they'd all gone to in order to save me. It was the most basic of survival rules among our kind, whether we counted ourselves among the rebels or not: *Don't trust the gods or any of their monsters.*

The *don't make deals with them* part was, of course, implied.

The only person not looking at me like I was a fool—or some sort of delinquent child—was Andrel. He remained quiet, still staring at the sky with a thoughtful frown on his face.

"What kind of deal did you make?" Saphiel asked.

I made my voice hard and unflinching despite the doubts trying to gnaw their way into my mind. "The kind that will get me close enough to the gods to destroy them from the inside out," I said.

Another round of gasps and whispers. Skeptical, amused, afraid—the tones I caught ran the gamut of emotions; it was hard to pick out a specific one from the flurry of noise.

I continued to recount the deal and all the plans I had made in that desperate moment.

Each word fell like a hammer stroke upon my old life, pounding away until it was entirely shattered. Nothing could truly go back to the way it had been before this moment. Even if I put the pieces back, the cracks between them would still be visible, diffusing a different sort of light over everything I'd known.

As my explanations trailed off, the whispers returned, louder and more urgent than before.

"Are you crazy?" Cillian asked, tilting toward me, his voice low and just between us. "I can't let you do this."

Guilt and fear coated my throat, too thick to swallow, but I somehow pushed a response out. "It's done, Cillian. I have to see it through; the mark isn't going to just go away."

"And apparently it knows when you start talking shit about

the gods," Saphiel mused, poking at the mark in question, which still shimmered a bit around the edges. "It seemed to react whenever you raised your voice against them."

I shivered at the thought of the brutish Fire God listening in on this conversation. "Just a coincidence, I hope."

"Terribly unsettling, otherwise," said Saphiel—a vast understatement.

I wondered again at what I'd truly gotten myself into, but I refused to dwell on it. Not here. Not now. The crowd around me would not see my doubts if I could help it. My sister wouldn't have shown any doubt; she would have been rallying them to the point of wanting to join her on a march to the divine realms or wherever else. Her shadow stretched longest in moments like this, making me more determined than ever to carry her weight without collapsing.

"Whatever becomes of the mark and the bargain, we'll see it through, as she said." Andrel's sudden voice was quiet yet commanding in the whisper-filled grove.

He was no longer looking at the grey sky; he was back to studying me, a strange emotion I couldn't name shining in his eyes. "I believe we should go to Hael, as Saphiel suggested, and plot our next moves from there. We need to get away from this city and its lingering unrest above everything else."

I nodded, grateful for the way his voice had pulled stares away from me.

Feeling a touch lighter, I breathed in deep and let my gaze wander back in the direction of Cauldra. The city was located in a valley along the Laton River; we were high above it now, and though trees blocked much of my view, I could still make out a few smog-veiled buildings.

I'd escaped.

Logically, I knew this.

But the heat on my skin and the smoke in my hair still made me feel as if I was burning, and I was beginning to wonder if the feeling would ever go away.

We traveled to Hael, as planned, and I spent the next several days preparing for...well, I didn't exactly know what.

How did one ready themselves to face the gods?

I'll send for you, he'd said.

Then what?

I needed a plan beyond whatever he had in mind as part of my indoctrination as his potential servant, and I hated—absolutely *loathed*—that I couldn't map things out with any sort of certainty.

I spent hours trying to decipher and diagram it all anyway, poring over the books and talking the ears off everyone who passed through our latest hideout, attempting to learn, to ready myself, to pinpoint weak spots I might be able to narrow in on once I was walking side-by-side with the Fire God.

A chill gripped me every time I pictured myself taking that walk, but I shook its ruthless hold off over and over again, forcing my attention back to plans and preparation.

There was plenty of fascinating literature to choose from. Saphiel's cousin—Zara, was her name—was as helpful as Saphiel had promised she'd be, both in hiding us and enlightening us; she was one of the elves most involved in the study of our kind's now-cursed and earthbound magic—a role she'd partly inherited, as her ancestors had once been among the most powerful magic wielders before the Fall.

I knew studies of this magic were growing deeper, the field

of this knowledge ever-expanding, but I'd seen little in the way of practical examples of it, and met even fewer actual scholars of the movement.

If anyone was going to discover how to bring down the gods with our so-called corrupted magic, however, I soon became convinced it would be Zara.

It felt like fate that I should find myself here on the eve of my mission. She and I spent hours by the fireplace in her cramped living room—often joined by Cillian—dissecting the brief conversation I'd had with the God of Fire, studying the mark he'd left and all the ways it came and went and reacted to the things I did or said. The most basic explanation seemed to be that strong emotions awakened its magic and made it appear, but Zara and I both suspected it went deeper than that.

Our conversations gave me hope. A proper direction to head in. A belief that if I could provide Zara and other scholars like her with more firsthand information about the Fire God and his brethren, then surely we could create some sort of weapon to bring those gods down.

Most days, I was so consumed with my thoughts and planning that I barely slept. Or ate. Or did anything else without a book in my hands or a notepad beside me, my hand cramping from all the thoughts I scribbled down in an attempt to untangle them. I wanted to believe my mind was absorbing it all, even if I was more closely resembling a walking, brainless corpse with every passing hour.

I didn't know how long I had before the Fire God would come for me, so I convinced myself I didn't need sleep or food as badly as I needed to prepare.

But the lack of these things, combined with the lingering frailty from my time in prison, eventually led to collapse—I lasted five days before it happened; one moment I was pulling a book from a shelf in Zara's office, the next, I was sprawled on the floor, blinking dancing lights from my vision, fingers digging into the weathered floor boards to try and keep my grip on reality.

My fingers eventually slipped away from the floor and reached instead for the bird hanging against my throat, and I would have sworn I heard my sister's voice floating down to me.

Don't let the gods win.

We can't let them win.

Unable to muster the energy to sit up, I laid on the office floor until Cillian encountered me, rushing to my side with an alarmed gasp.

"This has to stop," he muttered, scooping me up, carrying me to the nearest bed, and plopping me down upon it.

And though I tried to fight it, I was asleep before my head hit the pillow.

THE FOLLOWING MORNING, a burning sensation in my arm jolted me awake.

I shot upright, slapping desperately at my blankets, certain they were on fire. Certain *I* was on fire until I rolled from the bed, hitting the floor hard enough to jar myself fully awake.

Nothing was burning.

In fact, my skin felt cold to the touch—though the flame mark was once again shining on it, its color deep red with the faintest shimmer to it. Like wet blood. It took several attempts to slow my breathing as I stared at it.

After regaining my composure, I changed into clean

clothing and padded down the creaking steps to the kitchen. The sun had not yet risen, but Cillian, Andrel, and Zara were all awake, seemingly waiting for me when I walked in.

"You were shouting a few minutes ago," Andrel explained, rubbing the sleep from his eyes. "Nightmares, maybe? We were just debating about whether or not to wake you."

I didn't recall any nightmares. Only the fire that hadn't truly been there. I didn't mention this, however, because Cillian was already looking at the flame-shaped mark on my skin as though it was going to make him sick—a look that had nearly become permanent over the course of the past week as that mark became an ever more constant blight on my skin.

He'd stopped trying to convince me to change my mind at this point, but part of me was still afraid he might lock me away in some misguided attempt to protect me from myself.

Zara quietly fixed me a cup of tea that smelled strongly of lavender. Her heavily-wrinkled face scrunched in concern as she plopped the steaming cup in front of me and sat back down. I admired those lines as I sipped the warm liquid; the furrows around her eyes ran the deepest—likely from years of squinting at books and casting narrowed, disapproving glances at all her doubters.

The burning in my arm returned as I settled deeper into my chair, the sensation faint yet unmistakable.

Was it a signal of some sort?

Was this how the God of Fire intended to send for me?

I tapped my fingers irritably against the cup in my hands and sipped more adamantly at my drink, focusing on its warmth instead of the heat radiating from my new mark.

Trust a god to be cryptic and confusing.

No sooner had I thought of this when the hottest flash of fire yet seared through my arm; it felt as if the very blood beneath my skin was starting to boil. I jumped to my feet, nearly spilling what remained of my tea. Taking a deep breath, I sat the cup carefully back on the table. It rattled against the wood despite my best efforts to steady it.

"I...I think I need some fresh air," I said, backing away.

I needed much more than that, and we all knew it, but no one stopped me from leaving.

As I stepped outside, the heat pressing through my body began to fade. It grew cooler the farther I walked, and by the time I came to the edge of Zara's vast yard, the burning had reduced to nothing more than a tingling I barely noticed.

It still seemed annoyingly cryptic, but I was more certain than ever that this was a sign. One I had inadvertently answered by stepping outside.

The God of Fire was waiting for me, somewhere close by, somewhere beyond the edges of my familiar world. I felt him the way I felt storms approaching on a summer day—as a shifting pressure against my body, an electric pulsing that made the hairs on my arms stand on end.

But where was he?

Where was I meant to go from here?

I paced the yard for several minutes, searching, glancing occasionally at the faintly glowing mark on my skin while hoping for clearer signs.

The sun was low in the sky, sitting like an orange in the curved basket formed by the distant hills. A creek stretched along the edge of the yard, reflecting the growing daylight. Its brightly shining, vermilion streaked waves made me think of a building fire, which was the closest thing I'd seen to a sign since stepping outside.

I drew closer to the water's edge, chest tight with anticipation...and quickly realized that the bold streaks of red and gold were not a reflection of the sun.

The water was actually *burning*.

The waves did not bubble or gurgle, they hissed and crackled, moving with a viscosity more like mud than water. Above the churning flow of fire, orbs of silvery light danced in the air. The *Gatterlen*—also known as portal lights.

Legends said these lights were telltale signs to travelers that a pathway between realms was open and safe to use—a phenomenon that was once far more common, as there had supposedly been an age when elves could conjure up similar portals with similar guiding lights, when they had walked as freely between the divine and mortal realms as I walked between the rooms in Zara's house.

I heard footsteps approaching from behind me. Slowly, reluctantly, Cillian caught up to where I stood, and we both stared without speaking for several minutes. I couldn't bring myself to look at him right away, afraid I might lose my nerve if I saw his worried face.

"The Gatterlen," I finally whispered. "I thought they were nothing more than a myth."

"Me too," Cillian muttered.

Yet here they were, clearly heralding a portal—not even Cillian could deny what they were, though he did turn his back to the sight of it all.

I turned with him, doing my best to ignore the heat that the motion sent flashing up my arm. I understood Cillian's pain; I wanted one last moment without marks or missions or anything else between us as well.

A moment was, unfortunately, all we had to spare.

"I'll come back, you know," I said. "It isn't like what

happened to Savna. You know where I'm going, and why. And I have a plan."

He cut me a sideways glance. "You're the only one I know who could calmly plan a trip to visit the gods."

I managed a smile, which coaxed a partial grin from him too. "Just another day in our royally charmed life," I said.

He laughed, rolling his eyes.

"Also, *calmly* is a stretch."

The fiery portal flared brighter and hotter behind us, as if determined to draw our attention back to it.

Mesmerizing as it was, Cillian still refused to look at anything but me. "I'd go with you if I could," he said.

"I know." My heart clenched. "But I'd rather you stay here and learn more from Zara anyway. Between the two of you, I suspect there's some brilliant, magical, world-changing weapon just waiting to be discovered."

He seemed to turn the possibility over in his thoughts for a long time before acquiescing with a sigh. "I *do* have a brilliant mind, don't I?"

I laughed softly. "And it would be wasted where I'm going."

We stood for a few moments more, saying our last good-byes, until Andrel joined us. Zara watched the scene unfolding from her porch, staring at the Gatterlen lights and furiously scribbling notes. Cillian hugged me one last time before turning and starting a determined march back to the house.

Andrel made his way right down to the edge of the creek, swatting at the portal lights as though they were annoying gnats.

I followed him to the edge, picking up a handful of stones and tossing them into the fire, watching them sink. Trying not to think about myself sinking, and what might happen if this was all a terrible trick of some kind.

"It's really happening." Andrel gave the roiling waves of fire a disgusted look. "In a...flashy and pointlessly elaborate way. Typical divine nonsense."

"I expected Cillian would try and drag me away from it," I said, glancing over my shoulder to make sure he wasn't sneaking up on me to do just that.

Andrel gave a quiet, distracted chuckle. "I've been talking to him this past week, trying to convince him to trust you. Maybe it helped."

"So...you truly believe I can do this?" The question blurted out of me, and I hated how badly I needed to hear him say *yes*.

He didn't say it. Not right away. Instead, he took a few of the stones from my hand and said, "Do you remember the day we met?"

The words surprised me; it wasn't like him to wax nostalgic —and now, of all times?

I shook my head at him, giving a bemused smile. "I try not to think about it anymore than I have to."

He grinned. "Are you still embarrassed by the scene you made?"

The day my father snuck my sister and me out of the house to attend the rebel meeting at the Morethian Manor, I'd not exactly been on my best behavior. I'd spent that morning arguing with my mother about the incident that had left the burn scars on my face; she'd wanted me to go to the neighboring city, to a temple dedicated to the Healing Marr, to beg forgiveness for being so careless with our prayer shrine. To ask the Healing God to fix my scars in exchange for my repentance.

I'd refused.

It had been an ugly fight, and I'd leapt at the chance to

leave home with my father and meet the rebels I'd only heard whispers about.

I'd met those rebels, saw the state of the manor, heard the story behind it all, learned of all the things that had been lost. And with all the righteous indignity a twelve-year-old could muster, I'd formally declared war on the very idea of visiting any temple to any god—of healing or otherwise.

"The elders were shocked at how loud and blasphemous such a scrawny little kid could be, I think," Andrel recalled. "But me...I was too excited to sleep that night because I'd finally met someone who hated the gods as much as I did."

He skipped one of the stones across the fiery water. It nearly made it to the other side before sinking, pushing up a brief, bright fountain of fire as it went down.

"A hatred that couldn't be contained in all the endless political meetings and posturing so many of our older leaders insisted upon," he added after a moment.

A twist of that familiar fury unfurled in me as I stared at the portal ready and waiting to swallow me up, to take me away from him and everything else I knew.

"Promise me something," he said suddenly.

I inclined my head to show I was listening; I think I would have promised him anything in that moment, as foolish as it might have been.

He closed his fist over the stones still in his palm, staring at the spot where the last one had sunk for a moment before turning to me. "Don't lose your anger. And don't stop until you've destroyed them the way they've destroyed so much of us."

His hand reached for mine. The stones he'd closed in it had been crushed to dust by his cursed strength, and the gritty pieces that remained scratched my skin as he laced his fingers through mine and pulled me closer.

"I won't," I promised.

He pressed his forehead to mine, breathing me in for a moment before dragging himself away, planting a slow kiss on my scarred cheek as he went. "I'll see you soon, okay?"

I nodded, making myself stand still as he let go of my hand and backed away.

"I won't let you down," I whispered as I watched him leave —a promise to him, to Cillian, to my sister and all the others who were counting on me.

I ran my fingers over the scars he'd kissed, then down to the sparrow resting at my throat, willing its magic to cover those scars and my ears. I didn't expect the disguise to do me much good where I was going, but it had become like a comforting blanket that I couldn't help but wrap around myself.

As the magic settled, I took a deep breath.

With one final glance at the rising sun and mortal sky, I turned and stepped into the river of fire.

CHAPTER 12

I SANK.

And sank, and sank, and sank through strangely thick and warm water, bracing myself for an impact with the riverbed that never came.

My downward fall eventually slowed until I was merely floating.

I fell into light rather than the dark depths I'd anticipated —a fiery orange light so bright I could see it even though my eyes were tightly shut. The warmth around me grew to the point of sweltering, and I had the strange sensation I was sweating in the water, my skin growing uncomfortably slick and slimy.

As the suffocating heat pressed in, I gasped, sucking in not water, not air, but something in between that made my chest feel unbearably heavy. I started sinking again with the new weight, falling more swiftly this time until my feet finally hit solid ground.

I managed a normal breath. The water around me receded. A sudden, violent chill overcame me as the river I'd fallen through slipped away, and as I shivered, I couldn't help dropping to my knees, landing upon what felt like a beach of soft sand.

I steadied my pulse and opened my eyes.

Slowly, I staggered back to my feet, my mouth falling open at the sight awaiting me.

Ever since I was a child, I'd heard tales of the heavens where gods dwelled. Of mountains made of solid gold, roads paved with the same substance, of streams that babbled soft songs in strange languages and skies swept full of colors no mortal could properly name.

The tales really did no justice to the realm stretching before me now.

The air quite literally *sparkled*, bits of some sort of starlight-colored substance flittering down, coating the ground—and me—and making it all shimmer. The ground beyond my sandy beach was covered in rolling waves of blueish-green grass that looked so soft, so lush, I nearly sighed just at the thought of touching it. And the sky...pale lavender, I thought at first, but it kept changing before my eyes, dancing between shades of purple and blue until I gave up trying to decide on what color to call it.

I wanted to stare at it all forever, yet I felt unworthy of the beauty, smaller and more insignificant the longer I took it in.

I wasn't certain of where I was, but I suspected it was somewhere in the divine realm of Nerithyl—also known as the middle-heavens—the place in the universe where the Marr reigned most supreme. And if this was where the middle-gods dwelled, then what did the realm above it look like? I couldn't fathom the heavens the upper-gods must have lived in.

Giving my head a little shake, I saw to my clothes, expecting them to be damp and covered in sand. They were neither. The falling stardust, too, did not collect on my clothing or skin; instead, it sank into my body, melting as snow did—though it did seem to be creating a faint silver haze all around me.

I was alone, which seemed odd. Then again, what had I been expecting? A welcome party? It wasn't as though the gods were known for their hospitality.

I walked a short distance before I paused and decided to wait, somewhat awkwardly, while taking in more of my surroundings. I now stood upon the crest of a hill covered in the lush blue-green grass, and it *was* as soft as it looked. I plopped down into a particularly thick tuft of it. The air seemed to plop down with me, settling like a weighted blanket over my shoulders, and I had to fight the urge to curl up and take a nap.

Sweeping out from the base of the hill were countless paths leading in countless directions. I followed them with my eyes, one after the other, sketching the lines and destinations in a mental map. One led to a forest with trees that appeared to be made of colored glass. Another to a lake with impossibly blue water, and still another reached toward hills of silver-white flowers in the distance...

It would have taken a thick book full of detailed diagrams to chart them all. As far as I knew, no elf had laid eyes upon this realm since the Fall; what would they say back home if I mapped it all out and showed them such a thing? It wasn't why I'd come here, but the idea still excited me.

The grandest of the paths I saw—a winding walkway lined by lanterns flickering with bluish-white flames—stretched toward a walled area so large I was certain an entire city must have been contained within it. I searched my mind, trying to recall any mentions of such a city in Zara's books or any others I'd read, but I couldn't think of any.

Nevertheless, it seemed like the centerpiece of this place. A logical starting point. And if the God of Fire could not be bothered to greet me, I decided, hopping back to my feet, then I could manage a self-guided tour well enough—and I could take better mental notes without anyone distracting me, anyway.

The grand path seemed much longer once I was on it. No stardust fell upon it, and so it seemed oddly dark beyond the places where the lantern light fell, the shadows looming like beasts just waiting for me to stumble and fall fully into their darkness.

I finally reached the towering walls. There was a gate of iron and gold at the path's end with a somewhat familiar emblem in its center—that of a raven-like bird surrounded by thorns. It was the symbol of one of the Moraki...the upper-god of the Shade, in this case.

I knew there were three different courts of the Marr—one beneath each of the three Moraki—and I knew that the Fire God belonged to the Shade Court. Would I encounter other gods beyond this gate? Did all of the courts have their own separate homes within this same realm?

The gate was cracked open just wide enough for me to slip through, as though someone inside had been expecting me.

"I suppose leaving the gate unlocked counts as hospitality," I mumbled to myself. Either way, my curiosity was officially piqued, so I let myself in.

Within the walls, I found not a city, but a garden. Or perhaps *jungle* would be the better word, as it seemed to grow wild without any real structure—thick vines hung from the trees and wrapped around nearly every other solid structure.

Flowers of more colors and species than I could readily count bloomed everywhere I looked, several of the blossoms bigger than my head. I doubted any gardening tools had ever been used on the foliage here.

An attempt at a path had been made by someone, however; flat discs of sparkling stone wound a narrow trail between the spidery, gnarled tree trunks. I followed these stepping stones until I heard a peal of soft laughter that stopped me in my tracks.

I kept perfectly still, listening and inhaling deep lungfuls of the warm, thick air. I heard and scented plenty of things within that air, but few I could confidently name.

I needed to actually *see* the source of the laughter, I decided.

Carefully, I crept toward the sound, darting from tree to tree until I caught several unusual scents—something that reminded me of a stinging, wintry wind mingling with the aroma of metal and spice.

Following the strange smells brought me to a small area surrounded by trees with drooping branches covered in pink blossoms. The laughter had stopped. The only sounds now were my own breathing along with an odd humming in the air. The hum of magical energy, I thought; it sounded like bees buzzing in a far-off hive.

I leaned against a stone column wrapped in vines, and I stared.

A short distance away, two ethereal beings lounged in hammocks that appeared to have been spun from pure light. Or perhaps it was their bodies bleeding that glow; whatever the source, it took my eyes a moment to adjust and make sense of what I was seeing.

The being closest to me appeared to be a male. His skin was

ivory, his lean but muscular arms covered in faint markings in various shades of blue, the half-unbuttoned shirt he wore revealing similar markings upon his chest. His silvery-blond hair fell in straight, jagged layers just past his sharp chin. He was eating what smelled like some sort of fruit, tossing the dark pieces of it into his mouth between sips from a pewter goblet clasped delicately in his hand.

Stretched out in the hammock perpendicular to his own was a female with deep brown skin. A brush of gold paint covered her closed eyelids, and thin coins of what looked like actual gold decorated the scarf tied around her head, jingling a bit with every swing of the hammock—swings that made no sense, as there was no breeze, and she herself was perfectly still. Above her decorative scarf, her dark hair gathered in a thick poof, and her head reclined against a pillow of pink flowers.

They were both undeniably divine, just like their surroundings, and—just as before—I was torn between a desire to stare and shrink away.

Well, I hadn't come here with any plans to *shrink*.

I took a deep breath and crept quietly forward, keeping close to the various columns and trees spread throughout the space. I got close enough to study the details of the god and goddess, and I was gathering my courage to move closer when I accidentally stepped on a twig hiding beneath a pile of fallen flower petals.

I cringed at the sound, freezing where I stood.

The goddess spoke without opening her eyes. "Valas, do you smell something?"

The god beside her stopped mid-sip, lowering the goblet slowly as he breathed in a deep breath. His nose wrinkled in disgust. "Something from the mortal realm."

I pressed against the nearest tree, trying to decide whether to fully reveal myself or not. They clearly knew I was here. I didn't want them to think I'd been spying...but I *also* didn't particularly want to speak with anyone else until I'd spoken with the God of Fire; he was the one I'd made my deal with, after all.

The blond-haired god tilted his inhumanly beautiful face in my direction. His eyes were a pale, alluring yet unsettling shade of purple; just like the sky above us, I couldn't decide on a name for their true color.

"What a shame she's insisting on creeping about instead of coming to say hello," he said. "I'd love to meet her."

This last sentence dripped with such mockery and vitriol that I'm not ashamed to say it frightened me.

I stood up straighter anyway, stepping from the safety of my tree and marching toward them as adamantly as I'd marched into the river of fire that had brought me here.

I was standing between them for several moments before I realized what I was doing, that I had no real plan, and I needed to say something, anything—

"You are in the presence of the Marr," drawled the pale god. "Why do you not bow? Do you not possess any sense of decorum?"

And so the acting begins.

I lowered my gaze. "Forgive me," I said quietly. "I knew I was in the presence of gods, but I was overwhelmed by your power and beauty, and I was simply trying to find the right words to use, the right names to greet you by."

The god snorted disdainfully at this, not moving from his reclined position on the hammock.

The goddess, however, sat up, her amber-colored eyes fixing on me. She wore an ivory gown that pooled like rich layers of cream at her feet. Her lips curved in a smile—not a particularly kind one, but it was better than the scowl I'd been expecting.

"I am Mairu, Goddess of Change and Control," she said, her voice smooth and quiet, but with a promise of power, like a river gathering speed before it turned to rapids.

I'd suspected that was who she was, but a shiver still skipped across my skin at the proper introduction.

The Serpent Goddess, humans sometimes called her, as she often took the form of a serpentine dragon when she visited the mortal realm. They worshipped her out of fear as much as reverence, for she was known to be as cunning and violent as she was beautiful, capable of shifting into different forms with far more precision than any other deity. It was said she could split into various forms at the same time, even, and that some of these splintered pieces of her had posed as humans in various capacities throughout her history. Mortal rulers loved slapping her symbol onto things, too; they called her the Marr of both Control and Command, and liked to claim that she had granted them divine providence to wield these things themselves.

"And this handsome bastard," she offered with a wave toward her companion, "is Valas, God of Ice, Winter, Rebirth, and Getting on My Fucking Nerves."

The God of Ice yawned. "And I take all of these duties equally seriously."

I waited for either of them to elaborate. When they didn't, I broke the silence myself. "My name is—"

"We know who you are, child," interrupted the Serpent Goddess. "The one you mortals call 'Dravyn' has told us all about you, the game you're playing, and the...*amusing* things you offered him."

My skin crawled with heat.

I was not a child, and I had not come here to amuse him.

Though it was probably safer if these divine beasts believed as much. Let them think I was only here to play. I would make sure they regretted this assumption before the end.

"I came here to meet him, as we agreed," I said calmly.

The two of them exchanged a lazy glance.

The God of Ice said, "He was here earlier. But some urgent business pulled him away."

"What sort of business?"

Valas yawned again. "The godly kind."

"That's...vague."

"You should be thankful I'm not impaling you with spears of ice for inquiring about divine business."

I lifted my chin, refusing to tremble beneath his frigid gaze. "He knew I was coming."

"He didn't think you'd actually show up."

This irked me even more than being called an amusing child, but I still kept my voice level. "His portal revealed itself very plainly to me."

"Yes, but how many humans would be idiotic enough to actually step into a river of fire, hm?"

It seemed to be a rhetorical question, so I didn't bother replying.

Instead, I looked back to the Serpent Goddess, who was watching me curiously, her chin resting upon curled fingers laden with golden rings. Her eyes seemed to darken as she stared, from honeyed amber to the rust-colored tint of dried blood.

I fought the urge to reach for my sister's sparrow, which was tucked carefully underneath the layers of my clothing. The magic lacing the totem came from the Mimic spirit, I'd been told, but that spirit ultimately answered to the very goddess now staring at me. Under her gaze, the power I'd relied on to disguise myself all these years suddenly felt as flimsy and useless as a gauzy, translucent shroud.

She said nothing about the matter, however—a strange shadow overtook us before she could.

I thought I'd imagined it until both of the deities rose gracefully from their beds and looked to the sky, which had shifted from pale purple to a deep, foreboding violet streaked with black.

"Duty calls," said Mairu with a frown.

I studied the sky for a long moment, trying and failing to make sense of its sudden change. "Godly things?" I guessed.

The air chilled, and I braced myself for the spears of ice Valas had threatened me with earlier.

To my surprise, he only gave a dark, quiet chuckle and said, "At least she catches on quickly."

In the next breath he was changing, his form shifting to crystals of frost, then twisting and spinning into a panther-like shape.

The pale beast leapt straight up as soon as it was fully formed, landing on one of the nearest columns. He balanced delicately on the column's point for a moment before bouncing to the tops of several more pillars and trees—more bounces than seemed necessary, I thought. Likely an attempt to show off and further intimidate me, but I couldn't help being impressed by it.

The Serpent Goddess turned to me as he finally disappeared into the distance. "You will stay here until the god who sent for you comes to collect."

It wasn't a command so much as a sentencing; as she spoke, her hand rose, her fingers twitching with her controlling magic, and the vines wrapped around several nearby columns began to unravel. I watched, both mesmerized and terrified, as they snaked their way around us, weaving into bars that blocked all of the paths leading away from the clearing we stood in.

Before I could protest, the goddess changed as gracefully as her fellow Marr had, twisting into a dark and sparkling cloud that took on the serpentine dragon shape she was most known for. She didn't prance around as her fellow court member had; she shot directly up and over the trees, gone from my sight after scarcely more than a blink.

I stood completely still, barely even breathing. A long moment passed before it all truly sank in. I'd just had a casual conversation with two middle-gods. I was *here*. In their realm. Completely overpowered, essentially lost, and now I was alone, too. Trapped until the God of Fire came *to collect*—as if I was a piece of luggage he'd forgotten about.

I was grateful for the thorny vines trapping me; if not for them, I might have tried to make a run for it.

The air felt thick again, settling over me as it had earlier, heavier than ever. I hugged my arms around my stomach and leaned against a tree, closing my eyes and trying to think of everyone back home and all the things I had to fight for.

My eyes blinked open at the sound of footsteps upon stone.

The God of Fire stood less than ten feet away, burning the vines the Serpent Goddess had used to trap me.

I managed to keep from jumping at the sight of him, but I couldn't find my voice right away. I was too drowsy to think of anything to say, anyway; I don't believe I'd truly slept, but my eyelids felt heavy, my movements sluggish despite my best efforts to sit confidently upright.

"The magical energy in the air here is already proving too exhausting for you, I take it," said the god after a minute, sparing me a cursory glance. "Doesn't bode well for you surviving the tests to become a member of my court."

I tried harder to sit up straight and said, "I wasn't exhausted. I grew tired of waiting on you, that's all." It wasn't entirely true, but I wasn't about to let him know how exhausted I truly felt.

He grunted out a response before turning his attention back to the vines. They shriveled and twisted as he set fire to them, flailing so dramatically as they fell that I wondered if the Serpent Goddess's magic had made them sentient and capable of true suffering.

I took the opportunity to study him as he worked. He'd seemed out of place when we'd met in the prison—too big, too bold, too beautiful in the darkness. He still stood out even here, yet it was clear he belonged among the sparkling airs of this place; divinity seemed to drip from his bronze skin, from the red and black markings that were bolder than they'd appeared in Eligas. The silver in his eyes seemed bolder, too, bright as clouds caught in a full moon's light.

Beyond his appearance, there was something in the subtly powerful way he moved, too, something in the waves of fire unraveling as smoothly as silk from his fingertips, weaving through the thorny vines, warming the air all around us...

The longer I watched him, unconsciously committing the details of him to memory, the more uncomfortably intimate it felt with only the two of us here. I averted my eyes, staring in the direction the other Marr had disappeared in, wondering where they'd gone.

"Where were you earlier?" I asked.

My tone must have come off more accusatory than I'd meant for it to because his powerful shoulders rose and fell with a huff of laughter before he said, "Off slaughtering humans and setting fire to their forests and houses, of course. Sorry to keep you waiting."

I bit my lip. "I managed well enough without you."

"I'll stay longer next time, then. Burn a few more houses down."

"By all means. Don't let me keep you from your work."

He laughed again, but the sound was entirely devoid of humor. It sounded almost...tired.

That couldn't be right, could it?

I had never thought of the gods as beings who were capable of tiring. It made him seem a touch more human. Almost. I wondered if he'd purposely appeared quieter so as not to overwhelm me...

And I dismissed the idea just as quickly, as it would be a far too considerate thing for a god to do.

Was his distracted weariness related to the strange shadow that had drawn Valas and Mairu away, then?

I filed all my questions away for later; I'd pry no answers from him in this first meeting, I suspected, but I intended to find these things out soon enough.

He spoke again after a long silence, eyeing the goblet the Ice God had been drinking from. "They couldn't have shown you to your quarters, I suppose."

He seemed more than a little annoyed that he'd been left to deal with me on his own.

I thought of reminding him that he was the one who'd sent for me—*on his own*—but decided against it, trying my best to stay pleasant. "My quarters?"

"Unless you'd prefer to sleep in the dirt out here?" He gestured to the ground, now littered with scraps of the vines he'd burned.

I chose my words carefully. "I wasn't aware my preferences meant anything in this realm."

He turned to face me more fully, a storm rolling through his eyes, darkening them and passing just as quickly. "I suppose we didn't really go over the details of our arrangement, did we?"

"We did not."

He took a step closer, and all the magic and warmth in the air seemed to step with him, folding around me, pressing tight to my body.

I was intensely aware of every move he made within the warm cocoon of power he'd wrapped me in. Of his magic pulsing in the space between us, the marks on his skin flaring brighter, visible even through the loose shirt he wore. Of his hand moving, lifting toward my face. I fought the urge to unleash my claws, to violently swipe that hand away.

He never touched me.

Only the heat of his magic caressed my skin as a ball of fire spun into existence beside my head.

"Follow the wisps," he said, nodding to the ball, and then to a line of similar ones as they appeared and created a path leading into the distance. "They'll take you to your dwelling, and I trust you're smart enough to figure things out from there."

Maybe I should have stayed to ask more questions, but I felt lightheaded—and a bit stupid—from his closeness. Plus, I knew better than to argue when a potential opportunity to explore awaited me.

I gave a quick, polite bow before starting to turn away.

He was in front of me suddenly, his stormy eyes meeting my gaze and holding it fiercely as he said, "Don't stray from the trail the fire leads you on."

A lump formed in my throat. Had he heard my thoughts? Guessed at my exploration plans, somehow?

"I...I won't," I promised. I don't know if he heard me. Or believed me.

He was already striding off in the opposite direction, muttering to himself as though he'd forgotten I existed at all.

CHAPTER 13

I walked for what seemed like an eternity with nothing but the floating orbs of fire for company.

I tried a few times to stray from their beckoning light, to press deeper into the blackness beyond them. Each time, I was met with a crushing pressure that grew more unbearable the deeper I tried to go.

The fires were bright enough to illuminate the wide path I walked upon, but little else, and I suspected there was much, much more lurking in the dark parts I couldn't see.

How could I properly map out the bones of this place if I couldn't see more than the gods wanted to show me?

I did the best I could. The space seemed specifically built to discourage any further curiosity, but I'd always been exceptionally curious, so I noted every slightly darker shadow and counted the steps between every flare of light, searching for patterns.

Still, after several minutes, it all began to look the same; it was just the same grey path over and over again, occasionally dotted by tall, curved marking posts that served some function

I could only guess at. Even my usually curious mind eventually grew bored of cataloging the repetitive details, and all I could think about was getting to the end of things.

"One would think the gods could design a more efficient dwelling," I said to the wisp of flame that had just swirled into life closest to me. "Must everything be so spread out?"

It wouldn't have bothered me so much, except I also suspected the Fire God could have carried me instantly to the place he'd designated for me if he'd truly wanted to.

Why had he been so distracted, so indifferent to my presence when he'd specifically *sent* for me?

Perhaps the other gods had been telling the truth, and I *did* reek of the mortal realm—or something worse—and he just didn't know how to politely tell me the truth.

After a furtive glance around to make sure I was alone, I did a quick smell check under my arms and everywhere else I could crane my nose toward.

"You're a strange one, aren't you?"

I spun so swiftly toward the voice I nearly tripped and fell over my own feet.

A squat woman with thick curls of dark red hair and patchy, raised eyebrows was staring at me with her hand on her hip.

I was certain she hadn't been there before; it was as though she'd materialized from the air—an impossible idea made more plausible by the sudden appearance of a golden fence behind her, which I was sure had *also* just materialized from nowhere.

"I was just..." I fumbled for words to make the situation less awkward. Finding none, I cleared my voice and promptly changed the subject. "I'm sorry if I disturbed you and this... where exactly is this?"

Her intelligent eyes—a warm shade of brown, bordering

on red—narrowed on me. "You followed the fire here, didn't you, girl?"

"I...Yes." I peered at the fence behind her, my eyes following the lines of it for as far as possible; the golden railings seemed to curve at least a mile into the distance to both our right and left. "But I think I might be lost," I said.

The woman studied me for a moment before pointing at something behind her.

As if cued by the motion, the guiding flames ahead of and behind my path began to move, flying in the direction the woman had indicated. They soared over the fence before shooting straight upward and gathering into a point high above a yard of lush grass on the other side.

The gathered fire blazed blindingly bright for several moments before dimming to a more subtle glow and simply hanging there, burning as if our own personal sun, shedding soft light over everything contained within the fence.

Directly on the other side of that fence was a flower-lined walkway that led to a small house. It was a simple, one-story affair, unremarkable aside from its windows, which were made of colorful glass in every shade of yellow and orange and red imaginable. The windows immediately reminded me of the forest I'd glimpsed right after I'd arrived in this realm; they appeared to be the same sort of translucent glass. In the light of the makeshift sun, the colors were dazzling.

"Sometimes admitting we're lost is the first step to finding the way, isn't it?" said the red-haired woman.

She started toward the house, and I pried my eyes from the mesmerizing windows and followed her through the fence's gate, which she unlocked with a simple wave of her hand.

I couldn't help wandering toward the backyard before heading inside the house. Within the sun's light—which somehow only seemed to shine inside the fenced area before softly diffusing into the darkness on the other side—there were copious amounts of trees laden with flowers, birds flittering about, bushes full of fruits I couldn't name...it all went on and on.

As I stared, I felt as if my feet were truly beneath me for the first time since arriving in this upside-down world—because here was an abundance of things I could clearly see. Things that looked normal, that could be sorted, that I would be able to properly map.

Finally.

Moving with a quicker, more confident step, I followed the red-haired woman to the front door.

I paused on the threshold, as I always did when I was entering a new place where I'd be staying for any length of time, because I needed to make certain I stepped inside with my left foot first.

I'd always stepped into my sister's room right-foot first; it was a secret code we'd made up as children. Now I made certain I never stepped into any new room I'd be staying in the same way, because a repetitive, intrusive thought had convinced me those places would end up as bloody as my sister's room had—that it was a morbid pattern just waiting to reveal itself to me.

My host was staring at me, I realized.

I hurried through my ritual and averted my eyes, as I didn't want to explain this odd compulsion of mine to this woman I'd only just met.

I moved quickly past her, heading deeper into the house, where I found more simple things to match the outer appearance of the dwelling. Two modest rooms, one with a bed—I made certain to step left-footed into this space as well—and the other with a desk. I also found a small sitting area with screened doors open to the backyard, a tiny washroom, and pale wooden floors and bland colored walls throughout. The glass windows remained the only part of the place that seemed divinely extravagant.

Apparently, the God of Fire was not interested in showing off. Which was...interesting. And the opposite of the impression I'd gotten from the other members of his court.

As I wandered through the plain but cozy rooms of the house, I amused myself by trying to imagine what sort of houses all the different Marr might create. Based on our earlier meetings, the Serpent Goddess's house would have been colorful and full of beautiful, ever-changing things. The God of Ice's would have been cold and elegant, just like the beast he'd transformed into, with a touch of something whimsical, maybe.

I made my way back to the entryway, where my host was busy sorting through the drawers of a large pair of cabinets. I felt as though I should say something, so I cleared my throat.

"Thank you, um..." I realized then that I still had no idea who this woman was.

"Rieta," she offered without a glance.

I would have offered my own name in response, but I was certain she already knew it. Something about the way she looked me up and down when she finally turned to face me again made me think she knew much more than my name.

"Now, is there anything specific you'll be needing me to bring?"

I looked toward the backyard, thinking of all the light spilling so clearly over so many things. I wanted to diagram it all as soon as possible. I half expected it to change if I didn't keep my eyes on it; things seemed to come and go without warning here.

"Paper?" I said. "And some sort of writing utensil?"

She gave me a curious look. "I meant food and such, child. You must be starving? Most mortals don't last long in this realm without eating and drinking the proper fare—especially when they're made to march as far as you did. He meant that last part as a test, I believe."

"...A test?"

Her expression soured, as if she didn't believe I hadn't been aware I was in the middle of a trial.

I tried to shrug off her questioning gaze. "Right. Of course. I just thought...never mind about the paper and such. Food is obviously more important."

If it had been a test, surviving it honestly felt like no real accomplishment; I'd simply been too focused on my path to think of things like food. I tried to act as though I was starving now, though, trying to fit into whatever expectations this woman apparently had for me.

She didn't seem convinced by my act—she was still looking at me as though she thought *I* was the trickiest thing in this illusive realm.

However, when she left and came back some time later, leaving plates of food and pitchers of drink with me, there were sheets of paper tucked underneath one of the plates; I found a few sticks of graphite wrapped in one of the cloth napkins as well.

Rieta left again with only a few more words, including a blunt warning to eat slowly and drink even slower to give my mortal body a better chance at properly acclimating.

It had been an act to call for it, but I truly *was* hungry now that the possibility of food had presented itself.

Of course, I was also suspicious.

I picked at some sort of flaky pastry, breathing in the tart and fruity scent wafting from it, wondering if eating it would actually help me acclimate...and at what cost? I didn't want to admit I was exhausted, but the odd heaviness in the air persisted even here. I was more aware of it now that I was standing still—though it wasn't quite as crushing as it had been back in the garden of the gods.

Frowning, I reached for the paper and pencil, ready to recreate the lines and diagrams in my mind—as I so often did —to make me forget about the uncomfortable pit growing in my stomach.

I knew I couldn't go forever without eating the food of this realm.

But I was going to put it off for as long as I could.

CHAPTER 14

Days went by, I think; I was finding it difficult to mark the passing of time because my sun never moved.

There were certain hours when it seemed to grow dimmer, but nothing that I would call 'night.' These brighter and dimmer periods didn't appear to follow any set pattern, either, which was one of the worst kinds of torture I could personally imagine.

Before long I began to wonder if this was another test. If the God of Fire was trying to see if I could stay sane despite having no structure to ground myself within—something I'd never been good at.

I didn't like it; if I was going to be faced with trials, I at least wanted to know I was facing them.

There were worse explanations for what was happening, though. Maybe they'd already figured me out, for example, and I was being punished? Maybe I was dead, and the hell I'd been assigned to was personalized, reflecting the fears of my individual damned soul...

No.

That couldn't be it. I chose to believe I was being tested, and I tried to fight my way through it by staying busy.

There was no kitchen in the house, but I was still determined to cook, to find out how the different ingredients I gathered from the yard worked in different recipes, to take notes like I had back home.

Shortly after arriving, I constructed a primitive oven with rocks and slabs of stone I dug up from the yard, and I managed to set fire to it after a bit of experimenting with leaves and twigs and friction.

Rieta was unimpressed by my invention.

When I told her I *liked* to cook, that I actually preferred it to having all my food brought to me on a silver platter, she informed me I was being ungrateful and difficult, and the God of Fire would hear about it.

At which point I informed *her* that I would love the opportunity to tell him about it myself, if his godly ass could be bothered to come pay me a visit.

She'd glared in response to this—though her lips had twitched a bit, as if she'd wanted to say more on the subject—and she hadn't returned for what must have been several days afterward.

Frustration festered in her absence; I felt like I was breaking the rules of a game, only I had never been told the rules. Or even the actual name of the game.

Yet I persisted, still determined to win.

I went for long strolls around the inner perimeter of the golden fence, paper in hand, taking notes and making sketches. Soon I had created a small book full of diagrams and charts. The house and its yard and everything in it were all accounted for with utmost precision, so I could determine if anything changed or otherwise seemed amiss or worth the risk of exploring.

Once I ran out of immediate surroundings to diagram, I went back to the beginning of my time in this realm, trying to picture the things I'd seen when I first arrived. The view from the hilltop, the garden and the gods within it, the path I'd walked to get to my boring little house...

I usually kept all these notes tucked away in a drawer, but one night—or was it day?—I fell asleep at the table with my latest sketch underneath me, and I woke to the sound of the paper rustling in Rieta's hands as she looked it over.

"This is the Garden of Elestra," she said, eyes wide with intrigue.

"Yes." I did my best to feign casualness. "I passed through there when I first arrived."

"So detailed," she murmured.

I'd heard that tone before. What she really meant was *too detailed to have been created by a normal mind.*

I shrugged. "I have to keep busy somehow." My words came out sounding like an apology, though an unnecessary one; her expression was different from her usual cold, quietly judgmental stare. It was more...curious.

Her leathery fingers traced the drawing over and over. Her lips parted with thought. The quiet between us stretched uncomfortably until I decided that I should press her for information while she was distracted, her guard lower than usual.

"How long have I been in this place?" I asked.

She looked to the ceiling, calculating, and said, "Twenty-three days in mortal time, give or take."

Twenty-three days?

It had passed in a few blinks.

She lowered her gaze to me. "Are you not comfortable here?"

"I expected I'd see more of the God of Fire by this point," I admitted.

She folded my drawing into a small square, and I fought the urge to reach out and snatch it from her before she could pocket it. Was she planning to keep it? Would that god she served hear about this, too? Did she suspect I was plotting something?

"I did pass on your message to him from the other day," she said, casually.

My cheeks warmed, remembering our argument about the oven.

"And he asked me to inform you that his godly ass comes and goes as it pleases."

Bastard.

"I'll keep that in mind," I said with as much politeness as I could muster.

My polite tone didn't fool her. "You could do with some more patience."

Twenty-three days' worth of waiting felt plenty patient to me—though I guess to an immortal god and their servants, time had a different meaning.

"The sun above this house never dims, yet it feels like I'm entirely in the dark." I muttered the words more to myself than Rieta.

She didn't answer me right away, slipping my drawing into an inner pocket of her cloak before turning to the desk against the back wall. I feared she was going to start digging through its drawers in search of more of my maps and diagrams, asking more questions about why I was here and what I was after.

She didn't, thankfully; she only grabbed a basket of

supplies she'd brought, taking things from it and laying them across the desk's top.

I thought she was prepared to drop our conversation—that maybe she hadn't even heard my last words—until she quietly said, "Sometimes it's safer in the dark."

"I didn't come here to be kept safe. Or to be *kept* anywhere, for that matter. I am not a pet that needs to be fenced in."

She cut her eyes toward me and stared for a long, hard moment. "Did you ever consider that maybe we're not fencing you in, but rather fencing other things *out*?"

A shiver traveled down my spine.

I wasn't sure how to respond.

"Your mortal realm is not the only one that experiences strife, you know. You arrived here at a tumultuous time, and if it were up to *me*, I would have left you at home, deals be damned."

Strife?

The chills continued racing along my spine, but now they were partially excited ones. If there was discord in this realm, it meant more potential weaknesses to exploit. My mind raced with the possibilities.

I averted my eyes, afraid she might see the curiosity dancing in them.

"Patience," she reiterated, her wary tone dulling my enthusiasm a bit, "and hold your fire. You'll need it soon enough."

A FEW MORE SLEEPS CAME AND went until one day I woke up and knew that something had to change; I could no longer contain my restlessness.

I opened my eyes to a kaleidoscope of colors shining through the tinted window glass. My hand ritualistically reached for the sparrow resting against my chest, as it always did. Whether in divine or mortal realms, it didn't matter—it was always where I reached first.

All these years later, I still woke up wanting to tell my sister things, and it took me a minute to remember she wasn't there to hear them.

I swallowed down the rush of emotion trying to choke me and went to the washroom, which had a small closet full of basic but beautiful things to wear. The clothes had appeared just hours after the house had, all of them so finely tailored and luxuriously soft that I wondered if magic had been involved in their making. I hoped not. I didn't want to think about divine residue leaching into my skin from the fabric.

Either way, the clothes I'd arrived in had mysteriously disappeared when I put them aside to wash, which meant the alternative to the divine clothing was prancing around the realm naked. Not *exactly* the impression I'd planned to leave on the place.

So I grabbed a flowing, silver-trimmed tunic and a simple pair of straight black leggings without any fuss. Rieta's voice echoed in my thoughts as I pulled the tunic over my head, wincing as one of its buttons snagged on my messy braid.

Are you not comfortable here?

I couldn't say I wasn't; I'd been given everything I needed and then some. But I had not come here to be comfortable *or* safe, as I'd told her—I had things to accomplish.

I redid my sleep-mussed braid, then grabbed my charts and diagrams from their drawers and spread them across the table in the sitting room. My heart raced as I searched for…something. I still wasn't sure what; I just knew I needed to decide on a goal, a plan, and I needed to make a move. *Today.*

My fingers traced a darkly shaded area on the map I'd made of the backyard; a strange energy sometimes radiated from this point, and the trees here were always surrounded in long shadows no matter how brightly the false sun above them shined. It had caught my attention several times while strolling past it, and today I would explore it more thoroughly—even if it meant hopping the fence to search for a source on the other side.

I collected the small, makeshift spear I'd stashed under my bed; I'd whittled it from a tree limb with the help of a sharp-edged rock within the first days of my arrival, just in case I needed a weapon aside from my claws.

I hadn't tried to draw out my claws in this realm yet; I was doing my best to play the role of an ignorant human who posed no real threat, and the beastly nails would have been a dead giveaway that I was not who—or what—I claimed to be.

After securing the spear at my side, I headed for the back door. I was reaching for the socks and boots I'd left beside that door when I heard a sudden rustling behind me.

It sounded like a bird. My gaze darted to a nearby window, which I'd cracked open yesterday in hopes of disrupting the eerie silence of the house. The opening was technically large enough for something to fly through it, though it would have required twisting at a strange angle. Maybe—

Another rustling sound.

Definitely wings.

Definitely coming from inside the house.

I slowed my breathing and tried to calm my pounding heart so I could listen closer. I had no idea what sort of creatures lurked in this realm; it could have been another *test* waiting to pounce on me for all I knew.

Gripping the spear handle tightly, I crept backward, scanning every potential hiding place, more than ready to pour all of my frustrated, anxious energy into a deadly thrust.

Sudden movement flashed in the corner of my vision. I spun toward it just in time to see a small creature dart past the window.

I thought it was a cat at first; the thing certainly *moved* like a cat, slinking its way up and across the cabinets and shelves of the sitting room, circling me, squeezing into spaces it didn't seem to logically fit.

Then it leapt from the top of a cabinet, and I watched as tiny wings flared out to break its fall while sharp, talon-like claws extended, clicking across the wood to bring it to a stop at my feet.

I got a good look at its head as it came closer. Its ruby-colored eyes were wide and bright, more like a bird of prey's than a cat's, and its mouth was clearly a small but sharp beak. Its tufted ears still looked feline to me, however, and it let out a decidedly catlike purr as it weaved in between my legs, brushing both downy feathers and rough fur against my ankles.

I'd always been more of a dog person than a cat person, but I was so excited to have another living being to talk to that I didn't hesitate to crouch down and open my arms to it.

The creature seemed as eager to make a friend as I was, leaping into my lap and promptly burrowing its face into my shirt.

Smiling, I lifted it out in front of me to study it, my mind flipping through pages of a book I'd once read, searching for what to call this creature. It was the size of a large house cat, but weighed no more than a bird, as though its bones were hollow and its size exaggerated by a massive amount of fluff and feathers.

"You're a griffin, aren't you?"

Another purr, followed by the creature taking my sleeve in its beaked mouth. The gentle mouthing grew more violent as I drew him back toward my body, eventually nipping the skin underneath.

"Easy with the love nibbles," I chastised.

It spat my sleeve out and nuzzled against my arm instead, its purring even more enthusiastic than before.

"Well, you're a nice change from the monotonous drudgery of this place."

It agreed with another purr, its tail flicking excitedly; I thought I saw flashes of fire following the more enthusiastic flicks. I watched it more closely, so fully distracted by the intriguing little creature that I briefly forgot about my plans to explore the world beyond my golden-fenced prison.

Then the creature leapt onto the nearby table, snatched a pile of my diagrams up in its talons, and darted for the nearest open window.

"HEY!"

I tore after it, barefoot and furious.

There were definitely flickers of fire dancing off its tail now, which made it easier to follow. I kept my eye on the flames and pushed my legs as hard as I could, my energy draining too quickly for my liking. I felt slower and weaker after so many days in this place; I hadn't been eating or drinking enough of the things Rieta brought, as I was still suspicious of the ulti-mate effect it might all have on me.

I ran until stabbing pains in my side became too excruci-ating to ignore and my legs went wobbly, forcing me to stop for a few breaths or topple over. The brief pause was all it took to fully lose sight of the creature and its fires.

I crouched for a moment to keep my balance, wrapping an arm around my cramping stomach as I huffed out curses.

Finally, I caught my breath, straightened up, and looked around—and only then did I see how far I'd chased the stupid thing without realizing it.

Utter darkness surrounded me, so complete I couldn't see my hands in front of my face. I must have jumped the fence at some point, though I didn't remember doing it; I'd been so hellbent on catching that little beast that I'd lost track of everything else. Now the sun over my prison was nowhere to be seen.

Fire flared in the distance. Too far away to see if it belonged to a certain mischievous griffin or not. But I'd followed a trail of flames to my dwelling when I first arrived in this realm; what choice did I have but to follow this trail? I could see nothing else in the darkness.

Another flare of fire went up, as if beckoning.

I started toward it.

I didn't think I was traveling in the same direction I'd come from, and the feeling proved correct; the flickers of fire eventually led me to an entirely new area that was faintly lit, not by a fake sun, but by a floating orb of energy casting an eerie, whitish-blue glow over everything—more moonlike than sunlike.

The glow revealed a stone tower with a circular base. A wide set of stairs led up to this base floor, and sitting at the top of the steps was the griffin. The creature was busy pawing its way through the papers it had stolen from me, swatting them into the air and batting them about.

"There you are, you little monster," I said as I stomped up the stairs to it.

It didn't try to run away. It simply settled back on its haunches, perched in the messy nest of my drawings, looking incredibly pleased with itself.

"Have you had enough fun for the day, I hope?"

It responded by ripping one of the pages in half with its beak—almost mockingly—chewing it up, and swallowing it in one big gulp.

"We're going to have to work on your manners if we're going to be friends," I informed it.

It burped in reply, sending a puff of fire into the air.

"Oh, *that's* lovely."

I didn't bother trying to collect the scattered papers; I would have to redo them all at this point; my mind was finicky that way, sometimes—if one drawing in a set was lost or ruined, I had to start over from the beginning, or else nothing about it would feel right.

Too annoyed to focus on the fallen papers and my lost work, I lifted my gaze instead to what lay behind the purring thief.

The tower was so tall that I had to take several steps away and crane my neck all the way back to see the top of it. There was no lush grass nor golden fencing surrounding it, only cracked ground awash in pale light. As I stopped sweating from my run, I realized how strangely thin and cool the air suddenly felt.

Dark, cold, and foreboding, yet I couldn't deny the urge I felt to further explore the place.

It didn't take me long to make up my mind. I was here, now, and likely already in trouble for it; a little exploration couldn't make things much worse than they already were.

I felt a weight vibrating against my leg and looked down to see the griffin pressing against me, shivering and mewling softly.

"Are you honestly going to cower behind me now? You're the one who *brought* us here."

It gave a few pitiful flaps that lifted it up to my chest. I couldn't help catching it and wrapping my arms tightly, protectively around it. The extra warmth and weight against my chest helped combat the growing fear in my own heart, too, and I can't say I didn't appreciate that.

"You get away with a lot of things because you're cute, don't you?"

It chirped proudly.

"I thought so."

Together, we made our way to the tower's first floor, squeezing through a set of heavy metal doors that had been left partially ajar.

My footsteps echoed on the stone floor. The ceiling soared high above me, and several large, unlit chandeliers hung from it. There were plenty of tall windows around the space, but the light from the glowing orb outside was not bright enough to make much difference as it seeped through the glass. As my eyes slowly adjusted to the darkness, I managed to make my way over to a small side table where I spotted a few tarnished chambersticks holding unused candles. I grabbed one and held the griffin up to it.

"Help me out here, won't you?" I asked, giving the downy fur of its chest a little squeeze.

It gave a disgruntled snort, but eventually obliged, flicking its tail and then burping out a burst of flame to ignite the wick —and almost my sleeve with it.

I took the candle in one hand while the griffin clawed its

way up to my shoulder and wrapped around the curve of my neck, burying its face in the folds of my shirt.

Once my companion was secure and still, I walked deeper into the place, making my way into a second large room. This one seemed to be a strange combination of a study and a gallery. Tables covered in both strange equipment and books were evenly spaced throughout the room. There were countless paintings and tapestries brightening the stone walls as well, but they were all very practical in presentation; not art so much as instructions featuring diagrams of various creatures I didn't know the names of, and charts containing divine symbols I recognized alongside words written in a language that I didn't.

I studied it all, slowly making my way toward the largest of the tapestries in the center of the room. Candlelight washed over this tapestry's many, many colorful threads, over a creature with a lithe, muscular body covered in silver fur. It had long, elegant legs, and there were antlers protruding from its narrow skull. It was so large I had to take a step back to see the thing in its entirety.

I nearly dropped the candle as I did.

That beast.

I *knew* that beast.

I didn't know its name, but it was the same creature I'd seen outside my house in the weeks before my sister disappeared. The one that had died on my doorstep. The one we'd burned, whose ashes and smoke had lingered like a curse over my old life and home.

I slowly backed away, turning a slow circle, taking in the rest of the room and trying to make more sense of it.

The griffin lifted his head from my shoulder, its body tense, its feathers ruffling.

"Where have you taken me, little one?"

It made a clicking noise deep in its throat, sounding sorrowful, almost.

My instincts told me to run. Instead, I kept returning to the tapestry, inching closer and closer each time, despite my fear.

Eventually, I worked up the nerve to let my fingers run over the worn threads.

Where was I? What deity did this creature answer to? Was this a part of the Fire God's domain? The questions kept coming. Memories soon followed, clear and sharp as knives in my side—the claw marks this beast had left in the door; the smoke and strangeness that had followed in the days after; the tang of metal and magic in the air; my sister's empty bed...

And the blood, bright and burning and red.

So much red.

My knees felt weak. I knelt to keep from losing my balance, bracing a hand against the cold floor. The tiny griffin scrambled to stay upright as I dropped, eventually leaping from my shoulder and smacking against the tapestry. Its claws came out, digging into the woven artwork, trying to catch itself.

A wild thought seized me as I saw the threads coming unraveled beneath its claws—*don't destroy it. We can't let it die!*

It had been an omen before. It had died on my doorstep, and then my sister...*my sister...*

I grabbed for the griffin. It let out a screech and scrambled higher, completely out of my reach—

Right before bursting into flames, setting fire to both itself and the tapestry.

CHAPTER 15

The old tapestry fully ignited, filling the air with the horrible stench of smoke and burning dust. The griffin writhed about in the fire, tangling himself further in the fraying, burning threads. I snatched for him, missed, and watched in horror as more flames erupted from his body.

The brightness and fumes stung my eyes and throat, forcing me to cover my face and take a step back. I wafted the thickening plumes of smoke away as I did, still searching frantically for some sign of the griffin.

Embers showered down, landing on the rug at my feet. I stomped them out before darting around the room in search of something to extinguish the flames...a thick cloth to smother it, a basin of water, something, *anything*—

I heard a pained, animalistic cry and I doubled back to the fire, preparing to reach through the searing heat and grab the little beast before making a run for it.

I tried not to think about what sort of trouble I was going to be in if one of the gods caught sight of me fleeing from the burning building.

Cursing under my breath, I ran faster. As I approached the steadily building inferno, I nearly slipped in a puddle of water I hadn't noticed before. I thought nothing of it until I splashed through another, and then *another*—they were everywhere, as though the roof of the tower had peeled open to embrace a sudden rainstorm. I looked up.

It wasn't raining.

It was snowing.

I held out my hand, mesmerized, and watched as a few flakes landed and melted against my palm. A cold wind spun up around me, biting at my skin, lifting and playing with the loose strands of my braid.

"Setting fire to a sacred Tower of Creation is an interesting way to make an impression."

I spun around and saw the God of Ice leaning against the doorframe, a look of smug amusement on his handsome face.

"Then again," he said, propping a hand on his chin, "I suppose it makes sense, given the god you came here to try and impress."

"I didn't set fire to anything," I snapped, too frantic to have much patience for the gods and their games at the moment.

He pushed away from the frame and sauntered into the room, reaching a hand toward the wall above the blazing tapestry. A slight twist of that hand was all it took to cover a large section of the wall in ice. As the heat from the fire rose, it melted the new ice and sent a waterfall cascading over the flames.

He repeated this trick several more times until the fire was fully out. As the smoke and steam rolled away, I finally spotted the little griffin clinging to a swath of the ruined tapestry. The charred swath was attached to the rest of the cloth by only a few threads, and seconds later, it was ripping off and falling away. The griffin fell with it, tumbling lifelessly to the ground with a loud *thud*.

I let out a panicked cry, but the God of Ice only gave a snort of laughter and said, "So the troublemaker is revealed. *Now* the situation makes sense."

I ignored him and dropped to my knees beside the griffin, rolling it onto its side and laying a gentle hand against it.

To my relief, its breathing seemed normal.

"He's just being dramatic," Valas said, drawing my gaze back toward him.

As soon as I took my eyes off the griffin, the creature let out a low, mournful yowl, and when I looked to him once more, I found him on his back with his legs sticking straight up in the air, tongue lolling from his mouth.

Dramatic, indeed.

I heaved a relieved sigh while giving him a sharp poke in the side. "I don't appreciate you playing dead on me."

His tail flicked back and forth with increasing enthusiasm, more doglike than catlike for the moment. He rocked upright and leapt into my lap, tail still wagging.

"He ignited on you, didn't he?" asked Valas.

I reached for the piece of fallen cloth he'd been tangled in, nodding.

"Typical Moth."

"Moth?"

"That's his name."

"What sort of a name is that?"

The griffin nipped my arm and wriggled free of my lap, flipping into the air with a haughty flick of his tail, as though he was offended by my questioning. The tuft of fur at the end of that tail turned to flames, and I worried he might ignite once more.

"Well, it's Ramoth, actually," the Ice God continued. "After some sacred mountain in some human kingdom, I think. But most of us just call the annoying, fluttery little thing *Moth*."

It was fitting, I decided after watching the creature bounce about in the air for another moment; he did seem to flutter aimlessly—much like a moth unsure of how to get closer to a light it had glimpsed through a window. His coloring was similar to a common look of that insect, too; a mixture of different browns, with the palest shades featuring on his wings, his head, and the ruff of fur around his neck.

"And don't feel too bad about the whole spontaneous combustion thing," the God of Ice drawled on. "He just does that sometimes...particularly when he's experiencing strong emotions—whether his or otherwise. An unfortunate design flaw caused by an unskilled creator."

"An unskilled creator?" The God of Fire, he must have meant. What other deity would be responsible for a creature prone to bursting into flame? "Dravyn?" I questioned, making certain to use the expected, human moniker for him.

A corner of Valas's mouth lifted. "Yes, he would be the one I was referring to. And you can tell him I said he was unskilled."

The griffin let out a hiss, looking ready to fight on his creator's behalf. I grabbed him as I got to my feet, lifting his light body so our eyes were level with one another's.

"I'm sorry," I told him. "Moth is a lovely name, and you're a stunning creature. You know that, right?"

He puffed his fluffy chest out, flexing his wings to their full span and giving them a little shimmy.

Yes, I thought with a bemused smile. *He certainly knows it.*

He slipped free of my hold but didn't go far, bobbing up

and down beside me, occasionally turning lazy somersaults in the air.

I'd dropped the candle I'd been using for light, but even with both it and the tapestry's fire extinguished, the room was full of more light than before; the orb outside seemed to have brightened as if bolstered by the presence of a Marr, its pale blue glow stretching even to the shadowy edges of the space.

I bent and picked up the ripped piece of tapestry once more, studying it closer in the new light before I turned to Valas and asked, "You said this was a sacred Tower of Creation, didn't you? What does that mean?"

He didn't look at me or answer right away, focused on summoning and swirling crystals of ice around his hand. The soft purple shade of his eyes seemed darker as it reflected the sharp, cold crystals. "The upper-goddess of Creation, Solatis—"

"The Sun Goddess?"

"Yes, and don't interrupt me." He gave his hand a shake, scattering the crystals to the ground. Wherever the ice shards hit, more ice sprung up, some of it taking on intricate shapes that reminded me of flowers.

Show-off.

"Anyway," he continued, "yes. Her. She brought forth all life in all the realms, divine and otherwise, at the Creation. And the towers in this realm are full of her life-creating energy. Her gift to all the Marr, in addition to our respective magic: we're able to draw on some of the energy to create creatures of our own design and persuasion—simple beasts and the like. Moth was created of energy gathered from within this tower, along with many other experimental creatures. There are multiple such towers, one in all three of the middle-heavens, and also a fourth in—"

"All three? So there are three separate divine spaces at this level, one for each of the three Courts of the Marr?" This was a theory I'd read in a book once; I could still clearly picture the diagram that had gone with it: A map divided into multiple layers, both vertically and horizontally, each section intricately decorated with the symbols of the beings that inhabited the respective levels. It was one of the most complicated and interesting maps I'd ever seen—so, naturally, I'd hardly been able to take my eyes off it.

"Yes," Valas replied, "and you're interrupting me again."

"Sorry, I...my thoughts outrun my mouth sometimes."

"I'm noticing that."

I opened my mouth to reply, but shut it again as he arched a brow.

"This tower is called Eyrindor," he said after a pause. He circled the space as he spoke, studying the stone walls and all the charts and paintings as though it had been a long time since he'd seen any of it up close. "There are two more nearly identical towers among each of the other Marr's divine dwelling places, and also another in the center of all the court's territories in this realm, known as Amalith: The Tower of Ascension. The energy of that center tower is more complex; it's where chosen beings are sent when fully marked for divine status— the final step to becoming a middle-god or a Miratar spirit. If they survive the last round of horrors within Amalith itself, of course."

Those last words caused a numbness to sting from my skull down my spine...a reaction he seemed to have been going for, judging by the smirk that crossed his face.

That smirk didn't bother me; I had no plans to truly ascend as I'd told Dravyn I would, after all.

I *did* have a sudden desire to visit this Tower of Ascension, however—only so I could study it and find a way to bring it crashing down.

If I could cut off this source of creation...

The possibility excited me so much I could hardly keep still. I did my best not to fidget, quietly filing the new information alongside all the other things I'd learned since arriving in this realm.

There were at least a hundred other questions I wanted to ask after everything that had just happened, but I hesitated, cautious about seeming too eager about mining for information. I didn't trust this god before me—or any of them—and maybe it was too soon to press for more than they were willing to give.

The Winter God seemed eager to show off his knowledge, though. And I couldn't help myself; after weeks spent in the dark, I was desperate for all the enlightenment I could get. So I risked handing over the singed piece of tapestry, lifting a questioning gaze to the God of Ice, and said, "So this beast depicted on the tapestry...it was another creature born in this tower, like Moth?"

He nodded.

"Do you know what it was?"

He turned the cloth over in his hands, studying it, a bored expression dulling his purple-ice eyes. "Why so curious?"

"Because I...I saw one in the mortal realm, once."

He lifted his gaze to me without moving his head, considering me for a long moment before he finally said, "It's a veil-hound. A creation of the current God of Death, if I'm not mistaken."

The numbness itched over my scalp and spine again as I recalled the stories I'd heard about the Death Marr and his horrifying magic.

I swallowed hard. "And that god is a member of your court?"

"Yes."

"So he's here, somewhere in this area of the realm?"

He shrugged. "Often enough. He comes and goes as he pleases, plus he's young—the youngest of the Shade Court. And middle-gods tend to roam unpredictably in the early years."

It took the meaning of his words a moment to sink in. "Younger even than the God of Fire?"

Valas nodded. "It's been something like... a decade in mortal years since the one you call Dravyn went into the Tower of Ascension and was reborn as a middle-god. Our current Death Marr—the third of his order—has only been with us for five or six mortal years."

That was interesting. It was common knowledge that the Marr were not irreplaceable; they rose and fell at the discretion of the Moraki they served—partly by way of this *Tower of Ascension* and its magic, apparently. But this changing of the gods wasn't a frequent occurrence, as I understood it, so it seemed unusual that both Dravyn *and* the God of Death had ascended, replacing the old gods, in such a short timespan.

More evidence of that strife that Rieta had mentioned?

And the Death god...*five or six years*. That would have put him in charge of the veilhound beast that died outside of my home.

It wasn't fear shooting tingles through my body any longer, but the urge I felt to investigate this god and whatever creatures and questions surrounded him. The need grew more wild the longer I stood there, taking root deep in my stomach before twisting toward my limbs, trying to take them over. Trying to make me move, to go after answers at any cost.

Moth seemed to sense my anxiousness; he turned one last somersault before swooping down to perch on my shoulder. His beaked mouth closed gently over the side of my face. Not really a bite, but a definite pressure, like he was trying to give me a reassuring hug in his own way.

I tried to slow my racing thoughts, but I couldn't.

As if he could read my mind, the God of Ice said, "If he *is* here by chance, then you should go see him. He loves visitors." His smile was unapologetically...chaotic.

Was this another test?

And if it was, did he mean for me to refuse him, or dare to take him up on the challenge?

Yet again, I could only guess at the rules and objective of the game.

I looked to the nearest window. The pale blue light shining through it made me think of the moon in my realm, which in turn made me think of that Moon-marked girl who had given my location away to the king's soldiers.

My fists clenched.

The wild feeling taking root inside me dug in more deeply, securing me firmly in its grasp.

"Or, on second thought..." Valas began, his hand in front of him and his fingers dancing, summoning more crystals of ice to casually play with, "...maybe you should run back to your little sanctuary before your god realizes you ran off and started setting fires. He's not known for his patience or even temperament, after all."

He isn't my god, I wanted to snap.

Somehow, I held my tongue and shoved the thought away. I couldn't ignore the rest of what he'd said, however; the idea of running back to my so-called sanctuary with more questions than answers was maddening.

Valas reached the darkness of the hallway, stepping just beyond the glowing orb's light, before I gathered enough courage to speak again.

"Where can I find the Death Marr?" I called.

Moth grumbled and burrowed his head underneath my braid.

I gave him a reassuring scratch under the chin, my gaze still on the hallway.

The God of Ice glanced back at me, violet eyes glinting in the dark, and said, "I was hoping you'd ask."

CHAPTER 16

"This feels like a bad idea, doesn't it?" I asked Moth, who replied with a noise that sounded halfway like a growl, halfway like a purr, and all the way like agreement.

He insisted on staying close to me, however, his talons clinging tightly to my shoulder as I made my way down a steep embankment covered in white flowers.

"We won't stay too long," I promised him—and reminded myself. I didn't think I *could* stay too long; the air seemed to be growing heavier the deeper I moved into the Death God's territory. Each breath I took felt like it was coating my chest and lungs, bits of dark energy clinging to and decomposing me, slowly rotting me from the inside out.

I carried a gift from the God of Ice to help ward off some of the darkness—a chamberstick I'd taken from the Tower of Creation, which he'd magicked blue fire onto in order to create a sort of torch that burned indefinitely. Or maybe *burn* wasn't the right word; what I held resembled a torch, but the 'flame' was freezing cold to the touch, more dense than a true fire, and its edges did not flicker or shift no matter how fast I moved.

It gave off plenty of light, though, and with its help I had found my way down a long path running alongside a narrow stream of turquoise water, and then through a small forest of twisted grey trees. When I emerged on the other side of the forest, the sky had changed to an inky black canvas shining with spirals of light. Things had only gotten brighter as I walked onward—likely bright enough that I didn't need the torch I carried.

I clung to it anyway, prepared to brandish it like a sword if necessary.

Now, as I came to the bottom of the flower-strewn hill, I found myself facing a diverging path. To my left, far in the distance, stood a building crowned with glittering spires reaching so high into the sky the shining tips were lost among the stars.

Amalith, I assumed. The Tower of Ascension. Valas told me I might catch a glimpse of it when traveling this way, depending on how the energies in the air shifted.

Stay far, far away from it if you see it, he'd warned.

My curiosity burned as I stared, trying to determine the distance between it and where I stood. I felt it unfurling inside of me again—that wild desire to destroy, to find a way to bring the glittering tower down at whatever the cost...but I convinced myself to heed the god's warning for now; if he'd actually urged caution despite how little he obviously cared for me, then the danger surrounding that tower must have been very real.

Soon enough, I promised myself.

I could only focus on one objective at a time, anyway, and today I'd made up my mind to investigate the Death Marr and whatever connection he might have had to my sister's death.

Harithyn—that was what the area he'd staked his claim

upon was called. All four of the Marr in the Shade Court had their own respective areas in this divine realm, I'd learned, with the Garden of Elestra standing in the middle of each of the territories. I repeated these facts over and over to myself as I walked.

"Harithyn, Harithyn, Harithyn," I said, turning it into a soothing chant under my breath as I looked over the dark landscape. It comforted me to be able to label that darkness. Moth joined in, chirping to the same rhythm as he leapt from my shoulder, swooping about and bobbing up and down in the air alongside me.

We climbed another steep hill. At its crest, I could see for what seemed like miles in every direction—miles and miles of ground comprised of obsidian streaked with veins the color of starlight. The shining rock stretched on until, very abruptly, it stopped, cut off by a line of white, swirling energy far in the distance.

Beyond this line of pale energy, a churning mass of...*something* stretched and glistened like an ocean, though the water was an odd shade of mottled purple, pulsing from deep violet to green-tinged over and over. It made me think of a bruise rapidly healing only to immediately darken again. The longer I looked at it, trying to make sense of it, the less sense it made— and the more uncomfortable I felt.

Most of this realm felt foreign to me, but this bruised ocean felt...*wrong*.

Closer to where I stood, shadows stretched and swept over one another, cloaking most of my surroundings. I looked carefully, mapping out their shapes and the structures casting them, and I soon realized that some of them were more than mere disruptions of light; they were solid shapes in and of themselves.

Moving shapes.

As we started down the second hill, their movement grew more violent, the not-quite-shadows rising and falling so unnaturally that I became certain something was controlling them.

"Magic?" I wondered aloud to Moth, who responded with an uncertain whimper.

I probably should have expected such things at this point, but a small gasp still escaped me as the tendrils of darkness collided and exploded into a cloud which began to take the shape of a building. I took several steps back, but whatever magic my approach had triggered continued to unfold.

The not-shadows continued to work, weaving a foundation—a first story no less than a hundred feet wide—before stretching to form towers, turrets, and a roof edged in glowing blue stones that brought to mind eyes peering out from a haunted forest.

When the shadows finished and fell away, a massive house stood before me. It was as dark as the magic that had formed it, but clearly solid, complete with a low, gated wall surrounding its yard and a path of white stone leading up to a beautiful door framed in silver.

A palace fit for a king.

Or a god.

Lights shone in its many narrow windows, as though the dwelling and its inhabitants had been there all along, simply going about their business.

"It feels like the shadows were expecting us, doesn't it?" I said to Moth, trying to keep my voice light for his sake.

He let out another soft whine.

I walked forward before I could lose my nerve, pushing the

gate open with one hand while still tightly clutching my blue-fire torch in the other.

The gate creaked shut on its own behind me.

Moth leapt from my shoulder at the sound of it clicking into place, swatting anxiously at the floating bits of shadow and sparks of different colored magic in the air.

"Relax," I mumbled, calmly reaching for the griffin despite my own rising panic. "We just need to—"

A loud wind howled past us. The not-shadows lifted to life once more, weaving in and out of my legs. One of the dark ropes struck out and wrapped around Moth's middle, squeezing out a pitiful *squeak* before rendering him silent, suspended, and still in mid-air.

I reached for him again—

Cold fingers hooked around my neck and jerked me to a stop.

An even colder voice whispered against my neck a moment later: "A mortal soul prowling around my territory? This is unexpected."

The pressure against my throat loosened slightly, allowing me enough control to jerk free and spin around.

At first, all I could do was stare.

The voice had sounded like a man's, but such a label seemed inadequate for the being standing before me. He was vaguely human in shape, but the angles of him were too sharp, his skin too pale, and horned appendages curled away from the spots where his ears should have been. His arms hung well past his hips, ending not in hands, but merely in shadowy fingers long and curling like the roots of a tree.

Despite his odd angles and too-long parts, the same terrifying elegance surrounding the other middle-gods I'd met also surrounded him. He might have been beautiful to look at, even... if not for his eyes, which were pits of black with tiny slashes of white in their middles. Pure black would have been less unsettling, I thought; staring into his gaze now, I couldn't help but think of a last, desperate hope being swallowed up by utter despair.

"You're..." I fought to keep my words steady. "You're the middle-god of Death."

"That is one of my names." His voice remained just above a whisper. When he spoke, a faint, shimmering darkness puffed from his mouth like breath steaming in cold morning air.

All of the Marr had been human once, but it was easy to forget this fact while staring at him. It was hard not to forget *everything* I knew as I looked into those cavernous eyes. Why had I even come here?

What had I planned to say?

He inclined his head. The not-shadows rose up and began to weave once more, forming a net against my back, pulling me toward the god.

"A mark of the Flame," he murmured, taking my hand and twisting it so that flame-shaped brand on my arm was visible. His touch made the typically dormant mark itch and flash brightly before his gaze moved to the torch I clutched. "...A weapon of Ice." Wispy fingers reached from my wrist toward the sparrow hanging from my neck. I held my breath as those unsettlingly long fingers curled around the charm. "And a token of Control." His eyes shifted, the white sinking fully into the sea of black for a moment.

I'd been wrong—the pure darkness was worse.

He blinked slowly, bone-pale lids stark over the black, as he asked, "Are you here trying to collect a full set of the Shade Court's souvenirs, then?"

I slowly released my breath, trying to think of a safe answer.

I didn't know much about the politics of the divine, but the Marr likely shared some allegiance to the other gods in their court, didn't they? So this god before me would not be my enemy if I were truly planning to ascend to the Shade Court, as I'd claimed I was going to do.

Appealing to that court loyalty was worth a try, I decided.

"I was sent here by the God of Fire to acquaint myself with you," I said, "as a preliminary to my trials of ascension, as I intend to join his court."

Another slow blink. Another pair of white lights lost for several seconds in the sea of black. I lowered my gaze, feigning a respectful bow when truthfully I just didn't want him to notice how unsettled I was by those eyes.

Tendrils of the not-shadows caressed my cheek and chin, lifting my face against my will. One of them snaked across my jaw and up to my ear, weaving inside as if trying to find a way into my mind. It pressed harder and—eventually—deeper. My skull itched from the sensation, and I fought the urge to rake my fingers through my hair.

The God of Death smiled, revealing teeth like jagged rocks hanging from a cave roof.

"You're lying," he said.

My heart dropped into my stomach as I remembered a facet of the power he was known for: He was reading my mind.

"Let's try again," he said. "Tell me the true reason you're here, or you will never see a world outside of this domain again."

Moth started to shake free of whatever spell the shadows had held over him. The Death Marr let him go, but the dark ropes of his power continued to swirl threateningly around us as he added, "And neither will this little beast."

I managed to grab the griffin and secure him in my arms.

He hissed and pawed at the air but didn't resist when I jerked him behind me, positioning myself between him and the middle-god. He settled against my back, talons clutching my shirt, head occasionally butting anxiously between my shoulder blades.

Remembering Valas's words—that Moth was prone to bursting into flames when surrounded by strong emotions—I forced myself to breathe more calmly.

"I have a question about another beast," I said to the God of Death, staring at his pale forehead rather than his eyes. "One that I believe you created and unleashed upon my realm of Avalinth."

He didn't outright object to being interrogated, so I carefully took the burned tapestry from my pocket and held it out to him.

He barely glanced at the woven image before he answered my unasked question. "I've never sent the veilhound beasts to that wretched mortal realm you speak of."

I didn't believe him, but accusing him of lying didn't seem like a good way to get more information. He spoke again before I could reply, anyhow.

"But they're often *lured* there," he said.

"...Lured?"

"Mortals have a terrible, wonderful fascination with death. They like to play games with it. The veilhounds are sometimes drawn into the sport."

Sport? Indignant heat flooded my body. Nothing about what had happened with the dead beast, or with my sister's ensuing bloody disappearance, had felt like a game to me.

I couldn't mention these details, of course.

Instead, I gripped the torch I held more tightly and, as

calmly as I could, I said, "You speak as if the gods are guiltless—but they play plenty of games of their own, in my experience."

The god drew up straighter, his terrible eyes widening and his mouth curving as though I'd issued a challenge.

He said, "I've a game I think you'll enjoy."

I started to recoil at the unsettling tone of his voice. He stopped me with a quick motion, lifting one of his shadowy, root-like hands and sending the black ropes of his power circling more tightly around me. Several of the dark vines slammed against my shoulders, forcing me down to my knees.

Moth fluttered high above, frantically mewling and hissing, snapping uselessly at the shadowy magic. He was getting smaller, farther away, while I felt like I was sinking into the rock, cold dirt shifting down alongside me, burying me alive.

Moth's cries faded entirely into the distance.

Everything faded for a moment, only to rush back, jarring and shifting my stomach so violently that it almost made me vomit.

After settling the churning in my gut and then finally catching my breath, I shakily rose back to my full height and found myself alone on a cliff overlooking the strange purple ocean I'd seen from a distance earlier. It looked less like water up close, more like sludge, and it was nearly a straight drop down into the waves of it, broken up only by a few sharp, jutting rocks. A single misstep and I would meet a very painful, messy end.

You will never see a world outside of this domain again.

Terror gripped me, but curiosity wasn't far behind as I caught sight of the creatures pacing a stretch of shoreline down below.

Veilhounds.

The glowing line of white energy I'd seen earlier was emanating from them, it seemed like.

The God of Death materialized beside me as I crouched on the clifftop, his arrival heralded by a frigid, foul wind.

I braced a hand against the stone for balance as I leaned down and tried to get a closer look at the creatures below. "What is this place? Why are so many of the veilhounds here?"

"This is the edge of the middle-heavens," he said, as though this information should have meant something to me.

I briefly closed my eyes, trying again to picture the layered map of the realms I'd once studied. I didn't recall an ocean or anything of the sort on that diagram, but I doubted any mortal cartographer had ever captured this realm in its entirety—or even come close to it.

"The veilhounds guard the edge of this realm, as well as the space between it and the mortal realm—Eligas—and its pathways," said the God of Death. "They help me herd mortal souls into the afterlife when necessary. The pack before us is particularly adept at devouring the ones who attempt to cross into places they shouldn't—though they are guarding against a different kind of threat at the moment."

A different kind of threat...

Was it related to the trouble Rieta had mentioned?

"They seem to have noticed your arrival," he said.

I looked down to the sight of no less than ten of the beasts lifting their long faces toward us as if trying to better catch my scent in the chill breeze. A chorus of low, wailing howls rose from their throats, making me shiver. The trembling shook me inside and out; I couldn't suppress it no matter how hard I tried.

"We should get closer." The Death Marr smiled his jagged

smile at me again. "A quick *game* to see if you're worthy of even starting the process of ascension, or if you're wasting our time."

Warning bells clanged loudly in my mind. My involuntary trembling became so violent I worried it might shake the cliffs beneath my feet hard enough to start an avalanche.

I was finally realizing just how far I'd wandered from my safe little house and its golden fence, and the reality of the danger surrounding me officially began to overwhelm my curiosity.

"I...I don't want to get closer," I said.

"How disappointing," he tutted.

I took a step away from him only to nearly lose my balance as the stone beneath me crumbled as easily as sand, leaving the already too-narrow clifftop even smaller than before.

"Take me back to your palace, and I'll find my own way after—"

He cut me off with a dark laugh. "Very commanding for a mortal being, aren't you?"

The cold of his magic enveloped me again, but this time it didn't feel heavy; whereas before it had settled like chainmail upon my shoulders, pushing me down, now it felt more like it was howling through me, latching on to my very heart and soul, pulling out my will to stay conscious and on my feet.

Draining me.

I'd seen very little Death magic in action in my home realm, but I'd heard plenty of terrifying stories of how it could bleed victims dry of more than just blood. At the moment, all I could think about was the effect this draining power could have on other types of magic—how it could void those energies and render them useless.

Panic unfurled in my chest at the thought of my sparrow's

spell being fully undone. He'd read my mind earlier; what had he seen? Did he already know what I truly was underneath?

Was he trying to expose me more fully?

"Stop," I cried. "*Stop*! I want to go back—I need to go—I—"

"Go? Already? Have you gotten the answers you trespassed for? I don't think you have." His voice bordered on violent now, and I inwardly cursed myself for my stupidity.

Now what?

Almost as soon as the panicked thought crossed my mind, an orange light flared on an adjacent clifftop, drawing my gaze.

Fire.

And not the cold, pale blue flame like the torch I'd carried into Harithyn—this was bright and brilliant, almost blinding, even from a distance. It drew the attention of the Death Marr, too, and sent another chorus of howls rising up from the veil-hounds down below.

The fire didn't seem to draw any closer to us—only the heat from it did. I inhaled sharply as hot wind seared my face, bringing a swirling haze of ash and embers with it.

My mind, dazed as it was, still knew better than to touch fire—yet I stretched out my hand, thinking of catching one of the bright flickers as it twisted down.

After a long, mesmerizing moment of watching them, a single ember floated like a feather down into my upturned palm.

The draining cold of the Death Marr's magic was burned away almost instantly. I felt myself growing heavy again, but in a pleasant way this time—like the sort of heaviness that comes from sinking into a bed after days of no sleep.

Several moments passed in this pleasant, heavy warmth. My eyes fluttered shut. I don't know how long they stayed shut before a calm, deep voice pushed through the haze and said, "This one belongs to me, Death."

And Death replied, "Then why was she in my territory?" As he spoke, the terrible emptiness threatened again, blowing through my body like a cold wind.

"The reasons are irrelevant," said that same deep voice from before. "She's no threat to you. Release her."

My eyes blinked open to the sight of Dravyn facing the God of Death. The air was in a heated frenzy all around them, power and magic roiling off their bodies, creating an updraft that lifted pieces of their clothing and hair and whipped them about.

I started to reach for one of the embers surrounding Dravyn, desperate for even a burst of the warmth I'd felt a moment ago, but shadowy ropes of Death magic whipped between me and him, extinguishing the embers before taking aim at my throat and wrapping tightly around it.

"I have work to do," said the God of Death, his horrible cavern eyes fixed on Dravyn. He directed his magic more and more tightly around my throat without even glancing my way. "You know of the threats we face. Of the task that's been appointed to me and my creations—a task I cannot do while there are troublesome mortals poking around in my territory."

"She won't do it again."

"Can you be *sure*?" His voice was needling, like spiders crawling down my spine. "I think we need to teach her a lesson while she's here."

The shadows around my throat tightened.

All of the fire around us roared in response, even the tiniest embers swelling into a terrifying size. Waves of the gods' competing power overcame me. I shut my eyes briefly, trying to ward off the dizziness that followed. I opened them again just in time to see the God of Death taking a step back, his shadows retreating with him.

Threads of fire were advancing against those shadows, weaving in and out in a deadly dance of power.

I had never seen fire like this—it moved as fluidly as water, and the colors were incredible, a dozen different shades of red and orange and white. As I stared, I would have sworn I saw the flames twisting and taking on the shapes of beasts snapping at Death's shadows, burning them away whenever they managed to get them between their jaws.

The God of Death reached toward me one last time, his root-like hands lifting, magic rising up to drain the Fire magic separating us—but not quickly enough. It was clear he was being overpowered; I could only just make out his strange shape on the other side of the wall of solid flame building before me, and it was disappearing fast.

Just before the fire turned solid enough to block him completely from view, I felt his magic give one final, horribly cold surge, and I heard his voice one last time from the other side—

"*Take her and go,*" he hissed.

I was barely conscious, but my mind caught the word *go,* and I started to walk without another thought. I don't know how far I actually made it; I'd like to think I managed at least a respectable distance on my own two feet before I felt my legs crumpling.

A hand caught my arm, steadying me. Another pressed to my cheek.

Warmth flooded through me—the Fire God's magic, guarding against the deathly cold still lingering and trying to bite through and hollow me out.

He lifted me off my stumbling feet, holding me tightly

against his broad chest. He smelled of war. Of metal and fire and smoke. I shouldn't have found the scent comforting, but it was becoming familiar; the house I'd spent the past weeks in smelled of similar things—of his magic that had kept me safe multiple times now. Somewhere in the depths of my mind was a question that I was too weak to ask out loud—

Why?

Why are you keeping me safe?

I heard his voice then as I'd heard him in my prison cell weeks ago—a faraway voice echoing in my mind. Calm, powerful, pursuing me even as I tried to slip away into the dark.

You can't stay asleep forever, he'd told me in the cell, and he insisted on the same thing now. *Stay awake. You have to stay awake. Look at me.*

I did.

I don't know how I managed it, but I looked up and met his gaze. His strange silver eyes. In my mind I made a list of what the color reminded me of, picturing each object, holding to them like anchors to reality. *Clouds. Blades. Storms. Armor...*

My eyes stayed open and soon managed to focus on the things surrounding me instead—the things I was being carried away from. The howling veilhounds. The dark ocean. The magic—bright Fire and hollow Death vying for dominance in a world that, in that moment, seemed as bruised and broken as any mortal realm down below it.

CHAPTER 17

"Drink," the God of Fire ordered as he slammed a cup down on the table between us.

I took it with a slightly trembling hand but didn't lift it to my lips right away. Partly because I didn't fully trust what was inside, but mostly because I was still too dizzy to manage drinking anything.

I was in an unfamiliar room that was spinning alarmingly fast. I made out a faraway ceiling made of glass, several gold-accented columns, but little else before my stomach started to shift and I had to shut my eyes.

I took a few deep breaths and then tried again. My surroundings still tipped and swayed, but I concluded we were in an atrium of sorts. The table we sat at was in the center of a sunken-in space. Steps rose up to wide marble walkways all around us, and several grand, arched doorways were spaced evenly along these walkways.

There were colorful plants of all shapes and sizes soaking up the light filtering through the glass ceiling—light which came from what I assumed was another false sun like the one I had at my little house. The warm air smelled of a strange but alluring combination of smoke and citrus, and there was a sparkle to it similar to the shimmer I'd witnessed when first arriving in this realm.

Moth was here as well, curled up asleep on the far end of the table, each snore he emitted accompanied by a fluttering of his wings. I stared at him for a long time before forcing my gaze to the impatient middle-god sitting across from me.

The god's glare was fixed on the cup clutched in my hands. "Do I need to send for a servant to spoon it into your mouth?"

The thought alone was humiliating. I lifted the cup to my lips, a motion fueled mostly by stubbornness and spite. Maybe that was what he'd been going for? Stubbornness was the only thing that kept me from immediately vomiting the substance back up, too, as it tasted beyond awful—like pure alcohol and grass clippings.

Despite the taste, it warmed me from the inside out as it oozed down my throat, chasing away the lingering chill the Death magic had left in my bones. Getting rid of that hollow cold seemed like a fair trade off for a terrible taste, so I kept drinking.

Once I'd managed to down it all, Dravyn left the room and returned with another cup. The contents of this one tasted like plain water, albeit the clearest, most delicious water I'd ever tasted. I sipped it slowly, taking in more of my surroundings as their spinning finally came to a complete stop.

On the far end of the space, the stairs rose directly up into a room that appeared to be filled with colorful glass; I couldn't make out any distinct objects, but the light shining into the space was being thrown back out, refracted in endless colors and shapes.

Dravyn settled once more into the chair across from mine,

head tipping back and eyes narrowing at the light shining from above. Silence stretched tight and thin between us until, without looking at me, he asked, "Feel better?"

"...Yes," I said, cautiously, finding it difficult to believe he was truly interested in how I felt. The space seemed to rumble with his suppressed power—and anger. He was waiting to make sure I wasn't going to faint on him, I suspected, and then he'd unleash the true force of that temper Valas had warned me about.

I watched him closely, my body tensing, preparing to guard against whatever attack he launched at me.

He ran a hand through his hair, pulling it loose from the tie binding it. His face was smoother than it had been the last time I saw him, which filled my head with questions that were somewhat silly in the grand scheme of things: Did gods shave? Did they continue to grow and change? How much of their mortalness did they keep when they ascended? And what determined the level retained? The God of Death had seemed so... *monstrous* compared to this man before me.

I shuddered at the memory of the Death God and took another sip of my drink.

Dravyn cut his gaze briefly toward me, frowning as though he'd sensed the uneasy shudder curling through my body. He mentioned nothing about it, but after a moment he cleared his throat and said, "My servant tells me you haven't been eating or drinking nearly enough since your arrival. Which partially explains why you nearly fainted from the energies at the Edge. Even a fully acclimated, divine being would not have lasted long in that place. Only the Death Marr and his own creations usually trod there. They're more or less immune to the draining energies present in it."

I absently tapped my fingers against my cup, feeling a bit

sheepish. Rieta had warned me I wasn't consuming enough. I'd rationed my food and drink because I didn't want to trust or take in anything in this realm any more than I had to. It was a constant weighing of risk and reward, and it seemed I'd miscalculated this time.

"The Edgelands are a dangerous place, and the Death God is dangerous company."

"Aren't *all* gods dangerous company?"

I thought I saw the hint of a smile twitch his lips. It disappeared just as quickly. "Yes. But the younger the god, the more volatile their presence and powers. And Zachar is the youngest of us."

Zachar.

That must have been the Death Marr's true name.

"But I suppose the bigger concern and question," Dravyn went on, "is what you were doing in Zachar's territory to begin with. And in the Tower of Creation before that. Valas informed me that your adventures started early this morning."

"So the God of Ice is a show-off *and* a snitch," I muttered into my cup.

"Which is lucky for you," the Fire God said drily, "because otherwise I might not have been able to reach you in time."

I focused on sipping more of my water.

Though I still didn't look at him, I could practically hear the tight clench of his jaw as he said, "I told you not to stray from the trail the fire led you on, didn't I?"

I technically *had* followed a trail of fire to the Creation Tower—the trail Moth created—but I didn't say this, not wanting to incriminate my new winged friend.

Instead, I placed the cup delicately back on the table and said, "I didn't realize you meant for me to rely on their guidance indefinitely."

"Then you are not nearly as smart as I'd hoped you'd be."

I bristled. "I'm smart enough to know when someone is being unnecessarily cryptic with me."

"Unnecessarily?"

"Yes. And I'm not afraid to call them out on it, either."

Moth lifted his head, yawning.

The God of Fire glanced from the griffin to me, his eyes seeming to shift between silver and a darker, stormier grey as they settled on my face.

"It's been nearly a month since I arrived," I said, voice wavering only slightly under his challenging gaze. "Which might not be long to a god, but it's a long time to *me*—I can't be expected to just hide within a golden fence forever and not ask any questions."

He opened his mouth but closed it nearly as quickly.

"I'm not used to being caged in," I said.

He considered this for a long moment before he muttered, "Not by gold, perhaps."

"What is *that* supposed to mean?"

He sat up, fully abandoning the glare he'd had on the ceiling and fixing it completely on me instead.

Heat swelled in my chest, making me feel—as I had the first time I'd looked upon his godly form—that the fire in his gaze was scouring away all the things I was attempting to hide from him and everyone else.

He stared at my scoured-clean self for a long moment, clearly deep in thought, yet making no remark on whatever he saw hidden beneath the outer layers.

He got to his feet and started to walk away from me—but I was not going to be dismissed like last time. I didn't care if he was having second thoughts about our arrangement.

"We made a deal," I reminded him, my tone soft but savage, as I rose to my feet as well.

"I haven't gone back on anything we agreed to. I've simply been more preoccupied than I expected I'd be these past weeks."

"Preoccupied by what?"

"That's none of your concern."

"As long as I'm here, it *is* my concern, isn't it?"

Moth let out a low chirp, as if agreeing with me, and Dravyn's angry stare turned briefly toward the griffin.

"I don't like being surrounded by so many secrets," I said, drawing the attention back to me. "If there is something I'm not supposed to do, somewhere I'm not supposed to go, then of course I want to know *why.*"

"A written guide to the divine courts and all their problems?" he sneered. "That's what you want, I take it?"

I nearly threw up my hands and shouted *yes! That's exactly what I want!* But I knew that wasn't the reply he was looking for; sometimes I struggled to recognize sarcasm, but thus far, his had been obvious enough every time.

He walked away from me, moving to pluck a star-shaped fruit from one of the trees along the atrium's edge.

I followed closely behind. "You have to warn me about things," I insisted.

"I don't *have* to do anything, Little Sparrow."

"Then you can't get angry if I—"

He spun around to face me. I realized then how close I'd pressed to him. Stupidly close. He took a single step forward, and suddenly he was *too* close, the symbols upon his skin too bright as they blazed through his shirt, the heat from his dormant power building, threatening to erupt.

It was reflex—and maybe a touch of panic—that swung my hand forward, tossing the water from my cup toward his face.

Fire flared between us quickly enough to evaporate the liquid before it touched his skin. Steam billowed, and we stood in the clouds of it for several tense moments without speaking, chests heaving in search of calm breaths, hands clenched into fists.

Moth fluttered closer, perching on the branch of a nearby tree, leaning forward as if preparing for the climax of a dramatic play.

Dravyn flicked his wrist, tossing a last bit of fire from his fingertips. The motion felt laced with threat. I drew my arm back, preparing to strike before he could.

I was fast.

He was faster.

His hand struck forward—but only to swipe the cup from my grip and throw it aside. The pewter mug hit the ground with a metallic *thud* that echoed in the open space and made my heart thud just as heavily against my chest.

The air stayed hot even as he turned away from me. The tension slipped from my muscles, my adrenaline faded, and I felt annoyingly, undeniably fragile in the wake of even such a small display of his power, like a flower dangerously close to withering in the heat.

I wouldn't let myself wilt.

"I admit I made a mistake going into the Death God's territory without giving it enough thought," I said fiercely, "but *you* made a mistake if you believe I came here to be nothing more than your slave. I said I would serve in your court, not that you could lock me away and subject me to whatever you wished."

He went back to staring at the light shining through the ceiling, as if appealing to the gods above him for strength.

"And you said it yourself on the day I arrived here," I pressed, "we didn't really go over the details of our arrangement. And we *still* haven't."

He snorted. "*Details.*"

I fixed my eyes on his back, on the fiery patterns still glowing faintly beneath his shirt, staring until he finally looked at me once more.

Then he said, "Fine."

My mouth nearly dropped open in surprise. I didn't respond right away, afraid I might say the wrong thing and make him change his mind. I kept perfectly still as he reached out his hand, letting Moth flutter down and perch on his muscular forearm.

He stroked the griffin's tufted ears for a minute before he glanced over his shoulder and said, "Valas mentioned the Tower of Ascension to you, didn't he?"

I nodded.

"The only way to obtain its magic is to first pass the tests set forth by all three of the divine courts. The other two—the Sun Court and the Stone Court—will be first, and then this court you intend to join will also have its trial, but it will be one crafted by the Moraki we ultimately serve."

An image of that Moraki flashed in my mind—a drawing I'd seen in a book of a beastly, humanoid figure with tattered black wings and eyes the color of bone. Just one of many depictions of Malaphar, upper-god of the Shade. Like so many other divine things, my knowledge of him was limited. I knew just enough to feel my blood running cold at the thought of having to face any trial of his creation.

"And if I fail to pass these tests?"

Dravyn shrugged, his fingers moving to scratch Moth's fluffy chest. The griffin leapt from his arm to his shoulder to give him easier access. "From the moment you stepped into this realm," said Dravyn, "your eyes had already seen too much. You cannot go back to before."

"But I...I can't stay in this realm indefinitely if I'm not divine."

"Correct."

"So you mean...I either pass the trials, or I..."

I couldn't bring myself to say the word *die*. He didn't say it, either, but he didn't have to; the cold glint in his eyes said enough.

Failure meant death.

Dizziness threatened—I hadn't considered this angle of things. Not these trials, or the possibility that I might be subjected to them—and fail them—before I accomplished what I'd come here to do.

The God of Fire was watching me closely now, clearly trying to gauge how well I could stand underneath the weight of these *details* I'd insisted on having.

So I stood up straighter and asked, "When do I start?"

"Unfortunately, those other two courts are as preoccupied as I've been," he continued after a long pause. "We've been dealing with a rather large problem for some time now, so the whole process of ascension for gods and spirits alike has become somewhat...*chaotic*."

I was certain he wouldn't elaborate on whatever 'problem' they were having, so instead I asked, "If you knew this—if you've been preoccupied with this problem for so long—then why bring me into the chaos?"

He didn't look as though he wanted to answer, all of his attention focused on helping Moth fix a ruffled, out-of-place feather.

It didn't matter, really, but for some reason the question

sank its claws into me and would not let go; I had to know what he was thinking in that moment.

"Why didn't you leave me to die in that cell in Cauldra?" I asked.

He shook his head.

I chanced a step closer to him. The heat from earlier had lessened, so now only a pleasant, tempting warmth surrounded him. Without really meaning to, I found myself sinking toward it, drawing close enough that I could have reached out and touched him. His eyes met mine for a breath, then dropped to the sparrow hanging around my neck. I fought the urge to press my hand to my cheek, to make sure my scars weren't showing.

He lifted his hand, the motion slow and hesitant with thought, and gently grasped the necklace's charm. Turned it over. Studied it. His fingers brushed the hollow of my throat, leaving a tingling trail of heat in their wake.

"You wouldn't have died," he finally said, letting go of the necklace and turning away again.

He said it with such conviction that I couldn't help but ask, "How can you be sure?"

"Because."

"Because why?"

He scratched Moth's chin, causing the griffin to purr and rustle his wings. "Because I know a wildfire when I see one. And I don't think those villagers would have been able to put you out so easily."

"Was that a compliment?"

"No." The reply came insultingly quickly. "Merely an observation."

I tucked my hair behind my ears, my cheeks flooding with

heat for some reason. "You don't think I would have died, yet you intervened anyway. Why?"

He sighed. "Hasn't your curiosity gotten you into enough trouble for one day?"

I didn't have a convincing argument against that—and he wasn't expecting one, judging by the victorious smirk that briefly crossed his face.

I averted my eyes and muttered, "Thank you for saving me, by the way."

He didn't acknowledge the gratitude. "Just stay away from the God of Death," he said.

I wasn't in a hurry to see that god again anytime soon, so I nodded without arguing.

"You'll remain here in my palace for the moment," Dravyn went on. "I'm sure we can find a spare room for you. At least until I can make certain that god is placated, that he's forgotten about you and returned to the duties he should be focused on." He held out his arm again, letting Moth launch from it and shoot up toward the glass ceiling.

There must have been an opening in that glass that I couldn't see—one big enough for the griffin to slip through—because he kept going, twisting and turning higher and higher until he was completely lost among the bright sky.

I stared at the spot I'd last seen him for a long moment, an uneasy feeling gripping my chest.

When I'd first arrived, I would have given anything for a chance to worm my way into the Fire God's personal palace. But after the day's adventures, part of me longed to be back in my smaller, secluded little cottage. To have the privacy to map out all I'd seen and heard, and try to connect the dots between things. To revise plans and make new ones.

"I don't need surveillance," I insisted. "I could just go back to—"

He stopped me with a sharp look.

And, again, I couldn't think of an argument that wouldn't make my situation worse, so I swallowed down my words and nodded instead.

"Of course," I said. "I would be honored to stay here." I tried very hard to make my tone thankful. I don't think I fully pulled it off. Or even came close.

Nevertheless, he didn't retract his decision to have me stay.

He summoned servants—strange creatures with tall, dark bodies that made me think of scorched and skinny tree trunks —and instructed them to take me to a room and make me comfortable. He started to leave after his orders were finished, only to pause one final time at the top of the steps and turn back to me.

"I never intended to cage you indefinitely," he said. "Believe what you like about that, but I'm warning you now—tread more carefully. Because there are some things in this realm that I cannot save you from."

CHAPTER 18

I FOLLOWED THE STRANGE CREATURES DRAVYN HAD summoned out of the atrium and into the palace proper, keeping a safe distance as they led me down several long hallways full of more marble and gold—hallways that would have been dark and difficult to navigate if not for the bright flames swirling around the creatures' slender hands.

There didn't seem to be any other sources of light inside, and it only grew darker as we meandered farther away from the atrium and its glass ceiling; it appeared this place was not meant to be navigated by anyone or anything that couldn't summon their own torchlight. I was grateful for my elven eyes and their enhanced vision; a human would likely have been completely blind in here.

Maybe that's what Dravyn was hoping for.

The thought unsettled me, but I was grateful for this dark reminder of the sort of being I was dealing with. I'd thanked him for saving me earlier, and for an instant, I'd felt myself slipping, the line between the truth and my acting becoming blurred...a dangerous precedent.

I had to stay focused.

The room the creatures eventually brought me to was bright compared to the rest of the palace, with tall windows welcoming in what I assumed was the light of the same 'sun' that had shined upon the atrium's roof.

There were two sconces flanking each of the two doors, as well—both the door to the hall and to a connected washroom —and my escorts waved their flaming hands toward these sconces, setting all four alight with a *pop* and a small shower of sparks. As they blazed, the firelight stretched toward a series of strange glass receptacles scattered along the ceiling. The receptacles absorbed the light, I heard a soft *whirring* noise from them, and then they were alight as well, casting a more even glow across the space. It was fascinating to watch; my fingers itched to take them apart and see how they worked.

Once light had flooded the entire room, my escorts bowed their lanky bodies and left me alone to take in my newest prison.

The space was clean and comfortable enough, filled with fixtures that were clearly sturdy and well-made, accented with hints of yet more gold—elegant without being overly extravagant. There was a bed, a small dresser, and a long, empty closet that I suspected would fill up as mysteriously as the one at the other house had.

I briefly wondered why Dravyn would have such a large spare room, as I didn't think the gods regularly entertained guests. Maybe he didn't have these spaces, typically, but some sort of magic had swiftly created this room for the sole purpose of housing me? It was difficult to imagine such magic at work, but I was beginning to think nothing was impossible in this realm.

I stepped cautiously toward one of the room's three

windows, pushing its sheer curtains aside to get my first true glimpse of the yard surrounding the palace; I'd been too dizzy to take in much of it upon our arrival.

Staring at it now made me feel faint all over again.

Hills of silver-green grass rolled away from me, stretching on as far as I could see. They were covered in a shimmering ash, I concluded after a minute of staring. The same dust coated the pale flowers blanketing many of the hills, glinted off clusters of trees with crooked branches, and made the stone walkways around the palace shine brighter in the light of the false sun.

Farther in the distance, the grass gave way to scorched ground woven through with cracks of bright, molten rock. I couldn't tell from where I stood, but I imagined that fiery rock flowing freely like little rivers, crisscrossing each other in winding patterns. The air above it all wobbled, sweltering with heat, glowing bits of fire occasionally swirling through it.

Beautiful yet deadly in appearance—a quality I was starting to associate with all divine places.

The ocean of purple and black in the Death God's beautiful yet deadly territory kept resurfacing in my mind, fresh terror overtaking me every time I pictured it and those veil-hound creatures, and the uneasy energy surrounding it all...

What was happening in this realm?

And how was I going to survive it *and* pass the trials that apparently awaited me?

I needed to rethink my plans. To reevaluate now that I'd gathered more information. I didn't have my drawing materials from my former dwelling, but I made do by finding a container of powder in the washroom and spreading a thin layer of it over the countertop to create a sketching surface. It smelled pungently floral, and just a puff of it floating into the air around me made my skin itch; I was careful not to touch the layer of it with anything except for a single, briefly-extended claw.

I closed and barricaded the door before I went to work. Listening closely for any approaching footsteps, I hastily mapped out the new areas I'd seen, listed the new names I'd heard, and tried to recreate the scene at the eastern edge. The strange uneasiness that had overtaken me while staring out over that ocean struck me again as I drew.

When I'd finished my sketching and labeling, I stood back and studied it all. Even here, contained within the countertop of the small washroom, this realm and all I faced within it seemed so impossibly *big*.

I hugged my arms tightly around myself. I was beginning to think I was in over my head, as loathe as I was to admit it.

Yet the only option appeared to be to keep swimming, or else I was certain to drown.

DAYS PASSED. Or I assumed they were days, anyway; the false sun here actually came and went in a way that resembled the cycle I was accustomed to, so I counted these cycles as if they were normal days. I couldn't decide if I preferred this to the endless shine of my last sun or not; it made it easier to sleep, but also easier to realize how much time was passing without my accomplishing anything.

The God of Fire proved ever more enigmatic and aloof; another four days passed without a single conversation with him. We were under the same roof—I occasionally caught glimpses of him in the halls, which I was allowed to roam relatively freely—yet I felt no closer to him than before.

Rieta was a frequent visitor, and though her appearance often interrupted my plotting and thinking, I began to look forward to the sight of her barging into my room. She was not warm, nor pleasant most of the time, but she was familiar. She brought me paper and drawing sticks, and occasionally answered my questions in her snappish, matter-of-fact way.

On the fifth day, she knocked—only to open the door without waiting for my call to come in—and she pushed her way inside with a basket of linens against her hip. She grunted hello and trundled past with little more than a glance in my direction, but slowed to a stop as she caught sight of the sketch I'd just finished adding the final details to—one of the Death Marr and all his strange features.

"Drawing again, are we?"

I leaned away from the table I'd been working at so she could see my creation better; I had been anticipating her arrival, and I'd purposely brought this drawing out in hopes that she would see it and initiate a conversation.

"The God of Death..." I began, as casually as I could, "he looked so *inhuman* compared to Dravyn and the other gods I've met. I'm just curious about what makes him such a beast —and I can't help sketching things that make me curious."

She clicked her tongue as if she disapproved of that curiosity—but she snatched up the paper in her free hand and studied it closer, her warm-rust eyes scrutinizing each detail before nodding in a begrudging way, as if she was trying to decide whether or not I'd done the god's appearance its due justice.

"He may yet return to his more human self," she finally said. "The Marr are almost all beastly at first, until their magic and power settles down. Some are real quick about settling. Others take months. Years. Decades, even. They're still a relatively new being, you know—new creations from the Moraki —so I guess you could say we're still figuring out the specifics of how things work. Creation is a messy business, as it were."

I averted my eyes, determined not to betray any of my true feelings toward the gods and their *messy* creations.

"But for all their faults, the Marr are still far better than the Velkyn were."

The back of my neck burned. "The elves, you mean?"

"Yes, I suppose that's what they're better known by in the mortal realm, isn't it?"

I was struck with sudden curiosity about the way the beings in this realm saw the demise of my kind. So I played the role of a clueless human and asked, "Why did those first divine creations of the upper-gods fall from grace?"

Rieta frowned, clearly not up for an enthusiastic discussion on the complicated subject, but I decided to push my luck anyhow.

"I've heard stories that the Velkyn rebelled," I went on, still feigning curiosity and cluelessness, "but the hows and whys of it all are less clear."

She turned her attention back to the linens she'd carried in with her, unpacking the basket and organizing things, so quiet and intent on her work for so long that I didn't think she was going to oblige my questioning today.

Then she placed her empty basket on the foot of my bed and, staring toward the door, she said, "You know of the Moraki, Creators of all things, of course. Belegor, who formed the physical worlds. Solatis, who brought forth life, and Malaphar, who brought forth knowledge."

She glanced impatiently over her shoulder at me, and I nodded.

"And the beings you call elves were the first ones Solatis

created in her likeness," she continued. "But she made them too powerful. When the God of the Shade—Malaphar—gave them the entirety of his knowledge as well, the combination of it all proved too much for them to remain satisfied with their place in the world. They rebelled against the upper-gods and had to be stripped of their magic and power to prevent a total war that likely would have led to complete ruin for everyone involved."

"And they were relegated to Avalinth, stripped of their immortality, and left with nothing but curses and a few traces of divine power, correct?"

Rieta nodded. "And soon after, Solatis tried again, creating a new being. *Humans.* These were the complete opposite of the elves—weak, frail things this time. Too weak, it turned out, because though they were great in number, their gifted realm of Avalinth was not flourishing under their rule. So the Moraki made the decision to choose a few exemplary humans and elevate them to divine status in order to help things along."

"So came the Marr," I muttered.

"Yes," said Rieta. "Beings nearly as powerful as those elves once were, but far fewer in number. They are stewards of the mortal realm and others. Able to walk among mortals, occasionally gifting them small amounts of magic, while also frequenting the upper realms and sitting at the right hand of the Moraki as the elven-kind once did."

It was the same story I'd heard from countless human taverns and texts; the Marr were their last, most revered link to the almighty Creators.

The part that Rieta left out—and that I kept to myself just then—was how dramatically the number of remaining elves was reduced once the first Marr ascended. They had killed us off without hesitation, out of fear that we might threaten them or challenge them to try and regain our status as divine beings. They were just as violent and unpredictable as those ancient elves had been—if not worse.

Some stewards.

They were no better than us, and yet they flourished, worshipped and adored, while what was left of my kind barely managed to survive. They were monsters, as we'd supposedly been—the Moraki had simply found a better way to leash them.

"The elves still remain in the mortal realm, don't they?" I asked quietly.

"Yes." Rieta's voice was tense. "And some of them retain something like magic, which they continue to find new ways to corrupt and abuse. They've threatened the peace of the realms more than once with their meddling and warmongering."

I got abruptly to my feet, unable to keep still under these accusations. All my old, familiar rages threatened to surface, all at once, and I needed to move, to put space between myself and Rieta.

I made my way across the room to the largest of the windows, pushing aside its curtains and settling on the bench beneath it.

Several minutes passed. I kept waiting for Rieta to leave, but she kept finding things to do—new things to clean, to fold, to complain about while rearranging them.

"You seem troubled," she finally said to me, breaking the busy but uncomfortable silence. "Not at all like your usual spit-fire self today."

I didn't take my eyes from the window as I said, "It's simply a lot to think about. All that business with the gods and elves and magic and such."

"That it is," Rieta agreed, offhandedly, as she continued with her chores. "That it is."

"And there are many parts of it that likely aren't what they seem," I added, more to myself than her.

"I agree." She paused, and then added, "I would even go so far as to say that *most* things are not what they seem. Here in this room or otherwise."

Something in her tone unnerved me. I got to my feet again, excusing myself before heading to the washroom, hoping she'd leave me be if I disappeared into that private room for a while.

I made it halfway to the door before she called after me. "So tell me, Little Spitfire...are you planning on telling him what you are?"

I froze.

"You must realize you can't hide forever."

"I...I don't know what you're talking about."

"Oh, let's not play dumb, now."

I fought the urge to reach for my sister's necklace, afraid it might be snatched away from me if I drew attention to it. "How do you..."

"Child, it's *my* magic that's been hiding you."

I stared at her, heart pounding, unable to draw a deep breath.

And as I stared, the russet color of Rieta's irises changed, shifting to a vaguely familiar shade of gold. The mark on her wrist flashed, and then it shifted as well, twisting away from the flame shape it had been and becoming a winged serpent biting its own tail.

The symbol of the Goddess of Control.

"Why do you think your little *disguise* is so strong here?" she asked. "Did you honestly think that trinket around your neck had been keeping you hidden all this time? That it could manage such magic under the incredible power and pressure within this realm?"

I tried to think of a reply. An argument. An excuse...*something*.

I couldn't.

I was such a damn *fool*.

"I just wondered if you'd ever come clean about it on your own," Clearly-Not-Rieta said with a shrug.

Then she began to change in earnest. Her thick red hair deepened to black; her careworn face became smoother, darker; her slightly hunched and squat stature stretched into a tall, elegant form.

Soon an entirely different being stood before me, and she was not a servant of Dravyn or any other Marr—she was the Serpent Goddess, Mairu...and I felt like a complete and utter fool for not realizing it before now.

I stumbled away from her, a confusing storm of anger, shock, and betrayal roaring through me. Several moments passed before I finally found my voice. "You tricked me."

She turned to the mirror attached to the nearby dresser, patting a few loose sprigs of her plaited and coiled hair back into place. "The mortals sometimes call me the Goddess of Trickery, don't they? You should have expected no less. Let this be a lesson to you, hm? You aren't the only thing in this realm that is more than what it seems."

My blood remained at its boiling point, but I held my tongue. A reminder of this goddess's immense power still hovered in the air, the entire room full of an electrifying energy that made my hair stand on end. Hurling insults at her didn't seem like the wisest choice in this charged moment.

"Does it make you feel any better to know that Rieta actually *is* a real being, and the servant to the Fire God that she claimed to be? This is only the second time I've borrowed her appearance. And I only did it because she herself is busy elsewhere, and I was—quite frankly—bored."

It did make me feel better, although only marginally so.

"Did Dravyn order you to do this? Did he tell you to spy on me? To see if you could trick me?"

"As though I take orders from one of my own rank." She scoffed. "And, just so we're clear, were you not also trying to trick *us*?"

I opened my mouth to fire off a response, only to quickly close it.

She had a point.

We could have gone around in circles about the situation indefinitely, but it wouldn't have been a productive use of either of our time. I avoided her sharp and prying gaze, trying to think, to puzzle out my next move, even as my thoughts continued to spin.

"I assume you've told him the truth about me, though?" I asked.

"We do have some allegiance to one another," she said with a shrug. "I could not have kept it from him in good faith."

"So he knew. He's been playing a game with me this whole time."

"So have you," she reminded me again.

I bit my lip, still unwilling to engage in that particular argument with her. She might have been the one who had ultimately tricked me, but she was not the one I wanted to confront in that moment. "Take me to him."

The goddess arched a brow at the commanding tone of my voice, and I knew I was walking a dangerous line—but I didn't care. This particular game was coming to an end.

Now.

CHAPTER 19

Mairu brought me to the very center of the palace, to a grand staircase that led up to a bridge which stretched outside, high above an elaborate garden, and across to Dravyn's own private tower.

She instructed me to wait outside the tower doors, informing the creatures standing guard there—more creatures like the ones that had escorted me days before—that I would be here until the God of Fire returned. They were not to question or disturb me, or she would make them pay for it later.

Then she left, slipping gracefully into her serpentine dragon form and flying off to tend to something in her own territory.

And so I was alone again, shivering in the weak morning light of the fake sun. After a few minutes of this, it occurred to me how completely and utterly alone I was *everywhere* in this realm. What a fool I'd been to think I might find safe company in Rieta. I'd known from the beginning that nothing and no one in this realm could be trusted.

Why had I slipped?

Focus, I silently commanded myself.

Nothing mattered now except confronting the God of Fire, controlling the damage, and keeping all my plans from completely imploding.

No less than an hour passed while I waited, pacing the bridge for the first few minutes before settling down with my back resting on a column, huddling against the chill in the air. I pulled more and more tightly into myself, sinking into my anger and irritation, letting the waves of it warm me as they'd been doing for my entire life.

A tingling across my skin made me lift my head. The flame-shaped mark on my wrist itched. The air heated, and I leapt to my feet, ready to fight, more annoyed than ever after waiting so long.

I nearly lost my nerve as Dravyn arrived.

He descended not as a human-like being, but in one of his favored shapeshifter forms—that of a massive eagle that appeared to be made entirely of flame. Smoke and embers swirled as he landed in the center of the bridge, his massive wings folding around him and making his personal inferno build to the point of blinding.

Several pounding heartbeats later, he stepped from the blaze as a fully-formed man. The fire collapsed and extinguished instantly behind him, though its heat still lingered.

After the conversation with Mairu about elves and those who had replaced us, I couldn't help comparing myself to this other being, wondering what divine forms my ancestors might have taken—what sort of similar awe they might have inspired before the Fall.

And I hated the God of Fire even more because of it.

My words, after steeping in such vitriol for so long, came out in a snarl: "We need to talk."

"Yes, Mai warned me of as much."

"I won't be sent away until we've settled some things," I warned.

He met my challenging gaze and held it for a long moment. Hoping I'd flinch, maybe?

I didn't.

He gave the barest of nods toward the tower. "Shall we, then?"

He motioned, the guards pulled the doors open, and he headed inside without waiting for my reply.

I hesitated only a moment, wondering where he ultimately intended to lead me. Then I realized that it didn't matter; it wasn't as though I had any allies anywhere in this palace. I was in just as much danger on the bridge as inside the tower.

We passed through the large doors and went immediately to a spiraling staircase. It was steep, but I hardly noticed the burning in my legs as I climbed, as there were countless windows wrapping alongside the steps, drawing my attention outside. The higher we went, the better the view of the stark yet beautiful landscape. I wanted to study it more from this bird's-eye view, but Dravyn had pulled far ahead of me, so I gave my head a little shake and hurried on.

"You've been avoiding me again," I said, leaping the steps in sets of two and three to catch up to his long-legged strides. "It's been days since we last talked."

"I've been busy. Again." He gazed out of the windows and slowed his pace somewhat, though whether to allow me to catch up, or to better survey his domain, I wasn't sure. "And I still am," he continued. "But Mai insisted this couldn't wait. So if you have something to say, then say it."

"You know what I am."

He stopped walking as he reached the top landing, but he didn't reply.

I stepped closer to him. He turned his powerful gaze on me, but I still didn't flinch; I was finished with cowering under the heat of that glare.

"Well? Do you deny it?"

To my surprise, he didn't.

"Did you know what I was that day in Cauldra?" I asked.

He nodded. "I suspected it. Mai confirmed it. The two of us investigated the incident at the temple together, which led us to you in that prison cell. And then we sensed that you carried magic, despite what you were."

A ribbon of disgust curled through me; despite my constant efforts to bury that healing magic I possessed, to ignore it completely, here was an unwelcome reminder that it was still there.

"It's unusual for your kind to still carry such powerful divine magic," Dravyn said, "and I thought studying it more closely might yield answers to some questions I had. The upper-god I serve is aware of you as well, and I made my case to him before I sent for you—which, by the way...surely you didn't think you could hide from him as well?"

I didn't reply, my cheeks warming as much with embarrassment as anger, now.

"Such hubris," he chuckled.

I ignored this comment. "Are the rest of the Marr as aware as you? Does everyone know I'm here?"

"Only my own court," he said. "Most of the other middle-gods, if they realize what you are, will likely..."

"Disapprove of my very existence in any realm, much less this one?"

"...Your kind are not held in particularly high regard in divine circles."

I laughed. Coldly. "You can spare me the political wording; I know you hate my kind." I couldn't help the snarl slipping back into my voice as I added, "And that you fear them."

"And you feel the same about my kind."

"Not the fear part," I snapped.

"Noted." A muscle in his jaw twitched. I wasn't sure if it was from exasperation or amusement.

Our attention was drawn once more toward the windows as we both caught a flash of color moving fast over the landscape. A herd of golden-flanked, horse-like creatures galloped along a distant hillside, fire bursting from their hooves every time they made contact with the ground.

I fought the urge to press against the glass for a closer look, but kept one eye on the dazzling creatures as I asked, "So the other courts—the ones who will be partially responsible for devising my ascension trials—don't yet know what I truly am."

"Only because Mairu has been helping to hide you. That house you were staying in was filled with her magic; she's been subtly deepening the spell surrounding your appearance these past few weeks. It still isn't permanent, but it should take more quickly and completely now whenever we need to make use of it."

Another rush of mixed feelings flooded me. The alternative to being shoved into that protective cottage might have been death at the hands of those other Marr—or worse—but I still felt violated, angered by the Shade Court's subterfuge.

"The disguise is not necessary while you're here with me in my palace, however—unless we have visitors from elsewhere— so don't be alarmed if it begins to fade."

"Why didn't you just bring me here to begin with?"

"Because."

"Let me guess: You were too *preoccupied* by other things to have me distracting you as well?"

"That's the simplest explanation, yes. I couldn't be around to make certain every creature of, and visitor to, this palace behaved, so I thought you'd be better off set apart from any potential danger." Under his breath, he added, "Then you went and found yourself some danger anyway, of course."

I didn't fully buy this explanation, but I had bigger questions, so I let it go. "What other tricks have you been pulling on me since my arrival?" I demanded.

"None," he said, starting to walk again.

I pried my eyes away from the window and the golden horses and followed him.

He led me into a wide-open space at the very top of the tower. Its walls and floor were both made of white stone, making it appear more like an outdoor courtyard than anything. It seemed to be a central hub of sorts, with six closed doors spaced evenly around it. A table stood in the center of the room, surrounded by tall-backed chairs. It was easy to picture important meetings occurring regularly around this dark, elegant table.

The ceiling was the same as the one in the atrium, made of tinted glass letting in enough light to feed the plants growing all around the space.

I was surprised to see more things growing wild here, same as in that atrium; I had never associated the God of Fire with life. But there were living things everywhere in his palace, the most prominent here being flowering-vines that climbed trellises spaced evenly between the doors.

"I had no need for other tricks," he told me, reaching for one of the red flowers clinging to these vines. It was withered, barely clinging to life, and I watched as he summoned a tiny bit of perfectly controlled fire to his palm and turned the bloom to ashes. He did this to a few more shriveled blooms, burning away the dead things to allow room for healthy new growth.

"Can I trust anything you say at this point?" I asked.

"*Would* you trust anything I said to you at this point?"

"No."

He huffed out a laugh. "Then does it matter how I answer that question?"

I looked away, still fuming, yet silent for the moment; at least he seemed to be giving me answers now. There was no way of knowing if they were honest or not, but I still preferred them to silence and being shoved away, alone, in my room or cottage or wherever else.

He left me for a few minutes, busying himself with speaking to the few beings who were moving in and out of the rooms here. Some of those beings, like Rieta, looked human. Others were clearly anything but, and I wondered: Had Dravyn created all of these creatures? And if not, then where had they come from?

I started to wander after him, questions racing through my mind, when a dark blur hurtled down through the ceiling and stopped me in my tracks.

Moth.

He swooped down from an opening in the ceiling, flaring his wings and flapping for a moment before spotting me. He gave a happy squawk before darting forward and circling me, and despite all of my questions and lingering, festering anger, I couldn't help but smile at the sight of him.

The smile faded quickly as the God of Fire returned to my side. He held out his hand, which Moth didn't hesitate to land upon.

I watched the griffin preening for a moment, frowning. The pit that had opened in my stomach when I'd learned of Rieta's true form opened wider, threatening to swallow me up again.

"I suppose I can't trust this little beast either?" I asked. "Did you send him to spy and cause me trouble?"

"Him?" Dravyn chuckled. "I assure you I sent him nowhere; in case you haven't noticed, he very much has a mind of his own."

I watched the griffin for a moment—he was busy chewing contentedly on Dravyn's sleeve—and I couldn't think of any proof to the contrary.

"...It does seem like you could have sent a more capable spy," I admitted. "One that wasn't prone to bursting into flames at unfortunate times."

"You don't know the half of his unfortunate tendencies," Dravyn murmured.

Moth gave his hand a sharp nip in response, making the god curse, and I promptly decided that if I *was* going to trust anyone in this realm again, it would be this griffin.

"He was one of the first creatures I ever brought to life in the Tower of Creation," Dravyn said, giving his bitten hand a shake. "So the edges of him are admittedly rough." Moth attempted another nip, which Dravyn managed to dodge this time. He shot his creation a withering look as he said, "The magic in that tower is wild and difficult to take charge of and shape—a true test of a young Marr's grip on their divine power. Rarely is anything viable or desirable created on a first try; most gods destroy their first creations and try again, even. No desire to put their failed attempts on display..."

"But not you?"

He exhaled something between a laugh and a sigh, and the

griffin leapt from his hand to the air, tumbled through a few less-than-graceful flips in the air, and then crashed into my chest.

I instinctively wrapped my arms around his squirming, flailing body. When I had him secured, I glanced up and found Dravyn watching us with a curious gleam in his eyes.

"I suppose the sight of him—and his flaws—keeps me humble," he said.

I snorted.

A corner of his mouth lifted. "You don't think me humble?"

"...If what I've witnessed thus far is you *humble*, then I suppose I should be thanking the stars that at least you're not any more insufferable than you currently are."

Moth chirped in agreement at this, nuzzling his head into the folds of my shirt.

"I think he likes you," Dravyn commented.

My cheeks flushed a bit at the suddenly friendlier, almost admiring tone of his voice; I couldn't help it.

"Probably because you're both cantankerous, stubborn little assholes," he added, after a moment of thought.

"See, and now you've ruined the moment."

The god grinned fully at this, and the sight of it caused my cheeks to burn hotter. More of his tricks. I had not come here to fall for them, or to share any sort of smiling *moment* with him.

Tilting my face away to hide my frustration with myself, I lifted my hands to encourage Moth to fly away. As he playfully swooped and dove his way around the room, I went to stare out of the nearest window and collect myself.

I could feel Dravyn watching me. I heard him stepping closer, and then he said, "A truth for a truth?"

I kept my eyes on the hills, searching for the horses I'd seen earlier. "What do you mean?"

He moved even closer, his voice dropping lower so only I could hear it. "I told you the truth about what I saw when I found you in the prison cell. I also insisted that Mairu stop hiding in the guise of my servant and reveal *her* true self. So now you tell me: There was another reason you went to Harithyn the other day, wasn't there? You weren't simply bored, and you weren't fooled by Valas's charms. You're smarter than that. So what were you trying to find in the Death God's territory?"

I didn't reply right away, but my hand automatically reached for the sparrow hanging from my neck. I caught myself mid-reach and hugged my arms around myself instead.

"My curiosity simply got the better of me, I'm afraid," I said with a shrug. "It was foolish, I know."

He didn't argue. He simply stared out of the window with me for several minutes before he said, "I don't know what answers you were hoping to find in Zachar's territory or elsewhere, but this is not the sort of place where you can wander as you please. At least, not if you hope to survive long enough to have a chance to die in the official trials awaiting you."

The trials.

I didn't particularly want to think about them, but they felt like a safer subject than what had happened with the Death Marr. "So these trials..." I began, drumming my fingers against my arm. "...Are the other courts already preparing them?"

"They know I've collected a potential ascendant. Beyond that, I don't know their progress; we have a meeting this evening, in this very spot, on the matter." He gestured toward the table in the center of the space.

"One I can't attend, I assume."

He shook his head.

Silence settled between us, stretching until he said something I never would have expected, his voice still quiet and meant only for us: "I will give you one last chance to leave before it begins, no questions asked."

It took me a moment to reply. "What about the rules? I've seen too much, remember?"

A shadow of doubt crossed his face, but he quickly chased it away with a shrug and a confident, crooked smile. "It wouldn't be the first time I'd broken a few rules," he said. "We have other things distracting us here, and you haven't officially started any of the trials, so there's a case to be made, I think—and there's magic that can erase what you've seen, besides."

"Erase my memories?" I said, startled.

He nodded.

"That sounds worse than failing the trials."

"Does it?" He gave me a curious look. "Worse than death?"

My gaze dropped to my boots as I relived my final moment with Andrel by the river—the conversation, the crushing weight of expectation, the desperate way my heart had squeezed as he looked at me.

Don't lose your anger.

Don't stop until you've destroyed them.

I couldn't go home. I didn't *have* a home unless I succeeded at what I'd set out to do. If I went back now, nothing would change, and I would only be disappointing all of the people I loved. All the people I'd lost.

Dravyn was still watching me curiously as I searched for the right words. The smart words. The safe words. My hand pressed against my face, feeling for the scars I'd kept buried for so long. I didn't have to hide them in this palace, he'd said.

Don't be alarmed if it begins to fade.

I could already feel the scars starting to emerge beneath whatever magic Mairu had covered them in, I thought.

I clenched my fingers into a fist and jerked it back down to my side.

"I'm not going anywhere," I said, quietly but firmly. "I spoke the truth that day on the platform—I intend to serve in your court. I will become divine, or I will die trying."

CHAPTER 20

Dravyn didn't argue with my declaration, but his eyes grew distant, glassy with an emotion I couldn't name.

"Then it's settled," came the voice of the Ice God as he suddenly appeared at the top of the stairs. "How exciting."

"The doors below were left open for Mairu, not for you," Dravyn told him, tonelessly.

"That's terribly rude."

The God of Fire offered no apology.

They continued to chatter and bicker for a moment while I studied them, wondering how beastly they'd looked when they first ascended. How long had it taken them to settle their power? How long had they both been human-like, as they were now, and able to converse so easily as this? They seemed to fight like well-acquainted siblings, I thought.

"Don't look so worried about it," Valas was saying. "It's been some time since we've had an ascension trial, but I think this one will go better than the last one." He shrugged, and with his sly, chaotic smile, he added, "I mean, it can't go much *worse*, can it?"

Dravyn shot him a warning glare.

"What happened at the last trial?" I asked.

Dravyn shook his head. Valas appeared eager to keep talking, but neither had a chance to answer my question—the Serpent Goddess appeared as suddenly as her fellow court member had, interrupting us with her smooth, powerful voice. "Valas, my sweet," she called.

The Ice God lazily tilted his head toward her.

"Do you remember the time your magic slipped out of your control and encased your big stupid head in ice, mouth and all?"

He grimaced. "A painful, traumatic memory of my second divine year, yes—thank you so much for bringing it up."

"I wish it had been permanent," she informed him. "At least over your mouth."

He clutched a hand to his heart, and in a wounded voice he said, "You're both incredibly rude. We're supposed to be a team, you know."

Dravyn was, again, unapologetic. "We need to discuss some things before the meeting later," he said to Mairu. "If you'd like to be a part of the *team*," he added with a cursory glance at Valas, "then you can help the servants prepare for the arrival of our guests."

"Delighted to, of course," said Valas with a mocking little bow. "That isn't degrading work for a middle-god, at all."

Dravyn nodded toward me while keeping his glare on Valas. "And no more games with her," he warned. He was gone in the next instant, disappearing through one of the doors along the room's edge.

Valas wasted no time turning to me, looking all too eager to play another game. "So you met the God of Death," he said. "You two got along wonderfully, I assume?"

I narrowed my eyes. "If I'd realized you were also the God of Chaos, I never would have listened to a word you said."

His beaming smile was annoyingly handsome. "And then you never would have had this opportunity to move closer to the Fire God," he said, gesturing to the room around us. "He was going to keep you locked in that little cottage indefinitely, I'd imagine. I mixed things up on your behalf."

"On my behalf?"

"It's what I do," he said with a shrug. "No need to thank me."

"No one in their right mind is thanking you," Mairu said in a deadpan voice.

"Well they should."

"You just said there was no need," I pointed out.

"True, but I'm afraid I'm a creature of many *wants*."

"You could have gotten her killed," Mairu snapped. "As though we don't have enough things to deal with around here."

He waved a dismissive hand. "Nymth was in the Death God's territory already. I told him to keep an eye on our intrepid little court candidate."

"Nymth?"

"One of the two Miratar spirits that serve him," Mairu explained.

"And the one who informed me that Zachar was apparently in a bad mood, so a rescue mission might be in order."

I pondered the implications of this for a second, and then asked, "So it's true what I've heard—that you can communicate your thoughts through the connection you share with your divine court members?"

"Of course."

So, he was partly the reason I'd made the foolish decision to seek out the Death God...but also the reason Dravyn found me and rescued me when he did. This sent another ripple of confusing thoughts through me; I was veering wildly between feelings of gratitude and fury today.

Mairu appeared unimpressed by the Ice God's explanations. "It was still a foolish thing you did."

"Aren't you supposed to be in that room with Dravyn," Valas asked, "having that oh-so-important meeting that you two decided to exclude me from?"

"We both know you have no real desire to be in it."

"True. As long as you give me the highlights."

"Which we will."

"Then go already."

"Already gone," she said, flashing him a rude gesture before she turned and walked away.

Once she disappeared as Dravyn had, I wandered toward the closest window, bracing my hands against the sill as I peered out. The golden creatures I'd spotted earlier were back. Out of all the incredible scenery beneath me, nothing seemed to draw my eyes the way those horse-like beasts did.

"The *selakir*," Valas said, sidling up beside me.

I appreciated having a name to give them. If I was honest, I appreciated *most* of the things he'd told me, even if it had led to some unfortunate decisions.

He was a conniving, tricky bastard—but he'd made a point earlier: I never would have ventured into the Death God's territory and witnessed what I had if he had not given me the information he did. And he may have been chaotic, but I had always been good at imposing order upon chaos. So he could be useful, too.

I watched the doors Mairu had passed through, studying

the countless carved symbols decorating them until I found my voice again.

"What happened at the last ascension trial?" I asked.

"You really want to know?"

"I wouldn't have asked if I didn't." I turned to face him more fully. "Which god were they ascending to serve?"

"The Death Marr." The surprise must have been obvious on my face, because he added, "And it was arguably too soon for him to have been trying to create a Miratar spirit, given that he was so young and barely in control of his own magic. Nevertheless, the potential ascendant made it through the initial trials, and almost to the end, but...."

"But?"

"Then she failed the last test in the Tower of Ascension. She tried to flee back to the mortal realm afterwards, and, well..."

"You can't go back once you've started."

Unless the God of Fire wants to break the rules for you, I mused—and then immediately shook off the memory of Dravyn's words. I still didn't know what to make of them and his unexpected offer.

"Exactly." The Ice God's smile was grim, his expression the closest to serious I'd ever seen it.

I leaned against the window sill again, gripping it tightly to steady myself. "The trial that she failed...do you know what it was?"

"Not the details, I'm afraid. No one aside from the upper-gods really knows what goes on inside Amalith; even my own ascension is mostly a blur that I only occasionally visit in my dreams."

"And there's no way of knowing what trials *I* might end up facing, is there? Dravyn said the initial two are devised by the courts outside the one you intend to join, but he spoke as though it was up to the Marr of those courts to devise whatever they wished, whenever they wished, and there was no real way of predicting what would happen. It seems to be in the nature of all the Marr to keep me constantly guessing."

His smile turned sly again. "Ah, so you've noticed that."

I didn't return his smile. This conversation was making me sick to my stomach.

We were quiet for some time, both of us staring out the window. The herd of selakir had disappeared, so I focused instead on the black ground far in the distance, on the cracks of fire splitting it and the billows of smoke and steam rising up from it. I felt a strange kinship with that breaking earth, watching it buckle and try to resist the fiery rage building underneath.

"You look worried," Valas commented. "Don't tell me you're losing your nerve before we even get started?"

I narrowed my eyes on a particularly dark plume of smoke exhaling from the earth, shooting up into the sky. "I don't like not having all the facts," I said quietly. "Or *any* of the facts, in this case."

I could feel his gaze on me, and I braced myself for whatever other mocking words he had for me.

"Let me see what I can find out for you," he offered instead.

CHAPTER 21

Later that night, I found myself too restless to even consider going to sleep. Valas had stopped by my room after the Marr had their meeting and delivered what he'd been able to find out, as promised—but it wasn't much.

The Sun Court had insisted on leading the way, he'd learned, which meant my first trial would be devised by one of the four Marr who served in that Sun Goddess's court—Storm, Star, Sky, or Moon. Maybe some combination of the four.

"If I was the betting sort," he'd told me, *"I would be prepared to face something of the Star or Moon Goddess's design."*

I spent more than an hour after he left sitting cross-legged on the bed, trying to list the facts I knew about these goddesses, searching for anything and everything that might help prepare me for their trials.

Normally, making such lists brought comfort.

Tonight, it only seemed to be making me more anxious.

Tossing my notes aside, I went into the washroom, splashed

several handfuls of cool water onto my face, and took a long look into the gold-framed mirror.

With the meeting between the gods finished, and no more visits from any outsiders expected tonight, Mairu had let the cloaking magic around me relax. I knew this...yet my reflection still startled me, as it was the first time I'd looked upon my actual face in weeks. It wasn't much different, truly—my pointed ears and old scars were simply more visible now—but even the subtle change provided a glaring reminder of who I was and why I was really here.

More anxious than ever, I left my room, setting off without any real destination in mind. I quickly thought of one, however —the atrium I'd been brought to when I first arrived here. Or, more specifically, the room full of colored glass I'd glimpsed from the center of that atrium.

I moved like a ghost through the palace, passing only a few other beings at this late hour. Some looked my way, but none of them spoke. Nobody lingered, either. They all seemed to know who I was, but they hadn't yet figured out how to act around me, so they simply averted their eyes and moved out of my way as quickly as they could.

The doors to the glass-filled room were closed when I reached it. Two guards stood outside—more of those strange, lanky creatures with greyish-black skin and slender, flame-swirled hands. Even after a month spent in this realm, I realized now that I'd never spoken to their kind before, and they'd never spoken to me. I wasn't even sure they'd understand me.

I tried anyway. "Can I go inside?"

Their eyes—a red shade similar to Moth's—brightened and then narrowed as they looked me up and down. I felt like I was being scrutinized to my core, but they ultimately let me in without an argument. One of them even provided me with light, reaching his long arm up and cupping the torch beside the door, leaving a flame on its end when he backed away. He did the same with the torch on the other side before bowing out of the room, leaving me alone to take in the sight waiting for me.

It was incredible.

There were no overhead lights, but that seemed to be by design; the torches felt more intimate, their light dancing softly through the glass, illuminating it just well enough for me to see the unbelievable amount of detail and variation in each sculpture. And these glass sculptures...there were so *many*.

Glass-filled shelves lined the wall on either side of me, and throughout the room there were tables with bordered edges, organized like raised garden beds full of blossoming glass. Two of these gardens featured figures that were all the same color—one in all greens, the other entirely in shades of blue—but the individual figures were varied and followed no patterns that I could make sense of, no matter how hard I tried.

I stepped toward the blue garden. A particularly intricate figure had caught my eye—a willow tree with limbs that seemed impossibly thin and elegant. I didn't dare pick it up, as it looked far too delicate, but my fingers were stretching toward the trunk when I heard someone clear their throat behind me.

"The trials, whatever they end up being, will almost certainly be easier if you've slept beforehand."

I spun around to find Dravyn standing in the doorway. He looked a bit wild in the torchlight, his shirt half-unbuttoned and hanging loose, and his hair disheveled, as though he'd just returned from a hike through the hills of his territory.

And, for some reason, my heart started pounding as though I'd been hiking right alongside him.

"I...I couldn't sleep," I said.

He moved to the room's only window, peering through the tall, skinny opening and up at the glowing orb that had faded to a pale shade of moonlight. "The forgelight is simulating the mortal realm's day and night cycle well enough, isn't it? I thought that would help."

"It has been helping. Tonight is just...different. I've been busy thinking, trying to prepare myself for whatever lies ahead."

"Understandable, I suppose."

Talking about those trials wasn't going to help calm me down, so I gestured to the figures around us and asked, "Did you make all of these, somehow?"

He nodded but didn't elaborate immediately, instead moving to pick up the willow tree I'd been staring at. I held my breath as he did, certain his powerful hands would crush such a delicate thing without fail—even if those masterful hands had apparently been the ones to shape it.

He studied it for a long moment. I thought he'd forgotten I'd asked him anything, until, without a word, he placed the tree back down and beckoned me to follow him to the other side of the room.

There were two more torches here, which he lit with a simple flick of his wrist, revealing a door I hadn't noticed before. A small room lay on the other side, with what appeared to be an oven of some kind in the very center of it. He lit this oven as easily as he'd lit the torches. I drew closer, peering inside the deep well of it to see piles of what looked like broken glass and sand.

Dravyn wrapped his arm lightly around me, guiding me several steps back before he gave another flourish of his hand that caused the oven fire to build to a brighter, hotter temperature. The heat became so intense I automatically turned my face away, burying it against his chest.

Inhaling his smoky scent, wedged between the scorch of the oven and the powerful warmth he radiated, I felt myself briefly drifting closer to relaxation.

I stayed against him for longer than I meant to while he continued to manipulate the oven's fire, my eyes growing heavy with sleep, until his hand absently caressed the small of my back, sending a not-unpleasant shiver spiraling through me.

I quickly stepped away.

He let me go without comment, already on to the next part of his demonstration; there were various tools hanging from a nearby rack—pliers, tongs, rods of all shapes and sizes. He gathered a few of these things and carried them toward the oven.

I watched, mesmerized, as he rolled up his sleeves and then took a rod with a ringed end and swept it carefully through the oven. When he pulled it from the heat, a glowing, red-hot glob of melted glass clung to the end. He carried this to a nearby metal table and rolled the molten material back and forth against the shiny surface, working it until he had a smooth, elongated sphere at the end of the rod. Then he lifted it, blew gently into the other end, and the glowing sphere began to expand.

Once the material was sufficiently expanded, he took a second metal pole—this one with a sharper tip—and began to shape the inflated glass, pulling and twisting with quick, expert motions.

After he had a general shape worked out, he made use of several more tools to pinch and smooth more precise details into the piece. The heat was intense even for the god of these things, apparently; his loose shirt revealed sweat glistening on his chest, and he occasionally had to pause and swipe his forehead dry of the beads collecting on it.

It was worth the heat and effort, though, because when he'd finished, what had started as a blob of molten glass had become an elegant creature rearing onto powerful hind legs; it looked like one of the golden selakir I'd seen galloping across the hills earlier.

I stepped closer, not caring about the stifling heat, focused only on getting a better look at this extraordinary creation.

"I've heard of this art, and read about it," I said, "but I've never witnessed someone actually doing it."

"It's not that hard." He paused, considering. "Would you like to try?"

I hesitated only a moment before nodding. I couldn't resist; my love of learning and fascination with how things worked briefly overcame the disdain I felt for my teacher.

He removed his latest glass creation from the rod and carried it off to cool while I took a moment to familiarize myself with the tools before me. I touched nearly every one, picked them up, tested their weight, their sharpness, my ability to wield them.

I looked up minutes later and found Dravyn watching me as though he was trying to figure out how I worked as well—what sharpness and weight I carried, what shape I might leave behind.

"Ready?" he asked.

"Yes."

Together, with his arm steadying mine, we took the ringed rod and collected another end full of melted glass, carrying it to the same table he'd worked against last time.

Dravyn kept his arm braced against mine, guiding the first few twists of the rod, his body so close I could occasionally feel his heart beating against me. A beat that felt almost...human. I don't know why this surprised me; *human* was the form he held in this moment, after all.

I guess I'd convinced myself a god couldn't possibly possess a normal heart.

Yet his felt very normal, and the rest of him did as well, all flesh and muscle and warmth wrapping around me. My pulse skipped a few beats every time he pressed closer. It had been a long few weeks without being close to another like this—that was the only explanation for the twinge of desire that stirred deep in my belly, and for the way my mouth had gone so very dry.

Or the only explanation I was willing to accept, anyway.

Once I seemed to have gotten the hand of shaping my material, he took a step back and watched me work for a minute, offering occasional bits of advice until I'd managed to recreate a glowing sphere similar to the one he'd created earlier.

"It should be ready for shaping," he confirmed.

I nodded and, somewhat nervously, lifted the rod to my lips. It was heavy, and easier to hold steady while exhaling if I let him help, so I didn't protest when his arm braced against mine once more.

"Gently now," he instructed in a near-whisper, his mouth close enough to send warm air brushing against my ear.

It crossed my mind that my lips were pressing against the same metal that his had only minutes ago. Another spiral of something-I-refused-to-call-desire went through me. I shook it off and focused on exhaling.

The bubble I created didn't seem as even as his had been, but he assured me it was good enough for a first attempt; he handed me the first shaping tool he'd used and offered to hold the expanded glass steady so I could focus on sculpting it.

"You have to be quick but precise," he instructed, "the temperature and correct consistency won't last long before you'll have to put it back in the oven, which can make things trickier."

I did my best to follow his examples and advice, but quickly realized that he'd made this art look far, far easier than it actually was, and my end result was nowhere near what I'd been picturing in my head.

"That's...uninspiring," I said as I finished. "I'd been going for a cat. It looks a bit more like a slug though, doesn't it?"

His expression twisted in a way that I suspected was holding in laughter.

"Be honest," I chided.

"...It's a lovely slug, for what it's worth." His laughter escaped, the sound soft and hypnotizing, like a warm breeze brushing over my skin.

"Thank you for the lesson," I said, blushing as I looked away. "But I think I prefer watching you do it."

He finally managed to stop laughing and then went to work again, creating another figure. Though my cheeks still burned from my own embarrassing attempt, I was just as mesmerized by his movements as I'd been the last time.

When he finished this round, he presented me with another small, elegant animal—a sparrow. One with wings curled artfully around its body, its shape very similar to the one hanging around my neck—though its colors were much brighter, a swirling symphony of reds and oranges.

"It's...beautiful." It stung to admit that a god was capable of creating such beauty, but there was no other word for it.

"A good luck charm for whatever lies ahead," he told me, "though it will need time to properly cool in the kiln before you can take it."

"It would shatter if it cooled too quickly, I'd imagine."

"Exactly."

He showed me to the kiln. There were other golden horses here, along with the one he'd created earlier. When he caught me staring, awed once more, he plucked one from the herd and handed it to me for a closer look. It was still warm, but firm and clearly finished.

"The selakir?" I guessed.

"You've been learning, I see."

"Valas told me about them."

"Well, I suppose he occasionally says intelligent things after all."

I was determined not to return even the slight smile that crossed his face—we had already gotten too close to one another tonight. I focused only on turning the smooth, horse-like figure over and around in my hands, studying it.

I was so focused on memorizing its elegant curves that I didn't notice the blur of brown and white streaking toward me until it was almost too late.

I ducked while Dravyn reached out a hand and caught Moth by the scruff of his neck in mid-air, hardly flinching or taking his eyes from me as he did so.

I couldn't help but be impressed by his reflexes.

He locked eyes with the griffin and simply said, "No, you may not," before releasing him.

Moth flopped dramatically down to the ground, splaying out on his back as if the denial had killed him. Every few seconds he would twitch, and then lift his head just enough to fix one of his ruby-tinted eyes on me.

"He wants what's in your hand," Dravyn said. "He likes to collect shiny things. Precious stones, glittery rocks, bits of glass. Helpful when gathering materials to add to my oven," he said with a nod at that oven in the adjacent room, "but he can't seem to tell the difference between scraps and my works of art." Nudging the limp creature with his foot, he added, "Which I guess I should probably be offended by."

I found myself smiling at the wry tone of his voice, warmth bubbling up in me before I could guard against it.

"I've trained him to leave the gardens alone, at least."

I followed his gaze to a small sliver of those glass gardens that remained visible beyond the oven room. Their mesmerizing colors pulled me toward them just as before.

"What are all of these, exactly?" I asked as I wandered back into the room, studying the various tables full of figures. "Some of them seem organized with purpose."

He didn't reply, and I glanced over my shoulder to see he had followed me only as far as the doorway.

Moth had given up his dying act and now perched on Dravyn's shoulder, nuzzling against his cheek. The god was absently scratching the griffin's chest, a distant look in his eyes.

"A truth for a truth?" I pressed, borrowing his tactic from earlier. "I told you why I couldn't sleep. So you owe me some sort of honesty in exchange, right? So tell me what these are."

Another few beats passed before he seemed to shake off whatever thoughts had brought him to a stop.

"Memorials," he said, moving past me and heading back toward the atrium.

My breath caught at the word. I don't know what I'd expected to hear, but that wasn't it. Just as I'd never imagined a god with a heart...well, I guess I'd never pictured them as beings who would bother with memorializing anything, either.

He slowed to a stop just before the exit, glancing back at me and adding, "The magic I mentioned earlier today—the kind that erases memories—it doesn't work nearly as effectively on divine beings. I learned that the hard way, I'm afraid."

My gaze swept over the room; the number of figures seemed hauntingly vast, all of a sudden.

"So I tried to find different ways, different places, to keep things," he said. "The glass holds some memories of them so I don't have to hold them all in my mind."

"Who do you mean by *them*?"

He shook his head. "Our truths are unbalanced again, I'm afraid."

My brow furrowed, questions and concerns filling my head. Who was he trying to forget?

And more importantly, why did I care?

He looked toward the atrium. "Unless there's another truth of yours you'd like to give in exchange, you should probably just go back to your room and try to sleep."

"Another truth..."

"Those are the rules we've established, aren't they?"

"I guess they are."

"So? Do you have one?"

I shook my head. I'd already shared enough with him tonight. Too much, really. Far too much.

"As expected," he said, a faintly victorious smile crossing his lips.

I started to fire back a reply, determined not to give in so easily. Then I looked around at all the glass memorials surrounding us, and I decided—maybe just this once—to let him win.

He offered his arm.

I reached for it, but at that same moment my eyes caught on a third table of matching glass on the far side of the room. I hadn't noticed it before. Every figure upon this table was a shade of red, and—unlike any other table in the room—all the figures on this one were the same. Dozens upon dozens of rectangular-shaped sculptures. Like gravestones, I thought.

"It's late," Dravyn prompted.

I nodded and absently hooked my hand around his arm, letting him lead me mostly so I could focus on observing the things we passed.

He walked me all the way to my room, and he held the door open as he bade me goodnight; I hardly realized it all as it was happening, as lost in thought and observation as I was—but I recognized the absence of him as soon as he was gone.

My hand felt restless without his arm to hold on to, and a strange, uncomfortable weightlessness overcame me as I locked the door and turned to face my empty room.

I went slowly back to my bed and picked up the notes I'd tossed aside earlier. I used what little blank space I had left to draw miniature sketches of each of the glass figures I'd committed to memory, and then I tried—mostly in vain—to sort through them, to guess at what sort of memories they might have represented.

When I finally managed to fall asleep, I dreamt of the God of Fire. Of the two of us together in a dark room with glass walls, clothed in nothing but flames, our hands reaching, but not quite touching.

The closer we stepped to one another, the brighter the fires burned, until the heat became so intense that our glass surroundings shattered and fell over us like a sharp and deadly rain.

CHAPTER 22

I WOKE, IN NEAR TOTAL DARKNESS, TO FIND MYSELF in a room I'd never been in before.

My elven eyes adjusted quickly, but even my sensitive vision wasn't enough to fully see through the inky blackness surrounding me. I managed, through a combination of patience and still-half-asleep squinting, to feel my way from the couch I'd been laying on, around several tables and chairs, and eventually through a doorway and into a much larger room.

On the far side of this second room I saw what appeared to be a balcony. The door to it was open, a honeysuckle-scented breeze sweeping in, turning the gauzy curtains around it into swaying ghosts.

Outside, it was clearly night, but it still appeared much brighter than inside, so I headed toward the balcony in hopes of being able to better understand where I was and how I'd gotten here.

The frigid night air bit at my skin. I still wore only the thin nightclothes I'd fallen asleep in, and pulling the loose shirt more tightly around myself did little to ward off the chill. I tried to distract myself from the cold by looking up.

I'd never seen so many stars.

I nearly lost my balance craning my neck, trying to take in the vastness of it all, and I had to catch myself against the balcony's railing.

As soon as I touched that railing, the floor collapsed beneath me, swinging away as if on a hinge to allow me to fall through.

Except I didn't fall—not at first.

I floated.

I was suspended in mid-air as a powerful energy swirled around me, invisible aside from a strange shimmer I occasionally caught out of the corner of my eye. That power soon settled heavily against my chest, crushing the breath from my lungs...

Then it released, and I plummeted downward.

I opened my mouth to scream, but no sound came out. I reached upward, swiping desperately for something to catch on to, something to slow my descent, but there was nothing but emptiness.

Then the stars above were falling too, as if diving toward my outstretched hand. One of them brushed my fingertips. Its light scattered on impact, raining down as a shower of silver and gold upon me. What seemed like a thousand more stars cascaded down on my left and right, occasionally bursting with a similar show of silver and gold, and I was so busy being astonished by it all that I forgot about screaming—or even panicking—for a minute.

Just as I felt the panic returning, my body bumped gently against cold, sandy ground.

The stars continued to fall all around me, sinking into the

sand and making it glow for a moment before turning it to a deep shade of black. All around me the sand began to shift in this way; bright as the sun for a breath, dark as the depths of the earth in the next. The ground directly underneath my feet stayed the same, but everything else was changing, stretching into a wide expanse of black earth.

Once everything was dark for as far as I could see, pinpricks of light began to appear along the ground, popping up like speckles of shimmering paint splattered against a canvas.

Not ground, then, I realized.

No; it was becoming the night sky in its full, dazzling glory, and I stood breathless in the center of it all as it kept expanding, my heart coming a little closer to leaping from my chest with every new star that flashed into existence.

As I took in the sight of it all, I remembered what Valas had told me—that he suspected either the Star or Moon Goddess would be the one to test me.

This was not a dream.

It was a trial.

I still didn't understand how I had found myself in the middle of it, but I was wide awake, suddenly, and determined to survive whatever came next.

As I contemplated my first move, I reached up to run a hand along my ears. They'd been pointed when I'd fallen asleep, but now they were smooth; Mairu's magic somehow reached to cover me, even here—wherever this was—and the thought was oddly comforting and encouraging.

I cautiously stretched my foot away from the solid bit of ground beneath me, dipping it into the darkness around me as if testing the chill and depth of a river. The sky proved solid and even in a way that made no sense to my mind, but I didn't question it; I could move freely among the blackness, so this is what I did.

I wandered for what could have been minutes or hours, feeling terrifyingly small in the seemingly infinite sea of sky, with no clear idea of where to go and no easy way to mark where I'd been.

It didn't take long for thoughts—fears—of being lost forever in this infinity to start worming their way into my mind. With this fear squeezing tight on my head and heart, I made a point to try and counter it with reason and organization as I always did, seeking out recognizable patterns among the stars, searching for constellations that I could guide myself by.

The problem was that I would have sworn some of the stars were *moving*.

As I traveled on, studying and trying to memorize constellations, I came upon one that was, without a doubt, shifting. I slowed to a stop, watching the very clear outline of a woman shake out her long hair and then stride toward me. The outline pulled more and more stars toward it as it walked, so that by the time it stood before me the lines were solid and forming a tangible, beautiful woman cloaked in a long gown of silver.

A goddess.

She was not as monstrous as the Death Marr had been, nor did she appear as human as Dravyn and the rest of his court; her skin remained nearly as dark as the sky around us, but it occasionally pulsed with swirls of gold that sharply contrasted with the starlit outline of her body, reminding me she was solid. Her hair was the color of a pearl, rosy white and shining, and her eyes reminded me somewhat of Dravyn's—silver, but far lighter, shifting almost to white when glimpsed from certain angles.

A mark in the shape of a five-pointed star graced her wrist. The same symbol featured in the headpiece she wore, and it dangled from one of her many bracelets as well, further identifying her as Cepheid, the one often hailed as the Oracle Goddess—though I hardly needed to see such symbols to recognize her.

"Look closely, potential ascendant of Fire," she said, her voice slightly eerie and echoing, like a bell ringing out in the dead silence of a cave.

She waved a slender hand toward the sky behind her as she spoke, and as she did, a section of the stars upon her created canvas began to shift. They grew smaller, creating more opened spaces that were quickly filled by more stars, their positions all shuffling and shooting around until she held up her hand and slowed them to a stop.

"This is the beginning," she told me once the lights had fully settled. "That is, the way your home realm's sky appeared on the night you first arrived in this place. An exact reflection of our own divine sky, but less brilliant."

I did as she'd told me to, looking hard at the recreated sky, memorizing every detail I could, connecting the dots of light in a way that made sense to me. I searched, as before, for patterns among the chaos. I found them, too, and I felt confident I could make sense of any shapes or starry paths I might need to, if that was the test that lay before me.

As soon as that faint glimmer of confidence rose in me, the stars were moving again.

"And now, how they look in this very moment," Cepheid said, and with another sweep of her hand, the sky finished rearranging itself.

The stars retained the basic shapes and patterns of before, but those patterns had shifted far to my right.

"Past. Present. And now we must consider the future," said Cepheid, "and how they might move for you in that future." She lifted a hand. Splayed her fingers. The stars spun faster than ever before, their movement dizzying. Chaotic.

The spinning made my stomach churn, but I was determined to keep my eyes open and see all that I could.

"Seek their guidance," said the goddess, "and beware of taking wrong paths in the night."

"What happens if I follow a wrong path?"

"The stars can be cruel." She beckoned at the lights around her as if inviting them to demonstrate their cruelty. "And the darkness between them is worse."

Those lights all around us swept away. Even the goddess's skin ceased its glowing, encasing us briefly in a deep, hopeless night.

The solidness beneath me disappeared in the next instant. I plummeted once again, twisting and tumbling with more speed than before. This time the stars did not fall with me; they grew more and more distant until they winked out of existence completely.

I felt as if I'd ceased to exist along with them.

A soft, golden glow eventually swelled in their place, and I saw the Goddess of Stars falling alongside me, her body perfectly elegant and composed, feet pointed like a dancer's in mid-leap. Something like wings had flared out from her back, and the golden dust falling from them remained our only source of light for a long, terrifying moment.

She pointed at something below us. Our fall came to a slow end, the goddess landing delicately while I slammed hard onto my hands and knees. I staggered to my feet and fought to keep myself from vomiting.

A snap of the goddess's fingers, and we were back where

we'd stood moments before, once again facing the map of my realm's sky. It appeared to be just as we'd left it.

"Do you enjoy the feeling of falling? The thought of drifting forever among the stars?"

My mouth was almost too dry to speak. I swallowed hard and managed to say, "No."

"Then you must complete my task."

She waved her hand once more over the stars. This time, they seemed to keep their relative positions, but they grew larger, as did the darkness around them, creating a map that I could not only see but also walk through.

"Find the crown in your future sky," she said. "You have until the last of the stars in the beast's mane falls away."

The task delivered, she disappeared in a swirl of sparkling dust.

The silence following her disappearance was eerie; with the sky stretching endlessly around me, I felt like I was the only living thing in the universe. The sheer magnitude of my task nearly overwhelmed me before I could even start.

I gave my sister's necklace a quick squeeze, forced several deep breaths, and then began to break my task into smaller tasks, starting with the easiest of the goddess's riddles.

Until the last of the stars in the beast's mane falls away.

That was simple enough to puzzle out, I thought; I set about searching for a constellation that resembled a beast of some sort, and I quickly found it: the clear shape of a lion-like head. Stars circled around it, two clear layers set apart from the sea of lights beyond them. As I stared, expectant, one of the points in the outermost part of this circling mane flickered and began to fade.

So here was my timekeeper, then.

I watched it for a moment, feeling pleased at how easily I'd managed to untangle this first bit of my trial.

The satisfaction didn't last.

In the next blink, the light had disappeared. It happened so *quickly*—a precious fragment of my limited time already gone, just like that.

Wasting no more of that time, I started to search for the crown—though I still stayed close to the lion's mane at first, watching out of the corner of my eye until I saw another of its stars start to blink away. Then I calculated in my head, trying to determine—as accurately as I could—how much time seemed to pass between fading stars.

No more than a minute, I guessed.

A quick count found that there were only twenty of them left to go.

Palms sweating, I went back to my search for the crown. I walked as fast as I could through the sky map, noting the shape and layout of different star clusters I passed so that I wouldn't end up going in circles and wasting time. I combed methodically through row after row, and I managed to cover a great distance without getting too turned around, but it was fast becoming daunting.

How far did this sky stretch in each direction?

I looked back to the lion. It was hard to be certain from a distance, but it appeared as though three more of the mane's stars had already disappeared.

I shook off the sense of impending doom and walked faster.

I could do this.

I *would* do this.

Movement above drew my attention toward it. A star was falling toward me, and I reached up instinctively to catch it as I had when I'd been falling myself. It burst on impact just like the last one had, again showering me with silver and gold dust.

The particles seemed larger, thicker. What had seemed so beautiful before felt sinister now, reminding me of the shining, breaking glass from my nightmare. The bigger flakes of it scraped over my skin, leaving it feeling itchy and raw. Worse was the way the dust seemed to cast a fog over my senses, making the sky spin and stretch into something even larger, even more daunting.

More stars fell from somewhere up above, trying to distract me from the task at hand.

I pulled the rolled-up sleeves of my nightshirt down to protect my skin and trudged onward through the waves of stars, darting about to avoid letting them break against me. It made it more difficult, but I still stuck to the pattern of movement I'd established, still trying to be as efficient as possible.

At least five minutes had passed, if not ten, when the largest burst of falling stars yet fell over me. I couldn't avoid all of them.

I tried anyway, veering wildly to the right, tripping over my own feet in the process. Falling down as the stardust showered me was disorienting to say the least. I closed my eyes, but opened them almost immediately; it was too tempting to stay still in the dark.

Wiping the star's residue from my skin and clothing, I got back to my feet and continued my desperate search.

Until, finally, I saw it.

I spotted the base of it first, a curve of evenly spaced stars that connected to a vertical line of more stars on either side. The whole thing was tilted sideways, but it was very obviously a crown—one with five tall, distinct points.

I raced forward and reached for one of the points, bracing

myself for whatever unpredictable magic was to come after I completed this trial.

Nothing happened.

I took a step back. Blinked, and checked to make certain I still saw what I thought I did.

It was still a crown.

I reached for a different point. My hands passed right through the pale light, shaking as they went.

The shaking spread through the rest of my body. I had found the solution—I was so *certain* of it, and yet nothing I did seemed to trigger the Star Goddess's reappearance, or whatever the next part of her trial was.

Could there be another crown somewhere else? She'd said *my* crown. But what did that mean? I had no crown. No one in my family had since the humans and their new gods had brought so much ruin and death to us.

Was this some sort of cruel prank to remind me of that?

Maybe Mairu's magic had not hidden me at all. They all knew what I was, who I was, and now they were—

Stop it, I silently commanded myself.

Even if these things were true, I didn't have time to worry about them. Not if I was going to survive this.

I took a moment to memorize my location and the path leading to it, and then I sprinted a short distance until I was within sight of the lion once more. I knew my time was nearly up, but I wanted to know precisely what I had to work with.

It was worse than I'd feared.

My eyes fell upon the beast in the same moment the second to last star in its mane flickered out.

The ground beneath me buckled as though starting to give way.

I panicked and broke into a sprint, putting as much

distance between myself and my timekeeper as I could. I didn't go very far before I caught myself and slammed to a stop. I couldn't outrun this. Running would waste time. Running would mean certain death.

Tears streaming down my face, I stumbled back to the crown. I traced it with my finger in the air, double-checking its shape yet again. I briefly closed my eyes and mentally pictured every point, every edge, wracking my stardust-dazed mind for a solution.

Over and over, I repeated every single word the Goddess of Stars had said to me, searching for meanings I might have missed.

The ground swayed. My tears became so thick I could hardly see, the sob building in my throat so heavy I could hardly breathe.

"The crown," I repeated out loud to no one, trying desperately to keep focused. "The crown in your future sky, the crown, the crown..."

And then, very suddenly, I had the answer.

My future sky.

My sky was no longer the one in the mortal realm. The *divine* sky would be my future if I intended to ascend. It had been a trick question—and I'd nearly fallen for it.

I'd been looking for my crown in the wrong place.

I turned around and around, searching and—as expected—I noticed a section of much brighter sky far in the distance. That was what the goddess had said, wasn't it?

An exact reflection of our own divine sky, but less brilliant.

That brighter section must have been the map of the divine sky.

I ran faster than I ever had in my life.

I couldn't breathe, I could barely see for the tears, my skin itched and burned from the cutting stardust, and I kept stumbling on ground that was already sinking away, trying to swallow me up—but I pushed onward until I reached the reflections of the constellations I'd already found in the previous sky map.

I used these starry patterns to guide me until, finally, there it was: a tilted crown with five points, facing the opposite direction of the first one I'd found—a more brilliant reflection of the one in my old sky.

Running out of time, and not knowing what else to do, I leapt and reached for it as though I could simply snatch it from the sky. My hands touched something solid in the dark—something that I convinced my tired and terrified mind was a part of the crown.

The ground beneath me started to fall away. I shut my eyes tightly, bracing myself.

I didn't fall.

I dangled over the yawning darkness, watching as it sucked in star after star from the divine sky. With the light disappearing all around me, I gripped my invisible crown with one hand and all the strength I had in me.

I gritted my teeth, somehow summoned *more* strength from somewhere deep inside, and I managed to swing my other hand up and find another solid, invisible piece to grab. As my fingers closed over it, some of the stars veered from the vortex forming below me and streaked toward the crown constellation, creating a shining outline that soon turned tangible as the goddess had done earlier.

The sight of it fully formed sent another surge of strength through me. I pulled, and the crown moved, dislodging from whatever strange magic held it in place. A few awkward swings, throwing my weight this way and that, wrenched it completely free.

My stomach heaved violently as I hit solid ground a moment later. The air felt much warmer, and I heard what sounded like a collective gasp.

I opened my eyes and found myself in the circular room atop Dravyn's private tower, clutching a crown of silver to my chest, kneeling in the center of an entire circle of gods and goddesses.

CHAPTER 23

ALONG THE FAR WALL OF THE FAMILIAR MEETING room I'd landed in, a vision of the night sky was being projected by some sort of spell, casting constellations against the stone.

The stage where my trial had taken place, I realized after a moment of staring.

The gods had been watching me the entire time.

They were watching me now, too; I could feel their gazes boring into me, could sense their disdainful, doubting expressions. None of them spoke. None of them moved. I felt their combined power like a fist closing in around me, squeezing away my attempts to take deep breaths.

I'd never felt more intimidated in my life.

Yet I knew I had to stand, to somehow make them think I wasn't afraid. They had seen me crying on that projected stage; I couldn't let that be the only image of me they carried with them.

I clutched the crown in my hands more tightly and zeroed in on only one of the Marr—the Goddess of Stars. As terrifying and radiant as she was, at least I knew I could face her and survive. I'd proven that.

I rose, marched my way over to her, and tossed the silver crown at her slippered feet.

She didn't pick it up.

The god to her right spoke, breaking the heavy silence with a rumbling voice that made me think of waves colliding with rocks. "Was that *really* the best you could do, Cepheid?"

My gaze was drawn to that deep, resonant voice before I could help myself. The Marr it belonged to was even larger than Dravyn, with hair the color of the sea at night and a muscular body clothed in sleek armor in various deep shades of blue and green. Like Cepheid, he walked the fine line between human and beast. His face was triangular in shape, with sharp appendages sticking out from the upper points of it and elegant antlers twisting up between those appendages; without getting closer, I couldn't tell if these were all part of his anatomy, or a part of the hooded cloak he wore.

And I had no desire to get closer.

The sword hanging from his hip had a recognizable pattern carved all along its dark sheath—a long line of curling waves that were glowing softly. So this was the middle-god of the Ocean, then. Kelas was his name, if I recalled correctly.

His large eyes shimmered like sea-green water in sunlight as he fixed them on me.

I held his gaze for as long as I could, still determined not to show the fear currently making a mess of my insides. When I looked away, I did it slowly, calmly, searching again for something I felt like I could face.

My gaze settled on Dravyn. He looked somewhat unsettled —at least unsettled for him—his lips parted and skin flushed as though he'd been holding his breath for the past several minutes.

Something I couldn't name sparked in my chest when our eyes met, same as it had that day we'd locked eyes in Cauldra.

He didn't look away from me as he said, "I will speak with my ascending candidate in private, if you don't mind."

If the other Marr *did* mind, he gave them no chance to tell him. He moved confidently to my side, placing a hand against the small of my back and guiding me through one of the doors along the room's edge. On the other side was a small sitting area at the base of a narrow staircase. It smelled strongly of him —smoky metal and an undercurrent of cedar—and I wondered if his bedroom was located at the top of those stairs.

In private apparently meant with the rest of his court as well, because as he attempted to quietly shut the door behind us, Valas was suddenly on the other side, pushing it back open.

The God of Winter took my hand and gave it a businesslike shake. "You didn't die an unspeakably horrifying death," he said. "Well done, You. I'm so proud."

Mairu didn't say a word as she followed him into the room, but she did shove Valas aside and wrap me in a quick, awkward hug. The relief in her expression was obvious as she pulled away, even though she seemed to be trying to angle her face so I couldn't see it.

They were clearly pleased I'd succeeded—so pleased that they hadn't been able to resist following me and letting me know.

How strange.

Maybe the stardust had been more dangerous than I realized, and I was hallucinating all of this?

A chorus of raised voices began filtering in from the adjacent room. Dravyn's gaze shot back to the door, his jaw clenching briefly with concern, and then to his other court members he said, "I need you to stay out there and keep them under control for a few minutes, please."

Valas yawned, looking bored by the idea, but Mairu nodded and grabbed the Ice God by the sleeve of his colorful shirt, dragging him back through the door.

Once we were alone again, Dravyn turned to me and said, "You need to cleanse yourself."

I took a step back. "What?"

"The stardust on your skin," he explained. "The magic within it...it isn't good to let it linger on you."

I had a sudden urge to extend my claws and rake that dust from my body just at the mention of it. I'd been distracted enough to ignore it these past few minutes, but the second I started thinking about how badly it itched, I couldn't *stop* thinking about how badly it itched.

"You felt the disorientation it caused when it showered over you during the trial, didn't you?" he pressed.

"A little," I admitted.

"If it sinks through and enters your bloodstream it will lead to far worse—and longer-lasting—effects in addition to the superficial damage it's already doing to your skin." He gestured toward the stairs. "You can use the bath connected to my room if you like, so you don't have to walk back through the ones waiting on the other side of this door."

The thought of entering his private room—of using his private *bath*—unsettled me to my core.

I had no desire to walk back into that other room full of sneering deities, though. Not to mention my skin now felt like it was trying to crawl away from my bones, pulling and itching so badly that it was getting hard to think of anything other than finding some way to wash it off.

So I agreed, and I climbed the stairs alone while Dravyn went back to help placate the other Marr.

At the top of the short staircase, I found a heavy wooden door opened wide, as if the room had been waiting for me. I made certain to step inside left foot first; it seemed too important of a place—where too many things could go wrong—to not adhere to my comforting ritual.

It took me a few attempts—in and back out, in and back out—before I was finally satisfied with my left-footed entrance. Even then, I had to fight the urge to do it again. The stress of the last hours made my brain feel like it was looping endless, pointless thoughts, while my nerves were too aware of too many things that I couldn't properly give order to.

Between this and my awful, itchy skin, it took a moment for the reality of my surroundings to register.

I was in the God of Fire's bedroom.

I was staring at his actual bed, a massive four-poster centered between two tall, abstract paintings featuring a gold leafing technique. The bed was unmade, its piles of luxuriously soft looking blankets and sheets tempting my exhausted self to crawl inside.

There were balconies on both sides of the room, the curtains tied back from the glass double doors to reveal the sweeping landscape below. An open cage featuring a large perch and a cozy cushion stood beside one of the balcony entrances—Moth's, I assumed, based on the feathers littering the cushion. There were several more of these feathers on Dravyn's bed; I had a feeling the little troublemaker slept wherever he wanted to.

There were several high windows made of colorful glass, but no figures like the ones in the room attached to the atrium.

Maybe he didn't want to be reminded of those things he'd memorialized while he was trying to sleep?

Dark floors, soft, off-white walls, and lanterns with soft orange flames brought the space together. It was massive in size, yet cozier than I'd expected. The smoky, woodsy scent coupled with the flickering lanterns made me feel calmer, as if I was curled up beside a softly glowing fireplace, a book in one hand and a warm and steaming drink in the other.

It vaguely crossed my shaken and disoriented mind that this was not an opportunity to be wasted—there were so many pieces of him in this room, so many things that might prove useful for my upcoming battles with him.

Before I could work up the courage to start digging through these things, however, a familiar voice said, "We meet again."

I turned to find myself looking down into a pair of rust-colored, careworn eyes.

Rieta.

My already overloaded nerves sparked violently to attention, numbing away my words, but I lifted my hand and bent my fingers as if preparing to unleash claws. There was no point in hiding them from any servant of the Shade Court, it seemed.

She held up her palms. "Relax. It's truly me. Not a serpent in stolen skin, this time."

The reminder of her betrayal stung, but it was exactly the reminder I needed in that moment—that no matter how relieved Mairu might have seemed at my successful trial, I still couldn't trust her. I couldn't trust Rieta either, for that matter; she almost certainly knew Mairu had masqueraded as her, yet she'd said nothing to me.

I didn't ask her to leave only because my skin felt like it was in danger of disintegrating at this point, and I needed her help to work out how to fill the washroom's giant copper tub with water and whatever else might help cleanse me.

While that tub filled with water, pumped up through a pipe—that, fascinatingly, needed no more help from her after she got it started—she busied herself with picking through the various bottles along the shelf, muttering to herself as she searched.

"This should soothe your skin and help it back toward normal," she finally said, uncorking a purple glass bottle and pouring its oily contents into the tub. It turned the water nearly opaque, filling the air with a soft peppermint scent as it did.

I didn't need any more coaxing than this. While Rieta went back to the shelf in search of more remedies, I peeled my clothing carefully from my aching skin and stepped into the steaming tub.

The peppermint water felt oddly thick as it slid across my body, like a gritty mud scraping over me. It was unnerving, unexpected, but not entirely unpleasant. It felt like all of my bone-deep itches were finally being scratched.

I floated in that exfoliating water, oblivious to the rest of the world, until Rieta appeared, looming over me with a washcloth in her hand.

"You'll need to be rough with this to get at the deeper stardust residue," she told me. "I'll be back to check on you in a bit."

"I can manage without you," I said, somewhat coldly, as I snatched the cloth from her and sank back into the water.

She looked ruffled by my response, but she said nothing else before bowing her head and leaving the room.

I did as she'd instructed, rubbing my skin nearly raw in the process. Even after several minutes of methodical cleansing, my back still itched between my shoulder blades; I couldn't reach it well enough to apply proper pressure. Irritated, I closed my eyes and slid down deeper into the tub, trying to use the side of it to help slough off the damaged skin.

I was almost entirely underwater when I heard what sounded like claws skittering along the edge of the tub, and I resurfaced just as something small and brown plopped into the water in front of me.

A scream ripped from my throat before I could stop it— before a single pale golden wing stretched out of the water and gave a pitiful twitch, and I realized it was not a rat or some other nasty creature; it was Moth.

I scooped the griffin up and tossed him onto the shelf beside the tub. He seemed dazed, his face wrinkling in confusion every time he breathed in the peppermint-scented air.

As I opened my mouth to scold him for frightening me, I caught sight of the mirror on the far wall of the room, and I saw Dravyn standing in the doorway behind me. I nearly screamed again, grabbing the washcloth floating nearby and using it to cover as much of my chest as I could.

"*What are you doing in here?*"

"I—"

"Was this a trick?" I demanded. "Were you lingering in your room, just waiting for an excuse to come barging in?"

"Of course not," Dravyn growled. "I wasn't *lingering*, I just happened to be bringing up fresh towels, and I heard you scream."

I clutched the washcloth closer to my chest, still fuming as I considered his words. Why was he bringing towels himself? He could have gotten a servant to do that.

Had he been coming to check on me?

The moment shifted from heated to awkward in the span

of a heartbeat. I briefly considered sinking below the water again and never resurfacing.

"You...you've missed a spot," he muttered. "In the center of your back. Can you not reach it?"

I started to lie and say I was fine, but a fresh, terrible itch prickled down my spine at that exact moment, and I had to grit my teeth together to keep from crying out at the irritation. My discomfort was far too obvious.

"...May I?" he asked.

I clenched the washcloth more tightly to my bare chest and didn't reply.

"The skin already looks damaged beyond repair." I heard him take a step closer, and concern and irritation mingled in his tone as he added, "That fucking goddess and her fucking stardust..."

I gritted my teeth so tightly I thought I might crack them.

"It needs to be dealt with," he said. "I can send for Rieta if you insist, but we need to be quick."

Another painful itch rippled out from the spot in question, and I gave in and shook my head; I just wanted this all to be over with. "Don't send for her. I don't need any more company in here, just...just do whatever you need to do and then get out, please."

He went first to the shelf Rieta had been sorting through earlier. While he was preoccupied, I risked leaning out of the tub and grabbing a larger towel, so at least my entire front could be covered. Using that, as well as scooting closer to the back of the tub and sinking as deeply as I could into the cloudy, concealing water, he couldn't see much of me aside from the spot he intended to help with.

Even so, as he positioned himself behind me, I was very

aware of every inch of my bare skin and every move he made around it.

I sucked in a sharp breath as his hand brushed the side of my neck, lifting my hair and pushing it aside before his touch trailed back between my shoulder blades. His hands were usually warm, but compared to the steaming water, they felt cool. There was some sort of salve on his fingertips; it made my skin tingle as he swiped it on me.

"Bend over," he said.

"Excuse me?"

"So I can better see the spot I'm trying to tend to. The lighting in here is not ideal."

I squirmed where I sat, trying and failing to shake off the unwanted shivers his words had sent racing through me.

He tsked and muttered, "Where is your mind, Little Sparrow?"

Certainly not where I want it to be, I almost admitted.

He slid his hand toward the back of my neck, applying pressure and gently guiding me downward. His other hand brought more of the salve to my skin, covering a much wider swath than what I'd managed to scrub. Pain swiftly followed, like a scar had just been ripped off, fully exposing the wound to the elements. I cringed, and he pressed a strong, bracing grip against my shoulder.

"Be still, *miran-achth*."

The last word he'd said sounded foreign to my ears; I thought I'd imagined it at first, but then he continued in the same language, muttering under his breath as he worked.

"That language you're using...I've heard it before." It took me a moment of thought to come up with a name. "Galithi-an?" I guessed.

"Yes." He sounded a bit startled, as if he hadn't realized he'd been speaking out loud.

"It's only really spoken in the kingdom of its origin, Galizur, isn't it?"

He nodded. "It's an old habit that seems to come out when I'm...stressed."

I swirled my hand through the water, thinking.

He continued quickly, presumably before I could question him about why he was so stressed. "Everyone speaks the same language once they enter this realm—or any of the other divine ones—thanks to a spell created by the upper-god I ultimately serve."

The God of the Shade remained mostly a mystery to me even after these past weeks, but I knew he was the one who gave knowledge to all created beings; I suppose it made sense that he could make anything speak any language he wanted it to.

"But that doesn't mean we completely forget where we came from," Dravyn added. "Some things do fade over time, but lots of other things stick. What stays and goes is different for every Marr, I believe."

I considered this, more and more questions spinning through my mind. "Who were you before you became a god?"

He hesitated. I could clearly see his reflection in the mirror, dark as it was in the room; the expression on his face looked similar to the one from last night, when we were surrounded by his glass creations and I'd asked who they were memorializing.

"It will take my mind off the itching," I urged. "Because I still feel tempted to claw my skin off at the moment."

He sighed, but finally gave in. "I was... a prince. Of that kingdom you mentioned—Galizur."

"From a prince to a god," I mused.

"A lateral move at worst," he said with a slight smile.

"Were you an only child?"

"I was the second oldest of four. The spare heir, as they say."

I tried to recall anything else I'd heard about him and his siblings. I knew I'd heard of his kingdom, but most of the details about it eluded me now—unusual for my normally organized and hyper-retentive brain, and more proof of how badly the stardust had rattled me.

"And why did you make the move from prince to god?" I asked.

"Your curiosity never ceases, does it?"

"No," I answered honestly. "Though in my defense, I've lived a very curious life."

"Most people would be unconscious from all of the *curious* things you've been through tonight."

"Not everyone processes pain the same way," I pointed out.

His hand hesitated against my back at these words. I focused all of my energy on trying to breathe normally despite the heat radiating from his fingertips and shooting straight toward what felt like all the most sensitive parts of me.

He silently scooped several handfuls of warm water up and dripped them down my back, washing away the salve he'd spread across it, before he quietly asked, "Are you still in pain?"

I realized I wasn't. The itching was growing fainter by the moment, too. I shook my head slowly, still not quite believing how quickly it had disappeared.

"Good."

I glanced over my shoulder, watching him as he stood and turned his back to me.

"Our crowd of visitors downstairs doesn't seem ready to

move on, unfortunately," he said. "Some of them likely won't want to leave the palace until they've spoken with you. So prepare yourself. I'll have Rieta bring up some proper clothing for you."

I nodded, fighting the urge to sink beneath the water.

"You did well to solve the goddess's trial, by the way. They all thought you were going to fail." He started to leave.

"Did *you* think I was going to fail?" The question escaped before I could stop it. I didn't want to care about his answer. Or any of his thoughts.

But I couldn't deny that I did.

He paused in the doorway but took a long time answering —so long I assumed the answer was *yes*. Of course he'd expected me to fail. He'd probably *hoped* I would fail.

Rapping his knuckles against the door frame, he said, "I told you before that I knew a wildfire when I saw one, didn't I?"

I nodded.

"Wildfires are sometimes hard to predict," he concluded, shrugging, before disappearing into his room.

CHAPTER 24

THE CLOTHING RIETA BROUGHT WAS PERHAPS THE most beautiful outfit I'd donned since my arrival in this realm —or in any realm, for that matter. A peace offering, maybe. It was a delicate, ivory suit with trailing sleeves of gossamer fabric that made me think of the wings the Star Goddess had sprouted as we fell through the sky during her trial. They billowed gently, elegantly behind me as I walked, so although I didn't *feel* ethereal or worthy of walking among gods, at least I looked the part.

Several heads turned when I entered the room, though my steps made no sound in the soft golden slippers I'd been given to wear. Only two of the Marr from the other courts nodded in greeting—the God of the Ocean, and a goddess I didn't recognize with silver hair and white, shimmering freckles upon her dark brown skin.

I made a point to make eye contact even with the Marr who regarded me with nothing but disdainful looks, doing my best to move through the space as if I belonged in it. This was one of the first things Andrel and Cillian had taught me when they started to bring me along for rebel missions and demonstrations: act natural regardless of how I truly felt.

Not an easy feat in a room full of some of the most powerful beings in the known world.

I was still determined to try. I kept my head up and spoke when I was spoken to. I made sure to stare at them as if I wasn't afraid, and I comforted myself by thinking of later, when I could be alone in my room, sketching these divine beings and all their strange, fascinating features.

Very few of them actually spoke to me, but I could tell they were all observing me as much as I was observing them. Even those who couldn't be bothered to look my way clearly noticed every sound I made, every step I took; their bodies gave them away whenever their eyes didn't, subtly angling toward me or even mirroring my movements.

After what felt like nearly an hour of this mingling, I felt cracks in my fearless facade starting to form. I needed familiar company, I thought—Valas, or Mairu, maybe—and I had just started to search for one of them when a strange, heavy chill overtook me, wrapping like a damp towel around my body.

"Hello, Mortal." The cold, familiar voice of the Death Marr slid over me, stopping me in my tracks.

Perhaps I should have walked away. I'd been told to stay away from him, after all...but what was I supposed to do if he came to *me*? I couldn't exactly run away.

Surely I was safe within this tower, anyway. In fact, there likely would never be an opportunity to more safely converse with him than this—and there were still so many questions I needed to ask him.

I turned and faced him. He looked a bit less intimidating

here in the brighter, golden halls of the Fire God's palace. The shadows surrounding him were subdued; his complexion warmer, less corpse-like. His eyes looked more human in the firelight illuminating the room, too, the wide orbs more deep blue than black.

"Hello, Zachar," I said.

He seemed pleased to hear his name, as though he'd expected me to forget him. "You've shown impressive strength to survive tonight," he said. "Something in your blood seems to give you...*resilience*."

The way he said *your blood* made all the hairs on the back of my neck stand on end.

I lowered my voice, eyes darting about for eavesdroppers, and said, "You know what I am, don't you?"

Either Dravyn had told him, or he'd discerned it for himself when his shadows tried to force their way into my mind...what else had he seen when his magic pried its way into my thoughts the other day?

He smiled his jagged smile. "I know much more than that." He breathed out a puff of shadowy fog with the words, like he was exhaling a deep draw of pipe smoke. "Walk with me a moment?"

I hesitated until his magic made the decision for me, cold shadows weaving through my legs, caressing my back, urging me to move. It was much more subtle than the ropes of power he'd ensnared me with in Harithyn—I doubted he would risk anything more knowing Dravyn was close by—but it was enough to persuade me to follow him, especially when coupled with my own curiosity.

We moved toward the edge of the space, just out of reach of the light from the flaming chandeliers spaced throughout the room. I made it clear I wasn't going beyond that; I would speak with him in the shadows, and I would not show fear, but I was not leaving this room with him.

"The dead veilhound at your home..." he began.

I had an instant, visceral reaction as the memories of my sister's final weeks flooded my mind, and I had to lean against the wall to steady myself. This was not the conversation starter I'd been bracing for.

The Death Marr smiled and licked his pale lips, as if he could taste my discomfort and despair in the air and was savoring it. "I saw it in your mind the other day."

I forced myself to breathe deeply. Normally.

"I wanted to ask...are you the one who killed it?"

My throat was too thick with emotion to speak, but I adamantly shook my head.

"I would have been very impressed if you had." He cocked his head to the side, studying me. "The hounds are incredibly powerful. It would have been almost akin to killing a god, and would have required a very specific type of weapon to do the job...you know nothing of that either, I presume?"

I swallowed hard. "I don't know what you're talking about."

He licked his lips again. "No, of course you don't."

I tilted my face away, searching for something to focus on aside from his unsettling expression. All the other Marr seemed to be trying harder than ever not to make eye contact with me. No matter how hard I stared at them, it was as though I'd faded away in the shadowy folds of the Death God's energy.

"It's the company you presently keep," explained the Death Marr. "They don't want to look this way because they do not want me here anymore than they want *you* here."

"Why? You're a middle-god, aren't you?"

He breathed slowly in and out, exhaling more of that shadowy substance. "Harbinger, they have begun to call me. They see evidence of the destruction clinging to me, and they want me to keep it to myself. To carry on as though nothing is happening on the edges of our realm."

"What *is* happening on those edges?"

Another sharp smile. "I think you already know."

My forehead wrinkled in confusion. "No, I promise you I don't."

He inhaled slowly, strangely, almost drinking the air. I again got the impression that he was tasting the emotions in it, trying to determine whether or not I was telling the truth.

After a moment his eyes brightened with what looked like realization. I thought he was finally about to reveal something useful when his gaze jumped to something behind me and he took a step back.

"Come see me again soon," he said, "and maybe we can chat more in less...*constricting* surroundings."

"Wait a minute—" I reached for his arm; it was like grabbing a cold, weathered tree trunk. His smile became more of a snarl. His eyes flashed and turned to that terrifying shade of pure black, and I instinctively let go. He was gone in the next instant, disappearing with a sound like wind rattling through tree limbs, leaving nothing but a few lingering wisps of dark power behind.

I swatted absently at the dissipating shadows, pondering.

I think you already know.

What had he meant by that?

Had I missed some obvious answer to all my questions?

Annoyed at the very possibility, I turned back to the rest of the room, reminding myself of the role I still had to finish playing tonight. I immediately saw the reason for the Death Marr's sudden exit—Dravyn was staring at me from the opposite wall, seemingly ignoring the God of the Ocean who stood next to him, chatting with increasingly animated gestures.

The God of Fire did not look pleased.

His gaze followed the last wisps of Zachar's power as they disappeared. Then he was striding toward me, looking me over as if inspecting for damage or any lingering shadows.

"I told you to stay away from him, did I not?" His tone was calm enough as he reached me, but I could sense the frustration building underneath. The air heated a little more with each breath he took.

I stared defiantly back, too tired, confused, and ill to bother being careful with my reply. "He spoke to me first. Would you have preferred I offend one of your court?"

"You had no problem telling *me* to fuck off on the day we met, as I recall."

"I didn't realize you were a god at the time."

"Would it have mattered if you did?"

I bared my teeth in a smile. "No. As a matter of fact, it wouldn't have."

He leaned closer, his voice dropping low, meant only for me. "What must I do to convince you that you have no business with that monstrous god? He shouldn't even have come here tonight. He's only trying to stir up trouble."

"Why shouldn't he be here? Is he not a member of your court?"

"He is. But what he is beyond that...it's complicated."

"You asked what you must do to convince me. It's easy enough: You could tell me what is happening with him."

His jaw clenched.

"He's a part of your court," I said, as calmly as I could. "I don't see why—"

"Enough."

The word fell like an axe between us, heavy with a hint of violence, and for a moment, I forgot that I was supposed to be playing the role of a hopeful servant. I clenched my fists, resisting the urge I felt to unleash my claws and rake them across his face.

"In case you haven't noticed," he said quietly, "your every move is being watched, now. So I suggest you unclench your fists, lest you give some the idea that you don't care to join me and my court at all."

He was right; I could feel those watchers, and I realized then how quiet the room had become. I slowly opened my fists.

"Your focus should be on getting through the rest of this night and then surviving the next trial. Nothing else."

"Fine," I seethed. "But when I survive it, you owe me more explanations."

"*If* you survive it."

"*When* I survive it."

"We'll see." His tone remained sharply bitter, but the animosity in his gaze had shifted to...something else.

Concern?

I didn't know what to do with that concern, so I quickly excused myself and resumed my earlier search for a familiar face.

The God of Ice was easy to find; I only had to follow the sounds of his howling laughter.

He wasn't alone when I spotted him, so I wouldn't be able to try and make him elaborate on the things the Death Marr had said, which was disappointing. I drifted toward him anyway, the chaos in my soul drawn to the chaotic energy that seemed to constantly surround him.

Mairu was there as well, and six other beings were gathered around her and Valas—Miratar spirits, I thought. These spirits didn't radiate the same power as the Marr they served, but the energy they gave was much more intense than anything I felt around mortal beings, or even the magical creatures the Marr created.

If I *were* to ascend, I supposed I would be something similar to these beings. Some felt stronger than others, I thought, and I wondered if I...

No. It doesn't matter.

I would not get that far. This ruse would be over before that point. I didn't know how it would all end, but Dravyn had made one good point a few minutes ago: I needed to focus on surviving tonight, and then the next trial. The Tower of Ascension and its secrets would be next, and after that...

We'd see.

As I approached the group of gods and spirits, the Ice God put his arm around me and drew me closer. "I knew she could do it, of course," he told the small crowd before us. "She made the trial look easy, didn't she?"

Before the compliment had time to warm its way through me, Mairu cleared her throat and said, "Didn't I hear you betting several casks of wine that there was no way she would ever emerge in one piece?"

Valas's grin never faltered as he tilted his head closer to mine and whispered, "She's a dirty liar and a snake, don't listen to her."

Mairu rolled her eyes but smiled as her gaze fell on me, her expression brightening with the same relief she'd regarded me with earlier. I didn't know what to do with that relief anymore than I knew what to do with Dravyn's concern, so I just averted my eyes and tried to fade into the background, my head swimming with thoughts of the trials still waiting for me.

THE REST of the night passed in a blur.

I just wanted to go back to the privacy of my room and collapse into bed, but the visiting Marr simply would not leave. It felt like an extension of the Star Goddess's trial. Like they were trying to see how long they could keep me awake before I started begging for mercy.

I was close to dozing off while standing up when Valas gave me a pat on the head and wished me a good night, and I looked around and realized that nearly all the others had slipped away as well, though the simmering energy of the Marr's magic still lingered.

Of those Marr, only Dravyn remained. He was busy extinguishing candles, talking with a servant who was assisting him. When I started uncertainly toward the door, he looked over and caught my gaze, and I slowed to a stop before I realized what I was doing.

He didn't speak, but I could understand the meaning in his expression easily enough; I believe we were thinking the same thing: His palace was his own again, free of all the other Marr and their servants. *Finally*. The ordeal was finished. The meetings were over, the trial was done.

I could finally go back to bed. So the question was, why was I still standing in the middle of the room, feeling unfinished?

An answer struck me immediately, even though I didn't want to think it: I didn't like the way our conversation had ended earlier. The regret I felt over fighting with him weighed me down, even now, holding me in place as he dismissed his servant and then sauntered closer.

How stupid.

So what if we'd fought? I wasn't here to get along with him. Only to prove myself so I could get what I wanted. The more we hated each other, the easier it would be to betray him at the end of all of this.

I avoided his gaze and looked toward the window behind him, expecting to see a sky beginning to lighten as morning approached. It felt like I'd been up all night—but I suppose that meant nothing when this god before me controlled the sun itself. It was still pitch black outside, and who knew how long the night would last.

"You're angry with me," he said as I continued to stare at anything but him. It wasn't a question, but a statement.

Just anticipating your next lecture, I started to snap. I caught myself, however; there was no point in arguing or complicating things between us even further.

"Nothing to say?" he prodded. "This is a first."

I finally met his eyes but kept my lips pressed tightly together. I had *plenty* to say, but nothing good would come from any of it.

He folded his arms across his broad chest and tilted his head as he considered me, his silver eyes shining and an arrogant little smile flirting with his lips. "Or maybe you've just forgotten your lines, Little Sparrow?"

"My lines?"

"This is the part where you tell me to go fuck myself, isn't it?"

I glared at him.

He was going to insist on arguing and complicating things between us even further, wasn't he?

"Go on, then." He arched a brow. "Don't get shy on me now."

"I'm not shy."

"Your cheeks are flushed in a way that suggests otherwise."

"Nothing about you is responsible for any color in my cheeks, I assure you," I hissed. "And there's nothing you could do or say that would cause such a thing."

"Really?" His brows lifted higher, as though I'd just issued a challenge. "Nothing at all?"

"I am not some hapless, giggling virgin who's going to throw myself at your feet every time you flash a crooked smile my way."

"That's a shame," he said, "because I love it when hapless, giggling virgins throw themselves at my feet."

"I bet you do."

He took a step closer. Close enough that he could have reached out and touched me. For a moment I thought he might. His fingers brushed idly together, drawing sparks of embers into the air as they did.

I glared at those flashing embers for a moment before lifting my eyes back to him, "But if it helps you relieve some of the obvious burning tension you're experiencing, then by all means, you can go fuck yourself."

"I'm not usually a fan of the solo routine, as it were." He smiled brighter, clearly enjoying himself now. "You don't happen to know where I could find some giggling virgins, do you?"

"I can't help you there." I kept my voice perfectly even, determined not to seem flustered, as I added, "But I'm in a generous mood, so please feel free to think of me while you take care of yourself. Just know that it's as close as you'll ever get to the real thing. So I hope you enjoy it."

He stroked the hard line of his jaw as if considering my offer.

And I swear the bastard stopped just short of winking at me as he turned away, chuckling, and said, "I was already planning on thinking of you."

It felt as if my cheeks were close to igniting as I watched him leave.

CHAPTER 25

It was late the following morning—almost afternoon, based on the forgelight's glow—before I finally stumbled from my bed and made my way down to the main floor.

I had gotten used to having breakfast in a bright little room next to the kitchen, where I could stare through a row of windows into the small garden on the other side. Mairu and Valas occasionally joined me there; only the latter was present when I arrived on this particular morning, reclining on a chaise with a steaming mug of what smelled like herbal tea clasped in his hands.

I didn't usually mind the company, but, given how restless and irritable I felt, I would have been better off alone this time.

The memory of the stardust ravaging my skin still made me itch, even though I'd bathed again before falling into bed last night. It was all in my head, I knew, but I couldn't seem to shake the irritation—or the visions of myself lost in an endlessly dark sky with more shimmering dust pouring down and threatening to bury me.

I'd hardly slept, either, having spent entirely too much time tossing and turning while replaying the argument with Dravyn in my head. Every time I'd closed my eyes, I had thought of something else I could have said to him. Something better.

"You're even angrier than usual this morning," Valas commented in between loud slurps of his tea.

Was it that obvious?

I shrugged, helping myself to a basket of some sort of flaky bread on the table between us.

While I picked the bread apart, he spooned something that looked like honey into his cup—an alarmingly large amount of honey—and stirred it without taking his eyes off me.

"Did you even sleep last night?"

"Not as much as I should have," I muttered.

He stirred more slowly. Each circle of the spoon felt deliberate, loaded with unspoken commentary. "I noticed you and Dravyn were all alone when I left you."

"And?"

He took the spoon out and *ting, ting, tinged* it against the rim. "The two of you seem to be growing close."

"Not that close."

"Closer than I've ever seen him get to...well, anyone."

"I'm here to serve in this court, at his jurisdiction," I reminded him.

"True, true." He settled back against the cushions piled in the chaise, holding the mug with both hands, summoning a bit of ice to his palms to cool down the steaming contents. "I guess I'm just curious about other ways you might be *serving* him."

"It's a good thing I haven't eaten yet," I said, "because what you're suggesting is making me feel like I might vomit."

He grinned. I flipped him a rude gesture before getting to my feet and opening the window, trying to coax in more sound to drown out the memory of Dravyn's voice now playing through my head.

I was already planning on thinking of you.

My cheeks burned all over again as I pictured his mouth saying those words. I'd set him up for that comeback, and he had only been teasing, surely. He simply delighted in getting under my skin, nothing more.

I hated myself for *letting* him get under my skin. For not being quick enough to shut him up with a comeback of my own.

But worse—far, far worse—was how I didn't hate the idea of him thinking of me in that way.

What was *wrong* with me?

I had come here to prove myself, to assimilate into this realm so I could destroy its rulers from the inside out. I was successfully blending in...but at what cost?

"Probably for the best that the idea makes you sick," Valas commented. "The power dynamic would be too strange once you ascended. So I'd caution you to not get too close, now."

"I'm not worried about it," I said, slamming the window shut and excusing myself from the room.

"Just looking out for you," he called after me.

My gesture was friendlier this time—a dismissive little wave —but I wasn't going to humor his commentary any longer.

I wasn't worried about the idea of ending up in a subservient role to any god. Because it wasn't going to happen. I had drifted a bit from my course, maybe, but I had not forgotten where I intended to go.

And they had no idea how much power I intended to take from them before I was done.

I SPENT the rest of the day refocusing on my goals.

I took paper and drawing utensils and walked almost the entirety of the palace's extensive grounds, seeking out any and every nook and cranny I'd previously failed to document and making notes on them.

When I'd finished with that, I found a quiet, secluded grove of trees to sit in, and I started on the book of the gods I'd been thinking about making since last night. I recounted and recorded each detail of their appearances, along with every word I'd heard them utter, sifting through it all in search of useful things. So much of last night felt like a fever dream...

Had I really spent it walking and talking among all those divine beings?

My conversation with the Death Marr stood out most of all; he'd mentioned that killing a veilhound was close to killing a god—that it would have taken a very particular kind of weapon to do it.

Did such a weapon already exist?

Why would he mention the possibility if not?

As I sat there, scribbling and pondering, the wind changed.

The new breeze carried the scent of a flower I couldn't name, something musky and sweet that reminded me of the woods back home. I braced a hand against the dirt as I felt a lonely pit opening in my stomach, unbalancing me.

I tried to keep working on my notes, but once my thoughts of home started, I couldn't seem to make them stop.

I'd guarded against this longing so well over the past weeks, but I suppose I was too tired after the events of last night to keep my usual walls up. I soon gave up trying, putting my notes aside and drawing my knees toward me, huddling against the impending collapse of those walls.

It crashed over me all at once—how much I *hated* this place and all its trials and secrets. How I hated its smells, its magic, its confusing gods and shifting landscapes.

How I wanted to go home, to stay there until I felt like myself again.

I wanted Andrel to help calm my nerves and remind me of why we were fighting.

I would have given anything to share a drink with Cillian, to listen to one of his hour-long, excited rants about whatever latest weaponry or battle strategy he'd devised; he would have plenty to say about the sort of thing that might manage to kill a veilhound, I was sure.

My eyes watered. Trembling, I cursed myself and swiped the tears away—they would do me no good. All I could do was keep my head up and play my part like they'd asked me to. I couldn't let them down.

I *wouldn't* let them down.

"Crying is useless," I muttered, pretending I wasn't alone, that there was actually someone on my side, listening to what I had to say. "We have to get up," I told them. "We have to keep going."

We had to keep going.

So this was what I did—I stood and wiped the dust from my pants, gathered up my drawings and notes, and I went back to work.

Evening eventually rolled around, and, though I'd only been up for a few hours, I was more than ready to collapse back into bed. To put this angry, restless day behind me and start fresh tomorrow.

The only thing keeping me from heading straight to sleep was the fear that I might wake up, as I had before, in the middle of a trial that I was in no way prepared for.

As it turned out, a different sort of trial stood between me and my bed—one that was announced by the arrival of Mairu, who held a shimmering pile of green fabric in her arms.

"What is that?" I demanded.

"It's called a dress, Little Spitfire."

"Yes, but why do you have it?"

"Because we have to celebrate your first victory, of course." She hooked her arm in mine and steered me onward toward my room before I could protest. "We're going to have a proper dinner for once, and without the Marr of the other courts intruding like they did last night. Dravyn insisted on it."

I suspected I would enjoy whatever deadly trial those other Marr had planned for me better than sharing a dinner table with the God of Fire, but I didn't say so; I knew how to pick my battles. Mairu had locked an almost painful grip on my arm by the time we made it to my room, and I doubted she would be easy to shake off.

The thin-strapped dress was simple but elegant, and its deep emerald shade complimented my eyes and the light brown tone of my skin. It cut daringly low and slit dangerously high, and I would never have had the confidence to wear it back home. I wasn't sure I had such confidence now, either, even after successfully outwitting an actual goddess the night before.

I felt strange as I pulled it on, just as I'd been feeling all day...like I was succeeding at what I had come here to do, yet betraying myself and my allies at the same time.

I had set roles to play—a rebel; a destroyer; a last, desperate hope of my kind...

This dress didn't seem to fit any of those roles.

"It's too much," I told Mairu. "I'll endure whatever dinner you have planned, but I think I should change into something simpler."

I twisted toward the closet, but she held me in place by the locks of my hair she had started braiding. "There is nothing wrong with being *too much* every now and then," she said, matter-of-factly.

"I'm not used to it, though."

"You will have to grow used to it if you intend to take your place among the divine courts."

I bit my lip, holding back all the objections rushing to the front of my mind.

She guided me into a chair next to the bureau, and she worked in silence for several minutes, trying multiple hairstyles —only to undo them and start over—before she spoke again, through several pins she was holding on one side of her mouth: "You want to thrive in this place, don't you?"

"Of course."

"Then fading into the background won't serve you, I'm afraid." Her amber eyes seemed to sparkle as she regarded our reflections in the small mirror balanced upon the dresser. "If you want to prove you belong," she said, twisting and securing a thin braid against the side of my head, "then you must burn so brightly the gods cannot ignore you."

My heart pounded a little too hard—a little too loudly—at the thought.

"The other Marr will be looking for any chance to put out your fire. You can't give them that chance."

"So burn bright..." I mused, as much to myself as her, "...but not so brightly that they realize what I truly am."

She shrugged. "That will come out soon enough. As strong as my magic is, I can't disguise your appearance from them forever. But once you've passed their trials, it won't matter; the blessing they've extended to you cannot be undone, even once your true bloodline is revealed."

"So there's nothing—no law of magic or anything—that will prevent one of my kind from entering the Tower of Ascension?"

She shook her head. "The God of the Shade will determine the final trial in that tower. And he already knows the truth about your blood."

I picked anxiously at my nails, trying to picture what the meeting with that upper-god might be like. Should I take my ruse so far? At what point would I feel like I'd done enough?

How—and *when*—did this all end?

"There's a prejudice here against your kind, it's true," Mairu said, as she further secured the pinned braid behind my pointed ear. The majority of my hair remained down, curling in waves more defined than anything I'd ever managed; I would have sworn it was her magic shaping it.

"Most of the Marr are only repeating what they've seen and heard," she continued. "Those other two courts...the upper-gods who rule over them are disgusted with the elven-kind and their failures, and thus, their servants are, too."

I thought of Dravyn's comment from the other day—how most of the Marr would have destroyed a flawed creature like Moth in favor of trying to create something better.

To most of the divine beings, I was a flawed creature far worse than a griffin prone to spontaneous combustion.

"But you and your court don't harbor that same prejudice?" I asked.

She was thoughtful for a moment, pulling one of my hands into hers to stop me from picking at my nails. "Do you know," she said, "that when it came time to deal with the Velkyn, the only one of the upper-gods who resisted was the one I serve? He is the reason the elven-kind weren't simply wiped out of existence entirely. He thought it was possible for the elves and newly-created humans, and all other creations, to continue shaping the realm together, for better or worse."

The thought caused a strange tingling to spread through my skull. "Together?"

"His thinking tends to be less black and white than the other two, in my experience. He is the Moraki who gifted the world with knowledge, after all—all different shades of it."

She made the possibility of co-existing sound so simple, so obvious. Her effortlessly confident tone made me almost embarrassed to admit that I'd never really considered such a world. I'd been so busy struggling to survive—and hating the ones who threatened that survival—that it had left little time for anything else.

A month ago, I would have ignored the possibility and kept on hating.

Now, after all I'd seen and learned this past month, I felt compelled to at least sit with the idea for a few minutes, even though its newness made me feel uncomfortable. Uncertain.

I decided I didn't want to talk about it anymore just then, so I shifted the focus solely to her instead. "How long have you been a goddess?"

"I am the second oldest ascendant of the Shade Court," she

informed me. Fluffing her hair—which today fell in thick, dark ringlets well past her shoulders—she added, "Though I know I don't look it."

"Were you royalty as a human, like Dravyn was?"

She laughed. "Not exactly."

"But you live like royalty now, I suppose?"

"Of course."

"In a palace similar to this one?"

"But far more tastefully decorated. I'll take you for a visit if you like."

"Instead of going to this dinner, you mean?"

She gave me a wry smile. "Nice try, but no. Dravyn insisted on the dinner tonight. Tomorrow, perhaps."

Dravyn insisted on it.

Why was he so insistent on celebrating my victory? On getting *close* to me, if Valas was to be believed?

I shoved my questions about the God of Fire down as deeply as I could; I'd confront him about these things later.

"If you're the second oldest, then that means Valas is the oldest of your court," I thought aloud.

"Only a little older than me, but yes," said Mairu. "Hard to believe based on the way he acts, isn't it? I think he stopped maturing the instant he became a god." Despite the insult, the fondness in her tone was apparent—a fondness I'd never heard her use when he was within earshot.

"You two seem close," I commented.

She snorted at this, but her eyes had turned glassy, distant with thought. "I owe him...a lot. My very existence, I suppose. Though he'll insist he did nothing for me if you ask."

I didn't want to pry, to get anymore involved in their world than I already was, but I couldn't help my curiosity. "What happened?"

She sighed. Hesitated. Then she said, "I suppose I owe you some truth after deceiving you with my appearance the other day, don't I?"

"That only seems fair."

"It's not a particularly happy story. Might ruin our celebratory mood."

"I'm sure I've heard worse. And I'm not truly in a celebratory mood, in case you haven't noticed."

A side of her mouth quirked at this last part, but then quickly fell as she stood and walked to the full-length mirror in the corner of the room, studying her reflection as she spoke.

"My family was certainly not royalty," she began after a pause. "We barely scraped by for most of my life, and then my father became very ill shortly after my nineteenth birthday. Him and dozens of others in the village where we lived—so many that my mother ended up turning our home into an extension of the town's overwhelmed medical clinic.

"I helped her at this clinic, and together we found a treatment that was effective for the illness plaguing most of them. But winter was harsh that year, and the supplies were few, so I left one evening with the intention of braving the forest to find more in the towns beyond. I got lost trying to evade a pack of hungry wolves."

She had to stop and take several deep breaths before continuing. "I should have died that night. The last thing I remember was falling asleep in the snow, leaning against the base of a tree I'd been too tired to climb, listening to the sound of howling wolves drawing closer and closer."

A coldness settled deep in my chest, making it hard to take a breath, as though I was buried in that snow alongside her.

"I woke up and the snow around me was gone. As was the cold, the wolves...all of it. There were flowers everywhere instead—the very flowers we'd been using as part of our treatment. I'd dreamt of a man planting those shining white blossoms during the long night, and I thought I'd made him up... but once I found the strength to stand and walk out of the woods, I saw him again. Not a dream, but a true, solid god, accompanied by the higher being he served."

"The God of the Shade was actually there as well?"

She nodded. "He had apparently been searching for a fourth Marr to round out his court of servants, and for whatever reason, the middle-god of Winter and Rebirth led him to me."

"So there was no Serpent Goddess before you?"

"Correct; I am the first of my order."

"Did you have to go through trials like I am?"

"Something like that, except I had to prove my worth to the three Creators, not to any of the other Marr. And once I'd done that, I ascended, and I became the goddess over the very thing I felt like I'd never had in my mortal life."

"Control."

"Yes. And change." I watched as she pointed her hand at the mirror. A single twist of her wrist, and her reflection changed into an entirely different being—a young child with a gap-toothed smile and a head full of long, swinging braids—though her actual body remained the same for the moment; only the one in the mirror changed.

"People often overlook my power in favor of the brighter, bolder abilities of the rest of my court," she said. "But the ability to change things is a magic more potent than any other, I believe."

I sat in silence, thinking of her court and its magic and wondering at the history between them. The easy, almost familial way the three of them interacted was...unexpected.

She'd disguised herself and spied on me on Dravyn's behalf, and though I still had not forgiven her for that, it occurred to me now that I would have done the same thing for Andrel or Cillian if I'd been in a similar situation with her abilities.

"I've never really considered the reasons behind why humans become gods, I guess," I commented.

This was a lie; I *had* considered them—I'd just come to the conclusion that all of them had to have been selfish, destructive, power-hungry reasons.

"We all have our stories." She slowly waved her hand at her reflection, and it once more became her own. Glancing over her shoulder at me, she asked, "I don't suppose Dravyn has told you his?"

I shook my head, my eyes drifting toward the shelf beside my bed. The glass sparrow Dravyn had given me—my good luck charm—perched upon it, right next to the crown I'd pulled from the Star Goddess's sky.

"Give him time," Mairu said.

Time.

She spoke as though she fully expected me to have an endless amount of time with him. As though I was truly meant to be part of this divine realm—part of *them*—forever.

And again I wondered...*why?*

Why were they willing to get so close to me, when it was common knowledge that they hated my kind?

It felt like a trick.

Paranoia settled over me like an itchy and tight second skin. I didn't say anything to her declaration. Even when she came back to my side to finish preparing me for the evening, I just sat there, inwardly at war with myself as I stared into the bureau's mirror.

By the time she was finished, I hardly recognized the person staring back.

If I'd had a moment to dwell on things—to truly study my too-bright eyes, the odd shimmer of my skin, and to try and determine what parts were her magic and what parts were still me...well, maybe it would have scared me.

But a summons arrived before terror could truly grip me, and we were on our way down to the dining hall a minute later.

CHAPTER 26

A curious thing had happened during the past month I'd spent in this divine realm: I'd forgotten how much I loved food, and how I'd once loved to cook and challenge myself with inventing recipes.

There was no need to be creative with the food here; it was always abundant, always delicious—though it was an oddly controlled and consistent kind of deliciousness that never surprised or truly delighted.

I'd concluded that the gods only ate out of habit and a very occasional need for nourishment. The quality never faltered, of course, but they cared little for the *love* of eating.

The banquet waiting for us downstairs, however, seemed created for the sole purpose of tantalizing every possible sense.

I'd never seen such a variety of dishes gathered in one place. It truly did seem to be in honor of me and my success, too—for these were mostly recognizable foods from the mortal realm.

The war inside me raged on. I didn't want to be celebrated by them. I wanted to fit in to serve my purposes, but I didn't want to *belong* here. I didn't even want to enjoy any of this food...though damn it if I wasn't already salivating at the sight of it.

I reluctantly sampled a few of the plates that were placed before me. A hearty and perfectly spiced soup, roasted root vegetables, some sort of pheasant drizzled in a creamy sauce. I did my best to drown out my warring thoughts by trying to pick apart the ingredients in everything I tasted, mentally creating recipes I could add to my books back home.

When this mental listing of ingredients didn't calm me down, I reached for the wine—for glass after glass of it, despite Mairu warning me that my body had not acclimated to the point of being able to handle so much of the divine liquid.

I think I surprised her by how much I *did* manage to handle, and delighted Valas with the same dubious ability.

We ended up drinking our way through several bottles— though they both drank considerably more than me.

The hours passed by in a blur.

Eventually, things settled down at much the same pace as the night before, and I again found myself nearly alone with the God of Fire—though Valas and his servant spirits were still nearby, this time; I could hear them laughing and drinking in the next room over. Mairu had excused herself, but one of the Miratar who served her—the Mimic spirit—still lingered in the Ice God's company.

Dravyn was paying no attention to any of these other divine beings—or to me. All of his focus was on a golden chalice resting in his lap; he appeared to be trying to repair its broken handle, welding it back together with heated fingertips.

I took a deep breath and started toward him.

Perhaps it was all the glasses of wine I'd had. Or maybe it was the way he was sitting upon his chair like it was a throne, looking far too perfect and high and mighty for my taste. Or maybe it was the deeply-rooted need I was clinging to tonight —a need to make villains out of these gods, regardless of how much wine and praise they offered me.

Whatever the reason, I decided now was the time to confront him about our conversation from yesterday.

He glanced up as I approached, studied my wine-flushed face for a moment, then nodded toward the chair beside him.

I remained standing.

He went back to his welding project. "You seem to have enjoyed yourself tonight."

"I did, thank you. And did you enjoy yourself last night?"

"Last night?"

"While thinking of me." I'd meant it as a scathing remark, a harsh comment to try and embarrass him for his bold, teasing words.

It backfired immediately.

The look it drew from him made my stomach flip so violently I nearly lost my balance. Heat pooled too fast, in too many sensitive places, and my question from before—about whether or not he'd been serious about his plans to pleasure himself to me—was answered.

There was nothing teasing about the expression on his face.

His eyes burned with pure, unabashed lust. If we had been entirely alone, I wouldn't have been surprised if he'd grabbed me right then, and...

No.

I wasn't going to think about what he might have done.

A peal of nearby laughter reminded us we were not, in fact, alone, and he stayed perfectly composed aside from those wild eyes.

"Well?" I pressed for some reason. "Did you?"

"Immensely," he said.

It took me several attempts to manage a normal breath.

"You look nice, by the way. Radiant, even." He exchanged the chalice he'd repaired for the glass of wine on the table beside him. "For an elf," he added with a glance at my ears.

He sipped slowly from his glass, drinking it as he drank me in, as though he didn't have a single care in the world just then aside from studying me, complimenting me, confusing me.

I thought of all the things *I* cared about, all the reasons I was here, and it took a concentrated effort not to snatch the wine glass from his hand and fling its contents into his face.

"Have I rendered you speechless, yet again?" He smiled, obviously enjoying the idea.

Asshole.

"What would you like me to say?"

"You could compliment me back," he suggested.

"Why would I do that?"

"I don't know. For conversation's sake."

"Well, let me see..." I looked him up and down, trying very hard to appear uninterested in his appearance, forcing myself to be indifferent to the muscular cleft of his chest peeking out from underneath his loose shirt, to be unconcerned with his perfectly tailored pants clinging to his perfectly sculpted lower half.

All the beautiful statues the humans had built of him were —unfortunately—not entirely inaccurate.

If anything, they didn't do him justice.

"Your appearance doesn't make me want to claw my eyes out tonight," I informed him. "You're almost pleasant to look at, even. For a god."

His smile brightened.

Music drifted in from the room Valas and the others were in.

Dravyn glanced toward the sound, listening to the loud conversation taking place within it for a moment before rising to his feet and offering me his hand.

Against my better judgment, I took it.

We twirled around the room in a slow waltz, completely out of sync with the wild music next door. After a few minutes of moving to one another's rhythms, I don't think either of us even realized there was music playing.

The wine was settling in my blood, truly taking hold of me. It was making my balance questionable, but Dravyn's hold was strong, his movements fluid and easy to follow. With him guiding me, I didn't have to think about next steps, which left me free to study him more closely.

And even through the haze of divine wine, I noticed something strange.

"There are shadows moving under your skin." My eyes widened as I realized the energy radiating out with each pulse of darkness felt familiar—and it wasn't his. It was too cold. Too foul. "Death magic?" I guessed.

"The air of his territory occasionally leaves marks."

"You were there? Today? Why?"

He shook his head. "You haven't survived your next trial yet. That was the deal we made regarding more details about that dark place and its master, wasn't it?"

"What about this trial I'm surviving right now?" I asked under my breath. "I feel like I should get a reward for it, too."

"I'm not *that* horrible of a dance partner, am I?"

"I've had worse. Though not many worse, mind you."

"Well, I could likely think of a few ways to reward you for your suffering."

The low, suggestive tone of his voice sent heat creeping along the back of my neck.

"Are you imagining being rewarded, now?" A devious smile flirted with his lips. "I wonder...what are you hoping for?"

"That these rewards involve you going somewhere far, far away and not coming back for a few weeks."

"So bold tonight." He chuckled darkly. "I think you've had too much wine."

"In wine, they say, there is truth."

"There is. But often foolishness, too—at least in my experience."

"Are you afraid I might let some of that truth slip? Afraid to hear what I really think of you?"

"Afraid?" His eyes flashed to a deeper shade of silver as they fixed on me. "Nothing would delight me more."

"I promise you would not find my words delightful."

His smile turned a bit feral, a bit dangerous. "You try my patience, Sparrow."

It was in that precise moment that I realized he was right: I *had* drunk entirely too much wine; I couldn't seem to make myself shut up, even though I knew I was inching toward precarious ground. "Good. Someone needs to try you, and challenge your insufferable, arrogant—"

His gaze turned burning and wild once more, and all the fierce and slightly drunken words I'd planned to say died in my throat.

"Stop glaring at me." I swallowed hard. "You don't frighten me."

"I wasn't trying to frighten you. Believe me—you'd know if I was."

We'd stopped dancing, I realized. I started to take a step back but caught myself, clenching my fists at my sides and taking deep breaths, trying to cool myself despite the heat from his body, from his words, from the powerful magic that always seemed to be simmering just beneath the surface of him.

"Though if it's not fear, then I can only assume it's something else making you so flustered in my presence as of late," he said.

"There is nothing but an overwhelming feeling of disdain flustering me right now."

"Really?"

"Yes."

"I think there could be something else."

"I think you're mad."

"And yet *you* are the one who keeps insisting on playing games with a supposedly mad god."

"It's not a game, I—"

"Oh, I quite agree. I feel as if we moved out of the realm of pure games several days ago now."

I should not have responded to this, but the words slipped out of me before I could catch them. "And what *feelings* do you have about us now?"

He dropped his gaze to my mouth as his tongue slid over his bottom lip. "What a dangerous question."

I stood my ground. "Answer it."

He lifted his hand, trailed his fingers lightly across my cheek. "I don't think you want to hear my answer."

No, I don't, said the quiet, rational part of my brain.

The slightly drunk, foolish part of me whispered, "Yes, I do."

His fingers stilled against my skin. His lips parted, but he hesitated to answer.

"Tell me, oh great and powerful God of Fire and Forging: What do you *feel* toward me in this moment?"

My slightly trembling, slightly mocking voice made a

muscle in his jaw jump. His hand pressed through the waves of my hair, curving around and gripping the back of my head. A subtle movement that radiated power. Possessiveness.

"I feel…" he replied, slowly, "as though someone should have taught you not to play with fire."

"I thought we agreed this was not a game?"

"True." The hand against the nape of my neck held me in place as he leaned closer, while his other hand traveled down the curves of my body, coming to rest against the small of my back. "So let's keep the danger in mind," he murmured, "and please believe me, Little Sparrow, when I tell you that I could set fire to every inhibition you possess, and when we are finished it will only be you and I among the ashes. I will be the only thing you can think of, and it will not be *disdain* that you feel toward me, I can promise you that."

His lips swept over mine with the last word. The kiss was soft, yet certain. A promise. A threat. A taste of tart wine and heat that somehow left me both disgusted with myself and starving for more.

I held my breath as he pulled away.

He kept his searing gaze on mine as his fingers threaded back through my hair and along my jawline. His thumb stroked a path over my bottom lip, as though mapping out his next kiss, but that kiss never came; sudden awareness shimmered in his eyes, and the moment fizzled like the promising spark of a fire that had nearly ignited before giving way to nothing more than smoke.

My chest ached as though I had inhaled several lungfuls of that smoke.

"And now I feel like you and that dress should get out of my sight," he said, "before we do something we'll both end up regretting."

A traitorous thought flashed through my mind before I could guard against it—

I want to do regrettable things with him.

But the idea was gone in an instant, and I was storming from the room in the next.

CHAPTER 27

THE NEXT MORNING I WOKE UP EVEN ANGRIER THAN the last, hating the God of Fire more than ever, and—worse than that—hating *myself* for what I'd done with him. For the wine, for the kiss, for the traitorous thoughts and feelings he kept stirring within me.

All that time I'd spent trying to refocus yesterday had apparently been in vain. Nothing felt focused or right this morning. Even the simple act of walking downstairs to breakfast in the room by the garden triggered another wave of angry, restless feelings; I was getting too used to the rhythm of this realm and its rulers.

Valas was here, as he'd been so many times before. I couldn't decide if his presence made me feel better or worse. I wanted to hate him with the same ferocity I hated the God of Fire with, but I couldn't seem to. Chaos, hatred, misery...they all loved company, I suppose, and Valas seemed intent on being that company.

We shared a rigid, awkward silence for as long as it took him to drain the tea in his cup and fix me with a curious look.

"I'm beginning to think you aren't a morning person," he commented.

"Just another late night," I mumbled.

"Is it not *exhausting* to be angry all the time?"

"Is it not exhausting to run your mouth so incessantly as you do?"

"It's mostly an automatic function after all these years. Doesn't take much effort on my part."

I very nearly cracked a smile at this, but turned away before it happened, folding my arms across my chest and studying the garden on the other side of the window.

The flowers in that garden never changed. They had been the same brilliant shades of red and white since the first morning I'd spent here, their perfect petals never so much as curling on the edges.

They were beautiful, and yet this garden was becoming one more thing I hated about this place—I used to love documenting the flowers changing with the seasons around my home, watching for patterns in how they flourished and faded. It diminished the beauty of a bloom, I thought, if you never got to see what it looked like when it was barren.

I felt Valas staring at me. After a few minutes of this he asked, "Is it Dravyn?"

I didn't reply.

"He was in a bad mood this morning, too—you two are quite the pair. I think you should go talk to him."

The lack of sleep and everything else made my voice edgier than normal. "And I think you're underestimating just how little I care about your opinion," I told him. "So, *so* little. Like, so little you could not measure it with the world's smallest measuring stick."

"World's smallest measuring stick?" Mairu repeated as she

suddenly entered the room. "Are you two really in here talking about Valas's dick?"

The God of Ice yawned, and without looking at her he said, "Do you just lurk in doorways waiting for the opportunity to make jokes at my expense?"

"Sometimes, yes," said Mairu, taking a sip from the drink she carried before shrugging. "I have to entertain myself somehow."

"Have you considered doing work of some sort? Focusing on fulfilling the noble causes set forth by our Creator, maybe?"

"What, like all the time?"

"Just a suggestion." He stretched his long legs out before him, regarding her with a cocky look. "Also, let's be honest: I heard *zero* complaints from you about my measuring stick the last time we were—"

Mairu held up her hand, and the Ice God's lips puckered strangely together, sealing off whatever he'd been about to say.

"That's impressive magic," I had to admit.

The Serpent Goddess gave a little bow, but then she sighed. "Unfortunately, it never lasts."

As she spoke, a thin layer of ice formed on her hand and began to spread its way up her arm. She grimaced as it crept toward her throat, crackling and shining as it went. "Okay, okay—*truce.*"

The ice around her shattered, and Valas's lips were released from the goddess's controlling magic in the next instant.

Valas shook his head vigorously and rolled the tension from his shoulders. "That's such an unsettling feeling."

"I can do much worse," Mairu said with a sweet smile.

"Or you could try being nicer and using your powers for good."

She scoffed at this before turning to me. "Come on, Little

Spitfire. I think you need a change of scenery. You wanted to see my home in this realm, didn't you?"

I agreed after only a moment of hesitation, eager for a break in the too-familiar rhythms of the morning as well as a chance to take notes on new things.

She led me outside before turning to me with a concentrated look, smoothing my skin and rounding my ears with her disguising magic—*just in case we run into unexpected company*, she told me. Then she reached out her hand.

An odd energy rose around us, accompanied by a sudden, gentle wind.

I stared at her, uncertain.

"We'll travel faster this way," she explained.

I tentatively touched her hand, and I instantly felt an odd tugging in the pit of my stomach as the wind around us picked up. Everything was spinning a moment later, the landscape around us reduced to a blur that quickly bled into rich, autumnal shades of gold and orange.

When the spinning came to a stop, we stood in the middle of an orchard with rows of trees stretching beyond where I could see, golden leaves fluttering all around us. The warm air teemed with a delicious mixture of tangy and sweet scents.

I didn't know where we were or how far we'd gone, but it seemed far in a way I couldn't really explain...like we'd somehow just traversed an entire kingdom in the span of a few heartbeats.

"Can you travel anywhere like that?" I asked.

"Yes and no," she said, patting her crown of braids and checking for any strands the spinning journey might have pulled loose. "We travel to places by accessing the magical residue we leave behind in them. So, it's very easy for me to go to my own home, of course, because of how much of my energy resides there, but it takes more effort to travel to other territories I don't usually frequent in this realm."

"And what about in other realms? In Avalinth, for example?"

"We can travel easily to most places in the mortal realm," she explained. "The air is thinner, less constricting, for one thing—and our magic is spread throughout that realm by way of the humans who we bless with our power. It's getting easier with every new generation of those humans, as more divine magic circulates among them."

I had to avert my eyes to keep the goddess from seeing the fury that automatically roared through me at the mention of those divinely-marked humans.

That fury was becoming so *complicated*.

A traitorous new side of myself wanted to like this goddess I traveled with…but then she so flippantly spoke of the marks and magic destroying my kind and the world we'd once known, and the cycle of hatred and disgust began anew.

"My home is a little ways beyond this point," she told me, "but I brought us here because I thought you might enjoy a short walk." She gestured to the wide, slow-moving river winding its way through the orchard.

We followed this river for several minutes, leaving the wonderful smelling orchard behind and making our way through increasingly thinner tree coverage until we came to a wide open plain covered in long, swaying grass. The last bits of lingering fruit gave way to a briny scent as the air grew heavier, stickier. It felt like there was an ocean nearby.

The feeling was proven right after another half mile or so of walking, as we summited a hill and found ourselves staring at a seemingly endless expanse of blue.

A tremble went through me as I remembered my last

adventure alongside the water in the Death Marr's territory. This looked more like the oceans in my own realm, however, with waves that moved fluidly and were clear enough to reflect the divine daylight as they crashed upon the white sand.

I drifted down to the sandy beach. Mairu followed, and after we'd walked along the shoreline for some time, she slowed and pointed at something in the distance.

"My home," she informed me.

I looked and saw a shimmering ivory palace perched dramatically atop steep, dark cliffs. No less than a dozen staircases wound along the faces of the cliffs, most reaching up from the seaside and converging toward the center of the dwelling. At this center, a grand entrance pavilion flanked by flame-topped pillars awaited us, along with a front door so massive I could clearly make out its silver face and arched shape even from the beach.

A spiraling tower reached toward the peach-colored sky on either side of the palace, and circling around each of these towers were winged creatures that resembled much smaller versions of the serpentine dragon I'd seen the goddess shift into.

"The stairs aren't as daunting as they look," she assured me with a wink.

As we started toward the closest set of those stairs, a strange energy shot through my body, making all the hairs on my arms stand on end. The air grew oppressively humid, as though a thunderstorm was overtaking the area.

I turned toward the ocean, expecting to see white caps building, black clouds billowing, lightning flashing in the distance.

It all appeared perfectly calm.

A foreboding sensation skipped across my skin.

The Serpent Goddess seemed to have sensed something as well; she'd stopped several feet ahead of me and closed her eyes, her forehead wrinkling in concentration.

The air was becoming so damp it made my clothing cling uncomfortably to my body, while deep breaths were becoming increasingly more difficult.

"What is happening?" I asked.

A sudden, violent shifting in the water was my reply. We both took several steps back, watching as a whirlpool began to form with a twisting black hole at its center.

"Another one already?" The Serpent Goddess mumbled the words to herself, but I read the concerned expression on her face and quickly guessed the reason behind it.

"Another trial?" I asked.

She lifted her chin, clearly trying to appear calm and bold for my benefit. "The other Marr are restless and eager to continue with the ordeal, it seems."

Eager to be rid of me, I thought. *Eager for me to fail.*

I clenched my fists at the thought, looking back to the restless sea just as the whirlpool changed directions and ribbons of water began to peel away from it, reaching toward me like the arms of some sentient, horrifying monster.

Gasping, I tried to stumble farther out of the ocean's reach.

I wasn't quick enough.

The monstrous appendages wrapped around my ankles, pulling me toward the waves—I had to move with the monster or else I would have been ripped right off my feet. I was knee deep in the water before I finally managed to shake it off while still maintaining my balance.

Mairu started to rush forward but stopped just as quickly, reluctant resolve mingling with the concern shining in her eyes. She wasn't allowed to help me survive this.

I don't need her help, I told myself, fiercely.

I'd survived one trial on my own.

I would survive this one, too.

The whirlpool had calmed. There was no sign of any monster—yet.

Nerves buzzing and heart thumping, I waded deeper into the sea, putting a wide, clear space between myself and the Serpent Goddess. As I stopped and steadied myself, the water around me began to recede, pulling out toward the distant horizon with a violent swiftness, building into a massive wave at my back.

I should have turned around. Faced it. Braced myself for the deluge. But my gaze caught Mairu's again, and for a moment I couldn't move, couldn't pry my eyes from hers. Her lips moved, and on them I read the same advice she'd given me last night—

Burn brightly.

I swallowed hard, like I could ingest those words, absorb them, make them an intrinsic part of my very being.

Brightly, brightly, brightly.

The wave crashed down, ripping me off my feet and sending me tumbling aimlessly through a terrifyingly cold darkness.

CHAPTER 28

Once my directionless tumbling ceased, I thought I was back in one of the rivers between realms.

I floated steadily downward, just as I had in the river I'd traveled into the middle-heavens, and again, I could breathe despite being underwater—though each inhale was laborious and heavy, collecting like stones in my lungs and weighing me down more and more quickly.

My feet eventually touched a sandy and shifting bottom. I huddled there for a moment, gathering strength. Then I stood...and somehow broke immediately through the surface and came up gasping for air.

The water was shallow again.

It drained rapidly as I found my balance, sinking away until there was nothing more than a damp shoreline beneath my feet.

I was no longer on the same shore I'd been walking along with the Serpent Goddess. It looked vaguely similar, but Mairu was nowhere in sight. The water had shifted to a deep shade of turquoise, and an island had risen in the distance with a building made of grey and white stone standing in its center. The tide receded farther as I watched, revealing a rocky path stretching from where I stood to the island.

A wave crashed toward me, carrying something that glinted in the hazy light—a rusted sword. It washed to rest at my feet. The sapphires embedded in its hilt looked like eyes peering up at me, and I shuddered at the feeling of being watched by them.

I heard a low, threatening sound—something between a growl and a rumble of thunder—and I snatched up the sword and braced myself for an attack.

I turned in a slow circle, searching for the source of the noise. Not finding it, I lowered the sword, picked a direction, and started to walk with purpose. I was determined not to reveal how disoriented and unsure I felt to whatever gods might have been watching.

"Potential Ascendant of Fire," said a sudden voice, deep and cold as the depths of the sea I'd just tumbled through. "Where are you going?"

I spun around. Another wave rose behind me, and I stumbled back as a rush of power radiated out from the water.

This wave did not crash down like the one that had separated me from Mairu. It simply loomed for several beats, suspended and curling in a way that made no natural sense, before it parted to allow a being clad in sea-colored armor to step from within it—Kelas. The middle-god of the Ocean.

"I was going to look for you," I answered, forcing myself to keep still, to not show fear, as he came to stand before me.

He smiled mockingly at my bold words, his eyes flashing toward the weapon I'd picked up. "The sword you hold is Hydrus," Kelas said. "Forged by the sea itself, and it can be as powerful and as beautiful as that sea, or else treacherous to the one attempting to tame it… It all depends upon the wielder and their skill."

I swallowed down the lump trying to build in my throat. *Brightly, brightly, brightly.*

"And what am I supposed to do with it?" I asked.

His smile was wider this time, the flash of white like a quick glint of fish-scales in dark water. "It's simple: You only have to reach the fortress." He motioned toward the island at the end of the rocky causeway. "Beat the rising tide." Another flourish of his hand lifted the waves around the path, making them hover threateningly for several seconds before sending them crashing over the rocks. "And soothe the ocean-forged beast within the fortress's walls. The sword is merely a tool to help you on your way."

None of that sounds simple at all, I wanted to say.

Instead, I gripped the sword as if I'd always been its keeper —as if I knew exactly what to do with it—and I lifted my eyes to the goal awaiting me.

The space between the fortress and where I stood seemed much greater, all of a sudden.

"You accept the terms of this trial?"

'No' didn't seem like an option at this point, so I caught the bits of my courage that were trying desperately to flee, and I nodded.

"Then let us begin."

As he uttered the last syllable, it had already begun, the water around my feet already rising rapidly past my ankles.

I wiggled free of the sinking sand beneath my boots and sprinted for the higher, bridge-like trail of rocks leading to the distant island.

As my feet pounded onto the first stretch of the narrow path, the waves on either side of it began to churn, white foam gathering and bubbling in a way that felt threatening—like it could erupt and suffocate me, sink me back into the cold depths at any moment.

I didn't waste any effort wondering how long I had to beat the rising tide. I had a sneaking suspicion there was no rhyme or reason to its coming and going; the God of the Ocean seemed wilder, more chaotic than the Star Goddess, as if the tide would rise and fall at his command and nothing else.

Sword in hand, I leapt from rock to rock at a borderline reckless pace.

But no matter how fast I ran, the island and its fortress didn't seem to get any closer. I wondered if this could be some sort of trick. If the island was nothing more than a mirage—a goal that couldn't truly be reached.

Despair threatened at this last thought, so I stopped looking up for several minutes, focusing on the path itself rather than the destination. I would concern myself only with the few feet in front of me at any given moment.

Step by step, and I can make the whole journey this way.

I kept reminding myself of this as I stumbled and slipped and sprinted onward, onward, onward.

After several minutes, I felt as if I was making good time, and I lifted my gaze to check on my actual progress.

Something leapt out of the water behind me.

I slowed and twisted around. There was nothing there, but as I returned to the path ahead, I heard something in the water to my right.

The sea rose abruptly and violently, shooting toward me as if fired from a cannon, knocking me off my feet and nearly sending me into the water on the other side—water that appeared much darker than it had near the shore.

Much deeper.

I managed to grab a thin slab of stone at the last instant, clinging to it with one hand while the other desperately gripped my sword.

I was not a particularly strong swimmer. I'd never liked spending time in the water; there were too many unknowns, too few maps I could study of the deep depths of our realms. Those depths were one of the few places I would have been fine leaving to my imagination—and I certainly didn't want to explore the ones below me now.

More water rushed across my path, directly into my face. I coughed and sputtered, my grip on the rock faltering.

I slipped. Caught myself once more. Panic made me other-worldly strong for an instant, allowing me to hoist myself clumsily back onto the path.

The water continued to wash over me. It felt strange as it lapped against my body—sharp and tickling, like rats nibbling at the edges of me. As I caught my breath, I looked closer and realized I wasn't far off with my assessment.

The waves were, in fact...*creatures.*

Creatures with skinny-whip tails and rodent-like bodies shifting and moving with the fluidity of water, with claws and teeth made of sharp bits of the same rocks I'd been racing along.

I braced a hand against the ground as the watery vermin swarmed around me. More and more kept coming, a new body taking shape every time a wave crashed against the rocks and left bubbles of dirty, pebbly foam behind.

One of the rodents rose up from a glob of foam directly beside me and dove for my sword, claws outstretched as if to try and knock it from my grip. I whisked the weapon from its path, but its sharp stone teeth grazed my wrist and left bloody streaks behind.

Biting back a hiss of pain, I swung reflexively after the creature. As the blade connected with its body, a jolt of power shot out from the sword, and the water rat dissolved once more into sea foam and droplets that scattered into the wind.

I repeated this over and over, sending the rodents soaring and scurrying in all directions. But they kept coming back, three more appearing for every one I managed to send into the sea. There were simply too many; my arms were already aching from the effort of swinging my sword.

I looked desperately back to the path ahead, finally noting the distance that remained between me and the island I'd set out for—it wasn't very far.

The water rodents felt like a mere distraction that would never end as long as I kept giving them my attention; my true target was the fortress and the beast within it, so maybe I could shake these vermin off if I just kept going.

I gave one last mighty swing of my blade, knocking aside the rodents closest to me, and then I broke once more into a run.

The creatures gave chase, but they seemed to lose their shape as we went. Soon there were no fangs gnashing nor claws scraping the rocks—at least, not that I could see or hear.

I glanced back and saw what was left of the watery bodies turning away from the path, tumbling into the sea and swelling it to an increasingly threatening size. On both sides of me, water quickly rose over the rocks, spilling into my path and making it more slippery and treacherous with every passing second.

The fortress grew clearer as I approached. I spotted a set of stairs leading up into what looked to be the main floor; the door to it was open. Inviting, almost. And it was higher ground.

I vaulted up the steps and made a last, desperate leap through the arched doorway, landing painfully hard on the stone floor and rolling forward as far and as fast as I could.

A wall of water roared up and crashed in after me, flooding the space for a moment before receding at a crawling, almost hesitant pace, as if the sea was alive and reluctant to stop chasing me.

I rose shakily to my feet, watching the doorway to make sure the waters were done trying to claim me for the moment.

The ground trembled. An odd sound—a sharp, menacing sort of clicking—reached my ears, and suddenly the ocean and its rumblings were no longer my greatest concern.

Turning around, I found myself staring up at a beast many, many times larger than the rodents outside.

Its body was more solid, as well—though water still accented much of its appearance, shearing off its leathery, grey, muscular frame like rapids rushing over river rocks. When it moved, it left trails of that water in its wake—trails that rapidly evaporated, some of the droplets returning to bulk up its body once more. It was a constant cycle, restless and churning, contained yet unpredictable, much like the sea itself.

When the waters were at their most settled point around its frame, the monster vaguely resembled a cross between a large cat and something serpentine, with four powerful legs, a lithe body, and a head like a snake.

The clicking sound I'd heard had come from its long tail, the tip of which was covered with wet, shiny barbs. The barbs rattled against the stone floor with every swish of that skinny, reptilian tail.

It stalked closer.

My pulse quickened. My knees shook. I backed toward the

doorway only to stop at the sound of waves roaring louder outside, cutting off my escape.

There was nowhere to run.

The beast let out an eerie wail before it lunged.

I tripped as I tried to get out of its way, barely catching myself against the rough wall. It struck directly beside me, slamming into the stone with enough force to leave the wall buckling before it pushed off, then twisting after me with surprising agility for such a large creature.

My legs still had not recovered from my desperate sprint along the causeway. My breaths were still shallow, my sword arm still shaking. This was hardly a fair fight, and I could imagine the Ocean God's sadistic laughter as he watched me struggling to even know where—or how—to start.

Were *all* the Marr watching this unfold from some lofty, comfortable tower, like they had watched my last trial?

The thought sent indignant heat flooding through me.

If they wanted a show, I would fucking give them one.

I took my sword in both hands and rapidly circled the room, sprinting out of the beast's reach and moving in a weaving pattern to make myself more difficult to pin down. While I observed the water beast out of one eye, I scanned the room with the other, searching for something I could use to my advantage.

The space was large and mostly empty of furniture, save for a few cabinets housing rusted weapons. Stairs twisted along the curved walls on either side of me, leading to floors above and below. Through one of several tall windows, I could see the ocean rising and restlessly slamming against the fortress. With every wave that thrashed against the outside walls, the beast inside grew more restless. A particularly violent crash sent it into a frenzy, and it twisted toward me again, its jaws opened wide.

I instinctively started to lift my sword, but stopped as I recalled the Ocean Marr's instructions.

"*Soothe the ocean-forged beast inside the fortress,*" I reminded myself. "Soothe it, not slay it."

I pulled my sword in and leapt out of the beast's path at the last second. It swiped toward me, a powerful, watery paw catching on my hip and sending me sprawling. As I scrambled back to my feet and appraised the beast once more, I felt my heart drop into my stomach.

It was a long way from *soothed*.

What the hell was I supposed to do to calm it down?

Sing it a fucking lullaby?

It let out another wail before shooting toward me once more. I sidestepped its path. Its tail lashed out, trying to wrap around my ankles and jerk me off my feet.

I leapt over the lashing tail once, twice, three times until I finally lost patience and whipped my sword back, preparing to strike—only to again resist the urge to swing. I'd had an opening. I could have cut the beast's tail off and no longer had to worry about the sharp barbs on the end...but I'd hesitated.

I *still* hesitated as the monster crouched, tail whipping threateningly about, and watched me through its shining, deep-blue eyes. Its lips peeled back to reveal jagged grey teeth—almost like a grin. Like it was mocking me.

"*Soothe* it," I reminded myself.

The gods did not speak idle words, based on my experiences so far; if Kelas said *soothe*, then I had to believe doing the opposite would lead to terrible consequences—the least of which would be failing this trial.

I lowered my sword to my side and bolted toward the door, thinking a change of scenery might help me think more clearly.

The beast followed.

Would it keep following me, no matter how far I went?

Could I lure it to the shore and try to deal with it there?

I never found out; as I reached the door, a wave rose up and crashed into the fortress, cutting me off. I struggled for balance as water rushed in, reaching nearly to my waist.

The beast melted into that same water, its body shifting to the exact shade and consistency of the deluge. Though I could no longer see it, I could still *feel* its lithe body winding around the space, occasionally brushing against me. Playing with me. Mocking me again.

I looked at the sword I held, frustration rattling my breaths and shaking my hands. Why give me a weapon if I wasn't meant to kill anything?

What was I missing?

I searched the blade over and over for a pattern, for a clue, for anything I'd missed. The sapphire jewels of the hilt glinted wickedly, again giving me the unsettling feeling that I was being watched. Watched, and judged, and found severely *lacking*.

The beast's head poked above the surface as the sea began to recede. It seemed much calmer now that it had bathed in that sea. Its gaze became more calculated, less wild, and I noted how similar its eyes looked to the sapphires in the sword's hilt. They blinked every time I twisted the blade even the slightest bit. And its movements...

It wasn't following *me*, I realized.

It was following the sword.

Ocean-forged beast, the god had called it. He'd also told me that the sword I carried was forged of the sea. The two creations were made of the same energy...was that why the beast followed the blade so closely? Why the rodent creatures on the path outside had also kept diving for it?

Maybe it was similar to what Mairu had explained earlier—the way a place's gathered magical energies could pull her from one spot to another.

The energies pulled toward one another.

The water receded completely, and I straightened to my full height, twisting the sword this way and that. Whatever direction I moved it, the beast's body also moved, often reflecting the same speed and power I'd used. Its glare was fixed upon the sapphires.

"You want this, don't you?"

It answered with a hiss and a thump of its tail.

After testing my theory a few times, I grew bolder. Once I was certain I had the beast's attention, I swung the sword again...and this time I let it go, allowing it to clatter against the nearest wall.

The monster darted toward it as it fell.

I thought I could be quick enough to snatch the weapon back before it actually reached it.

I was wrong.

I dove for the sword and managed to get my hand on its grip, but the Ocean Marr's beast moved much more quickly than it had prior to this point. All at once it was *there*, curving toward me and lashing out with its barbed tail. It struck my legs, sharp tips catching and ripping through fabric and skin alike.

My blood sprayed the ground. I cried out, a wave of dizziness flooding in behind the pain, but I still clutched the sword —so I could still control the beast.

Stumbling from the burning pain in my leg, I ran again for

the door. Water roared up as before, but I didn't need to get outside; only the sword did.

I sized up the distance between the ocean and where I stood. Deciding it was too far for my throwing ability, I turned to search for another option.

I half-hobbled, half-sprinted for the closest staircase, my eyes on the large window partway between the first and second floors. Reaching that window, I wasted no time swinging the blade into it. Glass rained over me. I tucked my head in, draping my arms over it for protection, and kept moving. My sights were on the landing just above.

I leapt onto the landing, turned several circles to gain momentum, and then released the sword and sent it spinning out of the window below.

As it tumbled away toward the sea, flashing brightly in the daylight, a horrifying thought occurred to me: If this did not work, I'd just thrown away my only weapon.

Time slowed to a crawl as I waited for the beast's reaction.

It slinked up the stairs toward me, liquid shearing off it and turning the steps into a waterfall as it came. It stopped several feet before the broken window, rearing onto its hind-legs, its sapphire eyes flashing.

It gave a horrible shriek as it snapped forward with the speed and force of a crashing wave. I scrambled higher, dragging my bleeding self up and out of the way just as it turned and launched through the window, following the same trajectory as the weapon.

It was too big to fit through the opening, but it made a way just the same, its body slamming through the stone, popping it outward, sending several cracks twisting through the walls and the floor.

I cautiously but quickly followed it as far as I dared, side-stepping falling debris, glass, and fractured bits of steps so I could peer down and watch as the ocean-forged beast returned to the waves it had been made from.

It disappeared in a blink, leaving nothing but seafoam and ripples in its wake—and even these things soon settled, until only calm water remained. *Soothed.*

I watched for several breathless moments, waiting to see if it reformed or resurfaced.

It didn't.

Exhausted, I slumped down against the wall, eyeing the cracks left by the beast's chaotic exit.

One of those cracks began to widen. It overtook another crack, and then this second fissure also began to expand. All around the room the ripple effect continued—with a swiftness that seemed unnatural—until the foundation of the tower itself began to groan and shift under the weight of the damage.

The entire side of the fortress collapsed before I could get to my feet and escape.

I fell.

Stone and dust and glass fell with me, battering my body. By some miracle, I avoided the largest chunks of broken and breaking things, and I remained conscious as I hit the ground. I missed the sea by mere inches, landing at the very end of the path I'd been running along earlier. I slammed hard onto my side, striking a jagged edge of a large, flat stone before rolling to a stop.

Most of the fortress debris fell into the water on either side of me. Nothing more than a few stray stones struck me after my sharp landing, but an alarmingly warm wetness was spreading from my right side.

I couldn't move.

I could barely breathe.

The sky above me grew dark. I blinked and realized the blurry wall blotting out the daylight was a wave rising, towering over my landing spot, preparing to crash down.

I closed my eyes, squeezing out tears, waiting for the sea to finish me off. And waiting, and waiting, and waiting.

It never happened.

I finally found the courage to open my eyes just in time to see the water rolling harmlessly away, as if something had grabbed a hold of the waves and peeled them back. It felt like someone lifting the lid of my coffin, barely saving me from being buried alive.

My hand groped over my bleeding side, feeling for the damage while I watched the sea continue to peel back, certain I was actually dead, certain I was imagining this.

I felt someone pick me up. I didn't care who it was. I wouldn't have cared if they decided to toss me into the sea, either.

"You certainly have everyone's attention now, I think."

Mairu's voice.

Burn brightly, she'd told me. I suppose I had. But I didn't feel either bright or burning in that particular moment—I felt dull and cold, like the last foolish flower of summer clinging to life before the winter snows inevitably buried it.

The Serpent Goddess carried me across a stretch of receded sea and damp sand, back toward the shore. She wasn't looking ahead of us as we walked, but behind us, eyes narrowed as if she was giving the sea a stern reprimanding.

I concentrated—or tried to, at least—and I felt glimmers of her power floating around us. A hazy understanding dawned over me.

"You were controlling those waves a minute ago, weren't you?" My words came out in a quiet, breathless rush.

She lifted her chin, unapologetic. "I saw you in danger of drowning, and I couldn't let that happen. Not to you." Her gaze shifted covertly down the shoreline, to where Dravyn stood in the middle of what looked to be an intense conversation with the God of the Ocean and several other Marr. "Or to him."

We reached the shore. She laid me on the warm, dry sand, and I tried to lift my head and watch the conversation playing out between Dravyn and the other Marr.

"I don't think he would have cared if I'd drowned. I think —" I choked on the words as I tried and failed to push myself upright. I stubbornly tried again, and succeeded this time, though the pain in my side made me so dizzy I nearly fainted. "I think…" I gasped "…that he'd be happy to have the ordeal over with, honestly."

She placed a steadying hand on my arm. "He would be happy to have it over with," she agreed. "But I don't think you drowning is the ending he's hoping for."

CHAPTER 29

My recovery from the Ocean Marr's trial was agonizingly slow.

There was no peppermint bath, no special salve that could immediately erase the pain or draw the weariness from my bones this time. No amount of rest, and no amount of food or drink I consumed, made my weakness go away, either. I was given all manner of these things, but they merely dulled my suffering. I'd tumbled over the edge of my body's limits, landed hard and awkwardly at the bottom of the cliff, and the climb back up was proving steep and brutal.

Three days after the trial's end, I was tossing and turning in the throes of a restless slumber when I caught the scent of cedar and smoke. I jolted awake, cursing at the pain that throbbed through my ribs as I did so.

Dravyn appeared in my doorway a few moments later. He looked wordlessly to Rieta, who had been keeping watch at my bedside. Her concerned gaze lingered on me for a moment before she bowed to the god she served and left.

Once we were alone, Dravyn hesitated, one hand in his

pocket while he watched for something in the hallway, before he made his way into the room.

"I'm fine," I told him before he could speak. "You can stop checking on me."

"You still look horrible."

"That's rude," I mumbled, sinking deeper into my pillow.

"I was thinking..." he continued, drifting closer, "...I have a favor I can call in from the God of Healing. And I believe it needs to be done. I'm tired of seeing you like this."

I inwardly recoiled at the thought of him calling in any favors on my behalf. "I don't need any more divine encounters, thank you. If you don't want to see me like this, you could just leave."

His jaw clenched at the suggestion, as though maybe he *wanted* to leave, but something unseen was holding him back.

I refused to ponder what that something might have been.

He stayed for the better part of the next hour, neither of us paying much attention to the other. I continued to doze in and out of awareness while he occupied himself with increasingly pointless tasks, clearly looking for any excuse to stay in the room.

He finally broke the silence as he picked up and studied the sword I'd earned from the Ocean Marr's trial—which Kelas had begrudgingly collected and presented me with before we'd left the shoreline.

"They've subjected you to too much, too quickly," Dravyn said. "Which shouldn't have come as a surprise; the other courts *want* you to fail, and me to fail, by extension."

"Why?"

He sighed, some of the tension slipping from his jaw and shoulders as he turned back to me. "The divine have the same power struggles and hubris as humans...old habits die hard.

Each court wants to be the strongest, so they don't want me to add another powerful, capable member to my ranks."

"You think I'm powerful and capable?" I huffed out a laugh that sent another sharp pain through my bruised ribs. "That sounds an awful lot like a compliment."

"A statement of fact, more like," he said, tonelessly. "You would be dead right now if you weren't these things. I'm still not sure how you *aren't* dead after what happened at the end of the trial...so you're also incredibly lucky, it seems."

It wasn't luck, it was the Serpent Goddess.

He didn't seem to be aware that she'd helped me—maybe none of the other Marr realized what she'd done.

What would happen if they found out?

Her helping me was likely against the rules, wasn't it?

"When I saw that fortress collapsing around you," he continued, mumbling more to the sword than to me, "I thought for certain that was the end of you." He took the sword in one hand, adjusting his grip and testing its weight like he was preparing to swing it at some invisible enemy. At my enemies, maybe.

Mairu's words floated back into my mind.

I don't think you drowning is the ending he's hoping for.

After three days of him frequently showing up at my bedside like this, I was forced to admit that maybe she had a point. As much as I wanted to reject the idea, I couldn't.

What was less clear was *why* he didn't want me to drown.

When had he decided he wanted me to succeed? Was it merely because he didn't want my failure to reflect poorly on him and his court, or was there something more to this? To us?

Did I want there to be something more?

No. No, I didn't. But I certainly wanted to know what he was thinking in that moment—*needed* to know.

Unfortunately, the more time I spent with him, the more I realized that trying to pry information out of him was like trying to pry open the jaws of a dragon with my bare hands. It would take courage and precision—two things my addled and pain-wracked mind couldn't manage much of at the moment.

"It wasn't the end of me, obviously," I said, sinking into the pillow once more. "And I'm fine, as I told you. I mean, aside from the fact that it feels like parts of me shattered when I hit the rocks, and all those parts are now rattling around inside me in a way that probably isn't *ideal*." I gave him a slightly pained, half-hearted smile, which he didn't return.

"I know I sensed healing magic in your blood when we first met, but there's not a damn trace of it now," he said, eyes darkening with thought. "I wonder if being in this realm for so long has nullified it somehow?"

My reply came hesitantly; I had never imagined myself talking about such things with a god.

"...*Earthbound* is the term my kind have come up with," I said. "Our divine magic was stripped away a few generations ago, as you know, but such magic leaves a residue in the earth, and these weaker remnants still seem to be accessible for certain elvish bloodlines."

"Like yours," he said, settling into the chair previously occupied by Rieta.

"Yes. Some are better at drawing out specific residual types of magic than others—I've always been able to draw healing power from my surroundings without really trying, for example. That day you found me, I guess I'd been unconsciously reaching out for such energy to try and survive what was happening, and that's why you sensed what you did from me..."

I trailed off, my mind beginning to spin from the effort of

talking much more than I had in days. I wanted to close my eyes and rest, but I couldn't make myself; he was listening so intently, and I loved sharing knowledge, particularly with a captive audience—even if that audience *was* my sworn enemy.

"No divine being associated with the God of Healing frequents this part of our current realm, do they?" I asked. "And they never really have?"

Dravyn shook his head.

"So I wouldn't be able to call upon the traces of such magic like I can in my own realm," I said.

"That makes some sense, I suppose."

We sat there for another hour at least, puzzling over the things I'd said, discussing theories and swapping ideas. I still ached almost everywhere, but our conversation was somehow more invigorating than any of the remedies I'd been given thus far.

He finally fell silent and then stood, carrying the Ocean Marr's sword over and placing it beside the shelf that held the Star Goddess's silver crown and the glass sparrow he'd made. He carefully adjusted the bird's position on the middle of the shelf, his fingers tracing the edges of it, and without looking back at me he quietly said, "This entire realm is hard on mortal bodies as it is, as we'd already established in the past."

"I've been eating and drinking more to help with acclimation," I assured him.

"I know. But maybe..." He drew his fingers away from the sparrow, clenching them into a fist. "If you will not allow me to call upon the Healing God on your behalf, then maybe you should go back to your home for a bit and see if its energy helps."

I was so shocked by this suggestion that I promptly forgot about every other thing I'd been trying to make sense of.

Home.

He was offering me a chance to go home. To the broken but beautiful mansion, its sunrises, its cobbled-together kitchen. To Andrel. To Cillian. He was giving me a chance to talk to them, to see them and the rest of my world with newly opened eyes, and…

He couldn't have been serious.

I swallowed, pushing down the cautious hope trying to bloom inside me. "Is that…allowed?"

"I told you before that I was willing to bend the rules." He still didn't look at me. "And besides," he added, "you're useless to me while you're in such a state."

"Useless?"

"Afraid so."

"Well, I suppose it's lucky I've never based my worth on how useful I could be to a man. Or to a god, for that matter."

He ran a hand through his hair, eyes lifting toward the ceiling as they often did when he was becoming exasperated with me. But I thought I saw a corner of his mouth inch up as he said, "I can't believe I'm saying this, but I might actually miss that smart mouth of yours while you're gone."

Heat climbed into my cheeks. That—combined with the hope blooming defiantly in my heart—made me more bold than usual. Or more foolish. Or both. "Well, I would tell you to feel free to think of this mouth while I'm gone," I said, "but I'm sure you were already planning to think about it."

His gaze finally fixed on me, burning with possibility and promise as he said, "Among other things."

The heat in my cheeks swept over my entire body. I wanted to command him to elaborate on these *other things*, but I couldn't seem to find my voice.

"You'll have to come back soon enough, of course," he

continued without missing a beat. "I'm afraid we're stuck together until we see our deal through to the end, for better or worse."

I nodded. Despite our relentless bantering and bickering, the idea of seeing him again didn't make me recoil as it should have. Again, I didn't fully understand *why*. I didn't even want to think about it—so I was glad for the distraction of Moth's sudden appearance, heralded by the sound of his claws scrabbling against the sill as he tried to squeeze his body through the partially opened window.

He finally pressed his way through, tumbling clumsily inside and struggling to right himself for a moment before zooming toward me. He slammed into my stomach, sending fresh pain radiating through my ribs and causing me to let out a little grunt of pain.

Dravyn caught him by the scruff of his neck and pulled him away from my bruised body. "Behave yourself," he ordered, prompting Moth to twist and claw in vain toward his arm.

"He's okay," I insisted, holding my palms open for the creature to perch on. He fluttered down into my hands and stared up at me through big red eyes. "Did someone sense I was leaving?" I asked, scratching his chin.

He let out a sad purr, knocking his head against my hand. Dravyn left with a sigh, closing the door behind him, while I said my goodbyes to the griffin.

Thoughts of returning home had filled me with renewed energy. I managed to crawl from the bed and change into clean clothing, to wash my face and braid my hair, even as every too-deep breath and too-quick movement made me cringe.

Moth fluttered close by, mirroring each of my painful gasps and cringes with an anxious chirp and a worrisome flash of fire around his body, until I was forced to gather him into my arms and calm him down.

"No setting anything on fire while I'm gone, okay? You have to stay in control of yourself."

He squeezed out of my arms and shot toward my bed in response, burrowing himself under the pillow with a series of disgruntled little huffs. He stayed there while I packed a bag; when I glanced back at him, he'd fallen asleep. I was tucking covers around him when I heard a light knock at the door.

"Karys?"

My name, so soft and so clear from Dravyn's lips, startled me; I couldn't recall him ever calling me anything aside from Sparrow.

As I opened the door, my lips curved in a slight smile. "You actually do know my name."

He returned the smile, faintly, stepping inside and offering me what he'd apparently gone to retrieve—a bracelet comprised of glass beads.

I took it and held it up to the window for a closer look. The forgelight's glow ignited the translucent glass, revealing the true depth of colors swirling in each of the beads' centers.

"Your work?" I guessed.

He nodded. "And infused with a powerful dose of my magic. Whenever you're ready to come back, it will show you the way to me and help you get here."

Thoughts of *coming back* sent a myriad of confusing feelings twisting through me. Maybe we should have talked about those feelings—especially since he was being unusually forthcoming with his words this morning—but I only thanked him while slipping it onto the wrist opposite of the one that carried his flame mark.

He helped me secure the clasp. Once it was in place, his

hand stayed against my wrist for a moment, little pools of warmth building under each of his fingertips. I found myself wanting to stay for just another moment, to soak up more of that warmth. I'd already been here for so many weeks...what would a few more minutes hurt?

I looked up into his eyes and found their usual storminess settled, their silver color softer, their depths swirling with emotions I couldn't begin to name.

He brushed his knuckles across my cheek. I leaned into his touch. My heart fluttered to a stop and restarted at double its normal rate as he angled his face downward, bringing his mouth within a breath of my own. He paused just as our lips touched. Waiting for me to make the next move.

I nearly did.

Images of home flashed through my thoughts, followed by a single, sharp word—not in my own voice, but in the combined voices of all the ones I would be returning to.

Traitor, traitor, traitor.

I tilted my mouth away from Dravyn's, stopping the kiss. I might not have been able to stop the fire from kindling inside me at his touch, but I could still step away from him. I would not go back to my home with the taste of a god upon my tongue.

I licked the dryness and the tingling want from my lips and said, "I should head out, I think."

His gaze lingered on my mouth, but he let me go without protest. "You should," he agreed, giving his head a little shake, as though he'd just woken from a daydream. "Here—come with me."

He led me from his palace and into a small grove of trees just beyond the yard. A pool of silvery-blue water awaited us here, with five separate streams twisting out from it. We followed one of the streams for a few minutes, until it began to widen into a proper river. Its waters seemed to thicken, taking on the appearance of molten silver in some of the more shallow places, while all of the plants growing along the banks had a pale green, metallic sheen to them.

"Galim is the name for the pool we passed," Dravyn told me as we walked. "Its waters flow in-between the realms, and this river we're following now is only one branch of it. There are lots more, and through them, you can travel just about anywhere there's water, in the mortal realm or otherwise—as long as you have a clear picture of your destination in mind."

"How clear?"

"Just be sure you don't hesitate or have any confusing feelings about where you want to go."

"...Got it," I said, trying to sound much braver than I felt, in spite of the fact that *Confusing Feelings* could have been the title of a book starring the two of us.

"You don't need my magic to go back to the mortal realm," Dravyn said, eyeing that magic-infused bracelet he'd given me, "but you will need it to make the mortal waters shift for you when you want to return."

I twisted the bracelet around on my wrist, studying it again.

"Keep that close," he told me. "And...safe." His eyes flicked up to my face with the last word, concern—and maybe doubt—flashing in them before he quickly looked away. "Now, hurry up," he said, nodding at the water, "before Valas and Mai realize you're leaving and try to drag this out."

My heart swelled with an unexpected surge of emotion. "Tell them...tell them I'll see them soon, I hope."

"I will."

Not wanting to dwell on all of the confusing feelings

humming in the air between us, I quickly turned and walked without hesitation into the river—just as I'd done nearly a month and a half ago when I first crossed into this divine world.

I didn't know why the God of Fire had let me go. I didn't know what would happen in my absence, or what I would have to face when I returned to his realm.

For the moment, I didn't care.

The only thing that mattered was that I was going home.

CHAPTER 30

STEPPING OUT OF THE RIVER WAS LIKE WALKING INTO a dream.

I was in the Nightvale Forest, not far from Andrel's mansion, and I knew this place as well as I knew anything...yet none of it felt real.

Funny, and a little alarming, how easily my perspective of what felt normal and what felt surreal had shifted over the past weeks.

I moved cautiously, at first—partly because of my lingering injuries, and partly because I still was not convinced this wasn't some sort of trial or trick devised by the God of Fire—but by the time I reached the edge of the forest my doubts were disappearing, pushed aside by my growing excitement. I broke into a jog, no longer caring about the jarring pain each step caused me. The tears streaming down my face were from a mixture of aching injuries and relief.

Home.

I still couldn't believe I was home.

My mind raced with questions. What had happened while

I was gone? What had changed? What would my friends make of the things I'd seen and done?

As I reached the edge of the mansion's yard, I caught sight of a familiar silhouette tending to the lanterns by the front door. All of my thoughts crashed to a stop as an overwhelmed, overjoyed little cry escaped me.

Andrel turned at the sound. He was so stunned by my appearance that he barely moved in time to catch me; I collided with his chest, his arms circled around me, and we stumbled, falling together against the house.

We were lost in a tangle of laughter and breathless declarations for a moment before he finally caught my face in his hands and held me in place, taking a step back so he could truly look me over.

"You're...*alive*," he said, still breathless.

The impossibility of the situation overcame me all over again, and another laugh bubbled up through my tears. "Of course I'm alive."

He studied me for at least another full minute before he finally gave a grin to match my own, and he answered me in a voice thick with emotion, "I was worried I'd never see you again."

"So little faith in me," I chided.

He pressed his forehead to mine, his hands reaching to thread our fingers together and gently squeeze them. "It just feels like it's been forever," he said.

"Forever and a day," I agreed.

There were tears flowing freely down my face now. He reached to wipe them away just as we heard the door open, followed by Cillian's startled gasp.

Cillian—normally the epitome of grace and balance—nearly tripped as he ran to embrace me. He didn't speak for a long moment, as if he was afraid his voice might make me disappear.

"*How?*" he finally whispered. "You're here, and in one piece, and..."

"It's a long story."

His expression brightened at this; of all the people I knew, he'd always been the one most willing to sit and share a long story with me. The thought of spending entire evenings lounging around and catching up with him warmed the last bit of caution from my nerves.

"I'll tell you all of it," I assured him.

He gave me a wide grin. "And we'll do the same for you, of course. We've had a lot of company here lately—a lot of things have been happening while you were gone."

I didn't want to ask about what those things might have been. Not yet. It was exactly as it had been in my last moments with Dravyn—the questions were endless, but my only concern right then was walking through the door and back into my familiar world. I would reorient myself, heal, and then I would tackle all my questions, one by one.

For now, it was just so good to be home.

TWO DAYS WENT by before I truly began to feel like my old self again. I spent most of them catching up with Cillian and Andrel, swapping stories of the past weeks as we'd promised to do.

The only times I spent alone were brief, secret trips I took back into the Nightvale Forest. There were certain spots in those woods where the trees grew more wild, where the air shimmered, and animals behaved strangely—if they dared to enter the spots at all. These were the places where I knew magical residue had pooled in far greater amounts than average; I'd noted such hotspots in the past mainly so I could avoid going anywhere near them.

Even now, I was quick about my visits, lingering only until I felt the tingle of my dormant magic rising in response to my surroundings, sweeping over my skin, and tasted that distinctly salty and metallic flavor of divine power.

I didn't know how the others would react to me seeking out divine magic to heal myself rather than sticking to the remedies my kind typically used. Cillian would have been disappointed, maybe. Andrel would have wanted me to heal, I think, but he would have been angry at my decision to let magic aid in that healing.

At first, I was disappointed in myself, too, but it got easier with each trip into the wilds. Easier still when I started to notice my innate power actually engaging with the residual magic, working to erase my bruises and soothe my aches. It was like swallowing down a necessary but disgusting, horrible tasting medicine.

I was returning from one of my rejuvenating trips into the forest when I caught sight of Cillian pacing in the yard.

"There you are," he called, waving me in. "I've been looking all over the place for you."

"Sorry." I avoided glancing back at the forest, trying to sound casual as I shrugged and said, "It was a pleasant day for a walk in the woods."

He nodded absently. Luckily, he seemed too distracted to care much about where I'd been. Too excited. "I've got something to show you. Let's go find somewhere to sit down."

He offered no more explanation than this before turning and heading for the courtyard.

Curious, I followed.

The excitement rolling off him quickly proved contagious; my pulse raced as I caught up to him, and my face was flushed by the time we reached a leaf-covered table made of stone and he finally stopped, plopping down on one of the table's benches and indicating for me to sit across from him.

"What are you so excited about?" I asked, dubious.

"This," he said, simply, as he took a small knife from a sheath tucked under his coat and placed it on the table between us.

It was a tiny, dull blade, completely unremarkable save for the symbol carved into its handle—an upside-down triangle, dissected by a second, upward-reaching triangle, creating a diamond in the center. The symbol looked familiar, but I couldn't remember where I'd seen it before. As I studied it, my stomach twisted in a way I couldn't explain. The warm, healing magic that had been working through my blood seemed to stagnate as well, making my insides feel cold and hollow.

"One of Kinnara's envoys just dropped it off," Cillian said. "She heard about your return, and specifically asked that this be brought to our house so you could see it and test it out for yourself."

"My return... So she knows where I've been these past weeks?"

"Of course."

This wasn't all that surprising, I supposed; elvish circles were smaller than ever these days, and they'd never been known for their ability to keep secrets. "How many others know?" I wondered aloud.

"As many as we could tell," he said, offhandedly, as he carefully picked up the knife and traced the triangles on its handle with fingers that were stained with ink—as they often were.

"Really?" I frowned. "This is the first time you've mentioned this."

"We wanted to wait until you'd had a chance to catch your breath."

"It's caught," I insisted. "So tell me everything."

Cillian's focus was still mainly on the knife. As he held it up in front of him, I swore I felt the magic inside of me reacting again, twisting as if the blade had caught it and started to unravel it.

"Andrel wasted no time getting the word out after you left," he said, "and Kinnara was happy to help inform as many as she could about your dangerous encounters with the gods. People were eager to learn more after news spread about the Cauldra incident and your arrest and all that aftermath."

"I see."

"You're becoming something of a living martyr to our kind. You realize that, don't you?"

I stared at my reflection in the dull blade, trying to make my weak smile more convincing, even though he wasn't looking at me. "No pressure, right?"

"It's just good for our cause," he said. "The more who hear about how the humans wanted to sacrifice you to their new gods, and how one of those gods actually stole you away, the more it galvanizes them and makes them want to stand together against all of these evil things."

"But the God of Fire didn't steal me away," I said, my fingers absently slipping around the bracelet Dravyn had given me, squeezing it tightly. "I volunteered to go with him."

"Same difference," Cillian said, shrugging.

No, it isn't. The disagreement rang so loudly in my mind...but I couldn't bring myself to say it out loud.

How could I, when it would mean alienating myself from Cillian and the rest of my kind?

For as long as I could remember, the cause he'd spoken of had been mine, too, and I'd taken every chance I could to convince the world that the gods were synonymous with monsters—that was *still* my cause.

I'd been gone less than two months; it hardly seemed like long enough to change, to throw away nearly a lifetime's worth of beliefs.

"Anyway," Cillian continued, "hold this for a second." He handed me the knife and then disappeared into the manor, quickly returning with a small, cloth-wrapped object clutched in his hands. He placed the wrapped bundle on the table, and the knife in my hand briefly flashed black and began to tremble.

The change lasted only an instant, but its reaction was undeniable; I barely resisted the urge to throw it down in response.

"Cillian, this blade...why is it shaking? What is this?"

His green eyes were suddenly aglow with their strange, cursed brightness as he stared at the blade in question, looking like a starved man witnessing food for the first time in weeks. "It's the weapon that's going to change everything. One of several we're working on, actually."

"Change everything...?"

"When Kinnara and her group came to our home last month, before your capture and imprisonment, they actually brought a prototype of this with them. They told us we needed to change our tactics, remember? Well, it turns out they weren't all talk. They were already working on a change of tactics themselves. Unfortunately, things got complicated for you—and us, by extension—before we could all sit down and discuss things further."

"*Complicated* is putting it mildly."

He agreed with a wry grin. "Anyway, after you left, she stayed, and we spent the next weeks working on perfecting this knife. It's infused with a special essence they've been working on in her region for some time now—a sort of anti-venom, if you will, derived from the venom itself. The venom being divine magic, in this case." As he spoke, he uncovered the object on the table, revealing a smooth river stone beneath the cloth. A scent of salt and metal instantly assaulted my senses.

"There's residual magic gathered in that stone, isn't there?" My nose wrinkled. I'd spent weeks acclimating to a similar scent in the divine realm, but it was isolated here—the only rotten thing in our oasis of a courtyard—and that made it over-powering.

"Yes," Cillian said. "It's one of many similar materials I've collected from the Nightvale Forest, for testing purposes."

I squirmed on the bench, wondering if he'd collected these materials from any of the same places I was secretly visiting to heal myself.

"Now," he said, gesturing excitedly, "stab the blade into it and watch what happens."

My hand shook. Whether from my own nerves, or from the blade's power, I wasn't sure—but somehow, I managed to steady my grip enough for a quick, accurate jab into the center of the stone. The tip of the blade stuck into the surface in a way that seemed impossible, more like a knife into butter than rock. It didn't go all the way through, but it went deep enough to stick straight up and remain steady even after I pulled my hand away.

I watched as a dark, rotting energy unfurled from the

blade, wrapping around the stone. Ribbons of the energy criss-crossed their way through—following the veins of magic within, I guessed—and soon the stone was shriveling before my eyes.

"This is..." I didn't know what to say.

"A weapon with the potential to kill a god," Cillian finished for me, so excited he couldn't stay sitting down. He clambered to his feet and hovered around the table until the last threads of black energy dissipated, then he gathered up what remained of the stone and offered it to me.

I carefully cupped it in my hands. It had curled into a shape that vaguely resembled a small, crushed and withered heart.

A memory dropped into my head—the evening I'd spent with Dravyn in the room full of his glass creations. I'd been so surprised to feel the normal, mortal-like pulse of his heart that night...

Was this knife my allies had created really capable of putting an end to its beating?

"Well?" Cillian prompted. "What do you think?"

"I think," I said quietly, "that it would take something much more powerful than this to kill a god."

"Well, yes, of course—but this is the start of it. We've worked out the basic method, that's the important thing. We just need more 'venom' to create a stronger anti-divine spell, and then to take that spell and infuse it into bigger, better weapons...and then the possibilities are endless."

He settled once more onto the bench across from me, leaning forward in the eager, conspiratorial way he always did when we were getting to the most interesting parts of a plan. "And you're going to be invaluable for the next part of this operation."

"How so?"

"You've witnessed more magic than most of us could dream of at this point," he said, his tone filled with wonder and maybe a touch of jealousy. "I know we can use at least some of all this information you've gathered. You've told us much of it, but is there anything else we might be able to use?"

An answer struck me almost right away, but I felt too conflicted to voice it immediately. I gripped the stone bench beneath me, my claws extending and digging in, as I tried to keep my balance amidst my warring thoughts. I wanted to keep this potential idea to myself—at least until I'd had time to think everything through—but I also didn't want to let Cillian down.

"Karys?"

I couldn't remain silent.

I'd gone to the divine realm with a mission, and this was the clear, obvious next part of making sure that mission succeeded.

"There are...towers," I said. "I don't think I really told you and Andrel about them before, did I?"

He shook his head.

"The Towers of Creation. One in each divine court that has magic capable of creating lesser divine creatures, and then a fourth that contains whatever it is that allows for the ascension of humans, for their transformation into full gods or spirits. And I think...I think if we could somehow harness the magic within these places, then whatever reverse poison you could derive from it would likely be able to inflict..." I took a deep, bracing breath "...catastrophic damage to a divine being. Because the reverse of creation..."

"Is destruction." Cillian looked so excited by this idea I thought he might fall off the bench.

"I don't know how I would collect what we need," I said,

forcing my claws to retract as I rubbed the back of my neck, "but...well..."

"But I've no doubt you can figure it out." He jumped to his feet again, head tilting back and taking in the entirety of the manor looming over us as though he was staring at one of those Creation Towers, imagining all the possibilities. "Even just a *piece* from one of those buildings might be a valuable material for us. Do you realize what we might be able to build with it?"

I did.

I just wasn't sure I wanted to think about it anymore today.

I feigned an exhilarated expression all the same, mirroring his. We'd genuinely reflected one another's excitement so often over the past years that I was able to make my face convincing despite the uncertainties gnawing at my insides.

"It's going to unite us all, Karys," he said, breathlessly. "All the squabbles between our kind will be over, and we'll finally be able to stand our ground against the gods, the humans...all of them. We'll have power, and a place in this world again."

He walked circles around the yard, continuing to list possibilities and promises, and I gave a more earnest smile at this; the subject and implications of our conversation aside, it was nice to be back in his company, listening to his passionate ideas. Nobody shared my love of making plans and connecting the dots of things like he did—the ink staining his fingers was no doubt from notes he'd been studying all afternoon, and I was certain he was itching to rush back to his desk and start jotting down more thoughts about our conversation.

He eventually stopped his rambling, circled back to me, and picked up the knife. "You should take this with you when you go back to the divine realm. You can test it on things and take notes, maybe."

My perfectly composed reflection of his excitement cracked a tiny bit.

I pulled myself back together almost instantly, but he still caught the break, and his demeanor shifted quickly from excited to concerned.

"This is...a lot, I know," he began uncertainly.

"It is, but I can handle it."

"Are you sure you're okay?"

"Just tired." I plastered on another smile, brighter than before. "I don't think I'm fully recovered from my journey here, even now—turns out traversing the realms is an exhausting pastime."

He chuckled and offered his hand. "Who knew?"

He pulled me to my feet. We stood for a moment in the soft glow of the afternoon sun, both of us lost in thought. It had rained these past days, so the sun had been something of an afterthought—but it was bold and beautiful now, and I was struck by how different it was from the forgelight Dravyn had created. Less harsh. A much warmer shade of gold. And yet...

He'd created that light and regulated its cycles so they mimicked this mortal sun solely for my benefit, he'd said.

A monster, but a monster who had gifted me the sun. Who had offered me healing in every way he could after my trials... and then let me go when he saw no other way to aid in that healing. He was still the villain. I couldn't forget that. It was just...

In my head, I'd written our story much differently.

My hand reached absently for my ribs, testing their soreness. Still tender, but not nearly as bad as before. How much longer could I justify staying in this realm? I had to go back, and likely soon; every day I spent here was probably making things more complicated for the Shade Court—and thus, more difficult for me whenever I returned.

Cillian cleared his throat, interrupting my rambling thoughts, and then quietly said, "Savna would be proud of you, you know."

I froze at the mention of my sister, all of my questions and other concerns falling away. My hand started for my cheek. My scars.

Cillian—who'd witnessed me scratching those scars more often and more viciously than anyone—automatically reached up and caught my hand, gently guiding it away from my face.

Determined not to reach for them again, I fidgeted with the bracelet Dravyn had given me instead.

"I just thought you might need the reminder," Cillian said. "If she were here, she'd tell you the same thing." He smiled wistfully as he added, "And she'd have some rousing, encouraging speech to give you, too, I'm sure—sorry I'm not as good at that part."

"It's okay. I know what you mean."

He put his arm around me and we started toward the house. I tried to relax against him as I'd done so many times, sinking into his strength and his clean, citrusy scent. He had always been my confidante. My protector. The older brother who stepped in and carried me when the weight of my sister's memories and everything else got too heavy.

As I clutched the knife he'd given me, I hoped against hope that none of that would ever change.

CHAPTER 31

ANOTHER TWO DAYS PASSED. I KEPT WAITING FOR the God of Fire to lose his patience and call me back. For his fiery eagle form to swoop down from the clouds, snatch me up in his talons and carry me off. To steal me away, as all of my kind believed he'd done last time.

He never came.

I had mixed feelings about this. It would have been easier if he'd behaved as expected—a monster doing monstrous things, leaving me with no choice but to keep making plans to slay him.

Instead, I was allowed to linger in the mortal realm, to finish healing. To plot my next steps.

Each day, Andrel and Cillian came up with new theories and shared more thoughts about what those next steps should be. More experimental weapons appeared in our home. And as afternoon on the second day eased toward evening, visitors began to arrive—some I recognized, many I didn't.

They were all coming to see me.

To speak with their *living martyr*, as Cillian had called me.

Because word was spreading faster than ever; I was the warrior who had walked among our greatest enemies, survived them, tricked them into letting me come back.

Now they all wanted to know what I would do next.

I had a chance to rally and lift up my kind like never before. To give them hope. Encourage them to rise. To finish what my sister had started, which was the greatest vengeance possible for her death. It might not have been unfolding as I'd envisioned, but it *was* unfolding. Rapidly.

As the last rays of sunlight disappeared below the horizon, I was sitting in a patch of grass in the center of the eastern courtyard, studying the knife Cillian had given me and trying to prepare myself for the meeting with all our visitors.

My ears twitched at the sound of a familiar gait approaching—Andrel. He greeted me with a smile, his gaze snagging on the blade I held.

Cillian had looked at it as though it was food to fill his starving stomach. Andrel regarded it with a different kind of hunger, I thought; like a king looked at a territory he intended to conquer.

"Cillian's filled you in on all of the ones who will be here tonight, I assume?" he asked. "All the questions and topics to be discussed?"

I nodded. There had been comprehensive notes, arranged in the way he knew I would prefer. He'd spared no details. I had all the facts. I could recite them, study them to my heart's content...all the things I always did. All the things that usually made me feel calm and in control.

They weren't helping me today.

I felt like my world was spinning, even as I put the knife aside and dug my claws into the soft earth.

"He's been so excited about all these experiments and

breakthroughs that he's barely slept over the past weeks," Andrel commented, sitting down.

"Sounds like typical Cillian to me."

He gave me a crooked grin before tucking his arms behind his head and laying back on the grass. "You're not wrong."

I dug my claws deeper into the ground while Andrel studied the emerging stars, his eyes glassed over in thought.

"Can you imagine it?" he asked, after a few minutes. "That dagger of yours, plunged straight into the heart of a god? Or into whatever they have that masquerades as a *heart*."

I could imagine it. Vividly. Doing so made my vision spin even faster.

"I just hope I'm there to see the first strike," Andrel said. "The moment when everything changes."

"I probably won't start with the heart. I'd try something more subtle first."

He laughed as he sat up. "Ever the calculating one." His tone was playful, his gaze adoring. "We've missed that around here."

I blushed.

"I've missed all of it," he added. "All of you. I don't think I've told you that enough since you came back, but..." He trailed off, laughter still shining in his eyes.

The world's spinning slowed somewhat, steadying under the warm weight of his familiar, inviting affection. I'd been left lightheaded and unsure by that affection so many times in the past, but now it felt so...*simple* compared to everything else.

"I missed you, too," I said.

He reached and tucked a strand of hair away from my face, his touch lingering, caressing the edge of my ear. His tone dropped lower, filled with promise, as he asked, "Want to go calm your nerves before the meeting?"

I used to dream of these moments with him—of any chance for us to slip away from our larger battles, from the *cause* and the chaos that always seemed to loom over us. From everything. I wanted to live in that dream now, too. Wanted to lose myself in the feel of his fingers grazing my skin, in the taste of his kiss, in the heat of our bodies tangling together.

I wanted to go back to the days when these things—and the uncertain flutterings they caused—were my biggest questions. So I tried to; I tucked the knife into the sheath hidden beneath my shirt, and I took his hand and let him lead me across the yard, past the overgrown gardens scattered full of wild flowers, down the winding stone path that ran along the tumbledown fence.

I knew this path well. Knew where it ended—in the old guesthouse at the edge of the property, on the mattress that smelled faintly of dust and vanilla, where we'd given ourselves completely to one another on several different occasions. He hadn't been my first, just the first one that had mattered, and each encounter was still a fond memory.

But suddenly I wasn't sure I wanted to recreate any of those memories tonight.

My world was no longer spinning as we walked along. A sense of numbness had taken the place of the twisting, the unsteadiness. I wasn't sure which was worse.

Andrel must have read the lack of feeling in my silence, the hesitation in my step, because he slowed to a stop as the guesthouse came into view. "Is something wrong?"

I fumbled for an excuse and ended up giving him the same one I kept giving Cillian. "Still tired from my travels, I think."

His brows knitted together in concern as he took hold of my other hand and pulled me into a slow, gentle kiss.

Again, no nervous flutterings came from his touch or his

kiss. *Nothing* came from these things. And I couldn't help but compare it to the kiss I'd shared with Dravyn, the way the god's lips barely whispering against mine had made every inch of me feel alive and hungry for more.

I gave my head a little shake, trying to chase the images of the God of Fire from my mind. "We should probably get back to the house," I said, stepping away. "There are too many people waiting on me; we didn't really have time for this little excursion, anyway."

He studied me for a long moment before his concern gave way to another smile as he said, "We'll save it for another evening, then." His voice was quieter. Inching toward anger, I thought for an instant—but no. I was simply overwhelmed, worried about too many things and imagining problems that weren't really there.

We walked in silence back toward the house until we passed the gardens once more, at which point he said, "You haven't really seemed like yourself since you returned, Kare. I'm worried about you."

"I'm fine."

"What exactly did they do to you in that divine realm?" He seemed to be teasing at first—until I didn't answer him and kept walking, trying to keep my face angled so he couldn't see it. He cut in front of me, then, forcing me to meet his gaze.

All the amusement in his eyes had vanished.

"Karys? What did they do?"

"Nothing I couldn't handle," I said, pushing past him.

I felt him staring hard at my retreating back. "It doesn't feel like you've handled it."

I kept walking. I wanted to walk by the entire mansion, to sprint across the fields and into the forest beyond...but I couldn't. I was expected inside. Expected to lead, to reassure, to play this role I'd convinced myself I was meant for. I walked faster at the thought, as if I could outrun all of the doubts trying to creep into my head.

"Can we at least talk for a moment?" Andrel asked, jogging after me again. "Please?"

I slowed so he could catch up. I didn't want to talk, but I felt like I had with Cillian days ago—I couldn't stand the thought of letting him down.

So I stopped, and I tried to put all of my messy thoughts into words for him.

"I just...I've learned so much after spending so much time among the gods. I haven't been purposely keeping anything from you and Cillian, but I don't think I've managed to explain it all properly, either. And now everything feels like it's moving so fast. All these weapons, and all these people gathering to speak with me about them..."

"You don't think those weapons are a good thing?"

"It's not that. I do. I mean...I think I do, I just...I just wonder if we should slow down and more fully consider what effect such things will have on the realms in the long run."

He ran a hand along his jaw, as if considering—though the smirk he wore told me he'd already made up his mind about this. "The only effect I care about is how quickly one of our poison blades can wither a god's life-force," he said.

"I know." I took a deep breath. "But...what if not *all* of them deserve to be poisoned?"

I realized, instantly, that I had said the wrong thing.

His amused expression returned, but there was no brightness in it this time. It was strangely, terrifyingly cold. "You're joking."

"I'm not saying we should worship them as the humans do, but—"

"No?"

"Of course not, I—"

"Because it sounds like maybe you've already started to do exactly that."

I tried for more deep breaths, but they hitched in my throat, making my words come out as little more than a whisper. "That isn't fair. And it isn't true."

He let out a soft, incredulous little laugh. I thought we were finished; he seemed ready to turn and storm away from me, and I was more than ready to turn and storm away in the opposite direction.

Instead he went very still, his eyes locking on mine, as he said, "After everything we've been through together, and everything I've done for you..."

"I'm not throwing any of that away."

He didn't reply.

We stood in uncomfortable silence for a long moment. I clenched my fists—guarding against my claws trying to unleash themselves—but otherwise, I didn't dare move, afraid that so much as a wrong breath would escalate this beyond the point of no return.

"I just thought I was clear before you left, that's all," he said calmly.

"Clear?"

"I told you not to come back until you'd destroyed them, to not lose your anger over what they've done to us."

"I'm *still* angry, I just—"

He took a deliberate step toward me.

I stumbled back, warnings buzzing across my skin. "If you aren't going to listen to anything I'm trying to say, then this conversation is over," I snapped, starting once more for the house.

Just as before, I felt his gaze digging into my back.

Then he was following me, catching me by the arm and pulling me to a stop. The violence of the motion startled me, sending my pulse racing so fast it left me feeling faint.

"*Let go of me,*" I demanded.

"I think we need to finish our conversation first."

"I told you—I'm already *finished* with you at the moment."

His fingers dug more deeply into my skin. "I can't let you go inside and tell all our potential allies about the apparent affection you've gained for our enemies."

I tried to twist out of his grasp, but his cursed strength rose up and quickly overwhelmed me. Our brief struggle ended with him pushing me toward the manor, slamming my wrist into the wall with what felt like every ounce of that cursed power of his.

I heard the sound of bone snapping.

Pain blinded me.

It was a long moment before my surroundings came back into focus, before I looked down and saw bits of red glass scattered like drops of blood over the ground—the bracelet Dravyn had given me, shattered into too many pieces to count.

Sharp pain shot through my forearm, diffusing into a tingling ache that reached into my shoulders and neck. Head spinning, I lifted my gaze and tried to make sense of what had just happened.

Andrel's eyes were wide with the same shock I felt. His lips moved, but no sound came out.

Before he could find his voice, both of our eyes were drawn to the lanterns by the door, and then to the ones lining the path leading to that door; the flames in them had started to dance as though caught in a violent wind storm, even though no breeze stirred anywhere else.

One after the other, the lanterns went out.

Darkness overtook our surroundings—a swift, supernatural darkness that swallowed up the moon and stars along with everything else. The flame-shaped mark on my skin began to itch, to glisten as though coated in wet blood. I slumped against the wall, closing my eyes against the pain radiating through my arm, trying to find solace in the dark.

Light exploded into that solace seconds later, forcing my eyes open again. I half-expected to see the sun somehow blazing in the night sky.

It wasn't the sun.

It was a great eagle made of fire, and it was heading straight toward us.

CHAPTER 32

BRIGHT WINGS OF FLAME UNFURLED, STRETCHING nearly from one side of the courtyard to the other, as the fiery bird swooped to the ground.

Andrel crouched down in front of me as it did, panic making his eyes even wider than before. "Karys—you know I didn't mean for that to happen. I'm sorry, I just...I need you to *listen* and try to understand where I'm coming from, where *all* of us are coming from. Do you realize what's at stake for us? What your father and sister were trying to do? What we're *so close* to doing?"

I couldn't answer, shock and pain still stealing away every word I tried to think of.

The fire behind him started to shift.

His hand stayed against my knee, holding both of us steady in the rising heat. I heaved for breath and braced my uninjured arm against the ground as I watched the fiery wings folding around the bird, cocooning its body, creating a pillar of flames that shot up toward the dark sky. After a few seconds of spinning and reaching upward, the column abruptly collapsed and the fire extinguished, sending a whoosh of heat and wind toward us as it went.

Dravyn stood among the lingering, swirling embers, his eyes the most terrifying shade of red I'd ever seen, glowing like two hellish pits of molten rock.

Those terrible eyes flashed from the broken piece of bracelet scattering the ground up to the grip Andrel had on my leg.

His voice was quiet but deadly as he said, "Let go of her. *Now.*"

Andrel hesitated only an instant before he complied. He was furious, stubborn, powerful—but he wasn't stupid. He drew his hand back and took several steps away from me, his eyes never leaving the God of Fire.

Dravyn followed him.

The two of them squared up. I staggered to my feet. Movement caused pain, the pain caused dizziness, and I was forced to lean against the wall behind me for a moment to catch my balance.

A moment was all it would take for the Fire God to send Andrel and everything else in this courtyard up in flames. Panic gripped me at the thought, and I gritted my teeth, determined to go step between the two of them even as my eyes welled with tears.

Before I could, a second divine beast descended from the night sky—a cloud of mist and ice that took the form of a sleek white panther as it touched upon the ground. Its violet eyes gleamed as they fixed on me before it bounded over. Ice spread out from beneath its paws with every step, only to crackle and shatter in its wake, sending tendrils of mist up with every break. A blanket of fog soon hung over the area, cooling the air and making it a little easier to breathe.

The God of Winter and Rebirth emerged from a concentrated cloud of this fog, in his human form, his violet eyes still fixed on me. He headed straight to my side, completely ignoring both Andrel and the crowd of other elves—my allies—now rushing toward the chaotic scene.

For once, the middle-god had nothing to say; Valas merely stood like a sentinel at my side, one arm wrapped around me, holding me up, and together we watched my two worlds violently colliding.

No less than a dozen of my kind had rushed into the yard, all clamoring to make sense of what was happening. Some carried weapons, while the rest seemed to be looking around for something they could use to protect themselves.

I stood up straighter as several heads turned my way, trying to appear calm and in control, but unable to keep from wincing at the awful pain that shot through me with every tiny move I made.

Valas—still without speaking—reached out and subtly pressed a hand to my injured arm. A gentle cold swept out from his touch, soothing away some of the pain, dulling it enough that I could focus on what was being said between Andrel and Dravyn—though few words were being uttered just then.

The God of Fire had clearly not come here to *talk*.

As overcome by pain and confusion as I was, there was still space for fear to slip in. The stories of Dravyn's ascension and the destruction and death he'd caused rampaged through my mind. He looked prepared to set fire to everything around him without a second thought.

Adding fuel to that fire, Andrel had drawn a weapon from somewhere—a throwing knife. He'd wielded such knives with deadly precision for as long as I'd known him; I'd once seen him drive one into a target from well over a hundred feet away.

And I had a feeling this particular knife was laced with the same mysterious, anti-divine toxin as the weapon Cillian had given me.

Of the ones who had rushed out from the house, I saw two who were armed as well, only with bows, their metal-tipped arrows nocked and drawn.

I stared hard at all these weapons, watching closely until I saw the metal flash to black as my knife had done in the presence of divine magic.

Andrel spun the knife with the focus of a madman, looking all-too-eager for a chance to test the venomous blade out on an actual god.

I tried to squirm out of the Valas's hold, but he kept a gentle yet firm arm wrapped around my middle. "Be still," he urged. "You'll make your injury worse."

I watched, terrified, as Dravyn reached a hand toward Andrel and the spinning knife.

There was no more warning than this.

Flames erupted all around where Andrel stood, forcing him to stumble backward, arms flailing, to avoid catching fire. The knife slipped from his grasp and clanged against the ground. As the sound echoed through the stunned courtyard, Dravyn rushed forward and caught Andrel by the throat.

The ones pointing arrows at him took a few shaky steps forward, leveling their bows.

They fired.

Dravyn kept one hand on Andrel. He reached out again with the other, first to the left and then to the right, summoning fire to wrap up the shafts of each arrow, reducing them to ash in mid-air. The metal tips dropped harmlessly to the ground.

Fire swelled around the god, unfurling outward as his wings had earlier before sweeping forward to wrap around Andrel.

I could picture the inferno swallowing Andrel up, leaving nothing but ashes behind when the fires finally went out. Too clearly, I could picture it—and all of the violence that would follow it. I thought about nothing else. Not what Andrel and I had talked about. Not what he'd done. Not my own pain, my fury, my confusion. The only thing that mattered then was stopping this before it erupted and caused cataclysmic damage.

"Wait!" I shouted. "Please don't kill him!"

For a long, horrifying moment, I didn't think Dravyn was going to listen. The God of Ice held me more tightly than ever, though a quick, pleading glance at his face revealed he wore a torn expression.

"It's been a long time since I've seen him like this," Valas said, frowning.

"You have to stop him!"

The Winter God shifted his weight from one foot to the other, looking uncertain for the first time since I'd met him. A surge of frustration brought strength with it, allowing me to finally slip free of his hold, jostling my broken arm and sending fresh agony shooting through it.

It was my gasp of pain that finally caught the God of Fire's attention. The flames around him started to settle. His head tilted toward me, but his eyes were still terrifying, glowing with such a powerful brightness that I wasn't sure he could truly see my face through their burning.

I ran toward him anyway, clutching my arm to my chest, trying to stabilize it despite my unsteady steps. I made it to within a few feet before the heat became too intense, forcing me to stop and drop to one knee. As I buckled over, the hilt of the knife hidden under my shirt dug into my stomach, reminding me of the task I'd originally set out to do even as I tried to reason with the god before me.

"Please," I said in a voice shaky from pain and fear. "*Stop.*"

He blinked, and his eyes slowly began to change, as if he could sense the terror their burning glow had sent rattling through me. His darkening gaze fell to my injured arm and stayed there for a long moment.

Valas caught up to me, kneeling and helping me better stabilize my injury once more.

Dravyn turned his head slowly back to Andrel. Released him. Took a single step back, and in a voice tight with suppressed rage, he said, "If you ever touch her like that again, I will find you, and I will not simply *remove* your hands—I will carve them off in the most painful, gruesome manner possible." His voice slipped into a growl, so low I could barely hear it over the pounding of my pulse. "But don't worry: I'll be sure to cauterize your wounds when I'm done." A flame, wicked and blazing white, appeared in his hand. "I am a most *generous* god, after all."

His threat finished, he moved toward me. Though his stride was calm, the fires around him began to swell once more. They enveloped me as he approached, but didn't singe even a single hair on my body—they hadn't burned me on the first day we met, and they didn't burn me now.

As I slowly stretched back to my full height, I caught a glimpse of Cillian rushing to Andrel's side. I stayed where I was. With my arm throbbing despite the Ice God's soothing magic, I stared through the flames and watched my two oldest friends—the only thing I still had that resembled *family*—as they scrambled to find balance and calm the crowd that had gathered to witness this violent, divine show.

Cillian lifted his gaze toward me, and the look in his eyes...

It hurt worse than the pain in my arm.

I'm sorry, I mouthed.

I didn't know what else to say.

He clearly didn't either. He started to mouth several things in response, but in the end, he only stared at me in silence, looking like he was struggling to catch his breath. Then he averted his eyes and focused his attention on Andrel instead.

The rest of our allies gathered around the two of them, a few glancing uncertainly in my direction before hastily turning away from me, acting as though I wasn't even there. I didn't blame them; Dravyn's fires almost completely surrounded me —it would have been madness to try and get close.

I was an outsider looking in at my own life.

Valas gave Dravyn a pointed look. "We should go."

Dravyn nodded in agreement. Turning to me, he quietly said, "I think you should come back with us."

I was too numb, and in too much pain, to recoil at the suggestion. Even if I wasn't, how could I stay here in the wake of what had just happened?

Dravyn said nothing else, only watched me closely. Patiently. He wasn't forcing me. He was asking. Hoping, maybe. And I don't know that I truly wanted to go with him— I just knew I didn't want to stay where I was.

So when he held out his hand, I took it.

CHAPTER 33

With two middle-gods as escorts, the trip between realms didn't require the use of magical waterways or any of Eligas's other paths. Instead, Dravyn and Valas both held tightly to me, and we traveled the same way I'd traveled with Mairu prior to the Ocean Marr's trial.

Even with both of them helping to stabilize me, the pulling and spinning was as nausea-inducing as before, and sheer torture against my injured arm. I focused all of my energy on staying quiet. I couldn't keep the tears from streaming down my cheeks, but I refused to be reduced to a sick, sobbing mess.

We landed outside Dravyn's palace. Mairu rushed through the front door immediately to greet us, as though she'd been worriedly expecting us.

Before we could exchange a single word with her, the already horrific evening went from bad to worse.

It began with a curse from Valas, echoed by Dravyn. They glanced upward at the exact moment the sky began to turn black, shadows spreading out over it like ink spilled from a well. As darkness flooded every last bit of bright sky, I felt a power unlike anything I'd ever felt—in this immortal realm or otherwise. It was so immense I wanted to drop to my knees and curl into myself, to somehow become small enough to overlook. It crushed away not only what was left of the light, but also every sound outside of our breathing and my own raging, ragged heartbeat.

"I'll speak with him alone," Dravyn said, voice echoing strangely in the quiet.

I felt a hand against my back—Valas. His fingertips were the cold shock my body needed to start moving again. He guided me toward the palace; I couldn't see or sense much, but I recognized the stairs we climbed, and then the sparkling, patterned stone laid at the palace's entryway.

I heard Mairu's voice beckoning us inside. I stumbled forward, nearly tripping over the threshold as I fretted to make sure I stepped inside left foot first. Such a stupid, *stupid* ritual, but the urge to do it rose up and consumed me.

I felt like I'd misstepped in every way possible tonight, like I'd caused *everything* to go to shit. I had to stop it somehow. I couldn't change what had happened, but maybe I could control what came next if I could stick to this familiar ritual, if I could find some way to impose order upon the chaos.

The obsessive thoughts pelted my mind like a hailstorm, each hard, cold piece making me want to duck for cover. I realized I was standing oddly motionless in the doorway—all my attention on trying to stay upright under the deluge of my thoughts—and I hastily stepped inside so Valas could pull the heavy door shut behind us.

Even the light in here seemed dimmed, though flaming candles burned on the walls all around us. The room was illuminated enough to allow me to make out Mairu and Valas's faces, at least; they both seemed to be searching for something to say. I avoided their eyes as I cautiously approached the nearest window. I didn't expect to be able to make out much of what was happening outside, but I felt drawn to look anyway.

The darkness remained absolute, but within it I did see...*something*. Someone. A massive, dark-haired figure surrounded in a halo of hazy, greyish-white light. Feathered wings were folded against his back, occasionally rustling in a way that suggested a dangerous, growing impatience. The sword he held seemed to be absorbing much of the light his body gave off, the symbols carved into its blade pulsing brighter with every tense moment that passed.

The knife hidden beneath my shirt vibrated against my skin, as if in response, strong enough to feel even through the special, thick scabbard Cillian had given me. I shivered along with it, praying its power was too weak for the gods around me to take notice of it once all of our current distractions went away.

"That being out there, is that..." My brain couldn't seem to form words, as if struck dumb by his power, his presence.

"The God of the Shade," Mairu said, softly.

"Here to address what just happened," Valas said, steering me deeper inside, away from the window.

I briefly considered yanking the front door back open and going to meet this upper-god for myself, as foolish as that sounded.

Instead, I tucked my head toward my chest, trying to stop everything from churning around me as I asked, "Is Dravyn in trouble?"

"Not necessarily," Valas said. "But we have laws that govern our work within the mortal realms. And the Moraki we serve generally frown upon us descending upon those realms in a fiery rage."

"Which is why I tried to stop Dravyn from doing that," said Mairu. Leveling a glare at Valas, she added, "You were *supposed* to go calm him down, but it didn't feel like his power calmed after you left; I could sense it growing stronger. What happened down there?"

I stared numbly toward the window while they talked and argued beside me. Mairu managed to do several things at once, carrying on her conversation with Valas while simultaneously summoning servants and gathering supplies to tend to my arm.

Even as those servants worked, I still didn't move, drifting in and out of awareness, until I heard Valas say, "Her path back into this realm was broken—we would have had to intervene at one point or another."

An image of the bracelet's shattered beads flashed in my mind, and my entire body flooded with furious, confusing heat. "Is that why he came after me? Because he sensed the bracelet shattering?"

"That was the last trigger, yes," Valas said. "Even before that, he felt the magic in it growing restless—something about your own energy was setting it off. Then it was separated from you in a violent manner, and we suspected something was wrong. Well, he suspected it. I was busy enjoying a glass of wine, but I was nice enough to accompany him on his little rescue mission."

"Sorry to have disturbed your drinking," I muttered.

"I'll forgive you this time," he said with a crooked grin.

I wasn't in the mood to return it. I looked at my arm, now neatly wrapped up in a makeshift splint.

Broken, I'd heard one of the servants whisper.

These latest fissures in my life went much deeper than bone, it felt like.

I wrapped my uninjured arm around myself, trying to calm

my unsettled stomach while pressing my hidden knife more firmly against my body. The blade's vibrating had stopped, but the poison sleeping within it remained. As did the poison in my heart.

I no longer fit into my old world as I once had. That much was clear. Yet I still carried the weapons of that world. I still held to the hatred that had first brought me into this divine realm, because my sister was still dead, the gods were still dangerous, and the world down below was still changing, threatening to erase my kind from existence.

But now...

What was I supposed to do now?

"Karys?" Mairu said, taking an uncertain step closer. She was holding out a vial of some sort of foul-smelling tonic—she'd been offering it to me, I realized. "This should help with the pain."

It smelled like the same concoction Dravyn had given me after my first encounter with the Death Marr. Remembering how much better that tonic had made me feel, despite its off-putting taste, I accepted it with a thankful nod.

The Serpent Goddess lingered close to me, still looking hesitant. "If you want to talk about what happened with your—"

"I don't."

Valas let out an unimpressed snort. "Well, with all due respect—which is none—fuck him and his stupid pointy ears and beautiful face. If I were you, I would never speak of him again. Or *to* him, for that matter."

"*Valas,*" Mairu hissed. "You're not helping."

The God of Winter mumbled something indistinct in reply.

I downed the tonic Mairu had handed me in a few gulps,

then wandered away from the two of them, pacing the edges of the vast room.

I didn't disagree with Valas, but how could I simply *let go* of so many years of my life? It wasn't just Andrel. It was everything. Cillian, the place we'd called home, all our allies, the legacy of my sister, my father...

Had I severed my claim to all these things by disappearing in a flash of flames and divine power? It had seemed like the smartest thing to do at the time. Now it seemed like the most cowardly thing.

Coward. The word burrowed itself into my mind. I raked a hand through my hair as if I could claw it out—both it and the memory of Cillian's stare, of all the questions in his eyes that I had no answers for.

My pacing came to an abrupt halt as the front door swung open.

Dravyn stormed inside, still looking ready to burn something down.

The heat surrounding him fueled my own growing fury with the situation, and I did nothing to try and calm the rising fire—anger was easier than trying to process what had happened.

I wanted to burn something down, too, all of sudden.

"You told me that I could come back here when I needed to," I snapped at Dravyn. "Not that you would be *stalking* me through that bracelet you gave me."

"I wasn't stalking you," he shot back. "The bracelet was meant to make sure you returned to me in one piece, which is what I told you. And it did as intended, didn't it?"

"Yes, but what else were you able to feel through it in the meantime? To see? To hear? Have you been tracking me all along?"

He didn't reply, and my blood boiled even hotter as I marched toward him. "I gave you my word that I would return, didn't I? Did you not trust that I would? Is that the *real* reason you gave the bracelet to me?"

"That's not the reason. I did trust you. Tonight I just…"

"You just *what*?"

His voice lowered. Still annoyingly calm compared to mine, but clearly frustrated. "Tonight I just needed to make sure you were okay."

My heart stuttered in my chest, and for a moment I feared it might never beat correctly again. When it finally fell back into a normal rhythm, I was even angrier than before. Because this was all wrong. This was not part of any plan or goal I'd set —this apparent concern he had for me.

"I was fine."

His gaze darted to my arm, and the air around us grew hotter as he muttered, "Yes, clearly you had everything under control."

"I didn't need you to interfere!" Pain spasmed through my injury, edging my tone toward wild, unhinged. "I don't know what you were thinking, but I never needed you to swoop in and save me. I don't need you to burn the world down for me —if I wanted that done, I could do it myself."

"I was only trying to help."

"I didn't want your help!" I practically roared. "I don't want *anything* from you and your stupid court! I wish you'd left me alone—I wish you'd left me alone on the very first day we met, when I was burning on that platform!"

The Serpent Goddess shuffled uncomfortably.

The Ice God cleared his throat.

Dravyn shot them both a pointed look. "Leave us," he said.

Valas looked all too eager to go. Mairu hesitated, her hands clutched over her heart as she regarded me with pained uncertainty in her golden eyes, but she didn't resist when Valas grabbed her arm and pulled her out of the room.

Dravyn stared at the door they'd left through for a long moment before turning to me.

Neither of us spoke right away.

Why don't you leave with them? I wanted to scream at him.

But I didn't scream. I wanted him to go. I wanted him to stay. I wanted to be by myself, but I didn't want to be left alone with all the thoughts in my head, so I just stood there, feeling foolish about my outburst and everything else.

I didn't speak.

Couldn't speak.

The pain in my arm throbbed again. I wanted to rip it off and be done with it. I wanted to be done with *all* of this.

Another throb. The violent pounding of my pulse seemed to be making it worse. I turned away from Dravyn, trying to calm down, but it was useless. And just as my gasp of pain had caught his attention in the world below, one slipping from my lips drew his gaze now; I could feel his eyes following me even as I tried to ignore him.

"You should have let me kill the bastard," he snarled.

"It would only have caused more trouble."

"Do you think I'm concerned about such things?"

I didn't answer his question, my eyes lifting to the high ceiling as I steadied myself through another wave of pain. "He's never done anything like this before."

"If he did it once, he'll do it again."

"You have no idea what he's done for me, all the—"

"What he's done for you?"

"Yes."

"Does he remind you of those things often?"

I couldn't deny this.

His eyes narrowed. "So it sounds more like he did those things for *him*, in hopes of locking you into some sort of contract with unspecified terms."

I slowly lowered my gaze. I was too furious to speak right away—whether at myself or him, I wasn't sure.

"Get away from me," I hissed.

"Gladly," he replied. Yet he didn't move.

So I moved myself, relocating to one of the sitting rooms down the hall. There was no shortage of squishy, comfortable furniture in this room, but I opted for the cool solidness of the marble floor, collapsing next to the fireplace and dragging myself over to the nearest wall so I had something to brace myself against.

Dravyn followed moments later, and, without a word, he kindled a fire with only a slight flex of his fingers.

He left me alone with the crackling blaze for at least an hour.

I was disassociating, slipping into some blissful realm outside of my mind, when I heard him moving by the hearth, tending to the flames that had nearly gone out by this point.

"The tonic Mai gave you for the pain...is it helping?" His voice was an odd combination of sharp and soft, hardened steel tempered by concern.

I lifted my splinted arm, testing it for myself, and couldn't help wincing at the movement.

This was enough of an answer. He disappeared again, muttering about speaking to his servants—presumably about other remedies that might be more effective.

He returned to my side some time later and slumped down against the wall beside me. I didn't resist his closeness; there was something oddly comforting in his choice to meet me there on the floor, rather than to pick me up and try to carry me away from my misery.

All of my fight and fire had gone out by this point. He sensed this, I think, and didn't try to rekindle our argument. We sat silently in the wreckage of the day, like two equally lost souls, staring into the fire together.

At some point, I let myself fall more fully into the ruins with him, leaning my head onto his shoulder.

His arm moved, circling around me, gathering me carefully against his chest. I heard the same chorus of voices in my head as I had the last time we'd been so close.

Traitor, traitor, traitor.

Fainter now, but still clear, and now another insult joined it—

Coward, coward, coward.

I stayed in my traitorous, cowardly position because I felt too weak, too broken to move, to even hold my head up.

Another half hour passed. Dravyn and I still didn't speak. I started to doze off, sliding down until my head rested on his thigh. It was too muscular to make for a very comfortable pillow, but I was so exhausted I didn't care. I shut my eyes and sank into that exhaustion, concentrating not on the weight of all that had happened, but on the weight of his arm resting against my back.

At some point I was startled awake by the sound of ruffling feathers, scraping claws, and a sudden burst of heat that was soon followed by Dravyn's low voice—

"Not now, Ramoth."

I blinked my eyes open to the sight of him calming the flames around the ignited griffin with a wave of his hand.

"He really does have a bad habit of doing that at the worst moments, doesn't he?" I mumbled.

Moth gave a high-pitched squawk before dropping and rolling dramatically around on the floor, putting out the last bits of fire clinging to him.

"He gets that flaw from me, I suppose." Dravyn's voice was soft, more to himself than me. "I nearly ignited myself earlier. It's been a long time since I let emotions get the better of me, as they so often do for him, but..."

I sat up. The memory of my two worlds colliding, of his power rising in the courtyard of my home, threatening to engulf it, sent a fresh surge of fear and anger through me, making my next words come out sounding defensive and harsh. "Is that what happened with all the villages and people you allegedly destroyed after your ascension? Did your emotions get the better of you then, too?"

"Yes."

My breath caught. All the angry words I'd planned to say became dust in my throat, turning it unbearably dry. I hadn't expected him to admit to my accusations so readily. "So what I've read and heard about you is true. All the stories of the destruction and death you brought upon the mortal realm..."

He looked toward Moth as he quietly replied, "As I said, we are both flawed creatures."

"So flawed that perhaps you aren't in any place to pass judgment on any of the things my fellow elves have done, whether tonight or otherwise."

His gaze took mine again. We stared at one another, deeply and unflinchingly, a thousand unspoken things passing between us in the span of only breaths.

"Perhaps not," he said.

Mine was a flimsy argument—his offenses did not excuse Andrel's offenses, and I knew it. We both knew it. I was simply grasping at broken pieces, trying to convince myself that something of my old world and beliefs was still salvageable. I was not ready to admit that there was a chance I'd been wrong about who the greatest villain in my story was, even though the thought had certainly made its way across my mind.

My heart felt as if it was splintering, the jagged pieces of it sharp and piercing through my chest.

How had I ended up in this place?

Here, where I'd fallen asleep with my head in the lap of my sworn enemy. He was still the same enemy. He'd just casually *admitted* to some of the villainous, horrifying things I'd always suspected him of doing, and I was still holding tight to the hatred I felt over those things. We were both still the same. He had not hurt me personally, but he'd hurt plenty of others. I knew he was not safe. Not any better than the things that had broken me tonight, no matter how gently he'd been holding me.

Yet, tonight...tonight it felt like all of us were devils, and I just didn't want to be alone in this hell.

I thought I might vomit from the confusion. Or maybe it was the pain in my arm making me sick. Whatever the reason, I doubled over, holding my stomach as I felt bile rising in the back of my throat. I choked it back down, turning it into a cough that gave way to a whimper, and Dravyn shifted restlessly beside me.

"I am calling in that favor the God of Healing owes me," he said. "Be angry about it if you'd like. I don't care. I will not watch you suffer any more tonight."

I gave a barely perceptible nod, leaning back against the wall as he got to his feet.

Everything that happened next blurred together. There were servants. Whispers. Movement. I felt pressure, a pulling at my clothing and hair, and somehow I ended up in my room, in my bed, with a clean night dress draped over my aching body.

At some point, I opened my eyes and saw a divine being approaching me. He was dark-skinned, with eyes the color of daffodils, and faint halos of light surrounded his head and his hands. Shining gold and white ribbons twisted around him as he moved. Whether they were a part of his magic or his physical form, I didn't know; I couldn't tell with my blurry vision.

I heard his voice—a crisp breeze breaking through the oppressive heat of late summer—but the only part of his introduction I caught was his name. *Armaros.* I held to that name like it was the last rope tethering me to existence. I could almost sense the nightmares waiting for me to let go of it, crouched like beasts in the shadows, preparing to pounce.

Every time I blinked, they drew closer.

It continued like this throughout the night: The God of Healing was there when I opened my eyes, golden and bright, his magic weaving around me and soothing away the pain. But when I closed my eyes, it was nightmarish fire that met me— the same scene I'd dreamt of before, of Dravyn and me surrounded by flames, glass rain falling all around us.

Back and forth the images went, healing and heat all twisting more tightly together with every flutter of my eyelids until I could no longer tell what was saving me and what was destroying me.

CHAPTER 34

A week passed, and, with the help of the Healing Marr's magic, I was finally no longer in pain. Physically speaking, anyway.

Dravyn avoided me for most of the week, aside from occasional check-ins to make certain I was still recovering. I didn't go out of my way to see him, either. It was a strange sort of dance we did, moving through the palace, fully aware of and bound more completely than ever to one another, yet avoiding even the simplest bit of eye contact.

Even though we barely spoke, I couldn't stop thinking about what had happened on the night of my return—replaying the images of his fires surrounding me, his arms wrapping around me. Protecting me.

He was giving me space so I could heal without the complications of whatever feelings we had toward one another, I knew.

But as the days went by, an emptiness yawned ever wider in my chest—like my heart was clearing room for someone who never arrived—and I was forced to admit to myself that *space* was not what I really wanted most.

More than that, I wanted *him*.

It was different from the sparks of desire I'd felt when he'd kissed me. Deeper. More and more I found myself simply wanting to talk to him, wishing he'd linger longer when he came to check on me. Thinking of the mere possibility of these things brought me comfort, and I guess I was desperate for comfort after my disastrous trip home—even if it came with a side of guilt.

Meanwhile, the knife Cillian had given me remained close by. Buried in the closet of my room. Just waiting for me to test it.

To see what divine things I could kill with it.

Its blade had shifted to black—I assumed upon its exposure to this realm's magic—and it hadn't changed back. It hummed with a restless energy most of the time, too. Soft and subtle, but even as deeply as I'd buried it, my sensitive ears still picked up the noise when I was trying to sleep at night. Or I imagined it making noise, at least, because I was so paranoid it was going to be found.

Needless to say, I slept very little.

My nights were filled with visions of fire and knives and poison, while my days were marred by a haziness I wasn't used to feeling. I was usually so rigid, so organized, so good at outlining my goals and ideas...but how could I continue making the same plans as before?

Because Dravyn is only one god of many, was my mind's stubborn answer to that. *It isn't about him. It's what he represents—and what he represents killed your sister and threatens the very future of all your kind.*

As the second week after my return began, I woke with all of these thoughts already loud and tumbling through my head.

I ate a quick breakfast, alone in my room, before heading out for fresh air. As I stepped outside, I immediately looked up, shivers shooting down my spine as I did. Though the sky was clear, I still pictured black shadows spilling over the brightness—an image that was hard to unsee. To un*feel*.

The God of the Shade had not returned since his last harrowing visit, but it would only be a matter of time before he did. He was the one who would be responsible for my last trial, after all—though he apparently wasn't as restless and eager to get on with things as the Marr beneath him were.

I could only guess at the reason behind the delay, but—whatever the reason—I was grateful to have more time to figure out what my next moves would be.

I was meandering around the vast palace grounds, trying to commit to even *one* definite, precise next step, when I caught sight of one of the selakir—those golden, horse-like creatures I'd first seen weeks ago. It was galloping at full speed toward the palace, pale ribbons of fire trailing out behind it as it flew.

I watched as it disappeared behind the palace, hurtling into a fenced-in area that I was fairly certain was a dead-end. Curious about what was drawing such a wild creature in, I followed the flower-lined stone path that ran along the palace's edge, pausing at the corner and peering into the back yard.

At the end of the path, some ten feet ahead, several more of the selakir were gathered around Dravyn. He was busy brushing down one of the largest of the herd, making it gleam like polished gold.

Up close, I realized just how massive the beasts were; even the smallest ones were as large as the largest horses back home. Though they still reminded me of horses, even from here, there were subtle differences; the longer, leaner bodies; the small, antler-like appendages; the cloven hooves. And the color, of course. *Gold* seemed an inadequate name for all the different shades their coats shimmered between.

I was so mesmerized by the creatures that several minutes passed—easily the longest amount of time I'd spent near Dravyn for the past week.

"I was beginning to wonder if we'd ever share another space for more than a few seconds," he finally commented, his eyes on his fingers, which were busy untangling strands of silky white mane. "Seems one of us is always running the other direction here lately."

"I haven't been running away from anything." A week's worth of frustration and uncertainty made my tone sharper than normal.

He regarded me with a frown. "Put your daggers away, my Sparrow. You're not on trial at the moment. And everything I do and say is not meant to start an argument with you."

He went back to tending to the golden beast.

I stood watching him for a while longer, trying to decide what to do next. What to say. I didn't want to keep avoiding him. I didn't really want to fight, either—I just wasn't sure what I was supposed to do instead.

His words had plucked a long-buried truth from the dark and guarded places of my heart, and since I didn't know what else to say, I quietly admitted this truth to him: "I don't know how to put them away."

He stopped mid-brushstroke and looked over at me.

"What I mean to say is it's just...it's a habit. Always being prepared to fight." I slowly walked closer, gaze circling around, noting each of the six selakir who'd gathered here. Most of the beasts watched me with indifference—though the smallest one did take a few cautious steps after me as I passed it, lifting its long nose and inhaling my scent.

Its shining black eyes met mine, and I stared into them even as I continued to explain myself to Dravyn. "I feel like I've been holding my breath for a long time. For the past five years, at least—just waiting for the next attack against me and my kind. I don't know how to put down my weapons and stop fighting. I don't think I know who I am outside of the fight."

After a moment of considering this, he said, "The past five years?"

I hesitated.

The selakir I'd been staring at pranced closer, and I tentatively reached out a hand and let it examine me more closely. Its breath was hot against my skin—almost burning. I wouldn't have been surprised to learn it could breathe fire. Luckily, it didn't seem to be in the mood to do so at the moment; its silky tail swished—wagging like a dog's—and its nose shoved and snorted against my arm, the playful force of it almost knocking me over.

Something about the creature's accepting nudges gave me the courage to keep speaking. "My sister... she died a little over five years ago. I'm the one who found her blood-covered room. And the dead veilhound at our house weeks before—a harbinger of her death, I think. Even before that, I was always on guard. We were once one of the most powerful elven houses in Avalinth, and both my father and sister were leaders in the movement to try and restore that power. So we had no shortage of enemies."

Thinking of all those enemies—and all the violent, close calls I'd had throughout my childhood—I had to pause and take a deep, bracing breath before continuing.

"They were always heading off on missions to try and

undermine the rising human leaders and the gods those humans now worship. And I wanted to be with them, so I followed them as much as I could as I got older."

Dravyn was quiet for another long moment, then asked, "You wanted to be with them?"

"Of course."

"But did you want to be *like* them?"

The question felt like another chisel carving away at the protective walls I'd erected around my heart. It took everything in me not to recoil, to answer it honestly.

"I'm not sure. I never really felt like Savna. Though when she died, I...." I trailed off, absently running my hands along the selakir's smooth coat. *"Put down your daggers*, you said. But honestly, sometimes I'm not sure if the blades I'm carrying are hers or mine. And if they're hers, I feel like I..."

Like I can't put them down.

I couldn't bring myself to admit to this final part out loud, for some reason. I closed my eyes against the memories flooding me and tried to choke down the emotion bubbling up in my chest. I'd broken down enough over the past week. I was determined not to do it now. I clenched my fingers more deeply into the selakir's side than I meant to, trying to steady myself against it, and the creature gave a snort and stomped off, leaving a few golden threads of its coat in my palm as it pulled away.

Dravyn made a sharp clicking sound with his tongue, and the disgruntled selakir trotted over to him. He worked on soothing it for a minute before he said, "Sometimes we hold on to painful things, I think, because letting them go feels like letting go of the person who gave them to us."

I lifted my gaze from the flowers I'd been studying, and I was surprised to find him staring back at me with a look that bordered on gentle—an expression I didn't recall ever seeing in his eyes before. It was hard to believe these were the same eyes I'd recently witnessed burning with hellish, terrifying fire.

"Right," I said, softly. "And because sometimes it's all we have left of that person."

The moment stretched into a thoughtful silence. I knelt to more closely study the flowers—the scarlet-tinged, crisscrossing patterns on them were fascinating—while he continued to tend to the herd of his created beasts.

"The veilhound..." he began after a few minutes, "that's the real reason you ended up in the Death Marr's territory weeks ago, isn't it? You believed that creature foreshadowed your sister's death. You wanted to find out the truth about it, and what happened to her."

I picked one of the flowers and started plucking its petals off, one by one. "She was the only family I had left. My mother is alive, as far as I know, but she left me and my sister alone a long time ago. My father died several years before Savna did."

"And that elven male I...*spoke* with in your realm..." The air turned sweltering, hot enough to make the flowers around me start to droop.

"Andrel."

"Yes. Him." He turned his attention toward something in the distance, staring silently at it until the space around us cooled once more. "He took you in after your sister's death, I presume."

"Yes. Along with Cillian, who was my sister's best friend. The two of them both live in the mansion that once housed Andrel's family, along with various others over the years."

"So when you offered to become a part of my court," he said after a pause, "was this all so you could come here and find out what happened to your sister? And perhaps your father, too?" His eyes took mine, still gentle as they pleaded for sincerity.

For a brief, weak moment, I considered telling him everything.

My plans, my fury, my fears. All about the knife and the poison and the wars I was carrying. I wanted to come clean, to lay out everything before him even though I still didn't fully understand *why*.

But all I said was, "Yes."

"I should have known." He gave an amused snort. "You didn't exactly strike me as someone eager to become a divine servant."

Silence settled between us again, less easy than before. One of the selakir grew suddenly restless, bucking wildly and then bolting toward the distant hills. Several others followed it, until only two remained—the one Dravyn had initially been brushing, and the small one I'd tried to befriend.

"Are you going to cast me out for lying to you?" I asked, quietly. "Or kill me? Or smite me...or whatever it is you gods do when you've had enough of an untrustworthy mortal meddling in your business?"

"Smite you?" Dravyn laughed a quiet, humorless laugh. "No, Sparrow. I am not going to smite you. I'm not in the mood today."

"But maybe you will be tomorrow?"

"We'll see."

I tried to return his smile but couldn't manage it. Hugging my arms around my middle, watching the selakir turning to tiny gold dots in the distance, I said, "So on to the next trial then, I suppose."

He didn't reply. I looked over to see that his smile had

faded and his eyes had turned distant; I got the impression he was keeping a myriad of thoughts and concerns from me.

I started to ask him about those concerns when the smaller of the remaining selakir interrupted us, abruptly deciding it was interested in me again, nudging its slender head up under my arm and nearly lifting me off my feet. With a startled giggle, I took hold of its head and gently held it at a distance.

"Zell'thas," Dravyn informed me. "Or just Zell, if you prefer. And he likes to bite, so watch your hands."

I carefully slid my hands away from his mouth, giving his chest a gentle rub instead. "Hello, Zell."

"And this is Farak," he added, stroking the back of the larger beast.

I studied their anatomy more closely, memorizing each powerful line and curve so I could make a proper drawing of them as soon as I returned to my room. "Can you ride them?"

"I can, and I occasionally do. Some are more tame than the others. Farak here is probably the tamest."

I stepped closer to Farak, craning my neck so I could take in his full body, trying to imagine how sitting upon his back would compare to sitting on a horse. I froze when I heard Dravyn softly chuckling.

"What are you laughing about?"

"You have the look on your face."

"What look?"

"When you're curious about something, your forehead gets a very deep groove." He pointed to his own forehead, trying to mimic it. "And your lips part, as if you're trying to inhale it all in, in every way possible."

I tilted my face away from him, blushing.

"You don't have to hide it. I like that look on you."

I kept my eyes averted, focused on Farak. "I've often been

told I'm too curious for my own good." I didn't mention the person who most often told me that; Dravyn and I were actually talking again—actually getting along—and I didn't want to ruin the conversation by mentioning Andrel's name.

"Better too curious than willingly ignorant," Dravyn said. He considered me for a moment, then said, "Wait here. I'll grab some tack, and you can learn firsthand." He rushed off before I could question this plan.

So I waited, running my hands over the nervous bumps that had erupted along my skin. Farak stood stoically by my side, like a seasoned warhorse, while Zell galloped circles around the yard, occasionally leaping into the air and giving a wild, carefree kick.

Dravyn returned a short time later with the promised equipment—though it was only enough for a single rider, I noticed.

I frowned as he hoisted the saddle onto Farak's back. "Only one?"

"I'll teach you to ride on your own in time, but it would be irresponsible to let you immediately jump on the back of one of these creatures. So for now, I'm afraid you're stuck with me."

"I know how to ride a horse. I'm quite skilled at it, actually."

"But these are not horses," he said as he slipped the head-gear on and adjusted it. "They answer only to their creator—which would be me—and even then, only just. Even the tamest among them still have a deadly wild streak no matter how hard I try to work it out of them."

"More flawed creations of yours?" I mused.

"Indeed." He gave a wistful smile as Zell trotted over to us, tossing his head. "And yet I keep trying."

"Moth and I get along well enough," I reminded him. "I'm not afraid to try my luck with another of your failed designs. Zell seems to like me."

"The last time I tried to ride him, he nearly bit my foot off."

The selakir in question gave a loud, playful whinny, as if proud of his near-accomplishment. I caught a flash of teeth that were distinctly *not* horse-like—there were at least two rows of serrated fangs. I couldn't help but gasp at the sight, which drew a smug, victorious grin from Dravyn.

"...Fine," I mumbled as he knelt and offered me a hand up.

He boosted me easily upward with only the strength of one arm, holding Farak steady with the other, and then he hauled himself up just as effortlessly.

Farak seemed even larger from above. The distance to the ground was dizzying, and I quickly decided I'd made the right choice by agreeing to a tandem ride. Dravyn settled in behind me, pressing against my back as he reached around for the reins. The feel of his strength wrapping around my body was reassuring—though it sent a very different kind of nervousness rolling through me.

"Make sure you stay relaxed. They're very sensitive to any strong emotions, much like Moth." His tone was low and teasing, and though I couldn't see it, I suspected a wicked grin was spreading across his face. "Don't want them getting too aroused."

I released a slow breath before I replied, trying my best to sound unaffected. "Will they burst into flames as Moth does when he gets overly aroused?"

"I've never witnessed such a thing. Normally they just throw their riders, attempt to rip them apart with their teeth, or stomp their heads in...Valas was kicked in the head by one a few years ago; I think that's part of his problem."

"Oh good—that all sounds *much* better than being incinerated."

He laughed, the sound rich and rumbling against my back as he pressed closer.

Then we were off, launching so quickly into motion it took my breath away.

CHAPTER 35

I WAS A COWARD FOR THE FIRST FEW MINUTES OF OUR ride, afraid I might lose my balance—or my breakfast—if I tried to watch the scenery flying by us.

But my curiosity eventually won out, as it usually did; I peeked one eye open, then the other, and for a moment I was so stunned I forgot to breathe.

We were moving so quickly I couldn't make out distinct landmarks. I just knew it was beautiful—the colors of Dravyn's territory all swirling together—dark earth, occasional bright cracks of molten rock, hills of silver-green grass dotted with flowers. The air held a subtle scent of smoke, but there was also a hint of spice that grew more predominant as we made our way deeper into the wilds, farther away from the palace. The wind blowing through my hair—pulling it loose from the crown of braids I'd put it in—was warm, invigorating, sending pleasant shivers across my scalp and down my spine.

Several of the selakir herd had rejoined us. They raced alongside Farak, weaving in and out of our path, golden bodies flashing like shooting stars across the dark landscape. They left magic in their wake, sparks of red and orange that occasionally blossomed into brief, brilliant displays of fire that made me gasp every time.

Faster and faster we went, leaping over rocks and bushes and small streams of silver-white water. With every leap, I kept expecting the selakir to sprout wings and just keep going, maybe all the way to the upper-heavens above.

They never did—but after several miles the rest of the herd did pull ahead of us, and I lost sight of them against the distant horizon, their bodies blending into the pale-yellow sky.

Farak slowed to a trot once we were alone, and Dravyn offered me the reins.

I hesitated, but he insisted.

"Now that we've gotten some of the excess energy out of him, he should be easier to manage. Go on. Lead us wherever you'd like to go."

Farak tossed his head and gave an uncertain snort as I took over. But I found my courage, correctly positioning my hands on the reins and shifting so my legs could better squeeze and signal, and he settled quickly.

The selakir's gait felt much smoother than a horse's, and he behaved in much the same way as the mounts I was used to riding back home. This, combined with the way we were now moving slower, left little to distract me from the feel of the god pressing against me.

Dravyn's arms circled lightly around my waist. A casual, securing hold, but with each passing moment it felt heavier. Hotter. I was hyperaware of every inch of him shifting against me as we traversed uneven ground. Of every warm breath against the back of my neck. Every beat of his heart and flex of his muscles.

I tried to direct my attention to where I wanted to go, as he'd suggested, and not all the things I suddenly wanted to *do*.

After cantering along for another mile or so, something caught my eye—a small grouping of trees with leaves in what appeared to be every shade of blue and green in existence.

I guided Farak toward it. As we passed into the grove, the air cooled somewhat, and our surroundings grew dimmer, the forge-light's glow muted by thick foliage. Some of the darkness was offset by floating wisps of fire; a closer look revealed these wisps were actually insects similar to the fireflies of the mortal realm.

The wisps shined brighter, and the trees stretched taller, the deeper we went. Drawing Farak to a stop, I leaned back, marveling at the towering, colorful circle of branches overhead.

Dravyn sucked in a breath as I reclined into him, his hands sliding lower, following a natural path toward my inner thighs. He realized what he was doing and started to pull them back, but I reflexively pressed my hands over his and held him in place. For balance.

Mostly for balance.

The motion made him chuckle. He buried his face against my hair, breathing in my scent, nose and lips grazing the side of my neck. "Did you forget what I said about not becoming too aroused?"

"Did *you*?"

"I'm perfectly in control of my arousal, thank you." His hands moved beneath my palms, and I wondered—for the span of a shaky breath—what it might be like to make him lose that control.

"In control for now," I mumbled.

"Yes." His fingers massaged my thighs, moving closer to the center of them but stopping just short of stroking the sensitive spot at their apex—a demonstration of the *control* he touted. His mouth dipped closer to my ear as he said, "But we'll see what happens later, I suppose."

Farak stomped his feet and tossed his head.

Twisting around to face Dravyn, I cleared my throat and asked, "Help me down?"

He obliged with an unapologetically sinful smile, eyes dancing with thoughts I only dared to guess at.

As my boots hit the ground, I handed the reins back to Dravyn and then quickly put space between us, trying to give my thoughts a chance to clear.

The little bit of daylight penetrating the trees caught on the leaves in a breathtaking way, filtering through and making the colors of them shine more boldly. I ran my fingers along one and found it surprisingly hard.

"These leaves remind me of your glass art," I told Dravyn. "So thin, but strong, and the way they reflect the light..." I zigzagged in and out of the trees, gathering up the brightest of the fallen leaves and noting their textures, their colors, their shapes.

When I looked back at Dravyn a few minutes later, I found him watching me as though I was the only thing in the world just then—in this realm or otherwise.

A shiver skipped through me as I let the leaves fall and straightened back to my full height. My mind had felt clearer with the space between us...but all it took was one glance in his direction and every thought of him—all the frustrating, forbidden, confusing thoughts—came flooding back. All my attempts to turn away again, to find something else to distract myself with, were useless. This forest was full of indescribably beautiful things...

But nothing compared to the beauty of the god staring at me now.

And—for the moment, at least—I was tired of pretending otherwise.

Slowly, I stepped back to him. His gaze trailed over me as I came, the aching, sweeping look as intimate as any touch.

I stopped directly in front of him, peering up from under my lashes as I said, "You know, I don't think you're as in control as you claim."

He reached out and gathered a fistful of my shirt, dragging me the final few inches to his chest. His fingers remained clenched in the fabric, holding me in place, and his voice was quiet but frayed, teetering on the edge of losing restraint, as he replied.

"I will admit you test that control like no one I've ever met."

I felt a smile curving my lips.

His mouth crashed against it an instant later.

It didn't end there, this time—not as the soft, hesitant brush of lips we'd shared before. This time it was deeper, darker, as wild as the woods surrounding us. He took my bottom lip between his teeth. Not hard enough to hurt, but hard enough to make me feel like he intended to leave a mark, to claim my mouth and all the rest of me as his own.

The thought of being branded in such a way drew a soft moan through my lips.

He responded by bringing his other hand up and threading it through my hair, pulling me deeper into the kiss until I was breathless and forced to draw back for air.

"This is a bad idea," I gasped into his mouth.

"For so many reasons," he agreed, and kissed me again.

I wrapped my arms around his neck, clinging tightly, but

the force of his kisses still sent me staggering backward over the uneven ground. He solved this by guiding me toward the closest tree, pinning me against the smooth bark. With my tiptoes balanced on a thick root, I was taller than him, putting my breasts almost level with his mouth. His hand curved around one, massaging it, reveling in the weight of it as he pressed closer to me.

"I thought you were driving me mad when we were spending hours together in the palace," he growled. "This past week has somehow been worse—even though we've hardly spoken." His thumb stroked the peak of my breast, and even through the layers of my shirt and camisole, my nipple reacted, stiffening and rising to meet his touch. "Every time you saw me and turned the other way, I wanted to chase you down and pin you against the nearest wall, just like this."

"But you didn't."

He gave my hardened peak a teasing pinch. "I knew you'd come to me yourself. Eventually."

"Such arrogance."

"I thought you'd be used to it by now."

"Just waiting for me..." I gave another slight smile. "Like a lazy beast hoping his prey stumbles in to be killed."

Another pinch of my nipple sent a shock of pleasure deep into my belly.

"Or am I just a patient beast?" he suggested. "A clever one?"

"You're very good at complimenting yourself."

"One of my more underrated skills."

"Do I want to know what your higher-rated ones are?"

"Would you like me to show you?"

My lips parted at his offer, but no reply made it out.

He kissed me again, soft and slow and lingering this time.

His eyes locked on mine when he finally drew away, and they stayed locked on them even as he took hold of my hand and drew it up to his mouth, pressing his lips to my knuckles before moving to the flame he'd marked on my wrist. He kissed that mark before lacing our fingers and pulling us closer together, tilting his face toward mine as he said, "There are so many things I could show you, Little Sparrow."

Need throbbed through me. My body was opening for him even as I tried to keep myself closed off.

I was so *desperately* trying to close myself off.

Because there would be no going back from this. I felt like I was standing on a shoreline waiting for a tidal wave to crash over me; I could rebuild what it destroyed, but I'd never fully recover from the things I wanted to do with him in this glittering forest.

I cupped his face, fingers trembling against his strong jaw, heart threatening to pound out of my chest.

As I stretched up to meet his lips with mine, a sudden darkness overtook us, blocking out the dim light from above. It came and went so quickly I thought I'd imagined it.

Hoped I had.

But Dravyn's gaze tracked upward, and his hands stopped their teasing and roaming and came to rest in a strong grip on my hips.

"What was that?" I asked.

He was too focused to answer right away.

A foreboding wind swirled. The trees rattled around us, and Dravyn finally, reluctantly took a step away from me and answered my question. "Foreign company."

"Marr from other courts, you mean?"

He nodded.

"Should we go back to the palace?"

He considered the question for a long moment, his eyes still watching the little glimmers of sky visible through the thick trees. "Maybe."

He called Farak over to us, helped me into the saddle as before, and we set off without another word.

We galloped in silence for several minutes. His body wrapped around me in a way that now felt more protective than teasing, pressing close enough that the tension in his muscles seeped into my own.

It scared me.

I was so busy trying to watch the sky and our other surroundings for threats that I didn't realize, at first, that we seemed to be taking a completely different route than earlier.

"This isn't the way back to the palace, is it?"

"There's one more place I wanted to go before we went back."

He seemed like he was trying to find excuses not to return, which made me even more nervous.

"Should I be concerned?" I asked, jokingly, in an attempt to lighten the mood. "You really *did* intend to smite me, didn't you? But you're stealing me away to some even more remote corner of your territory to do it."

I felt his chest vibrate with a suppressed laugh. "You've caught on to me. Nothing gets by you, does it?" He pressed a kiss to my ear with the words, and I shivered.

We raced onward, climbing a steep hill and reaching a relatively flat meadow at the top. Far on the other side of it, across a swaying expanse of flower-dotted grass, I spotted two jagged, crystalline structures rising like miniature mountains toward the sky.

We rode toward them, our pace gradually slowing as we approached.

As we eased into a trot, I tried to think of another joking comment, but my mind was racing with too many questions, wondering about the other courts and all the other trouble that seemed to be building around us.

"You know, most of my kind believe you did steal me away," I said, wincing as I remembered the uncomfortable conversation I'd shared with Cillian.

"It did look that way, I suppose."

"And many of them think I'm a fool for willingly offering myself up as a slave to the Marr."

He stiffened a bit. "The Miratar spirits are not slaves. They have free will, same as you and me."

"But it's a hierarchy, correct? The Marr are always more powerful than the lesser divine spirits who serve them."

I don't know why I found myself curious about how it all truly worked—though gathering information was never a bad idea, in my opinion.

He shrugged. "The Marr has most of the say in how much power the ascendant in question receives—partly because it requires giving up some of their own power to make the ascension happen. So it's a much deeper bond than master and slave...more like, the Miratar becomes an extension of them. It's kind of hard to explain, and it's not an exact magic."

I pondered this as we came to a stop. "Does it ever...fail? The intended ascension, I mean."

He slid off Farak's back and offered me a hand. "Are you worried something might go wrong because of your elvish blood?"

"Something like that."

In truth, a potential idea had just occurred to me—how I *wanted* this all to fail at the last moment. I could survive my last trial, make it to the Tower of Ascension, gather what I needed from the tower as Cillian had asked me to do, and then the magic simply wouldn't work.

I wouldn't have really *failed* at that point, so maybe…

"I don't know all the details of what will happen, to be honest," Dravyn said. "But I suspect the gods above us do. The one I serve wouldn't have let your trials continue if he didn't."

I hugged my arms around myself, not wanting to think about what that upper-god might have seen or planned for me. I'd heard too many stories of the Moraki's nefarious scheming.

My eyes darted toward the sky as they so often had this past week.

Still no shadows streaking across it, but my body remained tense. "I keep expecting him to pay us another visit."

"You can relax for the moment," Dravyn said. "It won't happen here; the last trial will take place in the Tower of Ascension itself. You'll be granted access to it through the two relics you've earned from the two courts thus far. But you don't have to go there until you're ready for it—I've persuaded him to give us that much of an advantage, at least."

Persuaded him?

Protecting me again. Even while I stood there, trying to think of a way to steal from his realm and run away without regard to the damage I might do to him.

I felt sick to my stomach.

"So where exactly is *here*?" I asked, trying to change the subject, stepping toward the crystal structures to study them closer.

"It's my truth for a truth," he said after a slight hesitation.

I tossed him a curious look over my shoulder.

"You told me about your sister earlier, so I thought I would show you these."

Curiosity burning hotter, I circled the structures, tracing

the ridges of pale blue crystal, noting all the places where the forgelight caught and sparkled. "You made them, I'm sure."

"Yes."

"Two almost identical towers..."

"One for each of my siblings."

I froze with my hand against a sharp edge of crystal. "You had three siblings, I thought?"

"The oldest one still lives."

Understanding took a heavy grip on my heart. "You mean...these are more memorials, then?" I asked, softly. "To go with the glass gardens?"

A long time passed before he looked my way—at my hand still braced against the crystal, not my face—and said, "I tried to save them. I heard their screams, and I was one of the first to their rooms that night. My younger brother was dead when we found him. My sister, she..." He drew in a deep breath and closed his eyes for a moment before continuing in a practiced, steady voice. "She died in my arms while I was rushing her toward help. It was a blade laced with a quick-acting poison, in both cases."

"Dravyn, I...I'm sorry."

I didn't know what else to say.

Years of people telling me they were sorry about my sister had taught me that there really *was* nothing you could say— nothing that really made the pain go away. It was all just slapping a too-small bandage on a too-large wound, and it did little to heal the hurt festering deeply underneath.

"We had the antidote," he continued, voice so quiet it was nearly swept away in the gentle breeze whistling through the grass. "The most talented healer in our whole damn kingdom was employed by our very palace. If I could have gotten to her faster, my sister might have lived."

"It wasn't your fault," I said—more useless words people had also said to me. They were much easier to believe when you were the one saying them rather than receiving them.

He took another deep, bracing breath and nodded to acknowledge my words, but otherwise he didn't reply. He turned to Farak, instead, and busied himself with adjusting the saddle's straps and the bags attached to it.

I left him alone for a few minutes, gathering up flowers from the meadow and arranging them at the base of each monument. A question wormed its way into my thoughts as I worked. I wasn't sure I wanted to know the answer, but I couldn't seem to shake it.

"The third garden I asked about..." I began, gently. "Who was that for?"

He was staring at one of the flower piles I'd created, his eyes glassed over in thought.

"Dravyn?"

"You wanted to know about my ascension. Why I did it, and what happened in the days following it. And the truth is not far from whatever terrible stories you've heard, I imagine. Because the truth..." He finally lifted his gaze and met mine. "Is that I became the God of Fire because I wanted to burn it all down. The ones who had sent those assassins after my family. Every person those killers loved, every home they had ever had —*all of it*." His fists clenched and his eyes flashed briefly with their wild, fiery glow. "And so I did."

I straightened and took an uncertain step back, bracing a hand against the crystal behind me.

Dravyn blinked once, twice, and the wild glow faded from his gaze. "The God of the Shade came to me after the funeral. He offered me the greatest power imaginable at my weakest point imaginable, and I...I did not hesitate to take it."

"So the garden, those markers..."

"There are two-hundred and thirty-two graves marked by the glass in that garden," he said, confirming my worst fear. "Those are the ones whose bodies were actually found—the ones who didn't burn entirely to ash."

His gaze still held mine. We couldn't seem to look away from one another.

"Ederis," he said. "That was the largest of the towns I destroyed beyond repair. The rumors said the assassins who targeted my family had hailed from there, so that was where I went first."

After a brief struggle, I finally found my voice. "Ederis was once a...a..."

"A predominantly elvish town."

I knew that town—it was often referred to in rallying speeches by my kind, held up as a prime example of why the gods were monsters. Speeches that never mentioned the poisonous blades or murders we committed beforehand, of course.

The sick feeling in my gut twisted tighter.

"Ederis was a rebellious stronghold prior to my ascension," Dravyn continued. "My family was not the first to be targeted by the extremists from that area. The upper-gods wanted the place dealt with. They offered me a chance at immortality if I proved capable of using the Fire magic granted to me, destroying what they wanted me to, and then reining my new powers in when they called me to do so. These terms...it all seemed like a fair deal at the time."

"Two-hundred and thirty-two," I repeated faintly.

He was silent for a long time.

"How could you do something like that?" I was trying—and failing miserably—to comprehend all the messy layers of him.

"I don't remember most of it. Not that it makes it any better, but I was not the god you see before you now when it happened. I was a...a monster. For that first year or so, I forgot I'd even been human."

My knees felt weak. I wanted to sink into the ground and just keep going, to fall back into my own realm, away from all my confusing thoughts and feelings.

I stared at my hands, eyes tracing the faint flame mark on my wrist, as I asked, "Why are you telling me all of this?"

"After everything we've been through now, it only felt...fair."

Fair.

Except the gods were not supposed to be fair, or truthful, or remorseful about...well, *anything*. They raged without cause or reason, and they certainly didn't build memorials to the things they slaughtered.

A corner of Dravyn's mouth rose, but his voice was entirely devoid of humor as he said, "Are you thinking of smiting *me* now? If only you could?"

I slowly shook my head.

It wasn't that simple, unfortunately.

"Nothing about you fits the mold I had in my mind," I said after a long pause. "And I just...I struggle when I can't map things out in a way that makes sense. When I can't follow a clean line from one point to another."

He considered this, then quietly said, "Fire rarely follows a clean line."

Yet another reason why this was all wrong. Why *we* were all wrong, and I should have stolen Farak, raced away from the murderous god before me, and dove into the nearest waterway to take me back to my own realm. I wasn't sure where I would go at this point, but I needed to go somewhere other than here.

So why didn't I want to move?

What a damn fool I'd become.

Instead of running, I asked, "Your siblings...what were their names?"

He looked momentarily stunned, as though he couldn't fathom why I wanted to know this in spite of everything else he'd just said.

"Sylas," he said. "And Elora."

I went back to the monuments for the two of them, kneeling once more at the base of each one and continuing to arrange the flowers I'd collected.

I asked him more questions as I worked, and I listened as he slowly opened up about this painful part of his past. How Sylas had been on his way to becoming an excellent swordsman and soldier, but how his heart had truly been in horsemanship and taking care of animals. How Elora had hated the pressures and expectations of court life, but still excelled at it all, and how she'd planned to go away to distant kingdoms and study at the most prestigious of institutions when she got older.

The more he told me, the more compelled I felt to rearrange the flowers in ways that seemed more fitting. I couldn't have explained it if he'd asked, but sometimes I just saw things in my mind in a certain way—certain people became certain patterns as I got to know them. Sylas was woven circles of silver grass with blue-flower centers. Elora was wavy lines of white clover with smatterings of bold purple blossoms.

It took some time, but I was eventually satisfied with the way the flowers represented these lost souls, and I finally managed to stop my obsessive rearranging.

"I haven't talked about this much," Dravyn said as I stood and dusted myself off. "Mai and Valas know, of course, but only the basic details. I've never spoken with anyone who..."

"Knows what it's like?"

He went very still, as if I'd just blinded him with a sudden flare of light.

"When I found the blood in my sister's bed," I said, voice wavering, "I wanted to burn the world down, too." I lifted my eyes to his. "Did it bring you any peace, destroying so much? Even for a moment?"

His reply was soft but without hesitation. "No."

I wasn't surprised. In the years since Savna's death, I'd more or less come to the conclusion that anger was a strange well to draw from; the more you drank of it, the thirstier you became.

I crushed a few spare flower petals in my hand, absently tearing them to pieces. "Do you think it's possible that our kind could ever reach a peace of some sort?"

He watched the crushed petals flutter from my palm, waiting until the last one hit the ground before he said, "I don't know."

I nodded. I'm not sure what I'd expected him to say. I hated speaking in hypotheticals, anyway. I preferred to stick to the facts, the absolutes—the things I could map, as I'd told him.

He seemed to be trying to map me out as well, frowning as he looked me over. "I haven't been entirely forthcoming with you about some other things, either. There's more you deserve to know."

"Other things?" I tried to put on a brave face, to find some scrap of a joke as I had earlier. "I might need a glass of wine if it's going to get worse than what you've already told me."

He returned my grim smile before nodding toward Farak. "Come on," he said. "We'll talk more back at the palace."

CHAPTER 36

THE RIDE BACK TO THE PALACE WAS SILENT AND contemplative.

As our destination came into view, another flash of power briefly dulled the forgelight's glow, sending chills crawling over my body. Farak started to rear up, but Dravyn quickly settled him, turning the beast in several circles until he stopped his uneasy tossing and trembling.

His gaze narrowed on the tallest of his palace's towers—where the familiar, circular meeting room awaited us—and his body rose and fell with a heavy sigh against me. "I was afraid they were heading here."

He kicked Farak back into a gallop before I could ask *who*?

We rode first to the small building that housed the tack we'd used. Zell was prancing around in the grass outside of it and gave a happy whinny at the sight of us, bounding over, sticking his long nose into the saddlebags, sniffing and snorting in search of something.

"He often hangs around here, hoping for treats," Dravyn said. He shooed him away, but then pulled a small container from one of the bags, took out a dried strip of some sort of pale red fruit, and tossed it to the expectant creature—who caught it in mid air with a terrifying snap of his sharp teeth.

"Dried savos fruit," Dravyn said, distractedly. "He's crazy for them."

I took the container and cautiously offered Zell more of the strips; I wasn't above bribing the beast into liking me better.

Dravyn quickly put the equipment away before returning to my side. Together, we headed into the palace, making our way to the winding staircase that circled up to the meeting room at the base of his private quarters.

The last time I'd been in this tower was following my trial with the Star Goddess, when I'd inexplicably landed in the middle of the Marr's viewing party. Almost every middle god and goddess had been present to glare at me that night; was that what we were walking into now?

I shook down to my very bones at the thought, and I paused as I caught sight of my reflection in one of the stairwell windows. "Is Mairu here?"

"Yes," Dravyn said, after a moment of focusing, feeling for her power and presence. "But there's no sense in worrying about using her magic, if that's why you're asking," he muttered, continuing to climb. "I think that particular ruse is up."

He moved quickly enough that I didn't have time to succumb to my fears before we reached the top.

Mairu was waiting for us here, a worried frown on her face, and she wasn't alone.

A Marr I'd only seen briefly—during the last impromptu visit to this tower—was here as well. He stood on the far side of the room, arms folded across his chest, gazing out of the window. He was tall enough that his head nearly grazed the chandelier, but was vaguely human in appearance—save for the reptilian wings folded at his back, which brightened with sparks of electrical energy every time they twitched or otherwise stirred.

"I've been here for hours waiting for you two to return," Mairu told us in a low voice. "He showed up not long ago. I let him in on your behalf...mostly because he refused to leave." She fixed her eyes on Dravyn, and her tone sounded apologetic, almost—as though she regretted not fighting more fiercely to chase our visitor away—as she said, "They're restless, Dravyn. I don't think we can keep avoiding this conversation."

Dravyn waved the apology away, tilting his head in my direction.

"Halar," he informed me under his breath, "the Storm God." He casually moved to stand in front of me as that god strode toward us. Despite his attempt to be subtle, I didn't miss the tension tightening his muscles, or the protective heat that flared in the space around us—and neither did Halar.

"There's no need to hide her." An almost-laugh accompanied Halar's words—but not a pleasant one. A slightly unhinged one. "We've all seen enough already. We know what she is. What ties she has."

"You've seen all there is to see by spying, I presume?" Dravyn's tone was razor sharp, ready to draw blood. "And now you're showing up uninvited at my palace? Both rather egregious breaches of the laws we've all agreed to, wouldn't you say?"

"Terribly sorry about both of these things," Halar said, not sounding sorry at all. As he spoke, the electrical energy contained within his wings occasionally brightened his nearly black skin, sending cracks of white skittering across it. "But the one I serve requested I come pay your court a visit."

"On what grounds?"

"Solatis doesn't believe your court is as in control of the Edgelands situation as you claim—and the elf you've seemingly already welcomed into your court complicates the situation further."

"She complicates nothing."

"And what about the god *we* serve, and what he believes?" Mairu asked, stepping forward. "He will not be pleased by your unannounced visit."

"He is outnumbered two to one, I'm afraid."

Mairu glared at him, her fingers twitching as though she was considering unleashing her magic.

Halar only smiled at her, flashing teeth that were stark white, save for the black tips of his sharp canines. "More are coming from my court, and from the Court of Stone. We have much to discuss tonight. Including her." The Marr's unsettling gaze slid to me.

I stood up straighter, doing my best not to appear bothered by his stare even though I wanted to rake his unnaturally dark eyes out with my claws.

Dravyn shifted his stance to shield me more completely. There was nothing casual about the movement this time. "If there's proper business to be discussed about the Edgelands," he said, "then by all means, we will discuss it. But my ascendant is still recovering from her latest trials. She doesn't need to be subjected to any questioning this afternoon."

A tense moment stretched between us until the God of Storms acquiesced with a slight bow and another flash of his black-tipped teeth.

Mairu stepped forward to guide him away from us, while Dravyn took me by the arm and steered me toward the stairs that led toward his private quarters. He waited until we were out of Halar's sight before he quietly said, "These meetings with my fellow Marr can get...dangerous. I think you should go to my room and stay there for now; there are wards protecting it that will keep you safe."

I would have argued against being sent away from such an important discussion if not for the grim expression that had overtaken his features. I'd never seen anything like fear reflected in his eyes, but this...

This looked alarmingly close to it.

"Just for now," he insisted. "I'll explain everything as soon as I can."

Reluctantly, I nodded and headed for his room.

Once there, I couldn't keep still. I made several laps around the space, absently running my hands along the fine furniture, plucking a few books from his shelves and flipping through them, cleaning stray feathers from Moth's cage, all while listening closely, trying to make sense of what was happening down below.

I heard Valas loudly announcing himself, and several more following him in rapid succession. Soon the conversation between them all became a steadily rising roar of countless voices.

An hour passed. Maybe longer. More than once, I snuck back down the stairs to try and listen closer. Every time it proved useless; they were speaking in a language I couldn't understand.

Everyone speaks the same language here. Wasn't that what Dravyn had told me? The God of the Shade's magic at work. But apparently, there were multiple shared languages they made use of. It made sense, I supposed, that the Marr would have a way of communicating only between themselves, keeping the servants and any other outsiders in the dark if necessary.

Which meant I would have to trust Dravyn when he said he'd explain everything to me later.

Hopefully he was still in a divulging mood after all he'd already shared today.

I needed something to do—some way to distract myself.

My clothes stank of dust and grime and the selakir's sweat from the day's adventures, so I stripped them off and cleaned myself up in the attached washroom, then helped myself to some clean clothes I found on a shelf by the tub. Dravyn's shirt was large enough to fashion into a dress of sorts, so that's what I did, securing it with my own belt.

I looked silly, but it felt nice to be clean, and I couldn't deny the way being wrapped in his cedar and smoke scent settled my nerves.

Pulling the shirt more tightly around myself, I wandered toward the double glass doors that led out to the balcony.

I pushed the curtains aside, staring out over the landscape, silently wishing I could go back to this morning, when we were galloping so wildly that all I could think about was the wind in my hair and the feel of Dravyn's heart keeping rhythm with mine.

I was trying to mentally return there, lost in thought, when the sky flashed with a sickly green light. An uncomfortable pressure seized my chest—a terrifying feeling, though it lasted no longer than a few seconds.

Several more flashes of light and pressure followed.

I backed away from the balcony, trying, and mostly failing, to take deep breaths.

The heavens above me—and maybe the upper-gods them-selves—seemed restless.

The arguments down below me raged on.

And here I was, caught in the middle, wearing clothes I'd borrowed from a god I once considered my arch enemy.

What a confusing day it's been.

I turned away from whatever was happening outside. I tried to ignore what was happening down below me, too, but my hearing was too good, and my curiosity too great. My ears perked up every time voices started to rise.

I had just curled up on Dravyn's bed when the conversation took what sounded like a violent turn. Before I realized what I was doing, I had opened the bedroom door and started down the steps.

I hesitated, remembering the borderline fear in Dravyn's gaze.

Then I heard someone say my name.

Heart leaping into my throat, I couldn't help creeping my way farther down, trying to listen for any context I might be able to decipher.

Just as I came to a stop and settled in to listen closer, I sensed Dravyn storming toward me.

I quickly turned and raced back up to his room. I dove into the chair beside the fireplace and attempted to arrange myself into a relaxed pose—as though I'd been there the entire time.

He stepped inside, took one look at my flushed face, and a knowing little smile curved his lips.

"Eavesdropping, I presume?" He didn't sound upset. Just tired. "I expected nothing less. Though I doubt you could make much sense of what you heard of the Marr-speak?"

I shook my head.

He eyed the dress I'd made out of his shirt. "And thievery too? What am I going to do with you?"

He made the question sound like an invitation, and

thoughts of what he could do made my stomach clench with desire and left me momentarily speechless.

"You're welcome to the clothing, of course." His gaze slowly traveled the length of my body. "Even if part of me wants to demand you strip it off."

The knot in my stomach clenched tighter, but I stayed focused; I needed to know what they'd been talking about down below. "I didn't plan to eavesdrop," I told him. "But it sounded like it was getting violent, and I was...worried. What were they saying?"

"In short? They want you banished from this realm, disqualified from ascension and sent to Eligas to waste away as punishment. They claim it's because Mai helped you at the end of your last trial—yes, she admitted as much to me while you were off in the mortal realm—but it's more complicated than that. The fact that you two cheated just gives them something definite to sink their claws into."

He pointed to the fireplace, kindling it to life with a twist of his hand. He disappeared into the washroom after this, remerging several minutes later wearing clean clothing with his hair tied loosely away from his face.

I was in the same place he'd left me, staring into the fire while horrifying thoughts of being banished to the emptiness between realms played through my mind.

"It's not because we cheated," I thought aloud. "It's because of what I am."

He didn't disagree. "The other courts don't trust you, or the ones associated with you."

"But you and your court do?"

He hesitated.

There was a knock at the door, and I jumped to my feet; I

usually heard people coming, but I'd been too distracted to notice this one.

"Just a servant," he informed me. He answered the knocking and returned a moment later holding two glasses in one hand, brandishing a bottle of crimson liquid in the other. "The wine you mentioned a need for earlier today."

"Is that going to be enough, you think?"

He mirrored my sardonic smile. "I can always send for more." He poured both glasses and handed one to me before settling into the chair next to the fire. "And to answer your previous question...it's complicated."

I snorted at this as I stayed on my feet, clutching my drink, trying to figure out what to say next. "So what happens now? They want me gone, but..."

"But I insisted they reconsider."

"And?"

"They've left us alone, haven't they?" His gaze took mine, flashing with that wild, red glow. His eyes looked even more hellish as they reflected the fire at my back.

A shiver crept over my skull and shot down my spine.

"Sorry we were ambushed like this." He looked away from me until his eyes were back to their usual cool silver. "There have been rumblings from them, but I didn't expect them to show up, ready to fight, as quickly as this. I should have prepared you better."

"No need to apologize. I've been surrounded by fighting my entire life. I'm used to it."

"All the same, this is not a normal occurrence. I'm a bit rattled by it myself, to be honest. By this and everything else we've been dealing with."

"The trouble at the Edgelands, you mean?"

"Yes." He took a long sip from his glass, leaning back in the chair, stretching his legs out, and lifting his eyes to the ceiling. He didn't elaborate on that trouble. I think he would have if I'd asked—and I would ask, soon enough—but at the moment I didn't want to.

I just wanted to look at him.

He was beautiful in the dim light, stretched out with all his muscular lines on full display, his head tipped back and the strands of his hair more red than blond in the fire's glow. Vulnerable, yet powerful.

As I stared at him, a thought struck me—that what I'd told him was true. I really had been surrounded by fighting my entire life.

But I'd rarely experienced someone fighting *for* me the way he kept doing.

Andrel, Cillian, my father, even my sister...all their fierceness, all their countless, violent battles usually went back to the *greater cause*. The bigger picture. The outstanding obligations. I'd been a part of that cause for so long that I'd almost forgotten I existed outside of it.

How strange that this god I once hated would be the one to remind me of my existence.

"You can disregard whatever you might have heard them say," he told me, eyes still on the ceiling. "Our battle is not over, but you don't have to leave this realm—not for Eligas or otherwise. You don't have to go anywhere. Unless you want to, of course."

My breath caught.

Unless you want to.

Such a simple phrase, yet it completely undid me to the point that my hands started to shake.

I couldn't remember the last time someone had told me I didn't have to do something unless I wanted to do it.

"Karys? Are you all right?"

Karys. Not Sparrow. I was *me*, not my sister, not a rebel with a mission, not just a piece of something, but a *whole* something that he was willing to fight for—to protect—for some reason.

"I'm fine. And I don't want to go anywhere," I said softly. "I'd rather stay with...I mean...I want to be in here. With you."

He sat up, studying me closer, the weariness in his eyes giving way to brightness as he repeated my words on a breath. "With me."

I nodded.

He reached out a hand.

For once, I didn't hesitate. I took it and let him pull me into his lap. He placed his wine glass on the table beside him, and I did the same with mine. His newly freed hand reached to cup my face. His fingertips moved over my scars, caressing them as though the skin was unremarkable, unblemished. They were usually the first thing anybody noticed about me unless I kept them hidden.

He'd never asked about them at all.

He clearly saw them, felt them, traced every inch of them now. I kept waiting for the questions. For the disgust. But these things never came.

"Stay the night with me?" was all he asked. "Just in case we have more uninvited company."

Just in case I need to protect you.

I nodded, another clench of desire tightening my stomach as his fingers swept from my cheek down to the hollow of my throat. "Though I still don't need you to burn the world down for me," I said, "just so we're clear. The divine world or otherwise. Nothing has changed regarding that."

He smiled, his other hand finding its way to my lower back,

pulling me more fully into his lap. "You can do it yourself, as I recall."

"Yes."

"So perhaps I'll just stand among the ashes with you," he said, "and admire your work."

"I could allow that."

His nose brushed mine. His warm breath fanned over my skin, making my lips tingle. The hand against my back moved, trailing up my spine, while the other closed lightly around my throat.

"I find myself suddenly curious," he said.

"Curious?"

"About what else you would allow."

His lips hovered over mine. Waiting. Wanting. A god powerful enough to forge suns and level entire towns...was asking my permission.

I couldn't deny I wanted him, even though I now realized —more than ever—what I was getting myself into. What he'd done. What he was capable of. He was so beautiful, but so *dangerous*, so wrong, and everything I had ever believed felt like it was in danger of catching fire, disintegrating from the heat of his touch.

But gods how I wanted to burn with him.

I draped my arms around his neck, balancing myself more fully against him.

Slowly, I brought my mouth to his, parting my lips, giving him permission, inviting him in.

As his tongue pushed its way into my mouth, I felt his arousal stirring underneath me. The throbbing hardness made me inhale sharply, and he responded by deepening the kiss, devouring me so completely I could barely breathe.

One hand stayed against my back, holding me in place, while the one at my throat fell, slipping between my legs.

I'd had nothing to put underneath the clothing I'd borrowed from him, so it was bare skin that his fingertips found when they slid under the hem of his shirt and rubbed their way up my thighs to the aching center of me.

A low note of pleasure rumbled in his chest as he discovered the bareness, and he stopped kissing me long enough to say, "You were ready for me." His fingers trailed lightly across my ache, feeling the dampness that had gathered there. "And already wet, too."

He leaned back, pulling his hand away as he did. The evidence of my want for him glistened on his fingertips. He slipped that evidence into his mouth, sucking his fingers clean, one after the other.

I trembled. I needed him to touch me again. To go back to kissing me, devouring me.

"You look fucking beautiful in the firelight, if you weren't aware." He ran his damp fingers down the front of my body as he spoke, tracing the curves hidden underneath the much-too-large-for-me shirt. A wildness flashed in his eyes—different from his anger, but it still made my pulse skip and my breaths turn shallow.

He stood abruptly, taking me with him, spinning me around and placing me in the chair by myself.

Then he dropped to his knees before me.

He had hesitated earlier. A god, asking permission. And now he was kneeling before me, no longer simply asking, but seemingly prepared to beg, to worship—if the hungry glint in his eyes was any indication.

I was one of the weakest beings in this realm, but in that moment, I felt powerful beyond measure.

I didn't speak. I simply held his wild gaze as I beckoned him toward me. A soft gasp left my lips as his hands caressed my legs, followed by another as he pressed his lips against the inside of my thigh.

His fingertips made their way toward my center once more. He didn't push the shirt aside at first, working the silky fabric against my sex until the shirt was damp and I was shaking with need. Little by little, he pushed the cloth aside, and the combination of silk shirt and his rough fingers felt indescribably good.

Then came the heat. Deliberate, precise flares of his magic, burning through my sensitive nerves one moment, cooling off in the next, pulsing over and over until I wanted to cry out from the wicked pleasure of it.

My back arched with a particularly powerful spasm of pleasure, and he slid a hand around my hips and pulled me toward his mouth.

The heat of his magic was nothing compared to the heat of his tongue.

He worked through the fabric of the shirt at first, just as before, letting the damp weight of it cling to me as he sucked and teased, before finally swiping it fully aside and leaving me entirely exposed for him.

With nothing between us, he licked me fully, slowly, savoring each drop of my arousal, pulling back only long enough to roughly whisper, "You taste even more amazing than I thought you would."

I whimpered out something unintelligible in response. The noise sent another flash of fire through his gaze. He hooked my legs over his shoulders, lifting me up to his mouth as he dropped his head back between my thighs.

His hands roamed upward while he ate, traveling over my

stomach, my chest. While his tongue lashed at the sensitive bud at my center, his fingers pinched the ones on my breasts. Every time I squirmed, or gasped, or cursed his name, he smiled, pinched or sucked harder, or slipped his tongue deeper.

Just when I found myself approaching the edge, ready to shatter into the oblivion of my release, he leaned away, leaving me breathless and quivering.

"Take off the shirt," he commanded.

I didn't hesitate, eager to comply if it meant he'd go back to touching me, tasting me.

He admired the view for a moment—my flushed, pebbling skin, my heaving chest, the peaks of my breasts hard with need. Then he pulled me from the chair, closer to the fire's light and warmth. He leaned back onto the floor, dragging me over top so I was straddling him, my knees against the hardwood on either side, my wetness pressing against the heat and hardness of his body, my hair the only thing covering any part of me.

His hands stroked my curves for a moment before cupping underneath my ass and urging me to climb higher, to bring my center back toward his mouth.

I'd never been so aroused in my life, yet something made me resist movement at first.

"What is it?"

"Nothing. This is just..." I could hardly talk through my panting, needy breaths. "As a child I sometimes prayed to the Marr, and it's been a long time since I've done so, but this still feels a bit...blasphemous."

"If it's any encouragement, I am *imploring* you to commit blasphemy." His fingers tightened against me, and his tone dropped to a near-growl as he added, "Preferably on my face, while moving your hips like the proper fucking Wildfire I know you are."

His words alone were nearly enough to send me crashing back toward release.

When he pulled me toward his mouth this time, I didn't hesitate to rise up and settle there. I still felt hesitant for an instant—but all my apprehensive thoughts quickly burned away as his tongue penetrated me deeper than ever before.

His hands wrapped around my thighs, pulling them apart, opening my body more fully for him to explore. As he moved his mouth over me, I moved my hips as he'd asked, falling into a rhythm, guided and encouraged by his hands clenching increasingly tighter, by his strong arms rocking me faster, harder.

I soon felt a wild cry rising in my throat, followed by waves of building pleasure. He stilled, letting it build further, sending nothing but warm breath falling over me until my rising cry escaped and it was clear I was teetering on the edge between pain and pleasure.

He responded with one last deep thrust of his tongue, and I shattered.

I surrendered fully, and my body was no longer my own; I writhed and started to twist away from him, but he held me against him, drinking in my release, savoring me until I'd finished. It was a full minute, at least, before my thighs stopped shaking. Only then did he let me go.

I collapsed beside him, sliding down so my head could rest against his chest. His heart.

It still surprised me, the human-like beat of it.

He was quiet, contemplative, his fingers trailing up and down my bare back. When I shivered from a combination of aftershocks and nakedness, he heated the air to a soothing temperature with no more effort than an extra deep breath.

"Do you still feel nothing but disdain toward me?" he

asked after a minute, and I could almost hear the smirk behind the question.

I blushed at the memory of those words I'd said to him right before we'd kissed for the first time. We'd come a long way since that night, hadn't we?

"It's complicated," I replied.

He chuckled, sitting up and reaching for the glass he'd placed on the table, washing down the taste of me with the remainder of his wine.

I grabbed the shirt I'd borrowed and went to clean up for the second time that evening. When I came back, I found him opening the balcony door for an impatient little griffin.

Moth swooped in along with a cold, smoky breeze. He collided with my chest—as clumsy and unruly as ever—but I was getting used to catching him like this, so I managed to secure him quickly. I planted a kiss on top of his head, which made him purr deeply.

Dravyn closed the door but stayed next to it, watching the sky. It was flashing with the same sickly green color I'd first seen hours ago.

"This was happening earlier, too," I told him.

"Valla is restless," he muttered.

"Valla?" I repeated. "You mean the upper-heavens?"

"Mm." He pulled the curtains over the door. "The Moraki and their feuds often get violent, and sometimes it rattles us even down here."

"Their feuding...does this all go back to what the Storm Marr mentioned earlier? The Edgelands business?"

"That's most of it, yes."

"You told me you would explain more about the Edgelands troubles, and the Death Marr, after I survived my second trial," I reminded him.

"I know. And I intend to keep my promise." He glanced toward the bed, and I was overcome by a sudden urge to crawl under the covers with him, to pretend we were somewhere else for awhile.

"But let's rest tonight," he said, as if he could sense my unspoken desire. "Tomorrow, I'll take you to the Edgelands to see the truth for yourself."

CHAPTER 37

FOR SEVERAL MINUTES AFTER I WOKE THE NEXT morning, I thought I was still in a dream.

Dravyn's arms were wrapped tightly around me, holding me against his bare chest. His breaths were slow and easy, his heart thudding peacefully against my back.

I still wore his shirt, but it was untied, hanging open, bunched up and leaving my lower half fully exposed—I might as well have been entirely naked. In the bed of a god. A god who had given me the most powerful orgasm of my life last night.

I shuddered pleasantly at the memory of my release, and Dravyn stirred and pressed closer to me, nudging through the curtain of my hair, pressing his nose into the crook of my neck and exhaling a warm breath that sent shivers down to my toes.

His breath was all it took to make my body wake up completely, to come alive in hopes of picking up where we'd left off last night. Honestly, I'm not sure it had ever truly settled—nor had his. Spending the night tangled in each other's arms had done nothing to calm either of us down.

My one saving grace was that he was not as exposed as I was; he still wore the loose pants he'd slipped on before crawling into bed beside me. But that was *all* he wore, and the thin material didn't fully conceal the firmness—or the impressive size—of his arousal. That hardened length pressed against my backside as he leaned his mouth toward my ear and murmured, "You know, gods have little need for sleep...but I could get used to doing it if it means waking up beside you like this."

"I wouldn't get used to it," I mumbled back. "I'm still not convinced this is a good idea."

"Perhaps I could convince you?" His mouth tipped toward my ear again, giving my lobe a gentle, playful nip. "I can be very persuasive when I want to be."

"God of Fire and Forging and Persuasion...and what else, I wonder?"

"Why do you want to know? Are you thinking of praying to me again, as you mentioned last night?"

"You were the one praying at *my* altar last night, if I recall correctly."

"Very true." He buried his face into my neck, breathing me in, pressing his mouth against my skin and flicking his tongue against my pulse. "And now I would love to perform my morning rituals, if you don't mind."

I meant to protest.

I *should* have protested.

Then his fingers reached around my front and slipped between my legs, and I no longer wanted to do anything except surrender to him, just as I had yesterday.

His touch was lazy, almost, compared to last night, but he still knew precisely what he was doing; even half-asleep, he was still talented with his fingers, alternating between feather-light taps and deliberate, massaging touches until I was slick and pulsing with need.

He urged my legs apart. As I spread open for him, he stretched me even wider with one of his large hands, slipping just the tip of a finger inside as he did. He teased with that tip, dipping it in and out, playing at my most sensitive nerve endings for a minute before pushing deeper.

I arched my back and clenched my legs around his hand, and his hips lifted in response, pressing his hard length between my thighs. Feeling it twitch and throb drew a needy little cry from my lips. My head tilted back, and his lips fell upon my exposed throat, kissing even harder than before, his tongue lashing and teeth nipping hard enough that it would likely leave a mark.

And Gods help me, I *wanted* it to leave a mark.

He rolled me onto my back, and his eyes never left mine as he slid his pants down and freed himself. It looked as massive as it had felt, and as I watched him stroke the length of it, every part of me buzzed with need.

"Did you dream about me last night, my Sparrow?" He leaned over me, bringing his lips to mine, supporting himself on one powerful arm while the other rose and fell with more slow, deliberate strokes of himself. "About what it would feel like to have my cock between your legs, rather than my fingers? Rather than my tongue?"

I tried to reply, but my words became nothing more than a soft moan that rose into a whimper as his erection brushed across my thighs before trailing up to my center.

"I'll take that as a yes."

He kissed me again before settling back on his knees, pinning me between them. "We'll get there soon enough." His finger caressed my sex, circling through the added wetness he'd brushed onto me. "I wanted you to feel my tongue, and my touch, first. Just so you know I can make you come for me no matter what I use."

And then he started to prove his point, slipping his finger inside of me and thrusting deep, curling against my inner walls with increasing speed and pressure. Another finger soon followed, while his thumb continued to work against the outside, rubbing and gently pulling, opening me more completely.

I'd woken up with a ready ache between my legs, aroused by dreams I only vaguely remembered having while in his arms, and it didn't take long before I felt another release building, nearly as powerful as the one he'd given me last night.

It was what his other hand was doing that truly sent me over the edge—the way he had not stopped pleasuring himself even as he took care of my need.

My gaze flashed from his hands up to his face, and I saw something I'd never expected to see—a god kneeling before me, a picture of power and perfection coming undone in the early morning light. It was one of the most beautiful and most arousing things I'd ever seen.

I clamped my legs tighter around his fingers, urging them deeper, harder, and with a gasping cry I came completely undone.

I started to curl up as the powerful waves of pleasure overtook me, snapping the last chains of my self-control, but he pressed a hand to my chest and held me in place. "Stay on your back for me, Wildfire."

The low growl of a command sent another shock of release rumbling through me. I did as he said, stretching out on my back with my hands lifting above me, fingertips curling against the headboard.

"Just like that. Good..." He trailed off into a curse as I arched my back once more, letting my thighs graze his erection. He pressed me down into the bed and leaned over me, one hand roaming across my skin, pushing my shirt up to fully expose my breasts while his other hand moved furiously up and down his length.

He cupped one of my breasts, squeezing it, letting his thumb and forefinger circle my nipple and pinch and tease it into a hardened peak.

His touches soon grew rougher. Wilder. I lifted my hips again, pressing my still-throbbing center against him, and with a roar of pleasure he followed my release with his own, painting my bare chest and stomach in hot, glistening threads of white.

Once he'd fully emptied himself, he planted a slightly shaking arm on either side of my body. He leaned down, resting his forehead against mine for a moment. The weight of him was comforting. Steadying. It felt like everything I needed in that moment.

He planted a soft kiss on my cheek before leaning back. He grabbed a throw blanket, used it to clean off my stomach and chest. Then he tossed it aside and settled back on his knees again, still pinning me down, but just studying me now.

In the past, this would have been the point where I reached for the covers and pulled them across myself—not out of shame, but out of some deep need to regain control. I'd never liked the vulnerability of this moment, when I came back to my senses and the fullness of what I'd done—what I'd given— hit me. It frightened my sensible mind to think of giving up so much control.

But for some reason, I wasn't afraid of the way Dravyn was staring at me.

He continued to admire me, fingertips skating thoughtfully up and down my bare legs as he said, "It's been a long time since I experienced that with a mortal."

I didn't want to think about other, divine experiences he might have had—and how I compared to them—but I couldn't help but ask, "Is it different, doing this sort of thing with a...um...not-mortal?"

"Different is one way of putting it," he said, settling onto the bed beside me.

"I've heard stories of the appetites some of you gods have." I sat up, smoothing his rumpled shirt back into place over my body. "Insatiable lust, wild parties..."

A corner of his mouth quirked. "We were all humans once, and some of our very human urges carry over," he said with a shrug. "And yes—they're magnified at times. We can take many forms, too, so I suppose things can get a bit more...ah, *feral* compared to what mortals are used to."

I blushed as my imagination immediately ran wild, thinking of all the different forms he might take, all the different ways he might take care of those very human *urges*.

He arched a brow. "But I hope my mortal form was sufficient for you for now?"

I blushed deeper. "More than sufficient. I'm embarrassed I didn't last any longer than I did."

He grinned, and I feared I might melt right into the sheets at the sight of it. "Next time we'll take it slower," he promised.

Next time.

I felt dizzy, and I didn't think it was because of the lingering memory of my orgasm. I should have dropped the conversation then and there—for the sake of my own balance —but my mind still raced with questions.

And apparently, I had that particular, curious *look* on my face, because Dravyn smiled knowingly and said, "You have more questions about the gods and their wild sexual escapades, don't you?"

"Maybe."

He stood, redressed himself, and gestured for me to continue. "Out with it."

I cleared my throat. "If you and I were to truly lay together, and we were to fully, well, *finish*, and you were to..."

He glanced over at me mid-stretch, the trace of a smirk on his lips. "You're wondering if I can put a child in you."

"It's a fair question, isn't it?"

"It is." His smirk became more pronounced as he added, "And I do love that you're already imagining me coming inside of you."

"I like to be prepared for any and all potential disasters."

He chuckled. "Would it be disastrous? You truly think so?" He leaned back over the bed, bringing his lips to mine, and I couldn't resist meeting his kiss. "I can think of far more *disastrous* things," he mused when he finally dragged his lips away from mine. "But to answer your question, we're...*incompatible* in that way, as far as I'm aware."

I fiddled with my hair, twisting it into a messy braid only to untwist it again. "Good to know."

"I'd be happy to demonstrate things further, if you'd like. We can always test—"

I coughed. "We have other business to attend to today."

"We do, don't we?" He tried for another easy smile, but it didn't quite reach his eyes this time—a sign that he was as apprehensive about our upcoming business as I was, maybe. "I need to bathe first. You're welcome to join me, of course."

"I have my own room," I insisted, as tempting as the invitation was.

"Suit yourself. I'll see you downstairs in a bit."

I slipped on my pants from yesterday, cringing a bit at how dirty they were—at how dirty I was, in general. I pushed through the grossness, tucking his shirt in and smoothing it as best I could, and then made a beeline for the door. I planned to sneak as fast as I could to my room and jump immediately into the hottest tub of water I could stand.

Unfortunately, I ran into the God of Winter on my way down the tower steps.

He was in the middle of biting into a plum when our gazes met. He took one look at me, stopped walking and lowered the fruit, violet eyes dancing as a smile crossed his lips. "I'm guessing you know why the always-punctual God of Fire is late for the meeting he and I were supposed to have this morning?"

I lifted my chin and tried for as much dignity as I could muster. "He'll be downstairs in a few minutes."

"And in a very good mood, I suspect."

"He seemed happy enough when I left him."

Valas appraised me for a moment more, tossing the plum up and down as he did. "You smell terrible by the way," he informed me. "The shirt looks nice on you, though."

"Shut it," I grumbled.

"You should eat something." He caught the fruit and gave it a little shake. "I suspect you're famished after all the trouble you kids got into last night."

"I am," I agreed, snatching the plum and continuing on my way. "Thank you."

"I wasn't actually offering my own breakfast to you," he called to my retreating back.

As I bit into the soft flesh and wiped away the juice that dribbled down my chin, I smiled. I was in a better mood than I had been in a long time, despite all of the confusing thoughts swirling in my mind and all my uncertainties about what the day might hold.

A quick, hot bath improved my mood even more, as did the fine, comfortable riding clothes Rieta laid out for me to change into.

After I was dressed, I found her waiting for me at the bureau and its mirror, brushes and combs in hand. We tackled my hair together; she was talented at braiding, and she managed to tame my unruly strands into several sleek plaits that she pinned into a twisting crown around my head.

"I came to your room late last night to check in on you," she said as she worked, "and found you gone. Worried me for a moment."

I hadn't thought about causing concern to anyone—I was still not used to being expected anywhere in this realm. "I'm sorry," I said. "Last night was...strange."

She nodded in agreement. "I found out where you were soon enough. And I suspect you were safer with him than you would have been anywhere else, what with all the unrest and other nonsense last night."

Images flashed in my mind—the unsettled sky, the Storm Marr's dark gaze, the almost-fear in Dravyn's eyes when he sent me to his room.

My good mood deflated a bit.

"'Course it's none of my business, but it's nice to see you two are finally getting along."

I nodded absently.

We were getting along—I could hardly deny that after the things we'd done.

But the further removed I became from those things, the more they felt like a dream that hadn't truly happened. It had been so easy to slip into the dream when we were alone. Now the reality of my surroundings was settling in again, all my questions pressing into the places previously occupied by him.

My gaze drifted toward the closet.

I still hadn't taken the knife Cillian had given me from its hiding place. I couldn't hear its humming anymore, but I wondered if that was because I didn't really want to.

"Are you all right, dear?"

"Yes," I lied quickly. My gaze jumped up to my reflection in the mirror. "You've done a beautiful job."

Rieta waved the words off and smoothed her skirts in the slightly flustered way she always did when I paid her a compliment, and then she busied herself with cleaning up the mess I'd left in the washroom.

I normally would have told her to leave the mess and let me deal with it myself, but I was too distracted by my thoughts. My gaze circled the room.

A room that, at some point, I'd started to think of as *mine*.

The evidence of my settling in was appallingly apparent, now that I took a moment to see it. To admit to it. I saw all my drawings scattered about; the books I'd chosen and taken from the main library; a beautiful vase I'd fallen in love with, which Dravyn had insisted I could keep in here to look at whenever I wanted; the bed made up the way I always made it at home, with the same number of pillows arranged in exactly the same manner.

Then there was the shelf where I'd collected my most important artifacts of this realm—the crown, the sword, the glass sparrow.

My sister's necklace now sat on that shelf, too—it was as valuable as any god-given artifact, I'd reasoned—though I couldn't see it from where I currently sat.

Instead, my gaze caught on Hydrus, the sword I'd earned from the Ocean Marr's trial.

"An unsettling blade, that one," Rieta said, her gaze following mine as she reemerged from the washroom. "Its magic keeps me on my toes. Every time I walk in here, I can feel it rumbling."

"I can't really feel anything from it."

"No, I suspect a mortal wouldn't. But it's restless on that shelf, make no mistake. Maybe because the energy doesn't really fit in this territory."

Restless.

That made two of us.

I wanted to carry it with me today, I decided. To see it in action and watch how it worked when I *wasn't* flailing around and trying not to drown in the Ocean Marr's raging waves.

Rieta agreed, somewhat hesitantly, with my plan, and she went to fetch a fine leather baldric to go with my riding attire so I could carry the weapon properly. With it strapped into place, I *looked* more prepared to ride out and face the day, even if I didn't truly feel ready to do so.

I WALKED outside an hour or so later and found Dravyn already there, still occupied by his meeting with Valas. Both of their faces were grim.

Their conversation trailed off as I approached, and Valas's frown quickly gave way to a grin as his gaze fell on the sword I carried.

"Off to slay monsters, are we?"

"Or maybe middle-gods who can't keep their mouths shut."

His smile brightened. "You don't need a sword to slay me, love. Your looks alone are sufficient."

"Maybe so, but I think I'd rather stab you."

"Is it strange that your threats only make you seem *more* attractive to me?"

"Yes," Dravyn answered on my behalf, pushing past him and heading to the tack room. "Now if you'll excuse us, we have places to be."

"I think we're making him jealous," Valas said, giving me a wink.

I rolled my eyes but found myself fighting off a laugh; he had that effect on me.

All of them were having an effect on me, despite how I'd tried to guard myself against it.

The questions that had started in my room returned, louder than before. I was smiling, but only halfway listening to Valas as he listed off all the different ways we could make Dravyn jealous. I wanted to laugh and joke along with him. I wanted to feel like I belonged here—like I belonged anywhere at all. As if I wasn't caught between two warring worlds.

Today will bring more answers, I reminded myself. *More facts.*

Then I could put at least some of my questions to rest, and hopefully figure out what to do next.

Valas excused himself—off to go fulfill his duties of annoying Mairu, he told me.

Dravyn returned with our equipment a moment later. He summoned and saddled Farak quickly, avoiding making eye contact with me as he did so. We were riding rather than using transport magic, he explained, because the energies around the

Edgelands were difficult to navigate through, and he didn't want to risk making me sick when I was finally recovered from all my trials of the past weeks.

I hated the reminder of my mortal frailty, but I didn't hate having another opportunity to ride on Farak's back. It had ultimately proven therapeutic yesterday; maybe it would help calm my nerves today, too.

Moth soared into view just as we prepared to set off. He swooped around Farak's face, flicking his flame-tipped tail and swatting playfully at the beast's slender nose. The selakir snapped at him, coming alarmingly close to catching the griffin's backside with razor sharp teeth.

Dravyn scolded the fluttering creature, and Moth made a disgruntled noise before shooting off toward the sky.

He followed us as we galloped into the hills, staying high above and occasionally disappearing from sight; there were no clouds to get lost in here in this realm, but there were occasional pockets of brighter light that swallowed up his pale golden body.

I watched him, trying to see if I could spot a pattern to the bright places, trying to keep my nerves under control.

We kept a fast pace.

Dravyn said little. The passionate, almost playful god I'd spent the night with had been replaced by the stoic and powerful version I was more used to. He was clearly troubled but on a mission, determined to show me what I'd asked for at whatever the cost.

Finally, we came to it: A place where the rolling fields of silver grass and black earth ended in a steep drop down to a dark ocean—the same ocean of thick, purplish water I'd first seen in the Death Marr's territory.

To our left, several hundred yards away, was the Tower of

Ascension. To our right, far in the distance, I saw high cliffs; I wondered if they were the same ones I'd stood on the day I'd first encountered the Death Marr. This place felt familiar, yet altogether new, and I was more turned around than I cared to be.

We dismounted. I walked the edge of the steep drop-off, trying to orient myself, peering at the shoreline of white sand down below. I didn't see any of the Death Marr's veilhounds pacing today, and I said a silent prayer of thanks for that.

I gestured to the expansive shore in both directions. "So all of this is what you refer to as the Edgelands?"

He nodded.

"And that tower over there is the Tower of Ascension."

"Yes. Amalith," he said, reminding me of its proper name. "So this point is where ascension happens, but the area holds more significance than that." He picked up a broken tree branch and smoothed a patch of sandy ground with his boot.

He had apparently realized my love of maps and diagrams, because he took the time to sketch out a proper map of the realms in the sand—the upper-heavens, the middle-heavens, and the mortal world they sat above. He drew a line separating the upper-heavens from the middle-heavens, and then he divided the middle into three separate sections.

These three sections, I noticed, all converged toward a single point at the bottom.

"Where we stand is the point where the three courts' territories meet. A spot none of us fully claim." He circled the spot where the lines converged. "It's also the thinnest point between our realm of Nerithyl and the mortal realm of Avalinth. The only thing separating us from the mortals here is Eligas and its various pathways." He lifted his drawing stick and pointed it across the strange purple ocean.

"The Shade Court doesn't claim this point," he continued, "or the relatively narrow strip reaching out from it—that which we call the Edgelands—but the Death Marr has been keeping all these edges secure for some time now. A task appointed to him by all three of the upper-gods, for the benefit of all three courts."

"Right...I remember him mentioning he had a job to do. He claimed I was distracting him from his duties."

And then threatened to feed me to the veilhounds for it.

I shuddered at the memory.

"This ocean before us was not here in the beginning of this realm—it is a much more recent addition. The 'water' you see is actually a churning mass of the Death God's draining magic. An extra layer of protection preventing anything in the mortal realm from crossing over."

"Crossing over?" The idea was completely foreign and fascinating. "They can do that?"

"They shouldn't be able to. The magic of Eligas prevents it —redirects them. Mortal souls can rise to the middle-heavens after the death of their physical body, of course, but only into the designated Afterlands that run alongside the actual Marr territories. For a living being to cross into our personal territories, it requires a very specific kind of magic—which is what I gave to you when I placed my mark on your wrist. But something other than our magic is at work here."

I was still mostly confused, yet as he spoke, an uneasiness was building in my bones, shaking them, making me feel unsteady on my feet.

"Look harder, into the distance there," he said. "Do you see what's happening on the other side of this ocean?"

Breathless and buzzing with curiosity, I watched.

Several minutes passed before it happened, but when it did

it was unmistakable what he meant: a flash of jagged energy, like a bolt of lightning splitting a night sky.

I took an involuntary step back. I still didn't understand what I was seeing, but even I could tell it was unnatural.

Another flash quickly followed the first, but this time I held my ground. Narrowed my gaze for a closer look. Everything in the distance seemed to waver, to shake as though something was rattling the very gates of the heavens themselves.

Quietly, I said, "It's almost as if...as if something is trying to break in as we speak."

He nodded, his expression grim. "Something that threatens the very structure of our world and magic."

"What is it?"

"We aren't sure. We've tried to trace the source on the other side several times without success. But every day here lately, the strikes against the barrier grow more numerous. More violent. This past week has been particularly bad, which is part of what triggered that meeting of the courts last night."

The unease in my bones continued to deepen.

Moth swept down from the bright sky and made several clumsy loops in the air before dropping onto my shoulder. I absently stroked his wings as I considered all the things Dravyn had told me.

"The barriers between the realms exist for a reason," he said after a moment. "If they're compromised, if something else from the mortal realm crosses over..."

"Something else? You mean it's happened before?"

"Once." He inhaled deeply. Reluctance settled heavily in his features, as though we'd come to the part of the discussion he'd least wanted to reach.

But my questioning stare was insistent, and he soon relented.

"A little less than six years ago, a being of the mortal world succeeded in crossing into this realm uninvited. The breach caused a terrifying amount of instability—and not just to our own realm. It caused unchecked magic to flow out from our heavens and into Eligas, flooding its usually neutral pathways and creating chaos. We repaired it just in time to keep it from affecting the mortal realm, thankfully. And soon after, this 'ocean' before us was created by the Death Marr to better neutralize any potential future attacks. He's maintained it ever since."

"What happened to the person who broke through?"

"She remained here for a short time."

My unease sank deeper still, settling in the very core of my being, though I still couldn't properly explain what was causing it.

"Most of us wanted to destroy her for what she'd done—and what she'd tried to do. But she ended up in the Death Marr's clutches first, and Zachar loves to bargain; he offered the intruder a chance at becoming one of the Miratar.

"She was a clever being, he reasoned, to have found her way into our realm uninvited. She might have made a fine addition to our divine court, and we might have been able to convince her to explain how she'd managed to break through the veil between the realms, too. We held on to that hope for a little while, at least..."

"But she didn't work out," I recalled. "This was the same failed ascendant Valas told me about, wasn't it?"

He nodded. "And Zachar was afterwards relegated to this task of protecting the Edgelands because the Moraki were not pleased with his reckless decision-making."

"So he's being punished?"

"Yes. It's why he doesn't associate with the rest of the Marr very often, and I think it's part of the reason he still maintains such a monstrous appearance even several years after his ascension. So much of his power is poured into this ocean here that it's left him...unstable."

I couldn't help feeling a bit sorry for the God of Death. I still hadn't forgotten the way all the others had avoided even looking in our direction when I was talking to him.

Still turning all of these new facts over in my mind, I said, "And the failed ascendant was killed when she tried to flee, I assume."

Dravyn shook his head.

My heart skipped a few beats. "She got away?"

"And worse, she didn't go back to her realm empty-handed. She took several things from the Death God's palace that we know of—and likely more that we don't know of—for purposes that to this day we can only guess at."

The anxiety in my core twisted into something far more sinister.

Because I could think of at least one very good reason why a mortal would want to steal divine objects—a reason that brought me, unwillingly, back to the conversation with Cillian.

The knife hidden in my room flashed in my mind.

An impossible thought struck me, so sudden and sharp that I had to fight the urge to double-over as if I'd been stabbed in the stomach.

A long moment passed before I found the courage to speak my thoughts. "This failed ascendant..." I swallowed down the bile rising in the back of my throat. "What was her name?"

The silence that stretched between us was like a physical thing; a third person joining our conversation; an executioner aiming an arrow at my chest.

Dravyn stared out over the dark ocean of magic as he said,

"It was not a coincidence that I saved you from the pyre the day we met. I'd been watching you for some time before that, ever since the failed ascendant's death. Because though she was dealt with, we still didn't know what had become of the things she took—why she had taken them, what she had done with them. We needed more answers. And we hoped you would provide those answers where she had not."

I shook my head, fighting the urge to turn and run.

I couldn't make myself say the truth out loud.

So the God of Fire spoke it for me.

"The failed ascendant was your sister."

CHAPTER 38

"YOU'RE LYING."

Moth soared from my shoulder and took to the sky, startled by the sudden venom in my voice.

Dravyn took the furious accusation in stride, keeping his gaze fixed on the ocean as he quietly said, "You can't remember any time in the past when your sister might have disappeared without explanation?"

"She was always disappearing, going off on missions without me, that doesn't mean—"

"Some point around six years ago, specifically, when she was gone longer than usual? Long enough to make you curious about what she was truly doing?"

I tried to keep arguing, but my breath hitched and the words got caught in the back of my throat.

I didn't want to remember what he was asking me to, but I could.

Gods, I fucking *could*.

My stupid, obsessive memory was as relentlessly clear as it

ever was, and a particular moment in time stood out...one I could remember with nauseating clarity.

It was one of the first times I'd been left entirely on my own after our mother abandoned us. For nearly a month, I'd been left in our house alone, but I hadn't questioned it; I was simply doing what my sister asked of me—thinking of the greater cause. Trusting her more than I trusted anyone because she had been the only constant in my life, the point by which I set my compass.

She'd eventually returned as promised, haggard and haunted-looking, but still in one piece. Of course I'd been curious. But she'd assured me everything was fine.

So I'd believed everything was fine.

And I wanted to believe everything was fine now—that what Dravyn said was not the truth. The *gods* were liars. Not my sister. And this was just another lie from another god, just another attempt to trick me.

"She would have told me if she was involved in something like this." I backed away from him as the words tumbled breathlessly from my mouth. "She wouldn't have left me to go somewhere as dangerous as this without telling me the truth— she wouldn't have risked her life and left me there all alone. You're *lying*."

He started after me, reaching a hand toward my arm, but stopped when I shook my head and warned him off with a livid glare.

I froze in place. So did he. We stood mere feet apart, but it felt like miles. My hands shook. My heart felt like it was plummeting out of existence, the pull of its collapse drawing my lungs, my stomach, all my other vital organs into a freefall with it.

Meanwhile, the God of Fire stood there looking perfectly

calm and composed, and I hated him more in that moment than I ever had before.

"I'm sorry, Karys," he said.

His apology felt like a slap in the face. I didn't want an apology from him. I didn't want his pity. I wanted to go back to the beginning of things and try again, to not fall for him the way I had. To not let my guard down. I should have been focusing on trying to unearth this information he'd been keeping from me, instead of spending so much time kissing him and gods...I felt so damn *foolish*.

"How could you keep this from me?" I demanded. "You knew this yesterday. And last night. And this morning, every time we...we..."

"I can explain—"

"*How?*"

The air flared hotter around us, but he took a deep breath and quickly cooled it. "Because I needed to know what had truly become of your sister and what she took, as I said. There are things about the situation that don't add up, and you wouldn't have told me what I needed to know if I'd simply asked it of you in the beginning."

I'd been wrong last night. He didn't see me as I wanted to believe he did—I was nothing more than a means to an end.

"So you were using me." My voice was brittle, in danger of breaking.

His jaw clenched. "No. I was studying you. Trying to make sense of you. But what I found is not what I expected, and things got...*complicated* after that." He took another deep, calming breath. "Because I quickly realized you were just as clueless as anybody about all of the questions we had."

"I am not clueless," I snapped.

"I didn't mean it as an insult."

My claws itched and tingled at the tips of my fingers, but I kept them retracted. For now.

"I hadn't originally planned to bring you here to this realm, either," he continued, "but when you volunteered, I agreed because I thought I just needed to study you closer to get the answers we needed. The trials seemed like an obvious way to extend your time here, to give me longer to figure things out. I didn't think you—" He cut himself off, looking uncharacteristically flustered by whatever truth he'd nearly let slip.

"You didn't think I'd make it this far, did you?" I finished for him, and waited for him to deny it.

He said nothing.

My voice cracked completely despite my best efforts to hold it together. "You thought whatever trials I had to face would eventually finish me off, so you could take what you needed and then not have to deal with me after that."

Again, he was silent.

A hundred furious insults and curses exploded in my mind. None of them felt sufficient—and I was too hurt, too crushed, to speak anyway.

He remained calm, but all I could picture were the fires that had surrounded him on the day we'd met. Swirling flames that quickly gave way to the memory of my sister's blood. *Red.* All I could see was red, all I could feel was heat and fury.

I backed farther away from Dravyn. Slowly at first, but gaining speed with every beat of my increasingly angry heart until finally I turned and ran. I had to run. I didn't know where I was going to go, I just knew I couldn't stay beside him for another second.

My feet pounded relentlessly across the dry earth. I didn't look up until my lungs felt like they might give out, until the pain in my side became unbearable, a sharp stabbing with every step and breath I took.

I collapsed to my hands and knees, glancing up to see the Tower of Ascension looming just ahead of me. There was a patch of soft-looking silver-blue grass on the hilltop adjacent to the tower; I staggered my way over to it and knelt there, hands braced against the softness, trying to stop the world from spinning.

Had my sister made it all the way to this tower six years ago?

Had she taken magic from it, as Cillian asked me to do?

Was I the only one who didn't know? I couldn't understand why they would have kept me in the dark about these things. But I also didn't truly believe Dravyn would lie about something like this; what did he have to gain from it?

Everything hurt.

Nothing made sense.

I wanted to keep running, but where would I go?

Dravyn didn't follow me right away. I wasn't sure whether this made me feel better or worse. All I knew, in that moment, was that I wanted my old, simple anger back. I wanted to hate Dravyn and his entire realm, his entire court, the way I used to.

But that anger didn't feel the same now. Trying to wrap it around my body was like trying to protect myself with a coat I'd started to outgrow.

I shifted uncomfortably, stretching my legs out in front of me and adjusting the sword strapped against me—and I realized then that the sword was glowing.

It was moving, too, though barely. So subtly I thought it was my own trembling at first. I forced myself to go completely still for a moment, and the blade's rattling grew more obvious in the stillness, the tip of it lifting ever so slightly toward the nearby tower. Pulling toward it.

As if it wanted me to take it there.

I didn't have long to ponder over whether or not I should move before I heard Dravyn approaching. He stood at my side but didn't speak right away.

"I should have told you all of this before now," he finally said.

I didn't look at him. I'd stopped fighting against my tears, and I didn't want him to see them streaming down my face. I stared at my hands and quietly asked, "Do you know how she died?"

"Not all of the details, I'm afraid."

"Tell me what you know."

He settled down on the grass beside me, and another minute passed before he answered me. "When she fled this realm, the veilhounds gave chase. They're drawn to errant souls —a facet of the Death Marr's power at work. And her soul would have stood out in the mortal realm, I imagine, after all the time it spent acclimating to this one; she had no real chance to disappear. They never found the things she took, but they did find her, eventually."

The memory of Savna returning after her month away flashed in my mind again. Her ashen skin. Her sunken eyes. Her forced smile. No wonder she'd looked so horrible—she was being hunted down.

I pulled my legs to my chest and buried my face against them, feeling more frustrated than ever. Why had I not questioned her more than I did? For all my curiosity and the endless overthinking I always did, there was clearly a blind spot where my sister was concerned.

I felt so *foolish.*

"One of those hounds was killed during the hunt," Dravyn said. "We don't know how. But the second succeeded. Although..."

He fell silent for several beats, until I lifted my head from my knees and cut him a sideways glance, urging him to continue.

"They aren't usually violent when they kill. Typically, they leave only a shell of a body with no obvious cause of death when they drag a soul off...I was surprised to hear you say you found blood in her room."

"So she put up more of a fight than the hound anticipated."

"Seems like it."

"Good." I angrily wiped away fresh tears with the heel of my hand. "I hope she made the beast suffer, and I hope the Death Marr felt its suffering until the very end."

Dravyn didn't respond to this, which only made me angrier.

The only reason I didn't continue lashing out at him was because of Moth, who chose that moment to return to us. He swooped down and burrowed between my chest and raised knees, forcing me to rearrange myself to create a proper resting spot in my lap for him. He settled down into this spot with a heavy sigh, his eyes fluttering shut as though the conversation had been exhausting for him, even though he'd only observed most of it from the sky.

I focused on the solid weight of the griffin instead of the weight continuing to build around my heart, kneading his fur until he was purring softly, drifting toward sleep.

"You still don't know how she managed to kill that first veilhound, do you?" I asked Dravyn.

Out of the corner of my eye I saw him shake his head.

A memory of the Death Marr's words rang in my head.

It would have been almost akin to killing a god, and it would have required a very specific type of weapon to do the job.

I now had a likely answer to this question, I realized—the weapons Cillian had shown me.

More pieces of the bigger picture fell into place the longer I sat there.

The reason they had never found whatever my sister had taken from this realm, I guessed, was because these things had likely been drained of their divine energy, which had then been used to create the anti-venom Cillian told me about. Over five years ago, it seemed they'd already been able to create some version of these impossible weapons...and someone had used one to kill the divine creature trying to hunt my sister down.

I could think of no other explanation.

But who had wielded the weapon?

Had Savna herself truly slain the first hound, or was it one of our other allies? Andrel? Cillian? Kinnara?

The possibility that it was someone other than Savna made my chest ache all over again—because it was more proof that I'd been lied to by more people. That the ones I considered the closest friends I had left, my *family*, had kept me in the dark about the things they were truly doing, the kind of war they were truly planning to wage.

All these questions tumbled relentlessly through my mind. Meanwhile, I could feel Dravyn's eyes on me. The urge to tell him what I knew was eating at me again, but I couldn't bring myself to speak. Once again, I felt like I was standing in the very center of two entirely different worlds, the ground beneath me threatening to split and swallow me up if I didn't leap to one side or the other. I knew I couldn't stay in the middle, yet I couldn't move.

"Please talk to me," he said. "Tell me what you're thinking."

"That you were using me," I repeated, more broken than angry, now. "This whole time, you only wanted to bleed me dry of whatever information I carried. Nothing more."

"Karys, I..."

I finally turned to fully face him, narrowing my gaze, daring him to try and deny the accusation.

He sighed. "That's how it started."

That should have been the end of it. The last thread between us broken, the sign for me to stop talking to him, to stop trying to understand. I don't know why I kept looking at him. Why I stayed where I was and asked, "How does it end?"

He held my gaze, and I held my breath, though I wasn't sure why, or what I was even hoping for at this point.

"I'm not sure anymore," he said.

CHAPTER 39

THE NEXT MORNING, I REFUSED TO LET RIETA into my room when she came to do her usual cleaning routine. I locked her and everyone else out, and I sat at my desk and looked over all of the notes, maps, and diagrams I'd made about this realm, thinking through my next steps as best I could with a battered and bleary mind.

I'd cried myself to sleep last night. Tears had threatened again when I woke up, cold and alone, stricken with the realization of how different things had been this time yesterday. How different—yet how similar to the morning after I'd woken up following my fight with Andrel.

Physically, I was fine, this time. No broken arms or anything else.

Mentally was another story, entirely.

I had been lied to, kept in the dark by everyone I had ever dared to trust. I was trying to hold tight to my shredded confidence, but it was hard to trust even myself when it felt like I'd misjudged and overlooked so many things.

But I refused to be reduced to nothing more than tears and regret.

So I was going to *do something*—starting by following through with the idea I'd had weeks ago, when I'd first learned of the Tower of Ascension.

I was going back to that tower to see its magic for myself.

I would walk where my sister had walked, see what she'd seen, try to make sense of why she'd done the things she did. What she'd taken, and how she'd gotten away...I wanted answers, and though I didn't fully trust my own mind anymore, I still believed I was better off relying on myself to get those answers, rather than anyone else.

I didn't know what I would do with whatever magic or information I encountered in the tower, but the important thing now was *control*. If I had the facts, the firsthand knowledge and experience, then I could figure out the rest.

My plan started with the sword resting on its customary place in my room.

You'll be granted access to it through the two relics you've earned from the two courts, thus far, Dravyn had told me, and I assumed he was telling the truth in this case because I'd seen evidence of it—the way Hydrus had reacted to the tower when I got close to it yesterday.

I suspected the Star Goddess's crown might do the same thing. I would take them both back to the tower with me, and hopefully, they would help me find a way in.

Next, I had to devise a way to get to my destination—to travel quickly enough that I could get there and back without my absence being noticed. An idea for this struck me later that afternoon, when I spotted Zell sniffing around the tack building, clearly searching for something.

I remembered what Dravyn had told me about the selakir's love of dried savos fruit. I tracked down a large stash of these treats, and I spent the next few days feeding a generous amount of them to the creature. I spent hours with him, not just treating him but talking to him, brushing him, trying to gain his trust.

As an added benefit, it gave me an excuse to get out of the palace and avoid the God of Fire. I told him a partial truth when he inquired about it—that I was merely spending so much time with Zell because bonding with the creature brought me comfort.

He didn't argue or dig any deeper than this, as we had reverted back to the rhythms of the week prior—painfully aware of one another, but going to great lengths to avoid speaking any more than we had to.

Further hindering any chance at reconciliation was the continued unrest between the divine courts; he disappeared for long stretches to deal with various problems that popped up, often with little notice—so it wasn't difficult to find the time and privacy I needed to focus on my own schemes.

After three days, Zell began to anticipate me and greet me with enthusiasm. Affection, even. Later on that same day—after Dravyn and everyone else had retired to their rooms for the night—I risked fitting a saddle onto the selakir. He tolerated it well enough, so the next night I did it again, and this time I climbed onto his back and let him get used to the weight of me.

He seemed a bit disgruntled and confused, but he didn't so much as bare his teeth at me, so I considered it a success.

I kept up this strategy for another few days until, on the fourth day, an opportunity to move on to the next part of my plan presented itself.

I was rounding a corner when I nearly collided with

Dravyn. He caught my arm, steadying me as I stumbled back. His touch lingered against me. We *both* lingered, closer to one another than we'd been in days, for far too long before I came to my senses, pulled free, and took a step away.

I'd meant to take more steps, but something in his troubled gaze rooted me to the spot.

"You're up early," he commented. "Which is good, because I...I wanted to see you before I left."

"Left?"

"I have some business in the mortal realm to take care of. I likely won't be back until late tonight."

I didn't ask for details about the business; I no longer trusted he'd tell me the truth about it, anyway. All that mattered was he was leaving—so I had an entire day to work on my plans without fear of him interrupting.

"I'll see you when you get back," I said in the cordial, stiff tone I'd used in all our conversations these past days.

His tone had been much the same, and it remained so now —though it did falter a bit toward the end as he said, "I'd like to see you then."

My heart clenched.

"More than this brief passing in the hallways, I mean." He absently raked a hand through his hair. "We should sit and talk."

I swallowed hard. "When you get back."

He sighed, and then nodded. "Until then...please be safe. I'm sorry I have to go."

Another tight squeeze of my heart made my words quieter. "I'll be fine."

I'm sorry I have to go. It felt like a dozen more apologies were wrapped up in this one, trying to find their way out along with it. But I wasn't ready to hear any of them. They would only confuse and distract me from the things I needed to do, anyway.

I turned away from him first, and I didn't look back as I continued down the hallway.

As soon as I was certain Dravyn was gone for the day, I got to work.

I packed a bag with the Star Goddess's crown, various materials for collecting and recording whatever I might find in the tower, plenty of dried fruit strips, and a few provisions for myself. I slipped my sister's necklace on, strapped Hydrus to my body, then crept out through the darker, lesser-used halls of the palace, avoiding the eyes of the servants as much as possible.

Rieta was the only one who I worried might be overly curious about what I was doing, and she was usually still asleep around this time; thankfully, I didn't encounter her.

I stepped into the backyard and whistled. Zell galloped into sight a minute later, prancing up to me and immediately starting to nudge my hand.

I slipped him several treats before retrieving his riding gear and quickly outfitting him with it while he ate.

He cocked his head at me as I finished adjusting the last strap, intelligent eyes blinking, trying to understand why we were practicing our riding routine in the daytime.

I tried to stay calm, to give him confidence to feed from. "I need your help, Zell," I told him, stroking the bridge of his nose as I spoke. "We have to get to Amalith. I only sort of remember the way, but I know you can help me find it."

I braced myself for him to rebel, to show his teeth, but he stayed perfectly docile. If anything, he seemed eager to prove himself to me, even stepping so his saddle was better aligned with my body, making it easier to mount him.

I swung onto his back. I took the reins with steady hands,

optimism surging through me as I realized that my plan, so far, was actually working. Zell picked up on my optimism, too, setting off into the hills with an easy stride that shifted quickly into a fiery, full-blown gallop.

Without Dravyn anchoring me, I truly felt like I was flying as we gained speed and our surroundings blurred. I came out of the saddle more than once as we leapt over obstacles in our path, and fear and exhilaration danced a dizzying waltz in my stomach.

The journey was longer than I remembered it being. After an hour or so I briefly panicked, thinking we must have taken a wrong turn somewhere...but then they finally came into view: The glittering spires of the Tower of Ascension.

My breaths turned shallow, my heartbeats panicky, as we galloped closer. The structure seemed to rise up impossibly quickly before us—a distant pinpoint on the horizon one moment, an overwhelming stack of shadows and shining edges looming directly over us in the next.

Zell sensed my increasing trepidation and reared to a stop, letting out an uncertain whinny.

"We're okay," I told him, smoothing a hand up and down his neck. "We can do this." I was trying to comfort him as much as myself.

I'm not sure I fully convinced either of us, but he started to walk again with a slow, high-stepping gait, his dark eyes wide and searching, his large ears twitching.

I dismounted at the top of the hill overlooking what appeared to be the tower's main face. I wasn't sure how long I would be inside, and I could find no safe place to tie Zell, so I stripped the headgear from him and offered him several treats along with my thanks. I gave the bag containing the rest of his treats a pointed little shake—a bribe for him to stay close if he wanted more when I came back.

He stood perfectly still, head cocking in curiosity once more, but seemed to understand what I was asking of him.

Hydrus was glowing again, the strange, pulling energy taking hold of its blade and tilting it, pointing me toward the tower once more. I held my breath as I opened my bag and peered inside, checking on the Star Goddess's crown.

It glowed as well.

Another thing had gone according to plan.

I allowed myself a quick sigh of relief before I closed my bag up and steeled myself to approach the tower.

Zell tried to follow me down the steep hill, but I shooed him back. He circled anxiously, stomping his hooves, sending up clouds of dust and little flickers of fire.

My heart clenched at the loyalty he seemed to have developed toward me, but I still ordered him away; hopefully his reluctance to let me go meant he would still be waiting when I re-emerged. How would I get back to the palace, otherwise?

I pushed aside my concerns about *after* and focused on the trial directly in front of me.

At the bottom of the hill, the ground gave way to a stone pavilion with several engraved lines and patterns running through it. My footfalls echoed as I walked over it, as did any noise I made above a whisper; the air seemed closer and heavier here, as though I'd descended into a cave. I could still see the world beyond the pavilion, and even make out Zell's pacing golden figure at the top of the hill, but I felt a thousand miles removed from everything aside from the tower and its immediate energies.

There were three large but relatively plain doors along the tower's face. Beside each one stood a pedestal with strange markings. Each of the pedestals had a wide, deep iron bowl in its center—meant for offerings, it seemed like.

"Three doors and three offerings..." I thought aloud. "One for each court?"

That would make sense, I decided, but there were no labels to tell me which was which. What would happen if I placed the wrong relic into the wrong pedestal?

Maybe nothing at all—but this was essentially part of a divine trial, so I expected tricks and consequences.

As I turned in a circle, studying my surroundings more closely, I recalled the map Dravyn had drawn in the dirt for me. Similar to what I'd seen on that map, three lines ran away from the doors and converged toward a point at the edge of the pavilion, dividing the space into three distinct areas. I remembered the order of the territories from left to right—Sun, Stone, then Shade.

So it made sense to place things in that order, didn't it?

"Crown, sword, then open the door..." I recited to myself as I pulled the crown from my bag.

I left the bag, my sword, and everything else behind, and I clutched the crown with both hands and slowly approached the first pedestal. It trembled slightly in my hold, swirls of deep blue overtaking its tarnished silver surface.

The closer I came to placing it in the offering bowl, the darker the energy upon the crown became—though there were also pinpricks of silver interrupting the darkness, like stars winking into existence. By the time I reached the door, it fully resembled the night sky my trial had taken place within, as if the Star Goddess's magic was being drawn out more fully by whatever magic laced the offering bowl.

I hesitated only a moment before dropping the crown into place and taking several quick steps backward.

As I backed away, the iron bowl trembled and took on the same pattern as the crown—a pattern that quickly spread to the frame around the first doorway.

I held my breath as the door itself lit up with a pale, shimmering glow.

Nothing else rattled.

Nothing broke.

Nothing came crashing down even after at least a full minute passed.

Encouraged by this initial success, I moved faster with the second object, carrying Hydrus to the middle door. Like the crown, the blade's glow changed as I drew closer to the iron receptacle I intended to put it in, shifting into swirls of blue and white that reminded me of crashing waves. And again, the iron bowl took on the same colors and energies of its offering—an energy that soon surrounded the middle door and set it aglow.

Once more I held my breath. Watching. Waiting for some sign that I'd made a mistake.

None came.

The tower remained perfectly intact. The air around me seemed to be thinning, too, growing less oppressive.

Only one door remained.

I had nothing to place in the offering bowl beside it—but I did have the mark on my wrist. A mark that Dravyn had given me so I could walk into this realm, he'd said...was it enough to allow me to walk into this tower, too?

Would he be able to tell I'd accessed that magic?

I hadn't considered this last point before now. But the mark seemed to connect us, even across realms, in a way I still didn't fully understand. He'd felt my fear through it when I went back to the mortal realm weeks ago...so there was a chance he could feel it now, too.

Another reason I needed to hurry and finish this task before he returned from whatever business he was tending to.

The mark shivered as I drew closer to the door, the sensation growing more violent and unnerving with every step I took, but I pressed onward.

Though the bowl beside the door appeared empty, when I swiped my hand into it, it felt as if I was threading my fingers through thick plumes of smoke. The thickness seemed to cling to my hand, making it feel much heavier, as the mark on my wrist fully ignited.

The mark burned brighter and brighter, taking on the same hellish glow as the marks that sometimes appeared on Dravyn's skin whenever he accessed the deeper reserves of his power.

I kept my hand in the receptacle until the iron shifted colors as the other bowls had.

My breath left me in a nervous gasp as the final door took on the same color and then swung open, sending a blast of cold, damp air rushing over me.

I stood in the entryway, peering into the tower, trying to make out something—anything—in the darkness within. But I could see nothing, not even just a few feet inside; it was as though the tower's magic swallowed up all the light that attempted to cross the threshold.

At my back, far in the distance, I heard Zell whinnying loudly. Desperately.

A warning.

I ignored it and stepped inside.

The door slammed shut behind me, plunging me into total darkness—save for the soft glow still emanating from the mark on my wrist.

I tentatively held my hand out in front of me, willing it to burn brighter. I didn't truly feel like I had control over it, but it *did* seem to answer my silent plea. My elven eyes soon adjusted to the blackness as well, and between these things I was able to make out the basic shapes of my surroundings.

Soaring walls of sparkling obsidian rose higher than I could see all around me. The ground was the same pale stone as the pavilion outside, at first, but soon gave way to various different materials. A path of white crystal caught my eye, and I followed it as it sloped and twisted down into the tower's depths, eventually stretching into a flat corridor. Narrow rivers of turquoise water ran along each side of this corridor, the waters converging toward a single, shimmering pool in the center of a room just ahead.

And behind the pool stood a bright-eyed man dressed in a dark cloak with silver fastenings, smiling up at me as though he'd been eagerly awaiting my arrival.

CHAPTER 40

I THREW A GLANCE BACK UP THE SLOPING PATHWAY, toward the exit, but quickly decided I was past the point of running away.

The man continued smiling at me as I descended and approached the sparkling pool. His eyes had solid black centers rimmed by glowing white circles, making me think of ink bleeding out from the middle of a page. He was tall, subtly muscular, all the elegant edges of him suggesting power and grace.

His footsteps made no sound against the stone floor as he stepped to the very edge of the water, directly across from me. His finely made cloak was silent as well, swaying as he walked but without the *swish* of fabric or the clinking of fastenings that should have accompanied it; I wondered if he was merely an apparition of some sort.

"Who are you?" I asked.

"A keeper of the tower. Nothing more. Nothing less." His voice matched the rest of his demeanor—smooth yet powerful, twisting silk draped over a steel edge.

"And what is it that you're keeping?" I asked, gaze flickering to the turquoise water for an instant before darting back up to his face.

"This pool is known as *Berethryl*. To drink of its water is to forget the taste of all other things, to erase all that came before and start anew."

After the chaos and pain of the past months, I nearly trembled with the sudden temptation before me. My knees felt weak, threatening to buckle, to bring me closer to the water for a taste, a chance at having even just a part of my pain and confusion erased...

The Tower Keeper was studying me with interest, his handsome face bright in the light of the pool. "Do you wish to be divine, Karys Elendiel? To forget what you were before coming here?"

I jumped only slightly at the sound of my full name from the strange being's lips.

Of course he knew my name—it was hardly the most unsettling thing I'd encountered in this realm.

"Answer truthfully," he urged.

Truthfully, I *did* want to forget. I couldn't deny I sometimes wished for a blank slate, a chance to start over in some place where I wasn't caught between all the thorny questions and complications I was now.

But I knew better than to be quick to share my answers, my true desires, with any being in the divine realm.

Instead, I pondered both of his questions for a long moment, searching for whatever deception he was trying to conceal—until I realized that something he'd said didn't make sense.

I distinctly remembered the first conversation I'd had with Dravyn about his life before he became a god—how he'd told me that ascension did not mean forgetting what he'd been in his past. Mairu's story of her human family and hardships proved this to be true as well. What sort of god or goddess they became was directly tied to what they'd been through as mortals, in a way I never would have guessed at before these months I'd spent among them.

So this water, if it truly made one forget, was not the ascension magic most sought from this tower.

I met the Keeper's unsettling gaze, and I said, "I didn't come here because I wished to forget."

"Then why are you here?"

I wasn't truly here to ascend, either, so the question stumped me for a moment. His smile widened as the seconds passed, as though it had been his goal to stump me. I also had the distinct impression he was reading my mind—that he already knew why I was here—so it would have been pointless to try to lie to him.

"Because I want to understand," I answered, truthfully enough. "Because I want to know what fully became of the ones who walked in this tower before me."

His expression shifted into something unreadable, the white glow of his eyes overtaking the black for a terrifying moment. I braced myself and retreated a few steps, worried I had said the wrong thing.

Then he turned his back to me, pointing at something in the distance, and said, "If that is the case, I believe you'll want to venture deeper to find what it is you're after."

My chest tightened at the thought of having to descend farther into the darkness. But I managed a nod, and as I did, a path appeared where he was pointing—another sloping route twisting into the depths.

How far underground did this tower go?

I started to walk before fear could grip me more fully.

The path, which was made of translucent, faintly glowing blue crystal, led to another flat room with shining black walls that seemed to absorb most sound. There was no keeper here—only another pool that was much smaller, much brighter than the first.

I realized then that bypassing the first pool had likely been a test, and a chill shot through me as I wondered what would have become of me if I'd actually given in to the temptation and drank from its waters.

My shivering didn't cease as I approached the second pool. I peered into it, expecting to see my tired and scarred—but determined—face.

It was not myself peering back at me.

The reflection's dark hair fell in similar waves past her shoulders, but her eyes were blue, not green. Her skin was a perfectly sandy, unblemished beige, unmarred by scars or anything else. Her smile was bold. Unbothered. The confident, familiar expression I'd never managed to fully imitate.

My sister.

I blinked and she disappeared, leaving my face—and my face alone—in the water.

Another blink and she returned, only to disappear again in the next breath. Back and forth it went, the water rippling gently even though I never touched it—it was as though Savna was trapped beneath the surface, trying to break through.

I clenched my hands into fists and hugged them hard against my sides, fighting the urge to reach into the water and grab her. This was a trick. I *knew* this was a trick.

That didn't stop the aching in my hands and heart as I stood there uselessly, letting her drown.

I sensed the Tower Keeper approaching, though his footsteps and everything else about him remained silent.

"She's the one you're seeking, is she not?"

I couldn't answer with anything more than a numb dip of my head, an almost nod.

"She stood here, years ago," he informed me.

I spun around to face him, heart in my throat.

"Her reflection was much clearer than yours."

Of course it was.

My sister had always been so certain, so clear in her decisions. She would never have wavered as I did now. She never would never have questioned what she was meant to do, who she was meant to be, what she was meant to look like.

I glanced back at the water. At my reflection alone, now. Like a distant observer I saw my hands reaching for my scars, clawing a path across my cheek and throat. I dragged my fingers back down into fists at my sides and asked, "What is this pool called? What is its magic?"

"*Melithra*," he replied. "And its waters have the power to completely transform you with merely a sip."

"To trigger ascension, you mean?"

"It has such power, yes."

My pulse quickened. It couldn't be so easy as taking a drink of water. There had to have been a catch.

"The power to completely transform..." I repeated, "...but what will it transform me into?"

He took so long answering that I finally turned to face him again. His smile had become almost pleased. As though we were playing a game, and I'd proven a worthy opponent.

His approval did nothing to settle my nerves.

I watched closely as he stepped to my side and knelt down. His hand braced against the ground for a moment before he drew up a handful of dust, letting it trickle between his fingers. As it fell, it swirled into the shape of a large goblet with black jewels encircling it.

"What you become is, of course, up to you," he said, handing me the cup.

I took it slowly, marveling at it, trying to understand what sort of magic could create such a thing from dust—and with so little effort.

When I looked up again, the Tower Keeper was gone.

The cup shook in my hand as I turned my attention back to the water. This felt like another test. Another trick. I was not ready to drink anything I might draw from this pool. I was, however, ready to leave this place—and I couldn't go back empty-handed after all the trouble I'd gone through to get here.

After steadying myself with a deep breath, I scooped up a cupful of the magical water, taking care not to let even a drop of it touch my skin. I started to back away, but hesitated, unable to resist peering one last time into Melithra.

I'm not sure whose face I wanted to see—mine or my sister's.

I saw neither. Instead, the water frosted over as I looked into it, turning to an opaque glass that blazed with a bright energy for an instant before going dull, the dark shift causing a foreboding twist deep in the pit of my stomach.

I hurried back up the sloping pathway. My mark's light had dwindled, but the water I carried glowed brightly enough that my eyes could make out the way well enough, even once I left the path of glowing crystal behind.

As I reached the main floor once more, I braced myself for another trial, another fight to get out, just as I'd had to fight to get in.

The door was already open.

I could hear Zell whinnying, could feel the chill breeze rolling in, could smell the salt and dust in the outside air.

It felt almost too good to be true, but I was too anxious to leave to question it. I raced outside, taking care not to spill the elixir I'd gathered.

The other two doors, and the bowls and relics beside them, had ceased their glowing. The tower seemed darker than ever before. Duller, almost, as though taking even just a cupful of Melithra's water had somehow leached the dwelling of an incredible amount of power.

I grabbed Hydrus and the Star Goddess's crown from their receptacles, and I raced to the bag I'd left at the edge of the pavilion. Inside it was a waterskin; I drank all I could from it as quickly as possible, then dumped the rest of its contents out and carefully refilled it with the water from the tower's pool, securing it tightly before shoving it deep into the bottom of the bag.

I didn't look back at the tower as I raced up the hill. I wanted to. But I was afraid of what I might see. The foreboding feeling that had overtaken me as I watched Melithra's waters go dark was back, twisting more deeply in my gut than before.

As I reached the hilltop, I briefly forgot about the tower and its strangeness as I spotted a lone, familiar figure in the distance—the God of Death. He was walking along the steep edge overlooking the ocean of his dark energy. Maintaining it, I assumed, as was his punishment.

I froze at the sight of him.

Could he tell Dravyn and I had walked that same path days ago?

Had he seen me go into the tower just now?

No; he seemed entirely focused on his task. If he'd noticed

me, he gave no outward sign of it. Part of me wanted to go to him and *make* him notice me, to demand more answers about his relationship with my sister.

But another, much louder inner voice told me I needed to run.

I had not forgotten our last encounter near this territory. I was no match for the Death Marr if he decided he was in a bad mood today, and Dravyn was a world away, unable to come to my rescue.

I'd be a fool to linger.

I still hesitated much longer than I should have before I dug the bag of dried fruit out and fed several to Zell, urging him to be calm and quiet while I gathered the gear I'd set aside and prepared him for riding again.

By the time I finished and hoisted myself onto the selakir's back, the Death Marr was nowhere to be seen.

Of course, that didn't mean he wasn't there.

Palms sweating as they gripped the reins, I nudged Zell into movement. Luckily, he seemed ready to run, all the anxious energy I'd caused him unleashing all at once. He broke into a full speed gallop so quickly I was nearly thrown from the saddle.

He was moving so fast, and the wind stung so badly, that I couldn't stay upright. I leaned forward, pressing my body nearly flat against his back, trusting he knew the way back to the palace and would carry me there.

We made it only a few miles before a wave of bitter cold overtook us so swiftly it stole my breath away.

Zell veered wildly to the left before starting to slow. I shot upright, thighs gripping tightly to maintain balance, gaze searching. I immediately saw what was causing him distress: A strange fog had rolled in behind us.

Zell galloped faster, trying to stay ahead of it, but tendrils of the grey and white clouds were reaching out, swiping at our path, wilting every blade of grass they touched.

The tendrils grew thicker, heavier. *Colder.*

I heard a pounding within them, like the thunder of Zell's hooves magnified many times over.

This was no random fog, not some strange phenomenon of the magical landscape. Something concealed within it was alive and pursuing us.

Gaining on us.

The fog drew closer, and I recognized shapes emerging from the rolling clouds—silver fur, lithe bodies, antlered heads, long snouts snapping at Zell's heels...

Veilhounds.

An entire pack of them.

CHAPTER 41

I PRESSED CLOSER TO ZELL'S BACK ONCE MORE, urging him faster, shouting cries of encouragement. He lifted his head and his strides soared longer. Flames kicked up behind him, drawing multiple high-pitched yelps from the pursuing pack as the smell of singed flesh and fur filled the air.

I heard bodies tumbling, scuffling with one another and falling behind—but when I glanced back, I counted seven hounds still following us.

I made eye contact with the one leading the charge. It sped up, barreling closer as though fueled by the fear in my expression.

The flames building around Zell's hooves flared hotter and higher, nearly reaching up to his flanks and igniting my legs in the process. He could have ignited himself entirely and been rid of the beasts, I realized, and maybe he was thinking the same thing—that I was a burden keeping him from escaping.

I hastily scanned our surroundings for some way I could help.

After nearly a mile of searching, I spotted a river snaking its way through the tall grass. Hydrus vibrated against me at the exact same moment, as if trying to catch my attention and make sure I didn't overlook the water.

I wasn't sure I fully trusted the sword or the magic of the Ocean Marr that it contained, but I was desperate for help.

I guided Zell toward the river. He was obedient at first—until he got close enough to realize the waterway was too wide to leap across. It looked like a dead end.

But the sword was insistent, shaking so violently within its sheath that it nearly rattled free on its own. The hounds fanned out behind us. We couldn't turn around without turning into the jaws of at least one of them, so I urged Zell onward, whipping Hydrus from its sheath as I did.

The veilhounds on the outer edges of the pack sped up, racing nearly parallel to us and drifting closer and closer, pinching us in.

The river loomed.

Zell's cries were terrifyingly frantic as his hooves struck the shoreline.

He leapt.

I swung the sword forward, feeling its magic tremble through the blade. The waters parted for an instant—just long enough to allow us to bound across a drained riverbed of slippery stone and mud—before crashing back over the veilhounds, sweeping four of them off their feet and carrying them away.

The other three slammed to a stop on the shore behind us. They paced for a moment, long snouts lifting into the air, an eerie chorus of low-pitched howls rising between them. As the water settled back into an easy current, they began to swim across.

Downstream, one of the beasts the water had swept away

pulled itself from the river, gave a quick shake, then resumed the chase, quickly closing in on us.

"Faster, Zell!" I cried.

We spun away and broke into another gallop only to find ourselves facing a wall of grey and white clouds just ahead—more fog like the kind the hounds had emerged from.

I didn't want to know what would happen if we tried to race through it.

I changed directions—which slowed us down, giving the beast that had survived the crashing river time to catch up to us. It snapped and slashed at Zell's legs, growls and howls assaulting my ears in between its show of fangs and claws.

Zell let out a panicked bray as it leapt toward us. I swung my sword for the hound's neck. I missed, though I did manage to knock it off course and briefly disorient it.

Another lunge quickly followed the first. This time my attempt at parrying connected, but without the force to truly penetrate the beast's jaw like I'd wanted to—I only made it angrier.

It stopped attacking, throwing its head back and letting out a deep, gravelly howl.

The fog in the distance billowed, its movements growing more violent as the other three hounds answered the first one's sound. It was almost as if they were somehow controlling the mist with their eerie song. My eyes darted back and forth between the fog and the monsters, watching closer, trying to understand the connection between them.

The lower their howls, the larger the tumbling fog swelled.

Then came a series of sharp barks, and cloudy tendrils shot out from the churning mass and struck toward us.

Zell retreated, bucking wildly back and forth as the other three hounds closed in and circled around us. He slammed to a stop as he caught sight of them, throwing me sideways out of the saddle.

I dangled awkwardly, leg twisted in a gruesome, painful manner. In a panic, I swung Hydrus through the stirrup, cutting myself free. I hit the ground hard, knocking the wind from my lungs.

Zell bolted, narrowly avoiding stomping a fiery hoof onto my head as he went. Two of the hounds gave chase.

The remaining two narrowed their focus on me.

I stumbled to my feet, brandishing Hydrus in one hand and unleashing my claws on the other.

The tendrils of fog swarmed around me. As soon as I breathed it in, dizziness struck. I swayed dangerously, nearly dropping Hydrus as I flung my arms out beside me and snapped my eyes shut, trying to maintain balance.

The veilhounds rarely made violent work of their targets, I recalled—they drained them, leaving nothing but a shell of a body behind. It felt like they were attempting to do that now.

As the fog completely circled me and sank through my clothing and skin, the soul-deep chill of the Death Marr's magic came to mind. Except this was more painful. The fog pressed in only to immediately try to force its way back out, the wild back and forth pressure enough to make me want to collapse, to hug myself into a tight ball out of a desperate desire to just make myself and the world around me hold still.

But I stayed on my feet.

I had to stay on my feet.

These were the same sort of beasts who had been sent to hunt down my sister. For all I knew, one of them could have been the very one who had actually killed her.

Vengeance took a fierce, determined hold on my body, steadying me, fueling movement.

I broke through the disorienting fog, gasping for clean air, sword swinging at the curls of mist trying to reach for me. Hydrus seemed to have at least a minor effect on this mist, not parting it as easily as the river water, but scattering the reaching tendrils into thinner wisps that were easier to avoid.

One of the hounds lunged toward me, slamming their head into my side, trying to make me stumble once more into the mass of fog. I stopped myself just before the wall of grey touched my back. The hound charged again. This time I held my ground, catching it by the throat, my claws sinking deep into its rough, thick fur.

There was little blood, even as I flexed my fingers and twisted, deepening my hold. The blood that did spatter the ground was dark and purplish—shining almost the same way the Death Marr's ocean did.

I tried to wrestle the creature and pin it to the ground, but despite its light frame, it proved much stronger than me. It stood on its hind legs, digging its paws into the dirt, giving it leverage to jerk its head away from my claws. Its teeth grazed my forearm. As a steady stream of blood rolled down and collected at my wrist, I gave a vicious cry and violently dislodged my grip, throwing it off balance. It hit the ground with a yelp.

The second hound's eyes flashed brightly as it charged toward me and then stopped, crouching low, lifting its head with another low howl.

The fog behind me exploded in size, threatening to engulf us both.

Before the disorienting mist could overtake anything, a shadow overcame the entire area, long and twisting and accompanied by a low roar—

The shadow belonged to a dragon.

It took my fogged brain a moment to understand what I was seeing.

Mairu.

Her golden, serpentine form landed with enough force to shake the ground and knock the second veilhound off its feet. She lashed toward it as it tried to recover, and it rolled awkwardly, legs kicking and scrambling for purchase, before struggling to its feet and starting to run.

The one I'd battled staggered upright and followed, whimpering and leaving a trail of dark blood in its wake.

After they had fled far into the distance, Mairu arched her long body upright and began to shift, golden energy rippling around her, obscuring her in a curtain of light. Seconds later, the curtain fell away to reveal her human form. As her face emerged from the brightness, she wasted no time fixing me with a furious glare.

I met her fury with my own, clutching my bleeding arm, still on the defensive after my latest near-death experience. "Why are you here?" I demanded.

"Certainly not because I felt like going for a leisurely stroll," she snapped, adjusting one of her dangling, dagger-shaped earrings. "And I could ask you the same question, couldn't I?"

I didn't reply, busy watching Zell as he cantered back to me. The selakir immediately shoved his face underneath my arm, as if trying to use my body to shield its vision so it didn't have to see the bloody ground or other reminders of our battle. The poor thing was shaking all over.

"Well?" Mairu pressed.

"I actually *was* out for a leisurely stroll," I deadpanned. "Or a ride, rather. Obviously, the leisurely part didn't work out."

"As though I believe that for a moment," she hissed.

I kept my focus on Zell, trying to calm him—and myself—with slow, repetitive rubs of his sweaty, trembling neck.

Mairu's voice softened the tiniest bit as she said, "Just tell me the truth."

I glanced her direction, acknowledging the words, but I couldn't hold her disappointed gaze. I wanted to tell her the truth. My argument had been with Dravyn, not her, after all. But my hackles were still raised from my argument with the Fire God, and, even all these days later, I couldn't seem to lower them. "Did he send you after me?"

"He didn't send me anywhere. He's still in the mortal realm." She clicked her tongue in annoyance before begrudgingly adding, "Though yes, he did ask me to stay as close as possible to you until he returned."

"Spying on me again?"

"Watching over you," she corrected.

I scoffed.

She narrowed her golden eyes on my bleeding arm. "He wants to keep you safe. We *all* do."

"I would have been fine. I managed to deal with all except the very last of the hounds before you arrived, didn't I?"

Frowning, she pointed toward something in the distance. "There are more just over the hills there. A dozen, at least. I imagine they would have answered the calls of their fellow hounds eventually...do you think you would have been fine if they did?"

Chill bumps swept over my skin. Instead of answering her question, I asked one of my own. "Why did the Death Marr's beasts attack me?"

"I'd like to know that myself." Concern clouded her eyes, dulling their gold, as she added, "Dravyn will be furious when he finds out. We have enough problems with the courts outside our own, and now let's add intra-court feuding to the mix..."

I didn't want to think about court politics and posturing on top of everything else just then, so I focused on studying my latest wound, wincing a bit as I stepped away from Zell and twisted my arm around to get a better look.

The teeth marks didn't appear deep, but an alarmingly cold numbness was starting to overtake the area around them, as if the creature's bite had injected something similar to the fog summoned by its howls.

"I don't have to tell Dravyn everything you tell me," Mairu said. "I only wish you would explain yourself."

Zell gave a sudden snort, his nose no longer shoving against me but instead trying to reach the bag attached to his saddle. I moved to the bag—which thankfully had made it through the attack without any damage—in search of the treat container.

My hand brushed against the waterskin containing Melithra's water, and I tensed as if readying myself for an explosion, or some sign that the goddess before me realized what I was carrying...

Nothing happened.

Such power, in such an unassuming package, I mused.

I found the treat container next, but it was empty. Guilt gnawed at my insides. Not only for being out of them, but for putting Zell through what I had so soon after gaining his trust. And once the guilt started, I couldn't seem to stop it from spreading all the way through me; I felt it when I looked at the goddess, too—because we'd started to trust one another as well, hadn't we?

Sighing, I said, "I went to the Tower of Ascension."

Her eyes widened slightly, but she didn't interrupt.

"I know my sister did the same thing years ago," I continued, still somewhat reluctantly, "and I needed to walk where she had, that's all. To try and make sense of her and what she did."

Mairu was quiet for some time. "And did you get the answers you hoped for?"

"Not really," I answered, honestly. "Just more questions."

We stood in silence, the exasperation in her expression eventually giving way to concern, which softened the hard edges of my anger—at least for now. A tentative truce.

"You shouldn't have gone alone," she said.

"Would you have gone with me if I'd asked?"

"Of course."

I snorted.

"You don't believe me?"

Another admission fell from my lips before I could catch it. "I'm not sure what I believe anymore. Or who I can trust. I thought Dravyn and I..." I trailed off, shaking my head, and started to walk in the direction of the palace.

Zell followed dutifully at my side, nudging his head under my arm and lifting as if trying to pull me up onto his back. I didn't want to ride him again just then; I still felt bad about how I'd used him. And I needed to feel the earth beneath my feet, to ground myself against something solid.

Mairu followed as well, trailing at a short distance. "You actually rode that beast, huh?"

"We've gotten close." I gave him a rub between his stubby antlers. "Animals are less confusing when it comes to trust and affection, I've come to realize. It's much easier to care about them and not end up regretting it."

She nodded, though her expression was troubled when I glanced over my shoulder at her.

We walked for several minutes before she put that trouble into words. "The God of Fire cares deeply for you, you know."

I stiffened. "So he led me to believe."

She quickened her step until she was nearly in front of me, staring as if she could stop me with merely a look, with no need to employ her controlling magic.

I kept walking.

"If he didn't care about you," she said, "then the Death God would have broken you the first time you encountered him and his beasts—long before today."

I finally slowed, looking at her before I could help myself; I was curious.

Too curious for my own good.

"The Death Marr's magic can draw out even the deepest of a person's secrets," she said, "but he usually breaks the mind in the process."

Unpleasant memories of nearly crumpling on the cliffs, the God of Death looming over me, gripped my thoughts and made my pulse quicken.

"If Dravyn had not intervened when you trespassed in Harithyn, Zachar's magic would have taken the information we needed from you by force. This whole ordeal with the trials, with *you*...we could have avoided it all. We could have learned what we needed about your sister and the rest of your background, your allies—all of it—then discarded your broken body somewhere, simple as that. Valas and I were tempted to take this route in the beginning, to be honest. But Dravyn refused. So which do you think is more important to him in the end? You, or the information you carry?"

I started to walk again.

He was determined to protect me—I didn't doubt that. I

just wished he'd been honest about what he knew about me before now.

"The other courts were furious when they learned we'd brought one of your kind into our territory," she went on, catching up once more. "Another point where he could have—probably *should* have—broken and discarded you somewhere. But again, he didn't."

I still couldn't fully wrap my mind around whatever feelings Dravyn had for me, so I tried to stay focused on the bigger picture. "Do the others fully know who I am now? About my sister and everything? The God of Storms spoke as though he had everything about me figured out."

"Rumors travel as quickly through divine air as they do through mortal air. Quicker, maybe. Neither Valas nor I breathed a word, but Zachar lives for such gossip. And his relationship with the God of Fire is somewhat strained, if you haven't noticed. I wouldn't be surprised to learn he's been fraternizing with other courts in an attempt to hurt Dravyn. He likely saw it as a way to distract from the Edgelands business, too—get the other courts mad about *you*, and they might overlook any of his failures. Which is idiotic, as the Edgelands problem is a much more pressing matter. But there's no divine law against the gods being idiots, unfortunately."

Another round of chills went through me as I began to realize how messy the realm around me was truly becoming. I'd been so preoccupied with my own scheming that I'd been ignoring most of the growing unrest.

"I saw Zachar near the tower," I told Mairu. "Trying to tend to his appointed task, I assumed; Dravyn said these past weeks have seen more cracks in the barrier than ever before."

"Yes. All the more reason you shouldn't have been

anywhere near that place on your own," she said. "I thought we were past such foolishness."

"We were," I said, tersely, "until I realized how much Dravyn had been keeping from me this whole time." I tried to temper my voice into a more rational tone as I added, "I don't like being in the dark—and it feels as though everyone I've ever spoken to has been doing their best to keep me there. So you'll have to forgive me for wanting to go find some things out *on my own.*"

She shook her head but said nothing.

I finally gave in to Zell's insistent nudging and hoisted myself onto his back once more, gritting my teeth at the bite of pain that went through my arm when I put weight on it.

I could sense the selakir's anxious desire to run again, and I was tempted to let him take off at full speed—however rude it might have been—but I restrained him and let Mairu keep an easy pace alongside us.

"Dravyn should have told you sooner," she said, shaking her head again. "I could have told you, too, but..."

I focused on better situating my hands on the reins and muttered, "But none of us fully trust one another, do we?"

"The mistrust seems to have rooted itself deeply between our kind, unfortunately."

As though I needed the reminder.

"Do you remember what I told you about my magic?" she asked moments later, effortlessly demonstrating that magic by letting the dark skin of her cheeks transform into hard golden scales. "Change is perhaps the greatest power I possess...but unfortunately I've found it's often messy, too, ripping things out by their roots."

"And painful."

"Painful as shit," she agreed with a forlorn, sharp and partially-dragon-toothed smile.

I lifted my gaze, scanning the sky, some foolish part of me hoping to see wings of fire emerging from the brightness, as I asked, "You said he still hasn't returned...but where did he go?"

"Back to the kingdom he once called home, to check on what remains of the family he left behind."

Images of the memorials he'd shown me fell into my mind, and my heart sank into my stomach. However angry I was, however shattered my trust, I still didn't like the idea of him going home and facing his broken family alone, for some reason.

"Is something wrong in his old kingdom?" I asked.

"Hopefully not." Her tone was not reassuring.

I frowned, staring expectantly until she elaborated.

"Tensions are rising between the courts, as you know. When this happens, some of them fight dirty. Sometimes they target the things others care about, rather than dealing with one another directly. So Dravyn has had me and Valas watching over you during every moment when he can't do it himself, and he's been slipping back to check on his old life in the mortal realm occasionally, too."

"They would attack a mortal kingdom over such things? Really?"

"Many of the 'natural disasters' the realm of Avalinth deals with are actually the side effects of one god getting frustrated or furious with another." She shrugged. "It gets very dramatic at times. The Moraki don't intervene unless things get completely out-of-control."

This sounded more like the gods I'd once believed in—the ones introduced to me by my father and sister's fiery, impassioned speeches.

If only they had all proven to be so recklessly callous and unfairly cruel.

I continued to watch the sky as I trotted on, wondering what it looked like back in my old home. What it might look like if whatever was happening on the Edgelands escalated.

How had my sister broken through the barrier between realms? What sort of lasting damage had she done? Could I fix it, somehow? Or was my presence here only going to make things worse?

I was causing tension between the courts that needed to be working together on solving the threats they faced—which was bad enough—but as we drew closer to the God of Fire's territory, an even more unsettling thought occurred to me.

"Dravyn said the attacks at the Edgelands' barrier have gotten more volatile lately, starting around the time I came back from my visit home...could something about my return have triggered the escalation?" It sounded absurd when I said it out loud, I thought.

I wanted her to tell me it was absurd, too.

But she only said, "I wish I knew."

A lump formed in my throat, making it difficult to swallow.

"Just promise me you'll stay close to the palace for the foreseeable future, please?" The air tingled with her power, more hardened scales appearing along her skin, as she looked behind us and said, "Because it feels as though something big is about to break."

DRAVYN STILL HAD NOT RETURNED to the palace by the time we reached it.

Mairu brought me straight to Rieta, who helped dress the wound on my arm and fetched a tonic to rid me of the lingering chill of the veilhound's magic.

The Serpent Goddess made us both swear not to tell Dravyn what had truly caused that wound; if he asked, we were to blame the bite on one of the selakir. If he learned what Zachar's beasts had done—and tried to do—to me, *All hell will break loose*, Mairu warned, *and we have too many other things to focus on without inciting that battle.*

After we'd agreed to keep the secret, Mairu excused herself to return to her own palace—though not before promising that Valas would be by later to check on me as well.

Or maybe it was a warning, rather than a promise.

Hard to say which.

It was unnecessary, either way; I was done with my adventuring for the day, my courage and curiosity all used up. I was perfectly content to lock myself away in my room for the remainder of the night.

Luckily, Rieta wasn't in a prying mood. She largely left me to my quiet room and private musings, hardly even fussing when I insisted I wasn't hungry and wanted nothing to eat for supper. She was too distracted by the growing trouble outside of the palace to bother much with me, I think.

Even Valas was not his usual goading and playful self when he stopped by; he lingered only long enough to say hello, and— to use his words—*make sure I hadn't set anything on fire*. Then he was gone again, mumbling about needing to go speak with the God of Storms about something.

My heart stuttered as I watched him leave, as I thought about my last encounter with the Storm Marr. I nearly called

Valas back, the words *be careful* on the tip of my tongue. I stopped myself from speaking, but I couldn't stop the realization that slammed like a cannonball into my chest.

In a matter of months, I had gone from hating the gods of this court to worrying about them.

Caring about them.

Which made the weapons—and potential weapons—hidden in my room uncomfortable, to say the least.

Once again, I'd succeeded in the task I'd set out to do, but I didn't feel successful. I'd taken what I needed to take from this realm. I knew the way back to my own realm. I could have fled that very moment with my spoils, could have used them to carry on my sister's legacy, to get my revenge. The path to what I'd once thought would bring me peace lay before me, glittering and tempting and more clear than ever.

All I had to do was walk it.

Instead, I kept perfectly still, my hand braced beside the window, staring out over a world I was no longer sure I wanted to leave.

The tower, the knife, Melithra's water...these past days I had only been going through the motions, I was beginning to think. I'd been fueled by hatred and anger for so long that I'd walked the steps toward vengeance as thoughtlessly as I took my breaths.

Yet, no matter how hard I tried, I still couldn't clearly picture a different path.

Even if I could no longer bring myself to harm Dravyn or anything else in this realm, there was no happy ending in my future.

I couldn't go back to my home and tell them I'd failed, that I cared too much about the gods to follow through with our plans—I'd be banished from every place my kind dwelled. I'd be laughed at. Attacked. Or something far worse.

I also couldn't stay here in this realm that seemed perched on the brink of disaster, filled with danger and turmoil—turmoil that my presence was clearly exacerbating.

As night fell over the palace, the God of Fire still had not returned. And there was no point in denying my feelings about this; they were the same I'd felt watching Valas walk away earlier, only magnified.

I was worried about him.

So worried I could hardly breathe.

I kept pacing the room, inevitably returning to the window every few minutes. Watching the sky. Hoping for fire.

Meanwhile, I swore the shadows all around me were moving in impossible ways. Slinking in and out of the places where I'd hidden the evidence of my plans for betrayal, drawing my eyes unwillingly toward them. Paranoia coiled around me, making my breaths too tight, too shallow. Despite the tonic Rieta had given me earlier, I still felt as if the Death God's beasts had left a permanent mark on my body, chilling me so deeply that nothing I did seemed to warm it.

The cold made me feel unbearably heavy, and eventually, I drifted off to sleep right there on the floor beside the window, chased to exhaustion by visions of shapeshifting shadows and poisonous knives.

CHAPTER 42

A ROUGH HAND SHOOK ME AWAKE SOMETIME LATER. I mumbled curses as I sat up, rubbing my eyes and blinking until Rieta's face came into focus.

"You didn't look particularly comfortable curled up down there," she said, frowning. "And I know you were waiting for his return, so I thought I'd let you know he came back a half hour ago. And the first thing he did was ask about you."

I blushed as my sleepy mind slowly processed her words and realized she was referring to Dravyn.

"I wasn't really *waiting* for him, I just..."

"Spare me." She huffed out a laugh. "You'll find him in the gardens behind the eastern tower, I suspect. That's where he usually goes after coming back from a visit to our old home."

"*Our* old home? You mean you're from the same mortal kingdom he is?"

"Another story for another night." She sighed, and then nodded toward the door. "Go on. He didn't want to disturb your rest, but I think he needs to see you tonight."

"Okay," I mumbled, getting to my feet and stretching

before heading toward the door. I hesitated there, casting a longing look at my bed. It would have been easier to crawl into its piles of fluffy blankets and try to sleep off all my doubts and fears.

But I'd rarely taken the easy way out of things, and I didn't do it now.

I grabbed the cloak thrown over a nearby chair, wrapping it around myself as I stepped into the dark hallway.

It was late. I had no idea how long I'd slept, but most of the palace seemed to have retired for the night. My footsteps echoed on the marble, and the crackling torches lighting my way threw long, uninterrupted shadows across my path—much calmer and less unnerving than the ones that seemed to have taken over my room earlier.

These halls had been frightening when I'd first arrived, but now they felt familiar, like a place I'd called home for years rather than months.

As I made my way outside, I pulled my cloak more tightly against the slight chill. The air was tinged with its usual soft smokiness, but there was a sweet undercurrent of honey that I'd never really noticed before, too. The sky was a deep purplish-blue—beautiful, though I had to admit I missed seeing the stars of the mortal realm's night.

Could I ever get used to this strange sky?

Assuming I stayed here. Assuming there was any chance that I could ever call this place *home*...

Shaking my head, I tried to stop thinking about my future, focusing on remembering my way to the gardens.

I spotted the black iron gate that marked the entrance to the winding path I was searching for, and soon after, I caught a hint of cedar among the smokiness. I followed the scent and found Dravyn, as expected. He was reclining in a chair near a short, vine-wrapped wall with his head tipped back and his eyes closed.

He looked exhausted. I thought he might have been on the verge of sleep, but as I approached, I saw a corner of his mouth edge upward. Still aware of me. Still happy to see me, despite all the sharp words and arguments we'd exchanged over the past week.

"Hello, Sparrow."

"Hello."

He opened his eyes. They were beautiful in the light of the strange sky, their silver sheen shifting closer to blue as they focused on me.

My breath caught as I stared back, heart swelling painfully in my chest as I realized, all at once with a pounding certainty, that I cared more about being with him—making sure he was okay—than I did about continuing any of our arguments.

And maybe I could finally put down my daggers, as he'd asked me to all those days ago, if it meant freeing up my hands to reach for his.

I unclenched my fists and stepped closer to him, busying myself with tracing the vines along the wall while I tried to find the courage to reach, to say all the things I wanted to say.

"Are they all right?" I asked him after a minute.

He sat up more fully, giving me a curious look.

"Mairu told me you went to check on your family in your old kingdom."

"Ah. They're fine. Dealing with the typical threats and obligations of mortal politics, but otherwise, safe. Nothing to concern ourselves with."

"Do you go back to visit them often?" I asked, picking at the little white flowers interspersed along the crawling vine.

"From a distance. We never really speak, however. Not

since I ascended."

"Really? Never?" The thought caused an odd ache in the pit of my stomach. "Do they know what's become of you?"

"They...yes. They know."

"Is it against the rules for you to speak to them or something?"

He shook his head. "Not any rules I'm aware of. But my older brother and I never really saw eye to eye about...well, most things. And what I've become—the things I've done— only complicate our relationship. So I go back periodically to make sure they're still in one piece, but I avoid interacting with them as much as possible."

I frowned, the aching pit in my stomach widening, and he gave a humorless chuckle in response.

"I'm a coward, I know."

"I don't think you're a coward." I stopped picking at the flowering vine and leaned against the wall in front of him, folding my arms around myself and lifting my gaze to the starless sky. "It would be hard to go back to the past, I believe, after you've changed so...dramatically."

I didn't elaborate on why I believed this; I didn't think I needed to, and he didn't press the subject. Instead, his gaze fell to the bandage wrapped around my forearm. Just barely peeking out from beneath the sleeve of my cloak, yet he still noticed it.

"Never mind me," he said. "What about you? Are you all right?"

"This? It's nothing. I got too bold handling the selakir, that's all." I fidgeted with the bandage, forcing myself to meet his concerned gaze. "You warned me about Zell's teeth. I simply insist on learning things the hard way sometimes. Most of the time, actually."

He chuckled softly at this part, while I averted my eyes. I hated speaking yet another lie between us, even if it was a necessary one to keep the peace.

I pulled the sleeve of my cloak down and lost myself in thought for a moment, walking the garden paths, kneeling to study the more interesting plants I came across.

Dravyn named each one I asked about, telling me how they'd been created, whether they had similar counterparts in the mortal realm, and all about the magical properties that set some of them apart. Some were precise creations of his, while others had been part of the general shaping of this realm when the upper-gods laid their hands and magic upon it.

The conversation eventually shifted entirely to things we'd shaped ourselves—things we'd loved and lost and left behind, things we still held tightly to. We mostly avoided saying anything more about our families, but there were plenty of other things to learn about one another.

We spent at least an hour trading stories and occasional smiles until the sky had deepened to the color of an overripe plum, while the palace grew darker and quieter behind us.

At some point while we were talking, I lost my grip on whatever scraps were left of my rage, letting them float off into the ether until all that remained was a deeper, more nuanced kind of anger—one directed inward rather than outward. It was anger at a younger, more foolish me. One so blinded by hate and a desire to fill the empty spaces my sister had left that I'd never really stopped to question what I was filling those spaces with.

I still didn't know how to fix all the hollow places inside of me.

I just knew I didn't want to be angry any longer.

So where did that leave me?

Where did that leave *us*?

Our conversation trailed off, and I wandered through the flowers some more before settling in front of him again, the small of my back pressing against the wall, my hands close enough to reach out and take his—though I kept them fisted in front of me for the moment.

"You look terrible, by the way. For a god." I offered him a small smile. "Your kind have little need for sleep, you told me, but your face suggests otherwise."

He shrugged. "No rest takes its toll, eventually. Even on me." After a pause, he added, "And I haven't slept since the night I had you beside me." It sounded like a confession, soft and intimate.

"Why not?"

He said nothing to this, but the answer was evident enough in the look he gave me.

Can't you guess?

I could. I suppose I just wanted to hear him say it out loud —which he eventually did.

He took my hand, absently running his thumb along my palm as he said, "I fell asleep with you in my arms, woke up the same way, and now everything else feels unbalanced in comparison. You've ruined me, I'm afraid, and it's obvious to anyone paying attention—Valas won't shut the fuck up about it. He's been even more insufferable than usual."

I felt a blush warming my cheeks. "I haven't slept well lately, either." My lips parted. Closed. Wouldn't open again. There was more I'd planned to say. More I *needed* to say. To admit to.

If there was a coward between us, it was me, not him.

I kept my hand in his, determined not to let the coward

inside of me win. Finally, I managed to speak again. "Can we go for a walk?"

He smiled as he rose to his feet—the roguish, almost playful smile that I so rarely got to see. "We can go anywhere you like."

Not anywhere, I thought, holding in a sigh. *Because the place I'd like to go doesn't exist.*

A place where the wars between our kind had never happened, where we were all equal, where both our siblings were still alive... It didn't exist, but we walked hand-in-hand as if on our way to it just the same.

We strolled from the palace grounds and into the hills beyond. After climbing a particularly steep slope, we found ourselves facing an impressive view. The grass tickling my ankles was soft as velvet, the air teemed with magical energy, and the indigo sky seemed to stretch on for an eternity. I tilted my head back, frowning slightly, struck again by the difference between the skies of our respective worlds.

"What is it?"

"It's still strange to not see stars when I look up." I pulled my gaze back down to his. "I'm not complaining, of course. You gave me a kind of sun, after all—the forgelight is more than enough."

He considered my words for a moment before slipping his hand from mine, a mischievous glint in his eyes. He stayed on the peak of the hill but put some space between us, summoning fire into his palms as he walked away.

As I watched, huddling against the cold, he started to hurl handfuls of flame into the sky.

The fireballs scattered as they flew upwards, breaking into droplets that moved more like liquid than fire until they were mere dots against the vast sky—about the size of distant stars—at which point they fixed in place. Over and over he did this, until there were more fiery stars hanging in the sky than I could count.

Then he lifted his hand, made a sweeping gesture, and all at once the points flared brighter, bursting into bright shades of orange and red and white.

They stayed in place and continued to sparkle even after he lowered his hand and turned his attention back to me.

"Not exactly *stars*," he mused, strolling to my side. "But the best I could do on short notice."

I stared up at them, spinning in a slow circle, mouth agape as I tried to take in all their beauty at once. "I'll settle for them," I said with a soft, mesmerized little laugh.

I continued to marvel at the scene above me for several minutes. When I finally lowered my gaze, Dravyn was watching me with the faintest hint of a smile on his lips.

"Are all the gods such show-offs?" I asked with a wry grin.

"Yes," he said. "But I'm one of the worst."

Another quiet laugh escaped me, turning breathy as he closed the remaining distance between us, wrapping me in a loose embrace and planting a kiss on my forehead. I tucked my head against his collarbone, he rested his chin against me, and we stood like that long enough to make me forget the rest of the world.

My heart thumped, fast but steady. My hands splayed against his hard chest, bracing for balance. I kept watching the stars. One occasionally fell from its fixed point, but even the fall seemed beautifully choreographed, sparks and smoke trailing in a vibrant, spiraling pattern as it plummeted to the ground.

And as I watched the streaks of falling firelight, suddenly there were no doubts left in my mind about what I was supposed to do.

CHAPTER 43

I COULDN'T BECOME WHAT MY SISTER HAD BEEN.

I wouldn't be the pawn my kind insisted on, the rebel they needed, the martyr they wanted.

Instead, I would take the knife hidden in my closet and bury it as deeply as I could into the earth. I would tell Dravyn everything, and I would stay here—this was the side I would choose, and that crack between my worlds could split as wide as it wanted to. I would leap to this divine side and, somehow, I would find a way to stay here.

With him.

I'd wanted to burn with him before. Now I realized I wanted to build with him, too. I wanted to melt the broken pieces of both our worlds and all our wars down and shape them into something new.

I leaned back so I could see his face, ready to declare all of these things in that very moment, but I stopped short as I noticed his quiet smile had given way to a much more serious expression.

"Is something wrong?"

"No." He took a step back, hand falling over mine and grasping it tightly as he said, "But I think we should talk about what happened the other day."

A shiver of uncertainty crept down my spine, but I managed a nod.

He took a moment to decide where to start. "I've been thinking about the question you asked," he finally said. "*How does it end*? And I still don't know the answer, but I just...I need you to know that I'm not the same as I was in the beginning of this. When I realized you were truly unaware of what your sister had done—that your kind were using you in hopes of completing whatever rebellious plans she'd started—something inside of me...broke. Because you are more than a pawn. I realized that within moments of meeting you, and I cannot understand how the ones you consider your allies don't see the same thing." He dropped my hand and paced the length of the hilltop as he spoke, occasionally pausing to summon more flames and fling them at the heavens.

I stayed rooted to my spot. The moment was beginning to feel like a dream, a hallucination I was afraid might shatter if I moved too much.

"That day I took you to see my siblings' memorials," he continued, "when you asked me if I thought a peace between our kind was possible...The idea struck me as strange when you said it. Ridiculous, really. But I haven't been able to get it out of my head ever since. It made me remember something the God of the Shade told me soon after I ascended."

I swallowed hard. "Which was?"

"That fire destroys. But it also forges. I chose my own mark and magic when I ascended, and I swore I would hold to what that upper-god told me, but in truth, I've left out the forging part—unless you count the glass, the memories I keep trying to rebuild and replay in my mind." He stepped back to me, letting the flame he'd been summoning in his palm extinguish into smoke that rose and twisted between us as the wind caught it. "Then you came along, and the more time I spend with you, the more I find myself wanting to do more than just burn it all down. I can't explain it, but I—"

I stopped him with a kiss.

I didn't realize I was doing it until my lips were already against his, the electricity from our touch shocking me back to awareness.

I started to take a step back, startled by my own boldness.

He grabbed me and pulled me against him once more, wrapping my body in a tight embrace, crushing his lips so completely to mine that I forgot where I was for a moment.

We pulled away no less than a minute later, breathless, promise and heat sizzling between us.

He threaded his fingers through my hair, holding me still as he leaned in again, almost touching his forehead to mine. "I've missed you these past days. I've worried about you every damn second. Everything around us feels like it's moving toward chaos, and I should be focused on keeping order and solving problems, but for some reason all I can think about most of the time is *you*. It's maddening." His grip in my hair tightened, sending a bite of pain and a tremble of pleasure through my scalp. "So fucking maddening."

"I'm sorry I've been avoiding you," I whispered. "I'm sorry for...everything."

"It doesn't matter." His eyes fluttered shut as he leaned fully into me, pressing his face into my hair, breathing me in.

My hands came to rest on his chest again, right over his heart. Warmth pulsed in the air, and the stars he'd scattered seemed to shine more brightly, with every pounding beat of it.

"It doesn't matter," he repeated in a whisper, lips sweeping over mine. "Just tell me you'll stay. Tell me you're mine. At least for tonight."

I reached up and traced the strong line of his jaw, my hand and voice both trembling with anticipation. "I will. I am. And after tonight..."

"We'll figure that out when we come to it."

I started to ask how—I couldn't help myself—but he stopped me with another feather-light kiss that quickly grew deeper, hungrier, lasting several seconds before he pulled back, letting his teeth catch my bottom lip as he went.

"I love your mind." His laugh was low and rough, as though he was using it to suppress a growl. "Your endless wondering and interrogating." Another brush of teeth against my lips. "But right now I need you to stop asking so many damn questions and just let me kiss you."

I stopped.

Mostly because he had used the word *love*.

His mouth crashed back to mine. I let go of all my questions as he sank deeper into me, his tongue pushing in and dancing against mine, his hands tangling in my hair and clothing. My touches soon mirrored his—eager and desperate to unravel him, to touch every inch of skin I could.

As I unbuttoned his shirt, he slipped a hand around to the small of my back, cradling me as he dropped to his knees and eased me down along with him.

The grass was luxuriously soft, crushing easily beneath me, but he still slipped the cloak from my shoulders and spread it out behind me like a blanket. There was no need for the garment's warmth anymore; the air teemed with his aroused power, heated to the point of near-sweltering. There was a fire building in my blood at the same time, blazing so intensely that

I encouraged him to keep going until he had stripped away all but my thin undergarments.

I had a brief moment of self-consciousness reclining there, almost fully naked, on the hilltop; any of the gods or their servants might have stumbled upon us.

Then Dravyn shrugged his shirt off and tossed it aside, and I decided I didn't care who saw us—I only cared about digging my nails into the ridges of his muscles and feeling his warm, hard flesh pressed flush against my own.

I pulled my camisole over my head and added it to the pile of our discarded clothing. He watched me moving in the light of the fire-dotted sky, and I couldn't help feeling beautiful beneath his admiring gaze, all my scars and uncertainties, all the imperfect dips and curves of my body glowing beneath the stars he'd hung for me.

Our eyes met, and he lunged toward me like a man starved, pinning me against the ground, bracing an arm on either side of my body and leaning down to kiss me, engulfing me in his heat, his strength, his magic.

I traced the strong lines of his back with my hands. Wrapped my legs around him and tightened, pulling him in closer, harder, drawing a deep groan from his lips.

His mouth moved to the side of my neck, sucking and kissing until I was squirming underneath him. Then he went lower, lips and tongue trailing a path over my collarbone, between my breasts, down to my navel, fingertips skimming alongside as he went. As he reached my hips, he pulled the last of my clothing away. I inhaled sharply at my sudden, complete bareness. His eyes darkened at the sound, his expression flashing feral as he took in the full sight of me.

He ran a hand along the inside of my thigh, the caress light and teasing until my back arched, begging him to touch me more completely. He obliged, pressing a thumb to my aching center, tapping and rubbing in tantalizing circles. Two of his fingers joined in and, once they were fully coated with my arousal, they slipped inside as he leaned over me again.

His fingers plunged deeper as he brought his lips back up to mine, kissing me slowly, deeply, his touch matching the rhythm of whatever his tongue did.

His knees closed in against my thighs, pushing my legs together, clenching them more tightly around his hand.

I breathed out a curse.

His fingers worked faster in response, and he dipped his mouth to my ear and murmured, "I need to know...do you still think it would be a disaster for me to fill you completely? To feel me dripping out of you?"

My toes curled at the reminder of our conversation from days ago—and what had preceded it. "Maybe," I managed to gasp as his fingers curled inside me. "But it's a disaster I'm confident I'd survive."

He smiled at this—I felt it against my skin as he buried his face in the curve of my neck—and his voice dropped lower, wicked and full of want as he said, "We'll see."

My lips parted with a soft *oh* as his fingers slid out of me.

"I'll try to be gentle," he promised, nipping at the edge of my ear, "even though every part of me wants to show you what it feels like to be truly fucked by a god."

With this, he leaned away to finish undressing himself.

I could do nothing but stare for a moment, every nerve ending in my body alive and humming with desire, as he stretched to his full height with the fiery sky at his back, all the hard edges of him cast in perfect light, brilliant and bold and burning.

He took a deliberate step back to me, eyes never leaving mine.

I'd marveled at how human he often seemed, despite his power—but he'd never looked more like a god to me than he did in that moment.

He reached out his hand. I took it, let him pull me to my feet. As I rose up, he dropped to his knees before me, bringing his mouth immediately to my center. His hands clenched around my legs, spreading them wider while his tongue tasted me fully, dragging across my sex and down my thighs until I was quivering in his hold. He slowed after a minute of this, trading hot lashes of his tongue for gentle kisses and blowing the occasional warm, torturous breath across me.

My head tipped back, cutting off the cry rising in my throat. My legs started to buckle. He took my hand again and pulled me down, settling me into his lap, guiding me onto his erection.

I gasped as the hard tip of him slipped inside me.

He eased up only slightly, eyes wild and burning as they watched my lips part and he continued to press in, to stretch me wider.

"Onto your knees for me, Little Sparrow." His hands cupped my bottom, providing me with balance as I obeyed and sank lower, positioning my knees on either side of his.

An involuntary whimper escaped me as he pushed farther inside.

The sound made him pause and make an obvious effort to control himself; he dug his fingers into my skin and held them there, keeping me suspended and still as he asked, "Am I hurting you?"

He was, but I didn't want him to stop.

I shook my head, draping my arms around his neck, further

supporting myself as I dropped my knees fully to the ground and pulled him the rest of the way in.

He cursed, bowing his head to me, face briefly disappearing in the waves of hair cascading over my shoulder. "You're so tight," he growled.

His lips found the sensitive pulse of my throat. He kissed me roughly, and my hips moved of their own accord in response, rocking against him, desperate to match the intensity of his tongue and his touch.

With every rise and fall of my body against his, the pain faded a little more, until there was nothing left but pleasure. Nothing but his hard body colliding with the softness of mine, his powerful warmth radiating through me, his strong hands touching, securing, revering every inch of me.

His fingertips smoothed slow, deliberate trails up and down my spine, dropping lower each time, and a breathy cry escaped me as the first ripple of release curled through my stomach.

He felt me tightening around him—how close I already was—and his eyes took on the same wicked glint they had earlier.

He stopped being gentle. His godly strength was on full display as his hands slid to the backs of my thighs and easily lifted me up and down against him, pounding fully into me again and again until I couldn't think, couldn't speak aside from gasping attempts at his name.

He slowed, baring his teeth, pulling me hard against him, throbbing deeply inside while he held me still. "The sound of my name from your lips like that," he growled, "is going to be the end of me."

I let out a soft cry as he shifted beneath me, pressing even deeper, but managed to catch my breath enough to say, "Then I'll prepare for the disastrous end."

His laugh was savage as I braced my hands against his chest, squeezing my breasts together, drawing his attention to them. He buried his face between them while his hands unclenched from my thighs and roamed over the rest of my body, nails leaving a trail of pebbled flesh wherever they scraped across.

He finally let one hand rest against my lower back, holding me firmly in place as he thrust. The other hand took its time traveling up the length of my body, fingers pinching the swollen peak of a breast before continuing upward, lightly wrapping around my throat. Then he leaned back, bending just slightly at the waist, so his hips lifted and he penetrated even deeper.

I felt my control slipping, my muscles going rigid. His name became a cry rather than a gasp, and his grip on me tightened as he leaned up to kiss me, letting his lips linger against mine as he asked, "Are you going to come for me, Wildfire?"

Every syllable that purred from his mouth vibrated through my entire body in a way that felt torturously good. Words failed me, but I managed to nod in response. That response was all that mattered in that moment—there was only me and him, his question and my answer, the world reduced to nothing except the ending we were both chasing.

He stayed on his knees but hooked his arms beneath my legs, pulling them out straight beside him so he could better control the angle and speed at which he drove into me. I started to lean backwards, fingers clutching for ground, for balance, but he forced me back upright.

"Arms around my neck and eyes on me, Wildfire."

The edge in his voice was my final undoing; I could hear how close he was—closer even than me—and it made me feel powerful even as I followed his commands. The building waves of my climax rolled through me, and this time I didn't resist them. I let them carry me over the edge, and I dug my fingers into Dravyn's back and carried him with me, tightening my hold until I had pulled the satisfying roar of his release from deep within him.

As our cries faded, the night seemed strangely quiet all of sudden, with nothing but our too-fast heartbeats disrupting the silence.

The sky still flashed with occasional bursts of fiery, falling starlight.

Dravyn stretched out his legs behind me while I remained in his lap, facing him, the essence of him warm and dripping between us. He studied me like I was something altogether new —something he desperately wanted to know better—his fingers tracing the lines of my face, his lips moving slowly over mine as if memorizing the way his fit with them.

After our shaking stopped, we curled up together on the blanket he'd made of my cloak. He wrapped his arms around me, holding tightly, as though he was still afraid I might not stay as I'd promised I would.

A few minutes passed before his breathing slowed and he asked, "Do you feel as though you've just survived a disaster?"

I considered my response through the distracting sound of my heart still pounding in my ears. "No. But I feel as though tomorrow might bring bigger disasters."

"Don't think of tomorrow then, *miran-achth*."

"That word... You called me by it the night of my trial with the Star Goddess, too."

His body shook with quiet laughter. "Do you forget nothing?"

"Rarely. It's both a blessing and a curse."

He kissed my temple and loosened his grip on me somewhat, his attention shifting to something in the distance.

"What does it mean?"

"Can I keep at least one secret from your ever-curious mind?"

"I'll figure it out on my own, eventually."

"I've no doubt."

I twisted toward him, giving him my most persuasive pout.

He responded by wrapping me up in his arms again and rolling us both so we were more fully entangled in the cloak, so tightly intertwined that I could barely move—much less turn to pout at him.

It was such a silly, undignified and ungodlike maneuver that I couldn't help laughing and forgetting about my questions for the moment. I relaxed against him with a contented sigh instead, lifting my gaze back to the sky.

We lay together for some time, watching the last of the stars burn out and fall to the ground, until a new question tugged at the edges of my heart.

"When did this happen?" I wondered in a whisper.

"This?"

"You and me. How did we get from where we started to...*this*?"

He yawned, unraveling from me and sitting up and stretching. "Forever trying to map things out, aren't you?"

"You know I can't help myself." I sat up as well so that I could look him in the eyes. "Where did it start for you?"

He considered the question for several moments, taking my hand and absently threading his fingers in and out of mine. "The day we met. The first time we spoke."

"Really?"

Another long pause, then, "That day...I could smell the

fear on you. The blood. You could have given in—most in your position would have, I think—yet you stood in the rising flames like you still intended to set the world on fire, rather than letting it burn you down."

"And that was it for you, hm?" My smile was skeptical. "You really fell for that?"

"Wildfire..." He lifted my hand and planted a soft kiss on my knuckles. "I don't think I ever stood a chance."

ANOTHER HOUR—MAYBE more—passed in a blur of whispered conversation and quiet laughter. There was no one out here to overhear us, yet my voice stayed soft, and his mirrored it.

Whatever this was that was happening between us, I didn't want to share it with the rest of the world yet. I didn't want it to have to compete with all the noise outside of us.

We eventually agreed that we had to return to his palace, however, and we slowly gathered ourselves and reluctantly started back.

As we stepped once more into the gilded halls, our quiet conversation drifted to a stop, and Dravyn's hand tightened around mine.

Before I could ask what was wrong, I sensed it for myself: horribly cold energy, accompanied by a damp scent of mud and leaves—like a freshly dug grave.

The God of Death was here.

CHAPTER 44

Zachar came into view a moment later, rounding the corner just ahead of us.

Dravyn's demeanor immediately shifted at the sight of him, all his softness and vulnerability disappearing in a flare of heat and power as he strode ahead of me, intercepting the Death Marr, fire spiraling to life around his hands.

"Why are you here, Zachar?"

"Perhaps you should ask your companion?" the God of Death answered, coolly, in a voice that sent chills skipping through me.

I saw the muscles in Dravyn's arms twitching, and for a moment I worried he might wrap one of his fiery hands around the God of Death's throat, or else set the entire corridor ablaze —or both at the same time.

Then he clenched his fists, extinguishing the flames, and in a much more diplomatic—but still biting—tone he said, "I am asking *you*."

The Death Marr's black-abyss eyes shifted toward me. Despite the distance between us, I couldn't help stumbling back, desperate to put as much space between myself and him as possible.

Then he said, "She's blinded you to her scheming, you fool."

I froze.

Dravyn's gaze darted between me and the Death Marr, the impatience burning in them now darkened by confusion. A dangerous combination—though Zachar didn't seem to notice the danger he was in; his voice remained chillingly even.

"My shadows uncovered proof of her plans in the room she's been staying in."

"You sent your magic after me?" I stammered. "Into my room?" *That* was what I'd felt before I fell asleep. The shapeshifting darkness...I hadn't been imagining it.

Dravyn took one look at the fear and disgust on my face and his power flared again, making the sconces along the wall flicker and extinguish as he stepped closer to Zachar. "You dare slip your shadows into my palace? Into *her*? I warned you there would be consequences for attacking her mind, and now you've done it here, of all places?"

"I hardly glimpsed anything of her mind," Zachar said with a restless, popping roll of his bony shoulders. "I broke *nothing*. I needed to see no more than the surface of her thoughts to understand the fullness of her deceit."

Dravyn moved as if to attack, but in the same instant I finally found the courage to move, darting forward and wrapping my arms around his body.

The sudden weight of me startled him enough to stop him. I pulled my hands against his chest and peered around him, glaring at the chaotic god before us.

The slits of pale white in the Death Marr's eyes were more visible with the hallway lights extinguished. Like they had in the past, they brought to mind a last spark of hope being swallowed up by unfathomable darkness.

Our gazes fully met.

He smiled knowingly, and dread gripped me so tightly it likely would have knocked me off balance if not for the way I still held on to Dravyn.

"Search her room," he said. "You will see for yourself why I sent my shadows, and you will thank me for it when you realize the truth—that she means to destroy you. To destroy *all* of us."

Dravyn had started to pull free of my hold, but he paused at the word *destroy*.

Only the tiniest of hesitations, but I felt it.

"I will not search anything of hers," he said, somewhat quieter, but just as furiously as before, "and you will pay for doing so." His hand pressed against the one I had over his heart for a moment before he stepped out of my hold.

I couldn't just let him go. He trusted me over one of his own court—and it was trust I knew I didn't deserve.

Guilt surged through me, pushing a single word from my mouth: "Wait."

He paused and glanced back, uncertain.

The God of Death's gaze remained fixed on me. Challenging me to admit to everything I'd done, everything I'd planned, everything he'd seen.

I planned to. I was desperately trying to think of where to start, how to put it all into words—

Then came the eerie, echoing sound of claws upon marble.

Fog—similar to the kind I'd battled with yesterday—rolled into the hallway ahead of us, and a veilhound emerged from it, carrying the knife Cillian had given me between its jaws.

It stalked toward us and dropped its prize obediently at Zachar's side.

Before I could say a word, the Death Marr swooped up the knife and plunged it into the beast's side.

I watched in horror as the weapon had the same effect on the divine creature as it had on the magic-infused stone I'd first tested it on. Dark energy unfurled from the blade, seeking the veins of divine magic within the beast and choking them out, shriveling the creature's sides and stealing away its power, its energy, its very breaths.

The veilhound made almost no sound as it dropped dead, and no other sound followed for several moments after.

"Here is your evidence of my claims," Zachar finally said, his voice echoing in the space like a low peal of distant thunder.

Dravyn stood perfectly still, eyes locked on the dead beast.

I backed away from him until I hit the wall, bracing my hand against it, trying to catch my breath.

And though there was no real need for further explanation, the God of Death stepped forward, black eyes flashing between us as he said, "This weapon was hidden in her room, and its poison blade is likely the same kind that her beastly friends used to kill my hound years ago. This is what she intended to do to you. She's only been biding her time, waiting for an opportunity to strike."

Dravyn still didn't take his eyes from the dead creature and the knife beside it. "You *lie*. This evidence is—"

"I can show you what I saw in her mind, too," Zachar interrupted, calmly, his long, skeletal fingers lifting, the tips of them turning to shadows that lifted free and circled the god before snaking toward me.

Dravyn stepped in front of me, summoning a wall of flames that collided with the Death God's magic. The two powers wrestled with one another for a few seconds before disappearing in a violent implosion, sending shockwaves rushing over me, stealing away what little breath I'd managed to catch.

Zachar bared his teeth. "You protect her, even now?"

"Get out," Dravyn growled.

The Death Marr held his ground, his shadows shifting into javelin-like shapes that rose around him, all aimed threateningly at Dravyn's chest.

"OUT!"

With the roar of Dravyn's voice came a roar of intense, eye-waveringly bright power. Flames filled the hallway. They were everywhere, just as they'd been on the day we met. Still not burning me, somehow, even as they destroyed everything else—scorching walls, singeing rugs, melting paintings right in their frames.

When the fires finally dissipated, the Death Marr was gone.

His dead servant-beast remained, its body now charred, little more than a withered husk. The God of Fire stared at it for a moment longer before kneeling to pick up the knife beside it, taking care to avoid touching the blade, which still festered with black energy. His expression was unreadable as he turned to face me.

I wanted his fury.

I wanted his fires to come back, and I wanted them to burn me to ashes.

I wanted anything except for the quiet hurt and uncertainty in his voice as he said, "What is this? And why do you have it?"

I swallowed, trying to clear away the intense dryness in my throat. I knew what to say. I had decided I was going to tell him the truth. This was not how I'd planned to do it—but my decision remained unchanged. It was now or never.

"It's...it's what Zachar said it was," I told him. "A weapon created by the ones I considered my allies. I think it's how they killed his beast, as he said, and they wanted me to bring it here, to test it and see what else I might be able to learn. What other kinds of weapons we might create and I....I meant to tell you before, I just..." I trailed off, feeling like I was rambling, wishing he would say something, anything in response.

He was silent at first.

I stared at the scorched ground between us as I scrambled for something else to say, something that would make this look better than it did until, finally, he spoke.

"So I was wrong."

I lifted my eyes to his still guarded, unreadable face.

"You're exactly like your sister. I wasn't giving you enough credit before, was I?" He took a step back from me, as though I was infected with some horrible disease he didn't want to catch. "You're no pawn—you knew exactly what you were doing."

Months ago, being told I was like my sister would have been the greatest compliment I could have hoped for.

Now, it felt like he'd taken that knife in his hand and stabbed it directly into my heart.

"I'm not her. It isn't like that."

"This magic, this backwards, disgusting, corrupted *power...* is this the same power that's been threatening our borders?"

"I don't know, I was never told, I just—"

"Do you realize what this sort of thing could do, not only to this realm, but to all the realms connected to it? Do you even care? Or are you just like the rest of your kind? Rebellious, self-ish, *fools.*"

Your kind.

I'd been called by much worse slurs throughout my life, but

to hear him say it, and with such disgust...it stung more painfully than any insult I could remember.

But I'd gotten my wish. Here it was—the anger. The hallway was filling with heat that was making it hard to breathe, and I wasn't sure whether to sigh in relief or cower at the furious power building around him.

"If the one I serve discovers this treachery," he snapped, "then you will be dead before you can take another breath." His gaze flew to the window.

The Death Marr was long gone, not even a trace of his shadows lingering.

I think we both realized, at the same harrowing moment, where that god would likely go next—assuming he hadn't been there already.

Did that cursed middle-god know of the divine water I'd hidden, too? Had he made the connection between the weapon I already had and the grander ones my kind wanted to build? The ones they had sent me to gather materials for?

The evidence against me was damning enough, and if his shadows had penetrated deeply enough to see more of what I knew, more of what I'd originally planned, and he told those things to the God of the Shade...

A muscle worked in Dravyn's jaw. His eyes were dark and calculating, anguish occasionally flickering in place of his anger.

I knew what he was going to say next.

I desperately tried to think of something else I could say, something that could fix this, but nothing seemed like enough.

"I was going to tell you," I said again. "I *swear* I'd decided I was going to tell you."

"Tell me what? That you intended to stab me with this whenever you'd fully gained my trust? Whenever you got close enough to make it a fatal blow?" He lifted the knife between us, and for a moment I thought he intended to stab *me* with it —but then he flung it aside, throwing it so hard it left dents in the marble as it skipped across the floor.

I couldn't take my eyes off the blade as I said, "I had plans to test that weapon on the things in this realm, yes, but I changed my mind. It's like you said earlier: I'm not the same as I was at the beginning of this."

He met my gaze—truly met it—and hope flickered in my chest.

"We can fix this," I said. "Together. We'll think of something."

He shook his head. "You need to leave."

"I can't go, I—"

"You can't stay here. It isn't safe." He no longer roared. He didn't even sound angry. His voice was a wrecked whisper, and somehow that was worse, like the fire between us was wavering, in danger of flickering out.

Please don't let it go out. Please, please, please—

He turned away, heading toward the nearest exit, hesitating only long enough to glance back and say, "Follow the river that leads away from Galim...you remember the waterway that will take you back to your home, I assume."

I did. I didn't want to, but I did. "Where am I supposed to go after that?"

"I don't care," he said, "as long as it's anywhere but here."

I don't care.

The three words briefly paralyzed me, echoing over and over in my mind, the only thing I could hear, the only thing I could think—until I realized he was walking away.

"I'll see what I can do to lessen the damage and keep the rest of the courts from learning of this information," he said as he strode quickly through the door, his form starting to shift as soon as he was in open space.

I caught up to him as wings of fire unfurled from his back, watching helplessly as the rest of his body began to unravel, spiraling into threads of flame that twisted to form the outline of his massive eagle form.

I stumbled back toward the palace as the heat around him reached an unbearable level. His eyes met mine one final time before they were lost within the inferno engulfing him, and I heard his voice like an echoing, lingering memory from a nightmare—

"Just get away from here while you still can."

CHAPTER 45

I STOOD ON THE SHORES OF THE RIVER I'D previously taken back to the mortal realm, bag slung over my shoulder, heart breaking.

I'd been standing here for several minutes, unable to make myself dive into the strangely thick, silvery water.

Body trembling, I knelt, swinging my bag in front of me to check it one last time—as though this was just some normal trip I needed to make sure I'd correctly packed for.

In truth, I felt guilty about packing anything, and I was contemplating throwing it all out, letting the river wash every-thing away...all this evidence that could further incriminate me. All this proof I was a thief, just like my sister had been.

Except these things felt like they *belonged* to me now.

The Star Goddess's crown, the glass sparrow, the feathers from the bed Moth had made himself in my room... Everything I could fit of this world had been swept furiously inside, just as I'd done the night my sister died. I'd hardly paid attention to what I'd thrown in my bag then, either; I just knew I needed to hurry and get out, but I couldn't leave everything behind.

My hand closed around a small silver flask at the bottom of the bag—the container I'd transferred Melithra's water into.

I wanted to dump it out. I wanted to drink it. I didn't know what would happen if I did the latter—I assumed it would be fatal at this point. I'd failed to prove myself worthy of standing among the gods, after all, and the cost of failure was death. That rule had been made clear from the beginning.

I couldn't help thinking death would be easier than going back to my old home.

Gritting my teeth, I tossed the water back into my bag, burying it alongside everything else. I wouldn't drink it, but I couldn't let it go. Maybe it would help me return to this realm somehow; if things calmed down, maybe...

"You're a fool," I hissed at my reflection before swiping a clawed hand through the water, scattering it.

The sky flashed and rumbled above me.

I took a deep breath, and I waded into the river.

The time spent drifting between the worlds seemed to stretch on for hours. As I floated, it occurred to me that the other middle-gods might have gotten what they'd wished for, after all. They had banished me to the emptiness of Eligas— for cheating, for failing, for everything I'd gotten wrong— and I would never see the mortal realm, or *any* realm, ever again.

I twisted and tumbled, breathless and weightless for so long that I'd nearly made peace with the idea of purgatory when my back scraped against pebbly mud. Waves nudged me up and farther up. My face broke through the surface, I inhaled a sharp, painful breath, and I blinked my eyes open to a cold night sky.

Thousands of stars twinkled above me, welcoming me back. The stars I'd once missed.

I no longer wanted any of them.

I lay there, halfway in the water, halfway in the mud, while I tried to orient myself. I was not only heartbroken, but dizzy and nauseous now, too, the travel between realms taking what felt like a worse toll on my body than ever before.

Finally, I found the strength to sit up and look around.

This was clearly the mortal realm, but I wasn't precisely sure where I was. I was lucky I'd made it through at all, really; I hadn't pictured any destination clearly, as Dravyn had once instructed me to do—because I didn't know where in this realm I could possibly go.

I still didn't know.

But I wouldn't go back to my old home—of that much I was certain. Not with the divine things I carried and the knowledge I now had. I wouldn't let my old allies use these things. I wouldn't let them use *me*. I would hold my fragments of the divine realm close, and I would start over somewhere far, far away from everything.

I couldn't think beyond that; it was too daunting.

I tried to focus on surviving, nothing more. I was soaked to the bone, and the night seemed to be growing colder by the minute. I stripped my drenched cloak off in hopes that the clothing underneath would dry more quickly without it. I fastened it to my bag, secured that bag against my back, and then—knowing I'd dry quicker if I kept moving—I forced myself to stagger to my feet and started to walk.

I slogged on for a mile, at least, my dizziness growing worse with each step. For once, I tried not to think. I didn't map out my surroundings as I went. I didn't question any of it. I didn't care where I ended up.

As long as it's anywhere but here.

I was fighting the urge to vomit at the memory of Dravyn's words when I saw a strange light bobbing in the darkness off to my right, back in the direction of the river.

Fire?

Shivering, convinced I was hallucinating, I shook my head and trudged onward.

The fire followed me.

After a few minutes, I glanced over my shoulder. It was still there. I slowed to a stop. The dizziness I'd been fighting threatened to overtake me, so I leaned against a nearby tree, narrowing my eyes at the light now heading straight toward me. As my vision steadied, I realized it truly *was* fire—the flaming tip of a tail.

Moth bounded into sight seconds later, his wings drooping and his body darker than usual, his fur and feathers wet and dripping with what I assumed was river water.

His ears perked up at the sound of my surprised gasp. He spotted me after a moment of searching, and half-soared, half-stumbled his way toward me; his wings seemed to function even less gracefully while they were drenched, but it didn't slow him completely—he still managed to take a flying leap into my arms, colliding with my chest in his usual chaotic manner.

The sight of the divine creature was like a cold wind blowing into an open wound—a reminder of the pain I was trying desperately not to think about.

"What are you doing here?" I demanded.

He nuzzled his head against my chest, his beak closing around the damp collar of my shirt and giving it a little tug.

"First Dravyn thinks I intended to murder him, and now

he's going to think I stole his pet, too." I placed the griffin on the ground before me, steeling myself, knowing the painful words I needed to say.

He lifted his wide eyes to mine, cocking his head curiously to the side.

"You have to go back," I said, pointing him toward the river.

He let out an uncertain purr.

"Go away." I turned and started to walk. "I'm warning you."

I sensed him staring after me, and soon heard the unstable flutter of his damp wings as he took to the air. He followed me at a short distance, keeping up as best he could, occasionally tumbling to the ground and scampering along it for a few steps before flapping his way back into the air.

I tried to ignore him. Even as he butted his head into my back and tried to grab at my clothing with his mouth, I kept walking.

He eventually grew agitated, his collisions becoming harder and more frantic. He struck me hard on the shoulder, talons tangling in my hair, and I felt the heat around his body building, threatening combustion.

I swatted him away as I finally spun around, my words tearing out of me before I could stop them. "You stupid beast —*LEAVE ME ALONE!*"

He shrank away, tumbling to the ground as his wings folded to his sides. Flames danced around the edges of his body, but he didn't fully ignite. He just sat perfectly still, staring at me.

I said nothing else.

I couldn't; my heart was pounding too painfully to properly breathe, much less speak.

Moth let out a soft, mournful purr before flapping back into the air, hovering for a moment, then darting up into the dark sky. Seconds later, he was gone, his flaming tail disappearing within the wisps of a low-hanging cloud.

I was completely alone.

Another self-inflicted wound—and the last blow my heart could stand. The vertigo and nausea from my travels hit me worse than before. I sank to my knees, hands falling to the cold dirt, digging into it, trying to cling to something, anything.

I couldn't keep going.

I had nowhere to go, and it was my fault. I'd held on to my old beliefs and all my anger too tightly, too completely, when I should have just told Dravyn the truth. I should have told him how I felt. Despite all of the times he had proven himself to be completely different than I'd expected, I'd remained stubborn, blind, determined to convince myself I was right.

I'd been so, so wrong.

I realized it now, but it didn't matter.

Because I would never see him again.

And what would become of him when the rest of the gods found out everything about me? Would he be punished and shunned, as the Death Marr had been? All the times he'd protected me, cared for me...

They would be his undoing, while I was stuck here, a world away, unable to do anything to fix it.

My hands shook against the dirt. I felt my strength leaving me, all the things I carried growing heavier, pushing me down, down, down.

In a blink, I lost my balance. My face hit the ground. I couldn't summon the energy to lift my damp, trembling body from the earth, so I stopped fighting.

I let the dizziness overtake me, and my thoughts and everything else spun away, leaving me in total darkness.

WHEN I FORCED MY BLOODSHOT, weary eyes open again, sunlight was filtering through the trees. The air had warmed. Birds sang and tiny creatures stirred in the leaves all around me.

And I wasn't alone.

A woman I didn't recognize knelt beside me, her hand braced against my shoulder. "Are you all right, dear?"

The weight of the question made me want to drop my face back into the dirt.

When I didn't reply, she turned away and gestured toward someone I couldn't see in the distance, calling for help. Moments later, I heard the heavy footsteps and low, grumbling voice of what sounded like an older male.

Together, the two of them hauled me to my feet and dragged me to their nearby horse and cart, securing me in a wagon full of neatly packed supplies; they were returning from a visit to the market, it seemed.

We bumped and rattled along a dirt road for a mile or so before we reached a small cottage that smelled of dried flowers and wood smoke. They helped me inside, leading me to a small bed with cold, scratchy sheets.

I was too weak to protest much. The heady floral scent was overwhelming in a not-entirely-unpleasant way, and the bed grew more comfortable the longer my body warmed it.

Maybe I could stay here for a little while, I thought. Maybe I could sleep off my misery, and somehow find a way to start anew when I woke up.

I desperately tried to convince myself that such a thing might be possible.

Then I heard the woman say, "We should send word to the ones up near Habostad. All their kind seem wrapped in one another's business; they'll likely know who she is, at least."

No.

My lips formed the word, but the sound wouldn't come out.

"Don't worry, dear," she said, patting my shoulder. "We'll see to you in the meantime. You can rest."

I nearly snarled in response—it *would* be my luck that I would run into a human who actually had sympathy toward elves.

"Poor thing seems confused out of her mind."

No, no, no.

I wasn't confused. Not about this. I had to get up. I had to get away. I couldn't let them send word to any of my kind. I couldn't go back in the state I was in, carrying the things I was carrying.

I fought my way to my feet, grabbed my bag that was hanging from the bed's poster, and sprinted toward the door.

The woman let out a little cry of surprise, but she didn't follow me or try to stop me—not until I stumbled and was forced to catch myself against the wall. As I hit it, black dots swarmed in my vision, overcoming me completely as soon as I tried to force myself to keep moving.

I felt myself slumping against the wall, slowly collapsing, while the same word roared over and over in my thoughts.

No, no, no.

I'd brought my sister's necklace back with me; why hadn't I used it to hide what I was? Yet another foolish mistake.

The old woman was beside me again when I blinked back

into awareness, tentatively wrapping an arm around me for support.

She shushed my attempts to protest her help, and called over her shoulder to her companion, "Let's get the valerian root, love, before she hurts herself…"

I clenched my fists, preparing to summon every last ounce of strength I had to knock them away and make another run for it.

But then my eyes caught on the fire crackling in the nearby hearth, and all I could think about was Dravyn's form shifting and flying away from me.

While I was busy reliving the painful memory, something was shoved underneath my nose—a bottle filled with some sort of herbal concoction.

I inhaled deeply from it before I realized what I was doing.

My nostrils burned. My throat itched. My vision swayed, my thoughts blurring along with it. I was awake one moment, gone the next. Then awake again—but somehow back in the bed with its scratchy sheets, covered up, laying on my side.

I could see the fireplace from here, too, I realized.

So I watched the flames dancing, imagining myself lost within their warmth, and I slept.

I DON'T KNOW how long I was unconscious.

Long enough for my self-appointed saviors to send word to my old home.

Long enough for my body to grow numb and stupid from the side-effects of the herbal remedies they'd forced on me.

Long enough for my old world, my old allies, and all my mistakes to find me again.

When I woke, my nose was still burning from the herbs, all of my senses wrecked and half-ruined, but I recognized the scent of spice and sandalwood that had entered the house.

I would have recognized it anywhere.

My eyes fluttered open. I fought to suppress a groan, not wanting anyone to know I was awake. My muscles protested every move I made. I still felt the particular spinning weakness that came from traversing between realms, only it now seemed magnified. I had no idea what those stupid humans had given me, but it felt more powerful than a simple valerian root concoction.

I heard them speaking in the room down the hall, the woman's kind, warm notes calming me somewhat...until a familiar sound answered her—a clever, laughing voice that set every nerve in my body alight.

Andrel.

I slipped from the bed and grabbed my bag as quietly as I could. I didn't stumble in my escape this time, but I had to pause as I reached the door, already out of breath, my chest burning...

Those stupid, *stupid* humans and their useless remedies.

I was gripping the frame with all the strength I could muster when the conversation down the hall suddenly stopped.

Andrel appeared too quickly for me to change my plan.

"Karys." My name fell as a relieved sigh from his lips, like the sight of me was an answer to his prayers. "Thank the gods you're all right."

I gripped the frame tighter as he closed the space between us. Under my breath, I asked, "Since when do you thank the gods for anything?"

He only gave me his familiar, easy, confident smile in reply.

"Leave me alone," I hissed.

He flashed his charming smile back at my rescuers. "She's still a bit delirious, it seems."

I recoiled too quickly from the lie, losing my balance in the process.

He caught me just before I hit the ground, hands pressing hard against my body, fingers digging painfully into my sides.

"I've got you," he said, lifting me into his arms and holding me against his chest. "Everything's okay now."

CHAPTER 46

Andrel had not come alone.

Outside of the cottage, a small entourage of riders awaited us. Some I recognized. More I didn't. There were seven horses total, including Shadow—Andrel's own mare.

To the human couple who had taken me in, it must have been a welcome sight; clearly I had plenty of others to lean on, so whatever my mysterious ailment was, I was no longer their problem.

To me, it felt more like a show of force. A warning not to run or turn my back on Andrel and the rest of our kind. All the new faces...where had they come from? What had he told them about me? What sort of schemes were they plotting and planning to keep me in the dark about?

Outnumbered as I was, escape still crossed my mind. But I needed a more clever idea than recklessly sprinting for the hills. And at the moment, I could barely string two coherent thoughts together—much less an elaborate escape plan.

I felt like I was back on the ground where the humans had found me, face buried in the dirt, every part of me aching.

Since escape seemed unlikely, I instead tried to imagine myself someplace far away where none of the awful things happening were truly real. *I* wasn't real. I wasn't here.

Nothing can hurt me if I'm not here.

I kept repeating this to myself, over and over again, until my eyes glazed over and my body felt like someone else's, someone I didn't even have to look at if I didn't want to. I could make her disappear—all I had to do was close my eyes.

I barely flinched as Andrel lifted me onto his horse and climbed up behind me.

He was quiet for most of the ride back to his manor.

I did nothing to interrupt the silence until we turned onto the narrow path that wound through a thick stretch of trees before eventually opening onto his estate. As the scenery grew more familiar—even to my dazed mind and dead eyes—my pulse began to race, my instincts still alive somewhere deep within despite the thick coat of armor I'd tried to suffocate myself with. Panic floated slowly to the surface, lifting little bumps along my skin as it came.

I should have run.

I should have fought.

Even if I had no chance of winning, even if it resulted in violence...well, at least I wouldn't have died a coward. And maybe I could have found some way to destroy the bag of divine things I carried, too—a bag that was currently attached to the horse ahead of us.

My head pounded and my stomach churned, but I thought maybe I could summon enough energy for one last fight. There was a river less than a half-mile away. One swollen to ferocity, hopefully—the muddy ground we were trotting through suggested there had been a lot of recent rain. If I could snatch my bag and make a run for it, maybe I could get enough of a head start to have time to throw it into the rapids.

And maybe I could throw myself in as well.

Andrel's sudden voice made me jump, startling me away from my plotting. "I really am relieved to have you back."

I tried to settle my chilled skin and ignore him, but he was too close.

He leaned even closer when I didn't reply, as if punishing me for my silence.

"I know things ended badly between us last time." He took the reins in one hand and used the other to lift my arm, brushing the loose sleeve of my shirt up to inspect it closer. "I'm glad to see you healed...though it looks like you've sustained another injury since we last met."

He was referring to the marks left by my run-in with the Death Marr's beasts. The salve Rieta had put on the wound had erased the pain completely, but there were still faint scars where the veilhound's fangs had dragged across the skin.

He traced the marks with a contemplating, lingering touch. "The divine realm has no shortage of monsters with teeth, it seems."

"Yes," I muttered. "But I'm beginning to think the mortal realm might have bigger monsters."

He laughed, the low, dark sound causing another eruption of chills across my skin. "You have no idea," he said.

My eyes darted over the trees, searching for paths I could take to the river. The woods were thick here, their gnarled roots lifting and twisting above ground in more places than I could count. It would be a difficult slog through deep mud littered with tripping hazards; I doubted I could get to the water fast enough.

Andrel was well aware of how trapped I felt, judging by the

way he only bothered to keep a casual hold around my waist, and the arrogant, relaxed tone of his voice as he continued to speak. "So tell me," he said, "how did you find your way back to us this time?"

"I walked."

"You know what I mean. You left in such a dramatic fashion...didn't expect to see you back this soon. Did your heroic gods lose their luster so quickly?"

I didn't reply.

"Or maybe it was you who no longer shined enough for them?"

I stayed silent, but I couldn't keep my muscles from tensing, the memory of my last conversation with Dravyn flickering through my thoughts and making my breath catch.

"Seems I've struck the right note." Andrel brought his mouth uncomfortably close to my ear. "They cast you out, didn't they?"

I dug my fingers into Shadow's back, trying to resist the urge to slam my elbow into Andrel's gut.

"Of course they did," he answered. "It's the same story it's always been. The gods cast *all* our kind from their gilded graces, eventually; you didn't think you could stay in the divine realm forever, did you Karys? That they wouldn't turn on you? You're smart—you must have seen this coming. It was a game. One *you* initiated, in case you'd forgotten."

I bowed my head and closed my eyes.

Nothing can hurt me if I'm not here.

When I looked up again, the manor was in sight.

"Well, the important thing is that you survived their games, and you didn't come back empty-handed, did you?" Andrel continued. "And hopefully now that you're back where you belong, you can clear your mind of whatever confusion the gods filled it with…and remember why you started playing in the first place. Because we have important things to do, you and I."

I didn't dare ask him what he meant by that last part.

We reached the house, and I dismounted in the same numb, detached way I'd started the ride. As my boots hit the ground, I was overcome by a powerful wave of nausea. I tucked my chin toward my chest for a moment, just barely fighting off the urge to vomit.

When I managed to lift my head again, Andrel was watching me with a hint of a smirk on his lips.

"Stay close to the manor," he told me.

I stiffened and forced myself to meet—and hold—his gaze. "Is that a threat?"

"No. Just a friendly bit of advice to keep you safe." He smiled as he grabbed Shadow's bridle and turned him toward the stable. "Because there have been a lot of monster sightings in this realm lately."

I RETURNED to my old room because I didn't know where else to go.

I drifted like a ghost through it, haunting the paths of my former life, trying to understand how I'd died and why I'd been sent back to this dark place to relive all of my mistakes.

Exhaustion pulled at every part of me. I tried to rest but found myself unable to stop tossing and turning in a bed that suddenly felt too small, too stiff, too cold.

After my third failed attempt at a nap, I slipped away from the room and went to another of my old haunts, climbing the broken staircase of stone up to my tucked-away spot in the attic. I wove through the dust and cobwebs as I had a hundred times before, making my way to the section that jutted out over the rest of the manor and provided me with an expansive view of the yard and the marigold fields beyond it.

The sun was setting, brilliant and blood red, but the fields were dull, now, their blooms already ushered into hiding by the first frosts of autumn. There was still a stark, sweeping beauty to the view…but it was not the same.

Even if the flowers had still been bright, I had a feeling the sight wouldn't have made my heart race the way it once did. Everything seemed dull in comparison to the time I'd spent at Dravyn's side.

I sat down and pulled my legs to my chest, breaths shaky with my efforts to keep my emotions from overwhelming me, yet again.

"I thought I might find you here."

The sound of Cillian's voice sent a deep and drumming pain beating through me, like someone deliberately pounding against a bruise over my heart.

I kept my gaze narrowed on the faded fields as he came closer.

"Karys?"

I glanced his way, guarding myself against another surge of emotion. "What?"

He frowned at the curt tone of my voice.

I started to turn my gaze back to the fields, but stopped as I saw what was in his hands: The bag I'd carried from the divine realm.

"Andrel told me to sort through it and see if there was anything we could use," he said, offering it to me, "but it didn't seem right going through your things. So…I thought we could discuss any potentially useful objects and information you had —together. If you feel up to it, that is."

Wordlessly, I took the bag from him and pawed quickly through it, checking the contents. Everything was still there. It felt like a miracle after such a constant barrage of bad luck and betrayals, yet it did little to soothe the raw ache in my heart.

I mumbled something that sounded like *thanks,* cinched the bag tightly shut, and tucked it underneath my legs before I curled them back toward me.

Cillian sat down beside me. A few minutes passed, during which I tried to ignore him, and he sighed, readjusting his position multiple times, until finally he said, "I also wanted to tell you that I'm sorry about what happened the last time you were here."

I lifted my head from my knees but didn't look at him.

"I didn't realize the extent of what Andrel had done until I spoke with him later. And it happened so fast." He picked up a broken bit of plaster, breaking it into smaller pieces before hurling them at the spiderwebs clinging to the nearest rafters. "I didn't know *what* was happening, to be honest, and I was only trying to make sense of it all and keep control over the situation and everyone who was here, watching it unfold. I didn't mean to turn away from you."

The image of him doing precisely that—of his eyes meeting mine and looking away while Dravyn's fires closed protectively around me—fell into my head. Another pounding fist struck my bruised heart.

"Forgive me?" he whispered. "Please?"

I closed my eyes and breathed several deep lungfuls of the stale, dusty air. I wasn't sure my calloused and increasingly suspicious self was capable of forgiveness anymore. But I didn't outright dismiss him. I couldn't bring myself to do that, either, even though I tried.

Instead, after a moment of thought, I said, "Tell me the truth about something first."

"Anything."

"Did you know that Savna went to the divine realm shortly before she died? That she attempted to assimilate herself with the gods, same as me?"

He stared, mouth slightly agape.

"She earned their trust, stole from them, and then fled back to this realm," I said. "That's why they chased her down. That's why they killed her."

Shock glazed his eyes over as he shook his head and got to his feet, pressing a hand to his mouth. He seemed as confused and overwhelmed as I'd felt when Dravyn first told me.

It could have been an act.

I knew that.

But I desperately wanted it to be real—because if he wasn't acting, then I was not the only one my sister had kept secrets from, at least.

He eventually returned to my side, bracing an arm against part of the attic's exposed framework. "How did you come by this information?"

Slowly, little by little I opened up to him as I always had, telling him some of the things I'd learned. Not everything, as I would have months ago. Just enough to keep the words—and some semblance of our old friendship—flowing between us. If I was going to find any allies in this realm, I still believed he was my best chance. And whatever I decided to do next, I needed an ally in this place.

After I'd finished speaking, he was quiet for several moments, tapping his knuckles lightly together the way he often did when he was thinking. "What proof do you have of Savna's supposed crimes, aside from what the God of Fire told you?"

I opened my mouth to reply—only to close it quickly, realizing I didn't really have an answer.

"The gods could have been lying to you," he pointed out.

"Dravyn wasn't lying."

"How can you be sure?"

"Because I..." I got to my feet as if to leave, even though I had nowhere to go. "I just know. He wouldn't have lied to me about something like this."

"You trust him that much? Even after he sent you away?" His tone wasn't combative or mocking, as Andrel's likely would have been; it was merely concerned. Confused, perhaps.

But for all of the uncertainties surrounding my time among the gods, I wasn't confused about this.

Dravyn and I had both kept too many secrets from one another from the beginning, but things had been changing. Trust, and maybe something deeper, had been building between us.

He hadn't lied about my sister.

I knew it as surely as I knew I was breathing.

"Karys..." Cillian began, only to trail off. After several more false starts, he finally found the words he wanted. "You've been gone for what feels like forever. Please don't take this the wrong way, but I don't think it's possible for you to be entirely in your right mind, at the moment. I'm not sure you were when you came back last time, either."

A prickling heat itched over my scalp. "I'm more in my right mind than I've ever been before."

He shook his head as I began to pace restlessly. "You know the gods play tricks. You just spent months in their realm...you don't think they tried to trick you while you were there? That maybe they used some sort of confusing magic or illusions against you? Not even once?"

I didn't have to think about it.

I knew for a fact they had.

I had *befriended* the very goddess known for her ability to control the appearance of things, to shift them—and she had used her magic to trick me. Though again, it had been at the beginning of my journey. Things had changed.

I had changed.

My pacing came to a stop. I knew I trusted Dravyn, yet I couldn't find the words to explain why, to refute the things Cillian was voicing.

"You ate their food, I assume?" Cillian continued, gently. "You drank their wine? Hell, even just the air in that place is likely disorienting to our kind once you breathe it enough."

Maybe it was harder to dismiss his arguments because his concern felt so genuine.

But it was a misguided concern.

Wasn't it?

"They tricked you, Karys. Give it a few days, and I have a feeling you'll see the last months in a much clearer light."

It was the same thing Andrel had said, essentially. Only it sounded more logical coming from Cillian. And I had always been a fan of logic. Maybe that was where I'd gone wrong...the moment I started to let my heart lead where Dravyn was concerned, everything had gone to hell, hadn't it?

Sighing, I settled down on the floor and went back to staring outside.

Everything was still painfully confusing, but I felt better the longer I sat with Cillian. He was perhaps the one good thing I'd come home to; the one thing I would have missed if

I'd managed to make my initial escape and never returned to this place.

"So you didn't know about my sister's divine adventures," I thought aloud. "But there are still other things that don't make sense, right? Don't you have more questions about everything happening around us?"

He considered my words for a long time, eyes narrowed in concentration. Then, somewhat reluctantly, he said, "These anti-divine weapons that have suddenly popped up...I do think they came about too quickly."

My ears perked up at this. "Meaning what?"

More hesitation, but then he said, "The sort of craftsmanship that went into them...given my own experience with weaponry and such, I can safely say that the knowledge and materials required for such weapons didn't show up overnight. I was excited when Andrel and Kinnara showed them to me, but also a bit...confused? Skeptical?" He shrugged, a troubled look clouding his bright eyes. "They claimed they wanted me to help create a more finished product, but truthfully, I didn't need to do much; they already had detailed notes and everything."

"So do you think Andrel has been building something bigger behind our backs for years now? And maybe my sister was involved, too?"

The question brought even more disturbing ones to mind.

Had he tricked her into going to the divine realm, to find a way to help fuel his larger, more sinister plans?

Was he the reason she was dead?

"I don't know," said Cillian. "But I believe the ends will justify the means when it's all said and done." He tried to turn his frown into a smile that I don't think fooled either of us. "Your sister used to say that a lot, for what it's worth."

I took a deep breath. "I think my sister was wrong about a lot of things. And so is Andrel."

He was staring at me. I could sense his gaze like a weight hooking into my body and trying to drag me back to him, back to some place where he could keep me safe, as he always had.

But I no longer cared about staying *safe.*

And I wouldn't take back what I'd said. It felt too cathartic, finally saying it out loud.

For so long, I thought such catharsis could only come from destroying the gods, making them pay for everything wrong with my life.

Andrel used to tell me as much—that the only way to peace, to balance and healing, was through revenge. He was the one who had put most of the ideas about bringing down the gods into my head. And I'd been so desperate to find balance and meaning, to carry on my sister's legacy, that I'd eaten up every word he'd fed me.

Now I understood: He didn't want me to heal. He never had. Why would he, when my anger was so much more useful to him than my peace?

I still didn't know what *would* bring me closure, but I was going to try and find that out for myself from this point onward.

"I know you're mad at Andrel," Cillian began, uncertainly. "And you should be. But you can't go back to the divine realm, either, and if you start speaking up in favor of the gods, and against all the plans we've been making, it isn't going to be safe for you to stay here, either."

"Then I'll leave."

"I don't think it's that simple. Andrel is..." He cut himself off abruptly.

My gaze darted to his, fierce and expectant.

"You need to be careful," he concluded, simply.

"I am not afraid of him." It was a lie, but I made myself sound confident enough, I thought.

"Well, I'm worried on your behalf," Cillian said. "After you left last time, he was...difficult to deal with. I did my best to smooth things over, but if there's one thing he can't stand, it's looking foolish—and you made him look like a fool, running away from him after essentially attacking him with the gods you believe to be your allies."

"He made himself look like a fool," I spat, getting to my feet again.

The concern and uncertainty in his expression deepened.

I didn't care; I'd made my own mistakes, and I would admit to them—but I was tired of being blamed for things that were not my fault.

Cillian sighed. "Just try to keep things civil between the two of you, please? For all our sakes."

I started to walk away, determined not to even consider the idea, but I thought better of it. Glancing back over my shoulder, I said, "Fine."

The relief rolling off him was palpable.

I left before he could say anything else—before I could give my true thoughts away.

I had no intentions of keeping things civil.

I would never forgive Andrel for what he'd done, for the things he'd kept from me, for the poison he'd fed me.

But I knew how to channel my anger into more constructive plans. If I wanted to find the answers I needed, I was going to have to play the part they wanted me to for now.

A new game had just begun, and I had every intention of winning it.

CHAPTER 47

Four days passed, and I worked hard to appear as though I was getting used to my old home once more. I put my sister's necklace back around my neck, and I started my days as I had for most of the past years, walking through the same familiar rooms, eating the same foods, tending to the same chores.

There were still moments when I was tempted to pretend I'd never left this life, to act as though I truly *was* coming back to it. Moments when playing make-believe seemed easier than facing the changes in my heart and mind.

They never lasted long.

On the second day after my return, I'd successfully snuck off in the dead of night and found a place to hide my divine keepsakes, deep in the Nightvale Forest. I buried them close to the most potent pockets of residual magic I could find, reasoning that the energy in these places would help mask any that the divine objects might give off. The pockets weren't as far away from the manor as I would have liked, but they were as far as I dared to go at the moment; I was being watched too closely to risk more than that.

Once the bag and all its contents were buried, my mind gradually began to feel clearer. My weakness from traveling between the realms—and from the ordeal with my human 'saviors'—passed as well, and plans began to materialize once more in my head, though each one seemed more risky and less likely to succeed than the last.

By the time evening on the fourth day arrived, I had grown restless. I was terrified of failing, of getting more things wrong, but I couldn't keep going through the motions of my old life any longer.

So I slipped one of Cillian's impossibly sharp knives into a hidden sheath at my ankle, and I went to find Andrel.

I located him in the third-floor study—a longtime favorite spot of his. He was settled in one of two chairs next to a fireplace that I couldn't recall ever being lit before.

It wasn't lit now, either; the room was cold, drafty, darkening rapidly as the sun sank below the horizon and the last of its light slipped out of reach of the dusty windows. I convinced myself the draftiness was the reason for the shivers traveling up and down my arms as I stepped into the room.

I would not admit how afraid I was at that moment—not to myself or anyone else.

I wandered toward the nearest window, into one of the last patches of sun spilling across the weathered wood floors, and said, "Can we talk?"

Andrel closed the book he'd been reading and motioned to the chair across from him. "Of course."

Slowly, with as much casualness and confidence as I could summon, I took my seat. The sheath at my ankle, tiny and discreet as it was, shifted against my skin, reminding me of its presence, of my purpose, of just how much had changed between me and the one I sat across from.

I hesitated too long, trying to decide where to begin.

Always eager to fill the silence with the sound of his own voice, Andrel spoke first. "Have I ever told you why I spend so much time in this room?"

I shook my head.

"This is the main room I stayed in during the months after the manor was nearly burned down," he told me. "For a long time after that, it was the only place I felt safe, which is why I developed a habit of ending up in it, I guess. The door has multiple locks. My parents once used this space to store some of our most valuable possessions."

He got to his feet and sauntered to the fireplace, running his hands along the stone likeness of a wolf carved into the mantlepiece. He paused at its head and gave a few precise taps against the left ear.

I watched, mesmerized, as part of the beast's body broke away and swung inward, revealing a small room behind it.

"This is the only one that still opens," he said, "but there were once multiple ones in this room for us to store objects—jewels, art, that sort of thing. Turns out, small children can *also* fit inside the compartments. Lucky for me." He stood for a moment with his hand braced against the stationary part of the wolf's head, staring into the cramped and dark space.

I imagined it, though I didn't want to—a much smaller version of him, scared and alone, huddling behind the stone until the sounds of our enemies faded away and it was safe to come out. Though *safe* was always a relative term for us.

We had rarely been safe, even when we were all together; how much worse had it been before Cillian and our other allies found him? Before they helped him rebuild and breathe life back into the mansion?

How much time had he spent alone in the darkness?

It didn't excuse anything he'd done. Yet I still found myself wanting to know, as if better understanding how all his sharp and rough edges had been formed might lessen their sting when they cut into me.

I leaned forward in my chair, head bowed in thought for a moment before I remembered why I had come here, and I finally found my voice.

"I wanted to apologize," I said. "I don't know what came over me the other day. The divine realm was not at all like I expected, and I guess I got caught up in the magic and trickery of it. But you were right, of course—my place is here among our kind." I kept my head low, avoiding his gaze as I sensed it swivel in my direction.

After a thoughtful pause, he said, "Weaker minds than yours have been persuaded of worse things by the damnable gods."

"I know that," I replied, inflecting just the right amount of righteous anger into my voice. "I knew that going into things, too, and I don't know how I let them make me forget it, but I hate them even more because of it."

I'd lived with that hatred for so long that I still managed to call it up with little effort, even now—even as I was trying to move on from it—like an actress recalling lines from a long ago play.

Andrel studied me for a long time after the lines were recited, saying nothing.

I lifted a glare toward him and let fury shake my voice a bit more as I said, "If you don't trust me anymore, then so be it. I will find some way to continue seeking vengeance against the gods with or without your help."

With that I stood, letting my claws unleash, only to draw them back, clenching my hands into fists as I paced the room.

So many times, I had walked this same walk of barely-suppressed rage while in his presence, talking of revenge and impossible plots with him. So many times, I'd let him feed off my simmering violence, not realizing he was nothing more than a parasite trying to drain its host.

It made my skin itch and sweat, stepping back into this old version of myself, but I continued to play the part, trying to drag him into a sense of security, like everything was back to normal between us.

It eventually worked.

I carried on with my act until he finally chuckled and let a slow, approving smile spread across his face.

"There she is," he murmured. "I've missed this vicious version of you." He trailed his fingers down the wolf's neck, tapping along the waves of its fur, and the door swung shut once more. He stayed by the fireplace, leaning against the wall beside it, watching me closely as I returned to my chair and sank down into its dusty cushions.

"You mentioned we had things to do a few days ago, when I first returned here," I reminded him, voice still tight with anger—as were my fists. "I want to help with those things in any way I can."

He considered my offer for a moment before he said, "You already have."

"...I have?"

"The bracelet that broke during our last argument...do you have any idea how much magic was contained within its beads?"

My fists unclenched, fingers digging into the armrests to hold myself still. I couldn't show my fear.

Whatever I did, *I couldn't show my fear.*

"It held the power to let you return to the divine realm, didn't it?" he continued. "Each bead was like a tiny, concentrated version of the Gatterlen lights that first led you into the Marr's territory months ago—or that was Cillian's conclusion, anyway. He collected the shattered glass, realized the immense power it held, managed to extract some of said power..."

"And helped turn it into another weapon like the knife he showed me?" I guessed, somehow making my voice sound curious rather than terrified.

"Exactly," Andrel confirmed. "And our allies used it, along with a few other things, to create a sort of bomb capable of diffusing a negating energy over a relatively large space—an energy that had an interesting effect on the veil between this realm and the middle-heavens. It nearly made that veil collapse in on itself."

I held tighter to the chair as the smile dancing in his eyes nearly made me recoil.

"Next time," he said, in a voice dripping with dark promise, "we'll finish the job."

The attacks on the barrier.

Was this why they had gotten worse—stronger—soon after I returned to the middle-heavens?

It must have been.

I considered my next words carefully. Andrel didn't know that I knew about the compromised barrier, or any of the attacks I'd witnessed while on the divine side of things; I wanted to see what else I could learn by feigning ignorance.

"This veil you mentioned...it's a sort of wall separating us from the divine realm, you mean?" I began, in the most confused tone I could muster. "I didn't realize such a thing was accessible from our world."

"There are very few places where the phenomenon of a thin veil occurs."

"Is it possible to pass through it if you finish ripping it away?"

"Possible? Yes," he said, looking entirely too pleased with himself. "And it's all becoming more plausible by the day. As I said...next time our weapons will manage to peel it back completely."

My palms were covered in sweat by this point. I should have asked what he planned to do once that veil was ripped aside. I *needed* to ask. But fear had already tied my stomach into knots, and now it was working on doing the same to my tongue.

He pushed away from the fireplace, moving toward the window, hands clasped behind his back. "We've been working on doing exactly that for some time now."

"How long?" My nerves tingled, remembering my conversation with Cillian in the attic. "And who do you mean by *we*?"

"You already know of the cities in the north that Kinnara spoke of the last time she was here. The ones surrounded by protective, anti-divine magic? *Cowardkeeps*, your sister called them."

"Yes. You called them that, too."

"And I stand by it. Because most of the ones who live within the walls of those cities are content to stay hidden and forget everything about who we once were. But not all. Among the ones who created the city shields, there were a few scholars smart enough to realize the full potential of this inverse power they'd discovered. They saw that we could create offensive spells with it, too, and thought this was a discovery worth researching more closely."

"And you decided to join them?"

"The decision was your sister's idea, actually. She was one of the movement's earliest supporters, and she dragged me into it."

I wanted to call him a liar.

Something held the word back, and his revelation simply settled like another stone upon my back, casually tossed onto the weight I was already carrying, threatening to be the last blow that finally brought me to my knees.

"She was the one who showed me the first weapon," Andrel said. "And I didn't really believe in the potential like she did—that is, not until a few years ago."

The walls felt like they were closing in around me. Quietly, I asked, "What happened a few years ago?"

Even though I already knew the answer, I was determined to make him admit that he'd been keeping this devastating secret from me for years.

He hesitated.

My chest burned from the effort of holding in all my vicious words as I fought to maintain my act. Suddenly I had to work very hard to remember what these conversations had once sounded like between us—how we had spoken to one another when we were still allies trying to sort through plans together.

"I want to do more to help," I told him, evenly. "But how can I if you insist on keeping me in the dark about things?"

His eyes narrowed—with curiosity, more than suspicion, I thought. I hoped.

I held my breath.

"You want to know the full truth about your sister? Are you sure?"

I exhaled slowly. "It's all I ever wanted."

"Very well, then." He picked a loose thread from his sleeve, and in the same callously casual voice as before he said, "Your sister went to the divine realm six years ago. Much like you, she had a plan to assimilate with the gods and steal their secrets, find their weaknesses—and, in her case—to gather materials."

"Materials for these weapons she was experimenting with," I managed to whisper.

He nodded.

I closed my eyes. It wasn't difficult to appear rattled by what he'd just told me. Even though I already knew it, it still felt as though I hadn't recovered from learning it the first time.

Maybe I never would.

I rose to my feet, unable to keep still in the chair any longer. Hugging my arms tightly around myself, I tried—and failed— to meet Andrel's cool gaze several times before I finally managed it. "Why didn't you tell me this before now?"

"Because she asked me not to."

Another secret. Another deception by the sister I'd once loved more than anything in the world—and another stone added to the weight on my shoulders, threatening to make me collapse.

I wasn't sure how I remained standing at this point.

"She didn't actually *want* you to try and avenge her," Andrel said. "Not until you were ready...assuming you ever became ready. She didn't think you had the stomach to assist with these plans when you were younger, so she didn't want you getting tangled up in things until you could handle it."

"And if I never developed the appetite for it? If you decided

I couldn't handle this, that I was better off not knowing…then what?"

He shrugged. "Then I would have taken this information to the grave, as I promised her I would. She trusted only me with it; she didn't even tell Cillian, despite how close they were —probably because she knew he'd give in and tell you the truth the first time you got emotional around him."

Fury and grief danced a nauseating twist in my stomach.

What would my life have looked like if I'd never gone to the divine realm and learned the truth for myself? I would have become just another mindless puppet in Andrel's army, unaware of how tightly he held the strings of my life.

I considered storming from the room, but settled for moving toward the window, bracing a hand on the wall next to it and staring out over the dark yard, trying to imagine myself outside instead of suffocating in here.

In the reflection of the smudged glass, I saw my eyes shining with tears. I blinked them away. I couldn't let my emotions get the better of me right now.

Andrel followed me to the window, bracing his hand next to mine and pressing close. Too close. I forced myself to keep silent, to hold back my tears even as he gently grabbed my arm and turned me around to face him. His gaze dropped to that arm he held, studying my wrist. Searching for the flame-shaped mark, I guessed—a mark that wasn't there at the moment.

How *badly* I wanted it to appear, all of a sudden, to flare brightly and defiantly before him.

"I'd started to think you were never going to prove yourself capable of the sort of things your sister managed," he said, thumb tracing the veins along my wrist. "Then suddenly you had a divine mark on your skin, and you were charging so bravely into the middle-heavens...so you ended up a part of our grander plans, after all."

I stared at the chipped and weathered window sill, trying to ignore his closeness. Swallowing the lump in my throat, I said, "So Savna brought divine artifacts back for your use, same as I inadvertently did."

"Yes. When she came back from the divine realm, the two of us traveled north and gave those items to one of our allies doing research there."

"This was right before she..." I couldn't finish the thought.

It hung in the air until he shook his head and said, "We believed she'd be safe once she relocated the stolen objects—once they were hidden within the walls of those protected cities up north."

My breath hitched as he dropped my wrist and cupped his hand underneath my chin instead, forcing my gaze up to his.

"I tried to hide her, too, when she came back here. I truly did, Karys. We did everything we could to throw the gods off her trail. But they were...relentless. And smarter than we gave them credit for, I suppose. Because they found her."

Something almost like remorse darkened his bright eyes.

I didn't let it fool me. His only true regret, I suspected, was that my sister had died before he could finish properly exploiting her.

I was so disgusted by his words, by the way he was staring directly into my eyes as he said them, that it took me a minute to remember my own lines.

Finally, I managed to turn my head, and in a voice soft and seething, I said, "I hate those gods so much."

"I know. And you know I feel the same way." He went along with me so easily—no doubt because hatred was the only deep emotion we'd ever truly shared. My hate was toward him instead of the gods, now, but he was too arrogant to tell the difference.

He'd realize the truth soon enough.

I tilted my face back toward him and asked, "How did she get into the divine realm in the first place?"

"The earliest weapons—created from whatever traces of divine power we could gather in this realm—were weak, but efficient enough to allow her to carve her way through one of the thinnest points in the veil. She went alone, and most of us honestly thought we'd never see her again."

"Through the same veil you all are now trying to destroy completely, I assume?"

"Yes."

"It's near the northern territories?"

"Even farther north than the protected cities Kinnara and her clan claim. *Miralith*. That is the name those desolate lands are sometimes called by...most believe they're haunted—as are the mountains hedging them in—so they stay far, far away."

Miralith.

So now I had a location.

Was this the point of attack that Dravyn and the other Marr had not been able to pinpoint for whatever reason? And if I could get there, somehow, would I be able to do anything about it from the mortal side of things?

Andrel fell silent, studying me. Waiting for me to ask more questions. Hoping I would, maybe. Eager for a chance to wield his knowledge like a weapon against me, to make me feel reliant on him as I had been far too many times in the past.

I felt like a dog begging for scraps, and I hated it. Fury and stubbornness pursed my lips together for longer than I should have let them—long enough that Andrel left me and went back to his chair, resuming the relaxed position I'd first found him in.

After a moment, he even picked up the book he'd been reading and started to flip through it once more.

Cautiously, I returned to my chair as well, trying to extend the illusion that everything between us was business as usual.

After a few minutes, he glanced up at me and said, "Is there anything else you'd like to know? Or something you'd like to let *me* know, perhaps?"

I went very still.

"Anything you might have learned before the gods cast you out?"

"I learned a lot of things. You'll have to be more specific."

"Fair enough," he chuckled. "I just can't help feeling as though you might be keeping some of those things to yourself, that's all."

"I'm not hiding anything from you," I said, too quickly. "I'm just trying to figure out where I fit into all these plans you've revealed—how I can contribute to them."

He got to his feet, stretching. "Well, perhaps you simply need some time alone to think through your next steps."

"Perhaps."

"I'll leave you to it then, shall I? I need to go speak with Cillian about some matters, anyway."

I waved goodbye as he headed toward the hall, hoping my relief didn't show.

"It's nice to have you here again," he said, pausing at the door and glancing back. "We'll talk more soon."

I agreed, offering the most sincere smile I could dredge up from the dark and muddied depths of my broken heart. He beamed back, the sight making my skin crawl and my breaths turn rapid and shallow.

As he stepped into the hall, I found the courage to call out one last question: "What are you planning to do if we truly manage to shatter the wall between the realms?"

He paused and looked back at me once more. His smile remained, perfect and unbothered, but I instantly felt as if I'd gotten too reckless with my questioning.

"Let's talk more soon," he repeated, too cheerfully. With that, he left, closing the door behind him.

Dread settled over me like an uncomfortably heavy, itchy blanket, sinking me deeper into my chair.

I sat there for another hour, absently staring out the window, watching the sky shift from rosy twilight to a dark shade of indigo while reciting the things I'd learned to myself.

I now had a location to target—that was the biggest thing. I knew where they were concentrating their efforts, and I had an idea of what type of weapons they were planning to unleash. Now I just had to figure out how I could possibly stop them, and maybe fix the damage they had already done.

By myself, with no real weapons, a thousand questions and uncertainties ravaging my mind, and dozens of eyes watching every move I made around this mansion.

"Nothing to it," I muttered to the wolves around the fireplace. "It's basically impossible for me to fail, right?"

The drafty, depressing room around me was doing nothing to fuel my problem-solving abilities, so I decided to leave it behind.

As I wrapped my fingers around the cold iron doorknob, I glanced one last time at the wolves by the fireplace before turning my back on the room, steeling myself for the acting I knew I still had to do outside of it.

The door didn't budge when I pulled.

Something on the other side was holding it shut.

I willed myself not to panic. Took a deep breath. Tried again.

Still stuck.

I pounded my fist against the old wood. Lightly, at first, but growing increasingly harder, more frantic, as the seconds passed.

It was at least a full minute before I heard quiet laughter on the other side, followed by Andrel's voice drawing closer, finally acknowledging the sound of my fist.

"You know, I gave you multiple chances to prove your loyalty to us."

I pressed my fingers to the door. Extended my claws, digging them into the wood, stripping away several small chunks of it.

"I was so *hoping* you would come clean to me and admit that you'd buried that bag of yours on the edge of my land," Andrel went on. "Because surely you realize how helpful its divine contents could be to us? Especially after all I told you of our plans." He *tsked*. "If you were truly on our side, I don't think you would have tried to keep such valuable things to yourself."

The room reeled around me.

I couldn't seem to force air into my lungs.

If my shattered bracelet had given them enough power to create a massively destructive weapon...

Gods, I was such a *fool*.

I never should have brought any of those divine things back to this realm.

But that was so typically *me*, wasn't it? Unable to put the pieces of my past down until it was too late, forever dragging them along behind me and letting them trip me, weigh me down. Everything I had ever tried to let go of had claw marks on it, just like this door before me did now—markers of my stubbornness and refusal to change.

Even now that I desperately *wanted* to change, my mistakes kept holding me back.

But I refused to let them stop me.

My gaze flew toward the window, calculating. I was three stories up, and I hated heights, but I'd climbed my way down from worse.

Knowing I'd have to be quick—before he realized I was attempting escape and met me outside—I wasted no more time with the door. I sprinted to the window and tried to yank it open, cursing as I struggled with the damaged, rusted latches.

Before I could free the window, a strange sound—a metallic *clunk* followed by a low hissing—snapped my attention back toward the door.

Something small and grey had been rolled beneath it. I realized what it was, and I tried to snatch it up and fling it out of the window, but the latches still would not budge. I yanked my arm back, preparing to launch it through the glass instead.

But I was too slow.

The weapon ignited with a flash in my palm, filling the room with a white mist that smelled of damp earth and bitter herbs.

Wolfweed powder.

A variation of the same poison he'd used on the innocent humans the night at the Fire God's temple. Poison that paralyzed bodies but left the mind untouched, so they could remain aware of whatever horrors were befalling them.

It had acted slowly on those humans.

This was a much, much more potent version; the entire room was already hazy with it, and my muscles were already beginning to seize up after only a few breaths.

I fell against the window. My hands tugged uselessly at the bottom of it, trying one last time to free it even as I started to lose the feeling in my arms. Then my hands. My feet. My legs.

My vision remained mostly clear, and I couldn't seem to get my eyelids to close, so I saw—with horrible clarity—the window slipping farther and farther out of my reach as my legs crumpled and I tumbled backward onto the floor.

CHAPTER 48

THE HOURS TICKED BY IN A HAZE OF FEAR AND desperation.

Though I remained awake and aware, my senses were duller than normal, only growing more useless as time went by and delirium sank in. Bodies came and went and voices rose and fell in the hallway outside, but I couldn't tell who the sounds belonged to.

Every time the poison in my veins started to wear off, another bomb slid underneath the door, the room was eclipsed in shimmering powder once more, and the nightmare began anew.

The first rays of early morning light washed over me. I couldn't feel their warmth, but I could see the shadows shifting, retreating at the approach of a new day. I summoned all the strength I had to push through the numbness encasing me, rolling over so I could see the window and the sky beyond it, the swirls of orange and red painting the hazy blue canvas and setting the fluffy clouds alight.

The colors reminded me of fire.

I closed my eyes, squeezing out a few tears that had welled up within them.

I had to find clean air, somehow.

I forced my eyes open again and locked them on the window. I'd considered climbing out of it before, and I knew this would be an impossible feat in my current state, but if I could just get *to* the window, and breathe the air outside...

I quickly made up my mind that I was going to try, even though I would likely fail.

Every few minutes, I tested myself, trying to see if I could wiggle my fingers and toes.

The instant I felt something like control returning to my extremities, I started trying to move other parts of me. One arm, then the other, and then I twisted my torso and managed to wiggle a short distance across the rough floor. Though I still couldn't truly feel much of what I was doing, I pulled myself to the window inch by inch, dragging my upper body on to the sill that was wide enough to partially sit on before bending awkwardly forward and trying to balance there. As more feeling came back to my body, I found the position I'd twisted it into painfully uncomfortable, but I could press my mouth to the glass—and that was all that mattered.

I fumbled for the knife sheathed at my ankle. I dropped it several times, unable to get my fingers to close properly around its hilt. By the fourth drop I was in tears, but still determined, and finally I managed to clamp my fingers around it. I closed my other hand over it as well, and used both to lift the blade, slowly and shakily, to a corner of the window.

The blade was the same one I'd used the night I'd broken into the temple in Cauldra. It cut as easily now as it did then, slicing away the glass with little effort required on my part. I kept the opening much smaller this time—small enough to be unnoticeable if someone happened to walk into the room. I only needed it to be big enough to breathe through.

I pressed closer and inhaled deeply of the early morning air, greedily swallowing up the taste of grass and trees and what smelled like an approaching storm. I closed my eyes and imagined that storm falling over me, washing me clean of poison and past alike.

More hours passed.

More poison was slipped into the room, right on schedule, but I kept my face to the sunlight and kept breathing in the promise of cleansing rain on the horizon.

It was mid-afternoon, judging by the sun, before the dark clouds arrived in earnest. Thunder rolled in the distance. I jumped at the sound—

And I *felt* it.

I was aware of my muscles tensing and releasing, of the hairs on my arms standing on end.

Little by little, my body was becoming mine once more.

I heard voices in the hall. Whispers that sounded as though they were right outside the door, perhaps debating coming inside to check on me. Or torment me. I turned away from the opening I'd cut, not wanting to draw attention to it if anyone did happen to join me.

The latest dose of poison had nearly dissipated—it had been slipped under the door no less than four hours ago—but the room remained covered in a faint haze. The thickest of it had settled along the floor, however, so as long as I clung to the window and kept my head lifted, I could avoid breathing in too much of the nefarious air. Staying upright proved much easier than I could have hoped for. Proof that my plan was working, my strength and control returning.

Even so, the voices in the hallway made my stomach twist,

the impossibility of my situation settling fully now that I was no longer numb to my surroundings. My strength and clarity might have been returning, but my way out of this disaster was hardly clear.

Trembling, I bowed my head, trying to keep my composure.

And I realized then that the mark on my wrist was glowing.

Its light was so faint I wondered if I was imagining it—or if perhaps it was a trick of the storm-scattered sunlight. But no matter how I moved or twisted my hand, the flame upon my skin did not go out.

More tears leaked from the corners of my eyes as I pressed fingers to the mark, which felt faintly warm.

I'd wanted to dig my claws into it the first time I'd seen it.

Now I had the same thought—not because I wanted to claw it out of me, but rather because I wanted to trigger something. To feel Dravyn's magic burning to life in response, to somehow awaken that connection between us. He'd felt my fear and pain in the past. Could he feel it now?

Could I *make* him feel me?

Even if I could, I doubted he would be able to feel how deeply sorry I was for everything that had happened.

I needed to see him. To actually speak to him again. I needed to get back to him, somehow, if only to apologize and warn him of Andrel's plans.

I curled tighter into myself, still fighting against the urge to collapse under the impossible weight of the tasks before me.

My eyes flashed open at the sound of tapping against glass.

Moth was on the other side of the window, his head cocked and his bright, owlish eyes staring at me.

"You came back," I whispered, voice breaking slightly.

He latched more tightly onto the window ledge and started

to headbutt the glass harder than before—more of a pounding than a tapping—and the edges of the opening I'd cut began to buckle and crack.

The sight of him was still painful, just as it had been when I'd encountered him near the river. But he had come back to me, despite the things I'd said and done.

And the mark on my wrist was still burning faintly, a fire that even all my mistakes had not managed to put out.

I splayed my fingers against the glass, tapping lightly to get Moth's attention.

He stopped assaulting the window and pressed his forehead to it.

"You're being too loud," I warned.

He huffed.

"I can't go out this window," I told him. "I don't have wings like you, and I'm in no condition to climb down as quickly as I need to."

He narrowed his gaze on the cracked glass. Afraid he was going to keep attacking it until it shattered—a move that certainly wouldn't go unnoticed by my captors—I cast a nervous glance around the rest of the room, searching for alternative ways to let him in. I considered the fireplace behind me for a moment before gesturing toward it and then pointing him upwards, hoping he would understand what I was trying to tell him.

His head tilted from side to side a few times as he puzzled it out. Then he gave an excited chirp, flipped backwards off the ledge, and shot up and out of sight.

I held my breath until I heard a clattering in the chimney a minute later.

He descended into the room in a cloud of dust and cobwebs, bouncing off the stone hearth, tumbling and stumbling for a few steps before he managed to orient himself and bound over to me.

He sneezed and sputtered a few times as he breathed in the foul, tainted air of the room, but otherwise it didn't seem to have much of an effect on him, thankfully.

His leap into my arms was as uncoordinated but enthusiastic as ever. My body still felt weak, but I embraced him tightly, tears and apologies both flowing freely.

He settled in my lap, taking a moment to preen his feathers and clear the last cobwebs from them before looking up at me. Expectantly.

"You seem to think I have a plan," I whispered wryly.

He yawned and made himself more comfortable, apparently content to wait for me to come up with one—a rare show of patience from him.

As the minutes passed, however, we heard more and more people passing in the hallway outside. And with every new voice, Moth grew increasingly restless.

"We have to be calm about this," I told him. "Quiet. Smart."

He started to pull one of his dramatic flops in response, but I brought a finger to my lips, shushing him.

An instant later, I heard Andrel's voice rising above the others.

Moth cocked his head toward the door, a soft growl rising in his throat.

"*Hide*," I hissed at the griffin—and to my surprise, he obeyed, streaking away and back up the chimney. I heard his claws skittering along the stone, followed by a few clouds of dust puffing out of the bottom of the chimney, but then everything went silent and still.

I breathed in a few more deep lungfuls of fresh air from the hole I'd cut. The sound of locks being undone filled the room as I slid away from the window and braced my back against the wall.

I slumped down into what I hoped looked like a defenseless position, pretending I had neither control nor strength.

The door swung open.

I lifted only my eyes to watch Andrel as he stepped inside and shut the door behind him. He appraised me for a moment before sauntering forward.

"Have you had enough of this room, yet?"

Every part of me cringed as he knelt before me. I wanted to jump up at that very moment and make a mad dash for the door—and I felt strong enough to do it. But I kept still. Kept calculating my attack and escape plans.

"I can make this torture stop any time you like," he told me, producing a small vial of something from his pocket and holding it just out of my reach. "This concoction I hold is working wonders for me right now, protecting me against the Wolfweed; I don't feel a thing breathing in this nasty air. You just say the word, and I'd be happy to share it with you."

I said nothing.

"Hard to speak when your mouth and such are numb, I suppose." He canted his head toward my face, reaching and brushing a strand of hair from my eyes. "How about you blink once for *yes* and twice for *no*?"

I barely resisted the urge to reach up and snatch his wrist in my hand.

I wanted to do my best to return the favor of a broken arm.

But instead I bared my teeth at him, and in a voice faint from shallow breaths—the only kind I dared to breathe—I coughed out my answer: "How many blinks to say *fuck you*?"

He laughed. "Still full of that nasty fire of yours, I see." He stared wistfully out of the window as he spoke. "That boldness would have been useful for the next part of my plans. I had hoped we could rule alongside one another when that part came—the rebirth of our powerful houses. Our kind would still look to you as a leader, you know; it's not too late to spin your fate in that direction. You always wanted to be their savior, their hope against the gods, didn't you?"

Once upon a time, I'd tried to convince myself that was what I wanted.

Now I didn't hesitate to say, "No."

He tucked the bottle full of alleged antidote away in his pocket. "I had a feeling that would be your answer. What a shame."

I didn't reply. My eyes were on the door. Still calculating, listening for any nearby reinforcements he might have. The hall was silent. No voices, no footsteps—my path to escaping was likely as clear as it was going to get.

Andrel opened his mouth to speak, but I was done listening.

I lunged.

The sudden, unexpected explosion of me caught him off guard as I'd hoped it would; he stumbled and fell back, and I used the opportunity to knock him fully to the ground. I pinned him there, my knee in his gut and my hand around his throat.

"*How*?" he choked.

I didn't waste my precious energy explaining anything.

His choke turned to laughter as he shook his head, still trying to goad me, even now. "How disappointing that you can't do your part for your kind—that you can't even carry out the *simplest* parts of a revolution your sister was willing to die for."

"I'm sorry to disappoint you," I snarled, "but I am not my sister."

Her reflection had been clearer than mine in the tower.

She'd never wavered.

She'd always been so certain.

But I was beginning to think that a mind that was unwilling to change was not necessarily a strength.

"I am not my sister," I repeated. "And she made a mistake, trusting you."

He started to laugh again.

I cut him off by unleashing my claws, digging them into his throat. As the first drops of blood slid over his skin, all the amusement in his eyes disappeared in a flash of mad fury.

His hands shot toward my sides, digging in with a powerful grip as he rolled over, throwing me off balance before kicking me the rest of the way off of him.

I scrambled to put more space between us before stumbling to my feet. I was still more sluggish than usual after my poison-filled night; I saw his fist coming after me, but I only partially managed to twist away from the blow.

He struck me in the chest, knocking me back toward the chair he'd been sitting in yesterday. The corner of the iron side-table jabbed into my shoulder, causing a jarring, tingling pain to shoot through my entire right side.

I grabbed the table with my left hand and flung it at him.

He knocked it aside and continued to advance on me.

My eyes darted toward the hallway; I needed to escape before the sound of our battle drew more attention.

I tried to sprint toward the door.

He caught one of my arms. I briefly panicked, reliving the shock and pain of the first time he'd grabbed me like this—

But this would not be a repeat of last time.

His hands were stronger, but mine were sharper.

As he tried to wrestle me into his hold and slam me against the wall next to the fireplace, I managed to swing one last upward swipe toward his face. My claws struck skin, dragging bloody streaks across it. He roared in pain. His hold on me faltered. I still hit the wall hard as he let me go, but not nearly as hard as he'd intended.

Moth was there in the next instant, shooting out of the fireplace with a wild screech. His wings were already pure fire. As he twisted and tumbled toward Andrel, the rest of him ignited as well.

He collided with Andrel's chest. Andrel fell back into the chair, flames surrounding him. The rug beneath that chair caught fire, followed by the threadbare cushions, and while he was busy trying to put the fires out, I called Moth to my side and darted for the door.

"Where are you going to go, Karys?" Andrel's sudden voice stabbed through me like a knife into my back.

I should have kept running—I didn't owe him any answers—but I couldn't help pausing in the doorway, bracing a hand against the frame as I caught my breath and glanced over my shoulder.

He had stomped the fire out of the rug, thrown a blanket over the chair. He stared at me through rising smoke, blood streaming down his face, looking every bit like the dark, terrifying creature I now knew him to be.

"It's already begun," he said, voice chillingly calm. "We were so close to breaking our way in just days ago—the final blow is coming soon. We will breach the heavens and bring them crashing down, and if you want to run back to your precious gods, go ahead. You can crash and burn with them for all I care."

I glared back at him, and in a voice as cold and dark as his, I said, "We'll see which one of us ends up burning in the end."

I heard footsteps approaching from the stairs at the end of the hall to my right. I backed slowly in the opposite direction.

As soon as I was out of Andrel's sight, I ran.

With the scent of blood and smoke searing my nose, with the sound of my once allies' confused voices rising at my back, with stiffness and lingering poison in my muscles, I ran away from everything I'd ever believed, knowing that I wasn't ever going to be able to come back to it.

Knowing I didn't *want* to come back to it.

That newfound knowledge fueled my steps, pushing me faster and faster. I was running so fast by the time I reached the first floor that I didn't see Cillian rounding the corner ahead of me in enough time to stop.

We collided, hard, and he only just managed to catch me and keep me from hitting the ground.

"Cillian—"

A clamor of bodies and voices roared behind me, descending the same steps I'd raced down moments ago.

Andrel had said I could go back to my gods, but I had a feeling that was yet another lie.

Cillian seemed to understand everything that had happened—everything that was in danger of happening—even though I didn't say a word. He'd always been able to read my silences.

"Take my horse," he said, shaking me from my stupor. "Her tack is already hanging near her stall."

I couldn't find the words to reply.

"Get as far away from here as you can," he urged. "I'll distract him and hold him back for as long as I'm able to."

"If he finds out you helped me—"

"It doesn't matter. *Go*." He took my arm and pulled me into motion, setting me on a path toward the front door.

I didn't stop again. I didn't even look back. I raced out into the cool, misty evening air and sprinted directly for the stable, Moth soaring closely behind.

I found Nyxia, Cillian's barely-tamed mare, and I wrestled her into her riding tack. Then I grabbed a bag hanging nearby, threw some supplies into it, and hauled myself onto the horse's back.

We galloped for the forest.

I guided her to the places where I'd buried my divine keepsakes. They'd taken the bag, as Andrel had claimed, so they had the Star Goddess's crown, Moth's feathers, a dozen other things laced with the energy of the divine realm…and there was no telling what sort of power they'd be able to extract from them, what sort of anti-divine spells they'd derive by using that power.

But there was little I could do about those losses, now.

More importantly, the two most valuable things that had been in that bag—the glass sparrow Dravyn had made for me, and the waters of Melithra—I had buried elsewhere.

I focused on finding these two things; I had discreetly marked the burial spots with lines of berries pressed into the ground, so even in my rushed and panicked state I managed to track them down relatively quickly. But my hands still weren't at their full strength, the lingering numbness making my fingers difficult to coordinate. I spent far too long digging in the mud before I finally unearthed what I was looking for.

With a sigh of relief, I clutched the sparrow and the water to my chest, bracing myself for what lay ahead.

I heard shouting in the distance. Moth let out a soft, uncertain cry, while Nyxia stamped her feet and whinnied anxiously.

I hastily threw my things into the new bag I'd taken from the stable, tied it tightly shut, secured it to the saddle, and then hoisted myself up, my arms violently shaking from a combination of cold and poison.

With one final glance at the place I'd called home for so long, I turned and set a course toward the north, determined to fix all the things I'd gotten wrong.

CHAPTER 49

It was nearly a two day ride to Terrath, the largest of the two protected elven cities of the northern territories.

It seemed to take much longer.

I barely slept, and ate only what I managed to scavenge—which wasn't much. The ride was rough, climbing in elevation along roads that were eroded, rarely traveled, and ill-kept; the elves of these territories rarely ventured out of them, and the humans in surrounding places avoided venturing *into* them—save for occasional attempts at raids or other violent conquests—which left little need to maintain the roads in between.

As the hours pressed on, I became a ragged shell of a being, barely awake, all my energy narrowed in on the singular task of making it to the veil that lay north of Terrath.

I'd figure out the rest of my plan once I arrived, I'd decided.

For now, I just had to keep going.

Moth stayed close, loping alongside me at times, settling into my lap during others; if he had not been there to occasionally nip or headbutt me back into awareness, I likely would have toppled off Nyxia's back more than once.

But as the sun began to set on the second day, I finally saw it: The vaguely familiar skyline of the city of Terrath, made hazy by the anti-magic barrier protecting it.

The city may not have been my final destination, but it meant I was getting closer—the beacon of hope I needed to keep me upright on my horse for just a little longer.

As we approached, I ordered Moth to stay in a small clutch of nearby trees, out of sight, while I used my sister's necklace to shift the color of my eyes and hair to a soft shade of honey.

The disguise was necessary; I suspected Andrel had plenty of minions in this city, and there was a good chance he wouldn't be far behind me himself. I doubted the sparrow's spell would last long once I passed into the city—given the city's wards against divine magic—but hopefully it would endure long enough for me to find the information I needed from the local residents.

Once I had seen to Moth and my appearance, I guided Nyxia into Terrath at a quick trot.

The flame mark on my wrist—which until this point had mostly burned with a steady, soft glow—faded and began to itch as I passed through the gates.

I didn't dare scratch it or otherwise draw attention to it.

I found a shabby little tavern that looked like it would have exceptional gossip and passable food. After tying Nyxia to the hitching post next to a haggard looking old mare, I slipped inside and took a seat in the back corner. I kept the bag containing the glass sparrow and the water of Melithra with me, clutching it close to my chest as though it was the only true ally I could hope to find in this establishment.

It was strange, how out of place I felt in that moment,

surrounded by my own kind…as out of place as I'd felt months ago, when I'd first entered the divine realm.

Giving my head a shake—clearing it of musings I didn't have time for—I summoned the waitress, trying to look as inconspicuous as possible.

I ate an entirely too salty stew purchased with the few coins I'd found buried in the bag I'd taken from Nyxia's stall, and I kept to the shadows, listening to the conversations around me until I zeroed in on a table of patrons who were just the right level of intoxicated—drunk enough to not be suspicious of me, but sober enough to answer my questions about the stretch of supposedly haunted land that lay somewhere farther north. It took some patience, but among their enthusiastic rambling and laughter, I eventually picked out several useful clues.

Look for jagged rock formations and follow the trail of tall teeth.

The land will turn to the color of ash, and the sky will look brighter than it should, even in the dead of the darkest night.

If you spot the Sapphire Sea to the east, you'll know you've gone too far.

Mind the ghosts who guard it.

What sort of foolish elf wants to tangle themselves up with the evils and ghosts of Miralith, anyway?

I only smiled and deflected when we came to this last question. They went back to laughing and drinking easily enough afterwards, and now that I had a decent idea of where I needed to go and what to look for, I wasted no more time.

Nyxia was not enthusiastic about setting off again so soon, but she stopped protesting after I offered her a few carrots I'd saved from my meal.

"Just a little farther," I promised her, rubbing her neck before swinging into the saddle once more.

We rode onward, Moth swooping and diving just ahead of us; he seemed restless after being ordered to keep still, even though I'd taken no more than an hour in the city. I worried about him drawing attention to us at first. But after another hour passed and we encountered no other riders—or even signs that any riders had traveled our route—I relaxed somewhat.

The rough yet clearly-inhabited land gave way to wilder stretches full of overgrown fields, unspoiled swaths of wildflowers, and clear streams that looked like pure, bubbling silver in the moonlight. Anything resembling a path ended, leaving us to pick our way through increasingly rocky terrain.

Another hour came and went. I still had not noticed any trails of jagged teeth, nor any of the distinct color changes I'd been told about. I began to worry that I'd chosen the wrong targets back in the tavern—that perhaps I was the victim of some drunken prank or dare between them.

The sky grew darker, thousands of stars flickering to life against the black canvas and making the world seem too big, too vast, too overwhelming—and all the plans I was trying to formulate seemed equally overwhelming against this backdrop.

Where *was* I?

What the hell was I doing here?

The farther I went, the harder I tried, the more lost I felt.

Yet I soldiered on, encouraging Nyxia to do the same, until I finally spotted jagged rows of rocks popping up with increasing frequency and forming a road of sorts between them.

I followed these sharp 'teeth' as I'd been told to do, keeping a mindful eye toward the east, hoping I wouldn't see the sea that meant I'd gone too far.

The stars above started to disappear, lost against a sky shifting closer and closer to the color of a polished pearl. The increasingly white atmosphere made a sudden expanse of grey in the distance immediately noticeable.

I'd actually reached it.

'Veil' was a fitting moniker, it turned out, because that was what it looked like—a thin, gauzy cloth of grey stretched across the world ahead of me, rippling slightly as if caught in the barely-there breeze.

Realizing I was holding my breath, I forced myself to slowly exhale. I pulled Nyxia to a stop and rolled the tension from my shoulders. Moth soared back to me and dove into my arms, huddling against my chest, a low, uncertain mewl rising from him.

"Courage, Ramoth," I whispered, stroking the ruff around his neck. "We'll be all right."

I dismounted, took my bag and strapped it securely across my body, then started to relieve Nyxia of her tack. I planned to let her go her own way from this point; she'd grown up wild before meeting Cillian, a part of the massive herds that ruled the vast Windscar Plains south of our home. I wasn't worried about her surviving on her own. And I strongly suspected she'd eventually find her way back to Cillian—she'd roamed farther distances than this and made it home in the past.

I watched her trotting briskly away, eventually breaking into an eager gallop. She didn't look back. I didn't blame her.

I turned to face the veil.

For several moments, I was perfectly still and silent, marveling again at the sight of it, wondering how such a thing could exist in this world without my ever having seen it—or even *known* of it.

Then again, I'd been blind to the truths within my very own home, hadn't I?

I'd closed my eyes for too long against too many things I didn't want to see.

But I wouldn't do that anymore.

I marched forward, determined to take in the full sight of everything before me, no matter how terrifying it was.

The scent of campfire smoke caught my attention. I cautiously followed it and, while crouching behind the first bush I came across, I scanned the distance, searching for the source.

The hairs on the back of my neck rose as I spotted it: A small encampment lay a few hundred yards away, bustling with noise and movement. Some of the so-called *ghosts* the tavern patrons had warned me about, no doubt.

I wasn't surprised to see them; I imagined there were plenty of elves—allies of the movement Andrel and my sister had apparently helped lead—who regularly patrolled to keep prying eyes away from the experiments going on here.

I was only surprised there weren't more of them.

Despite the lack of bodies, there was a violent, bristling energy surrounding the small camp, and it seemed to be building by the minute. It made me think of the sea pulling back, gathering into something altogether more massive and violent before crashing destructively over the shore.

Cautiously, I moved in the opposite direction of the camp, searching for any more who might have been guarding the barrier, while simultaneously trying to study the veil itself. I tried to ignore the ache growing in the pit of my stomach as I drew nearer to that veil.

I was closer to Dravyn's realm than I had been in days, supposedly, yet the space between us felt more impossible than ever.

What would happen if I tried to cross through right this moment?

It seemed reckless, but I couldn't help myself; once I was well out of sight of anybody at the encampment, I paused. Took a deep, bracing breath.

And I reached tentatively toward the wall of magic.

The veil felt cold at first. My fingers came away covered in a faint, dewy, silvery substance that made my skin tingle. It absorbed quickly into my skin, a subtle warmth spreading out from the mark on my wrist as it did. Otherwise, nothing of consequence seemed to happen.

Feeling braver, I reached out again, pressing deeper this time. My hand didn't make it far before seizing up. I reflexively jerked back before the paralysis could spread, but my hand remained numb for several moments afterward.

I hadn't really expected to just be able to push my way through, as nice as that would have been. Still, I couldn't help feeling disappointed.

Moth caught up to me, chirping eagerly. He'd seen me reaching, and he wasted no time joining my efforts to cross over, diving headfirst into the veil and disappearing with a flick of his flame-tufted tail.

He was gone for nearly a full minute. The ache in my stomach deepened as I feared I'd lost the last of my companions —but then he re-emerged, rolling out from the bottom of the veil, his body covered in a shimmering silver glow that slowly disappeared. He didn't seem paralyzed or otherwise affected as he shook out a few rumpled feathers before looking up at me expectantly.

I gave him a sad smile. "If only it were so easy for me. But I'm not divine like you, unfortunately."

Disheartened, but not ready to give up, I continued traveling parallel to the veil, searching for more clues, trying to decide what to do next.

I'd come here to find proof that this place existed and could be accessed. To map it out and gain useful information that would help stop Andrel and all the mad plans he had.

But that information would be useless if I couldn't get to the other side, if I couldn't find some way to tell Dravyn and the others what they were truly up against.

As I was pondering, a strange, warbling sound—like a sheet of metal being battered by the wind—filled the air.

I dropped instinctively to a crouch, scanning my surroundings for threats.

I was still alone, out of sight of anyone.

But the veil was...*changing*.

The waves of grey were smoothing out in places—as though something had grabbed the edges of several sections and jerked them taut—while its color deepened to the shade of a heavy storm cloud.

Another metallic warble sounded. The veil radiated with a strange, densely cold energy, a pressure reaching out and crushing over me so rapidly, so intensely, that I had a hard time straightening back to my full height.

Then came a *BOOM* loud enough to shake the ground. It rattled the rocky hills all around me, sending streams of pebbles rushing down and stirring up storms of dust.

Moth let out a high-pitched shriek and shot for the cover of trees on a distant hilltop. I sprinted after him, but couldn't help slowing down after a few seconds, turning and jogging backwards long enough to gape at the veil.

Something was spreading across its face—an inky black darkness that caused a sharp, devastating sensation of despair to rush through me.

Another *BOOM*.

The inky dark cracks lit briefly. Like lightning. Similar to the attacks I'd witnessed alongside Dravyn the day he'd told me about my sister—only these were brighter. More powerful, maybe.

Pulse racing, I abandoned my decision to follow Moth and instead crept my way back toward the encampment I'd first seen, hiding once more in the bushes to spy.

My fears from earlier—that I had only been witnessing the start of a building wave—were confirmed.

The encampment had already grown, nearly tripled in size.

There were several people gathered in a circle near the veil, holding something between them. They seemed to be reaching into the barrier as I'd tried to do earlier, only they moved with much more confidence—and they weren't reaching with empty hands.

As a few of them took a step back, I was able to see the object they'd been gathering around—a small, pale weapon with a faint trail of smoke wafting up from it.

That smoke twisted into the veil. As I watched, it became the darkness I'd seen farther down, a shadow that spread with a sinister slowness, spiderwebbing this way and that, laying claim to a large section of the grey.

It seemed to be creating a path; once the trails of darkness had eaten away whatever magic existed within the veil, the chaotic energy had room to surge—which it then did, flashes of brightness crackling violently into existence, heralded by the warbling and booming that made me jump nearly every time, even now that I was expecting the sounds.

Boom. Boom. Boom.

With every flash and explosion, the veil's face looked more

uneven. More unsteady. Little by little, it was being scraped away.

Panic rushed through me, like a bitterly cold wind, while a single question beat against my mind, over and over—

How long do I have before it weakens to the point of total collapse?

I sank back into the bush, trying to collect myself. As soon as I dared, I again raced away from the encampment. This time, I kept running all the way to the very end of the veil—nearly a mile away—where the grey wall of energy dissipated against rolling hills that rose steeply into mountains just a little farther ahead.

Perpendicular to this ending stretched the edge of a cliff. Bits of smoky energy rolled off the veil and tumbled over the edge, streaming down into the canyon below; it almost looked as though the excess magic of the veil had been responsible for eroding the rock, creating that canyon in the same way rivers slowly carved them out over time.

The cliff edge felt like a cruel metaphor—a dead end at the crossroads of the two worlds I'd been caught between for so long. They'd intersected in the most violent manner possible, and now I had nowhere to go.

I stood there, heaving for breath. I wanted to shout loud enough for the gods to hear me. I wanted to claw the veil down myself, peel it away bit by bit until my nails broke and my fingers bled and I could at least glimpse the heavens I'd left behind, even if it was only one last time.

Moth caught up to me once more, his big eyes wide and sorrowful as he took in our surroundings with the same sort of despair I felt.

I briefly considered sending him through the veil without

me; could I put what I needed to say into a note for him to deliver?

But I had nothing to write it with, no confidence that Moth would leave me to deliver it, and no time to come up with a more foolproof plan.

I looked to the mark on my wrist. Pictured Dravyn's face and his fires wrapping around me, protecting me, carrying me away from the trouble I'd found myself in the last time I came to this realm.

He'd felt my pain, my desperation, and he'd answered it.

I was not in any extreme pain at the moment, but maybe...

After a deep breath, I extended my claws and dug them into the flame-shaped mark, biting back a cry as I broke through skin and felt warm blood bubbling up, oozing around my fingers.

Please let him feel me.

Please let him reach back for me.

Please let him feel how sorry I am, how much I—

I gasped as the mark flared to life, brighter than I'd ever seen it in this realm. Another thorn of hope dug into me, catching me and dragging me back from collapse at the last possible moment.

My gaze darted back to the veil, seeking another sign, another flash of brightness coming to life in the darkness— hoping, not for the chaotic lightning I'd been witnessing, but for fire. For some sign that the god of it was near.

The veil remained unchanged.

I stared at it for several minutes.

Still nothing.

Meanwhile, I heard voices in the distance, steadily growing louder. Closer. The air grew heavier. Tendrils of shadows started to snake their way through the veil, coming closer to where I stood. No chaotic energy filled these dark paths yet, but it was only a matter of time before it did, before everything shattered and the world would be forever changed—and not just for me.

Chest heaving, I pried my gaze away from the veil and fixed it on the damage I'd done to my wrist, watched the blood dripping from it. Each drop of crimson against the mud was another moment gone, another second ticking by with no answer, another sliver of confidence lost.

Yet I kept looking back to the veil. Kept clinging to my threadbare hope. I would have bled myself dry as long as I still had a chance, any chance, to set things right.

The minutes crawled on.

The shadows breaking across the veil grew bolder.

I knelt, wrapping my arms around myself, and huddled against the sobs trying to rise through me, not caring about the blood or dirt smearing across my already filthy tunic.

Then I looked up, and I saw lights.

The same wisps of flame I'd seen at the beginning of all this. The lights that had led me into the river of fire. To the divine realm. To *him*.

Now they were leading me toward the cliff before me.

Cautiously, I crawled to the edge of it, my gaze following the fires. Down into the canyon they went, disappearing into the hazy scraps of the veil's grey energy that had collected at the bottom. Or what I assumed was the bottom, anyway.

Was there really something down there—some path I couldn't see?

I rose to my feet, readjusting the straps of the bag fixed across my body, and backed uncertainly away from the edge.

The sound of someone shouting jerked my attention behind me.

The fires I'd summoned—which still blazed brightly alongside me—had not gone unnoticed. They were essentially a spotlight drawing attention to where I stood, and now two males on horseback were racing my direction, their armor and weapons flashing in the moonlight.

Moth fluttered frantically around me.

I dashed toward the cliff again only to lose my nerve at the last instant, my boots barely catching the edge, sliding and scraping, sending pebbles and dirt bouncing down into the canyon as I fought for balance.

The sound of hooves pounded closer. An arrow hit the ground immediately to my left, so close to striking my shoulder that I felt the wind from it as it shot by.

I looked to the bloodied, glowing mark on my wrist, then once more to the flames stretching alongside me.

All of my instincts, my logic, my years spent not trusting the gods or anything related to divine magic told me that I was a fool to even consider following the path of fire over the edge.

But my heart said *jump.*

So I jumped.

CHAPTER 50

THERE WAS NO RIVER THIS TIME—NO PEACEFUL floating in the water, nor gradual heaviness dragging me slowly to the other realm.

There was only falling, fast and furious, while I was excruciatingly aware of each of my body's flailing twists and turns and failed attempts at control.

I finally struck dust-covered ground—hard—and lay motionless for long enough to draw a concerned purr from Moth as he glided down beside me and nuzzled my cheek. I lifted my head quicker than I should have, trying to reassure him. Dizziness struck, bringing the urge to vomit with it.

After heaving up essentially everything I'd eaten for the past day—which wasn't much, for better or worse—I crawled for a few feet and tried to focus on making sense of my new surroundings.

I no longer smelled campfire smoke.

I no longer heard pounding hooves, or shouting voices, and the crackling, booming energy of the anti-divine weapons was muted at first...and soon the unsettling sounds stopped entirely. Everything was strangely quiet. Each of my rattling breaths seemed to echo.

Had I really managed to cross back into the divine realm?

I lifted my head and gazed upon miles and miles of parched, cracked ground that I didn't recognize.

Where the hell was I?

Why had I jumped so recklessly into this?

Fear wrapped around me like a heavy chain, threatening to hold me in place. But I knew staying here wouldn't do me any good, so I got to my feet, double-checked that the bag I carried was still secure, that its contents were safe, and then I started to walk.

The ground was mercifully flat and smooth, but seemingly never-ending. The only disruptions of the desolate landscape were strange, low-lying black clouds that were scattered about. A stench of sulfur surrounded them, and Moth let out a low growl every time one drifted too close to us.

We walked on and on, and nothing seemed to change—until a jagged tower took shape in the distance, its dark spires reaching up in a pattern that seemed familiar even to my exhausted and slightly dazed mind.

I slowed to a stop, Moth hovering anxiously alongside me. "Is that...the Tower of Ascension?"

The griffin turned a few loops in the air in response.

And I realized—with sudden, horrifying clarity—where I was. What I was walking through.

The ocean of the Death Marr's magic.

Except the ocean of magic was gone. In its place was this new wasteland, completely empty of the power that was supposed to help keep dangerous, destructive things from crossing over.

Those clouds of darkness, the foul stench surrounding them…

Were they more signs of the weapons my kind were using to attack the veil?

I looked back in the direction I'd traveled from. The barrier between worlds continued to shiver and flash with cracks of pale light. Though it remained mostly silent—the sound apparently unable to travel through whatever divine energies remained here—the ongoing attack was apparent. It looked just as it had the day Dravyn and I stood together on the shore near the tower…

Only now it was ten times as active.

I started to jog, and then to run, chased by increasingly vivid thoughts of the ground beneath me collapsing.

But even if I got away from this wasteland, what then? It would take at least a day to walk all the way back to Dravyn's palace on my own two feet, and by then, it might be too late.

I kept running anyway, eyes frantically scanning my surroundings for help. The gods came and went so easily throughout this realm—Dravyn could be here in an instant, if only I could catch his attention. I pressed a hand against the dried blood on my mark, and I looked to the sky, hoping against hope that I might see wings of fire appearing just as the wisps in the mortal realm had.

It was not fire that answered my silent pleas.

It was lightning.

Not the faint cracks of light I'd seen destabilizing the veil, but a hot, jagged bolt that struck from above, hitting the ground directly in front of me, searing a black scar of no less than thirty feet into the dry dirt. I tripped as I scrambled backward, flailing to avoid the sizzling destruction, and landed hard on my backside.

Gasping, I looked again to the sky, trying to see where the attack had originated from.

I saw no more bolts of lightning, only flashes of white and blue energy similar to what I'd seen the first night I'd stayed in Dravyn's room. He had said they were signs of unrest in the upper heavens—but this was closer than any conflict that might have been happening between the Moraki in Valla; the very air around me sizzled with electricity. And a haze of different energies filled the sky directly above me, gathering into a thick cloud with a sick, yellowish color.

Something was happening in the skies of *this* heaven, above that cloud—a battle I couldn't see.

Moth soared down beside me, grabbing my sleeve and tugging anxiously.

I fought my way to my feet and started to run once more, keeping an eye out for anything I might be able to shelter underneath in case of more errant lightning.

We made it nearly to the Tower of Ascension before the next bolt struck uncomfortably close to our path. The air remained charged long after it hit, buzzing so intensely that it hurt just to stand within it. Moth dropped to the ground, flexing and shaking his wings as if trying to rid them of numbness.

I ran to scoop him up.

As I did, a dark shadow overtook us. Moth panicked and squirmed free of my hold, shooting off toward the tower, leaving me alone as another bolt of white-hot magic raced through that shadow above.

Before the bolt could strike toward the ground, a blur of white and silver charged out of seemingly nowhere, hurtling straight at me. I felt arms close around my torso, an intense cold biting through my entire body, and then suddenly I was swept off my feet and flying through the air.

Lightning hit where I'd just been standing an instant later.

The close call hardly registered in my mind at first; I was too numbed by the cold sinking into my bones—so numbed that it took a moment to even question how I was currently *flying*.

Finally, I gave my head a little shake and looked up to the sight of a pale, handsome face framed by even paler hair. Wings of jagged silver and white feathers stretched out behind him, sending ice crystals shimmering into the air with every powerful beat they made.

Valas.

He deposited me unceremoniously on the stone pavilion surrounding the Tower of Ascension, behind one of the thickest of its columns. Then he turned away from me, his eyes narrowing on the sky and his body braced for attack. He looked brilliant and terrifying in this warrior-like stance, his normally carefree expression hard and focused, his powerful chest rising and falling with deep, focused inhales, his wings folded in like crossed blades against his back.

I held my breath as he continued to scan the sky.

Moments passed, thick with tension.

Nothing happened.

Still breathing hard, Valas turned a wild gaze on me. "Sparrow, my love, ever-favorite object of my heart," he said, forcing a smile that came across a bit feral, "what the ever-loving *fuck* are you doing back here?"

"I can explain why I'm here, I promise—"

Another lightning strike hit the column I was huddled under. Valas grabbed my arm and flung me aside as bits of stone showered us along with balls of electricity.

I stayed on the ground, crouching and trying to make myself as small as possible, watching in awe as Valas stretched out his hand and summoned a swirling, icy mist around his fingers.

The mist built and stretched into a sword-like shape, its blade glistening in the light of the unsettled sky as he used it to knock away chips of stone and orbs of lightning alike. Every time electricity struck it, melting away part of its edge, he would simply repair it with more hastily summoned freezing mist.

The column remained standing even after the damage was done and the chips of stone stopped falling. The electric strikes became less frequent and farther away, as though something in the distance had drawn their attention.

Valas remained vigilant, sword still in hand, for several minutes after the last spark faded. Then he finally turned and continued his questioning. "Never mind the *why*," he said. "*How* did you get here?"

"I...I followed the Gatterlen lights down a path near the veil between our realms."

"Near the *what*?"

"A place where the barrier between our worlds is thin—the spot my kind have been trying to tear down in order to attack this realm. I tracked it down. I saw the damage being done, and I got desperate, and somehow I...I managed to cross over so I could warn you all."

He was quiet for nearly a full minute, his forehead creased in thought as he continued to watch the sky. Then something like understanding flashed in his violet eyes, followed by fear, and his gaze flew back to mine. "Wait...you passed directly through from the mortal realm into this one? Just like that?"

"Directly..." My thoughts reeled. I hadn't considered much

beyond the fact that I'd gotten here—that was all that mattered —but now that he said it out loud, it raised several questions.

"There were no waterways?" he pressed. "No paths? Just this veil you said they were trying to weaken...you walked directly through it into here?"

"Yes. Well, I *fell* directly." I swallowed hard. "None of you have managed to travel in such a way before, I'm guessing?"

"Not any of the times we've tried in the past. That's why we haven't been able to pinpoint the source of the damage that's being done ourselves. The realms don't run directly beside one another, normally."

I remembered Dravyn telling me they hadn't been able to find the source of the attack; I'd never understood why until now.

Valas shook his head in disbelief. "Besides that, you should have stepped into Eligas, not here. Its paths should have guided your mortal soul away from this realm."

"If I made it here so easily, then that means..."

"That they've essentially destroyed the protective layer between our worlds, making a direct route where there wasn't one before. So we have even less time before everything all goes to shit. Fantastic." He continued muttering curses to himself while I cautiously got to my feet and gazed out at the wasteland before us.

"What's happened to this place?" I asked. "And that lightning a moment ago...was that Halar?"

"Yes." Valas scanned our surroundings, as if making certain no one was watching us, before ushering me farther into the shadows of the tower and continuing his explanation. "The Death Marr's magic started failing completely two days ago, the entire ocean of it drying up because of some strange fog that started seeping in through the edges of the realm. The other courts caught wind of this, and one of the Miratar spirits who serves the Storm Marr was sent to investigate on his behalf. The investigation ended...badly."

"How badly?"

"The spirit is dead."

Horror gripped my throat, squeezing away my voice.

Valas waved a flustered hand. "Or maybe that's not even the right word? I don't know—because this sort of thing is unprecedented. But his body was found, completely drained and shriveled around the edges, and he sure as fuck isn't what I'd call *alive* anymore."

Shriveled at the edges.

Just like the stone I'd stabbed with the knife Cillian had first given me all those weeks ago.

"How did it happen?" I asked, hoarsely. "Was he exposed to the same fog that dried up the Death Marr's magic?"

"We can only assume. And since it happened here, in the territory Zachar was supposed to be keeping safe and under control, the God of Storms came demanding answers from our court—hence his stupid rampaging. The Marr have started wars over much less. And we're trying to *avoid* a full-blown war, so Mairu is with the God of Death back in her own territory, keeping him out of sight and under control so he doesn't antagonize anyone further. Dravyn and I have been doing our best to keep the Storm God from destroying a bunch of shit while he's pitching his tantrum."

The sky flashed wildly in the distance, and he grimaced before adding, "And it's going pretty fucking poorly, if you couldn't tell."

I frowned, thinking of how fast the encampment by the veil had been growing, of the weapons clasped between the soldiers there and the sinister trails of poisonous smoke spiraling into the grey, carving out paths ripe for destruction...

It was going poorly now, but it was about to get much worse.

"We need to get away from this place," I told Valas. "I think another attack is building in the mortal realm. A massive one. Whatever drained this ocean and killed the Storm Marr's servant...more of that poison could start flooding into this territory at any moment. It's not safe for you or anything divine to be here."

Valas was still watching the sky. His hand was absently twisting back and forth, tiny drops of snow trailing the movements, as though he was thinking of shaping another sword.

"You shouldn't be fighting each other," I snapped, "you should be fighting the growing threat on the other side of the barrier."

"No kidding," he muttered. "If you'd like to go inform the Storm Marr of that, be my guest. But I think you'll find he's not really in a listening mood."

"Then we need to *make* him listen before it's too late."

"As though we haven't tried."

"You haven't tried with the knowledge that I've just given you," I pointed out.

The God of Winter finally pulled his gaze back to me.

We stared at one another for a moment, the impossibility of the situation settling over us, frustrating us both into silence —until I caught sight of another wild flash of energy in the distant sky. Not the color of lightning this time, but bright and burning shades of orange and red.

The color of fire.

I realized then why the God of Storms was not tracking us down—because he was busy fighting with someone else.

"Dravyn is here too, isn't he?" I took a few dazed steps in the direction of the flashing sky, watching the streaks of orange and red fade.

Again, he felt so close, yet so impossibly far away.

Valas grabbed my arm and held me back. "Yes, he's here. But he's had a long few days, and his temper is worse than the God of Storm's. So I *really* don't think you want to step into the middle of that battle."

I pulled my arm out of his hold but didn't take another step.

The warring gods were too far away to see clearly, but the effects of their rampaging stirred the air even where we stood. The electricity made all the hairs on my body stand on end, while waves of heat occasionally washed over us, leaving me breathless.

I spotted a wave of gold in the nearby hills—a herd of the selakir, racing together in an oddly frantic yet synchronized manner, drawn toward the flashes of distant fire only to be driven away when lightning threatened, over and over again.

Valas started in the direction of the battle several times, but doubled back every time, clearly not wanting to leave me by myself.

A particularly violent collision of static and flame lit up the sky and shook the air.

Everything went eerily still afterward, and I couldn't help fearing the worst.

And I could no longer stand it; I wouldn't wait here, doing nothing, while this realm and its rulers collapsed into complete chaos—all while a quieter, more sinister threat was slipping in, waiting for the opportunity to destroy them.

"I need to talk to Dravyn," I told Valas, already turning in the direction of the circling herd of golden selakir. "Please.

Just go after Halar, distract him, try to explain to him what's really happening. I'll get to Dravyn myself. Maybe we can draw them apart and calm them both down long enough to listen and make a better plan besides destroying one another."

Valas looked doubtful.

"No matter what happens next, no matter the ending, I need to see him before that end," I said, quieter, pausing long enough to look back and meet his gaze. "I need a chance to explain myself."

Valas studied me for a few beats, then let out a long-suffering sigh. "Fine. Just don't die, please. I've grown fond of you, and grief is not a good look on me. I'm an ugly crier."

"I'll do my best to survive," I promised with a small, nervous smile. "If only for the sake of your good looks."

Our eyes met one final time before he backed away from me, letting the icy mists of his magic overtake him and shape his form into the familiar shape of a lean, powerful panther.

He bounded off in one direction.

I ran in the opposite.

With everything left in me, I raced across the dead, drained land, pounding up dust as I went. I knew I had no hope of catching a god on my own two feet, so I instead ran toward the selakir, eyes desperately searching through the restless herd in hopes of spotting a familiar, relatively tiny beast among them.

It took an exhaustingly long time before the group finally shifted directions and galloped closer to me, and I caught sight of the one I was looking for.

I whistled, shouted, called his name until I was too hoarse to call it anymore.

The herd raced on, trails of fire whipping out behind them. But one golden beast had stayed behind, listening closer, his ears twitching—and then his whole body was trembling and bursting into motion as he caught sight of me.

Zell.

I pushed my dead legs onward, meeting him at the bottom of a nearby hill. He shoved his head under my arm so enthusiastically it lifted me off my feet. I wrapped him up in a quick hug —one that was interrupted seconds later by a wave of heat washing over us.

I caught a glimpse of red lighting up the sky far in the distance.

Zell's head lifted toward it, and he gave a concerned snort.

Stroking the bridge of his nose, I asked, "You can feel your creator's magic, can't you? You could follow it?"

I didn't know if he could understand what I was asking of him, but he seemed eager to try and please, circling around me and lowering himself to make it easier for me to climb on.

I tightened the strap of the bag I carried before pulling myself up onto his back, weaving my fingers through his mane, and speaking a command, a whispered plea—

"Take me to Dravyn."

We shot up the hillside.

I had little experience riding bareback, and what I did have had been unpleasant. But Zell's gait was smoother than a normal horse's, and I was so grateful to be off my feet and moving so quickly through the bleak landscape that I didn't care about the discomfort I felt.

I simply held on, pressing nearly flat against his powerful back, encouraging him faster and faster until finally—

There.

I saw the God of Fire in the distance, standing on a hilltop in his human form, eyes glowing with the same fire as the marks on his skin.

Beyond him, drawing his gaze, were dark clouds dancing with electricity. I couldn't see the Storm Marr, but when his power lit up the sky I saw the God of Winter beneath it—a sleek white beast leaping and chasing the lightning, sending daggers of ice shooting upward with every twist of his slender body.

I slowed long enough to watch the battle unfolding, to see the God of Storms finally emerge from his clouds. Bolts of his magic came first, weaving into an outline of a winged beast with a long, jagged tail.

He dove at Valas.

The two of them became a tangled mass of shifting forms and energies, moving so violently and quickly I couldn't tell them apart.

After several heart-pounding moments, Valas emerged from the chaos, breathing a frigid mist over the God of Storms before turning and darting away.

Halar shook the icy glaze from his form and gave chase.

They disappeared into the distance—the God of Winter keeping his promise, drawing Halar away from me and Dravyn.

Dravyn's fiery marks flared brighter as he watched them leave, wings unfurling from his back as he prepared to join the fray himself.

I clung tighter to Zell and urged him faster, racing onward until I was close enough to be heard over the lingering, uneasy energies from the gods' battle.

"Wait!"

Dravyn spun around at the sound of my voice, a whirlwind of fire spinning with him.

The flames around him extinguished the instant our eyes met. I drew Zell to a stop, and everything else seemed to stop with him, save for a few lingering embers drifting and swirling slowly to the ground.

I leapt from the selakir's back and strode forward before I could lose my nerve.

The fire in Dravyn's eyes gave way to silver as I approached, but his expression remained fierce, a painful combination of anger and disbelief.

I nearly stopped at the sight of that anger, a flood of confusing emotions overtaking me. Maybe I needed to regroup, to rethink, to better plan what I could possibly say—

He grabbed my hand and pulled me the rest of the way to him.

I buried my head against his chest. He wrapped his arms around me, and for a moment—just a single, breathless moment—nothing was chaos, nothing was breaking, nothing was burning.

When I finally made myself lean away from him, his gaze caught on my wrist. He took it gently, studying each of the jagged claw marks.

He was still staring at the dried blood on my skin as he said, "You came back."

I swallowed hard, chasing away the distracting butterflies that swarmed through me at his touch. "Of course I did. You sent for me. I saw the Gatterlen lights."

"Lights?"

"The same ones you sent months ago, when you first called me into the divine realm."

He continued to study my bloodied arm, his brows furrowing in thought.

"You seem surprised?"

His gaze lifted to mine. "It's just...I didn't do it on purpose, like last time."

I opened my mouth to reply but couldn't find the words.

He hadn't done it on purpose?

What did that mean?

"You didn't feel me calling for you, then?"

"No—I did." He let go of my wrist as his eyes scanned the broken ground and sky all around us. "I felt you, even among this chaos. Something in my blood, in my bones, calling for my attention in spite of it all. And I couldn't get away from the God of Storms to answer right away, but I..." He trailed off, shaking his head at himself, as though he'd just realized something that he should have known all along.

I didn't know how to reply.

I'd heard little of what he said after those first words—*I felt you among the chaos.*

He turned back to me, cupping a hand against the side of my face. "I felt you reach for me," he said, "and it seems as though something inside of me couldn't help but reach back."

I placed my hand over his, pressing it more firmly against my cheek. He leaned his forehead into mine, and all the world outside of the two of us was reduced to nothing but blurs of meaningless sound and color.

"I didn't think I'd ever see you again." He whispered the words, his voice slightly unsteady. "After what happened, after what I said...I didn't think you would ever dare set foot here again."

"Wildfires can be unpredictable," I reminded him, my voice mirroring his hushed tone.

He smiled a bit at this, pushing his hand through the waves of my hair. He started to pull me into a kiss before catching himself, taking a step back and shaking his head. "It's not safe for you here."

"It's not safe for me anywhere. Send me away afterwards if

you like, I don't care, but I needed to see you again. I had to warn you, and to make things right between us because I...I..."

Somewhere in the rush of emotions and adrenaline tumbling through me, I lost the words I'd been trying to say.

Then his gaze took mine, and I remembered them just as quickly—they struck me like a blow to the back, knocking the breath from my lungs.

Because I'm falling in love with you.

That was why I had come back in spite of the danger, the questions, the confusion. Why I had jumped off that cliff, even though I hadn't been able to see the bottom.

But before I managed to tell him this, several things happened all at once.

A violent *crack* sounded through the air, Zell let out a high-pitched cry and bolted, and the air began to sizzle and spark.

Dravyn pulled me against his chest, wings of fire flaring out wide before folding protectively around us and burning away the shower of electricity raining down from above.

Another *crack* echoed around us.

Dravyn looked to the sky, calculating, his grip on me tightening. "Brace yourself," he said, drawing me closer, "and don't let go of me."

CHAPTER 51

WE RETURNED TO HIS PALACE IN A FLOURISH OF smoke and fire, and my knees promptly buckled and gave out. Dravyn caught me as I fell, cradling me in his arms as he frowned down at me.

"I'm okay," I mumbled.

"The energies around the Edgelands are more unsettled than ever," he said. "I'm sorry; I tried to smooth the passage through them as best I could."

"It would have been fine, if not for all the other, um, *rough* trips I've already taken lately."

His eyes fixed more fully on me, concern shining in their silver depths, but now didn't feel like the time to recount my harrowing escape from my old home.

"The battle in the Edgelands wasn't over," I reminded him. "Valas is still back there, and Moth too, I don't know where he went—"

"I'm going back for them," Dravyn said, setting me on my feet. "You're staying here for the moment." He lifted a palm toward the palace. A look of concentration briefly crossed his face, and two things happened in quick succession—first, the forgelight above us glowed to life, illuminating the grounds that had, until this point, been the darkest I'd ever seen them.

Then I saw a series of strange, fiery symbols flash in the air all around the palace. They were gone in the blink of an eye, but the air still teemed with new warmth and a threat of power—spells that would be triggered by anyone trying to trespass, I suspected.

Light and protection for me; but what about him?

"Inside," he said, nodding toward the nearest door. "And don't come out until I get back."

I didn't want to separate from him again so soon, but I couldn't argue that I'd be an asset on the battlefield he was returning to. I didn't want to slow down his return to it, either; I was worried about Valas and Moth.

He was gone again before I could speak, anyway.

I hurried inside. Walking into the familiar halls soothed the ache of our separation, somewhat—though not for very long.

With anxiety thrumming through my veins, I briefly returned to my room and found it completely untouched, the evidence of my hasty exit still scattered about.

I placed the bag I'd carried with me from the mortal realm on the chair in the corner, relieved to finally be in a place where I felt I could safely put it down. I took my sister's necklace off as well, placing it on its customary spot on the shelf; the last spell had worn off hours ago, and I didn't feel like I needed to hide in this realm anymore.

I started to head into the washroom to clean myself up, but I couldn't focus very long on anything I tried to do; I just wanted to keep moving. I felt as if the electricity from the Storm God's magic was still lingering in my skin, shocking me into motion every time I held still.

An hour passed.

Dravyn still hadn't returned.

My restless wandering brought me from one end of the palace to the other, and Rieta and I eventually stumbled into one another.

I expected a full scolding from her—assuming she even knew the half of what had happened before I fled the palace—but I only received a stern look, a painfully tight hug, and then one of her favorite questions: "When was the last time you ate?"

"I'm not hungry."

"I swear you've lost more weight off that scrawny frame of yours in just the few days we've been apart."

"I haven't," I insisted, knowing it didn't matter; she dragged me toward the small dining nook beside the kitchen regardless of my protests. I sat in the familiar, light-filled space while she continued to drop plate after plate of food in front of me.

I tried to appease her, but couldn't stomach much; I ate little, drank even less, and sank into a quiet, thoughtful pose while she flittered about.

How many times had I sat in this place, by this same window, staring at the garden on the other side? Now the blossoms I'd once tried to convince myself I hated...they were wilted, most of their petals lying on the ground.

"The flowers died," I said, surprise making me voice the thought aloud even though I was alone in the room.

Rieta was within earshot, however—carrying yet another bowl of some sort of food my way—and she answered me with a frown as she came closer. "He stopped tending them after you left, I suppose."

That was why they never wilted; I'd assumed magic was in

some way responsible for their creation, but I hadn't realized he'd been tending to them every day—and for me, apparently.

I got to my feet and went back to the door I'd first entered through, hoping he might have returned to the same spot as before.

There was still no sign of him.

I didn't leave the palace. I wanted to, but instead I only moved from window to window, watching through the glass until I finally saw the first sign of fire against the pale-yellow sky.

I rushed outside to greet him, reaching his side just as his eagle form touched down, stepping back as the flames around him flared, twisted, and fell back into his human shape.

As the flames extinguished, he blinked several times at the sight of me—as if he still couldn't quite believe I was actually back in his realm—before wrapping me in a quick embrace, his hands traveling along my body, testing the solidness of me.

I spotted Moth soaring down from the sky a moment later, looking rattled, but otherwise healthy.

There was no sign of the God of Winter.

"Where is Valas? What's happening at the Edgelands?"

"Valas went to check on Mairu," Dravyn replied, letting go of me and taking a step back. "The situation at the Edgelands appears to be stable for the moment; the attacks on the veil have slowed, and Valas managed to make Halar listen to a bit of reason—enough to get him to leave and go speak with his own court about the latest developments. Apparently, he was intrigued by the information you gave Valas."

I took the first deep, almost normal breath I'd taken in forever, glad to have done something right after so many disastrous decisions. "That's the reason I had to come back here— to deliver that information. Well, part of the reason..."

My voice trailed off just as it had back at the Edgelands, and I found my courage failing me again when I thought of telling him my true feelings.

Now isn't the time, anyway, I tried to reason with myself.

He eyed me curiously for a moment, then beckoned me to follow him into the palace. "We should sit down," he said, "and you need to tell me everything you know."

He led me to a small office on the second floor. I headed for the desk next to the window, drawn to it by the stacks of paper and drawing utensils collected on it. My hands were already reaching for these supplies as I sat down, preparing to map out the things I'd seen for him.

Meanwhile, Dravyn moved toward a mirrored cabinet in the corner, studying his reflection with a frown, then twisting to better examine his right side. His shirt was singed all along that side, and when he pulled the damaged fabric aside, it revealed a jagged shaped wound of seared, bloody skin.

I jumped immediately back to my feet. "You're injured."

"Barely." He smiled through a very obvious bite of pain. His gaze darted toward the doorway, where Rieta had just appeared. Her eyes were filled with unspoken questions; he simply nodded, and she seemed to understand what he needed.

She disappeared only to return a short time later with a bundle of healing supplies. I intercepted her as she made her way toward Dravyn, taking over the things she'd brought; after all the lies and trouble I'd put him through lately, the least I could do was help bandage his wounds.

I pointed him sternly toward a chair next to the bookshelf in the corner. He obeyed with a slightly amused grin, shrugging out of his shirt as he went.

I held in a gasp as I saw the full extent of his injury. The bloody burn traveled nearly the entire length of his side, branching out like lightning against his skin. It made me think of the cracks of energy branching out across the veil, too, and I suddenly felt lightheaded.

"So the gods are capable of bleeding after all," I mumbled, kneeling beside him and dabbing away some of the blood. It was darker than human blood. Thicker.

"At least in this form," he said. "There's a price to pay for holding on to your humanity, I suppose."

I bit my lip, trying not to lose my nerve. I used to hate thinking that the gods might be invincible; now I only wished it was true.

"It's not as bad as it looks." His eyes were closed, voice slightly faint, as he took my shaking hand and pressed it against his chest for a moment, steadying it.

I steeled myself with a deep breath and continued to work.

I should have been focusing solely on that work, but it would have been a lie to say parts of me weren't buzzing over the chance to touch him again. Just days ago, I'd been certain I would never see him again. But here he was, real and solid and warm beneath my fingertips.

And the thought of anything happening to this solid, real body filled me with a terror unlike anything I'd ever known. I just kept staring at the dark, burned edges of his wound and thinking of the dark, shriveled edges of the stone I'd stabbed weeks ago.

My hand pressed against a particularly rough patch of burned skin.

He sucked in a breath.

"I used to think gods weren't even capable of feeling pain," I said, trying to keep my voice light and even.

"It isn't the same sensation as when I was a human," he replied after a pause. "But...yes. It still hurts."

"A flaw in your Creator's design?"

"An intended feature, I've always thought." His eyes fluttered open, and he stared at the ceiling as he continued, "As long as we can at least vaguely remember what it feels like to be in pain, it makes us less likely to inflict pain upon mortals." He was quiet for a long time before he continued. "Pain is one thing, though. Death is another. And not a thing I believed our kind were subject to, unless it was at the hands of the upper-gods we serve...but apparently, I was mistaken."

"Yes," I said softly. "Valas told me about what happened to the Storm God's servant."

His brow furrowed. "The situation has certainly escalated."

All my mistakes flashed through my mind again, relentlessly loud and bright.

"I should apologize again," I blurted out. "More thoroughly. I feel like I caused so much of this. I know I should have told you what I knew sooner, but I was confused. Afraid. And I understand why you sent me away, but I just...I just hope we can..."

He shook his head. "That isn't the main reason I sent you away."

I froze with my hand hovering just above his injury. "It wasn't?"

His face tilted toward me. "It would have been somewhat hypocritical of me to banish you over the secrets you kept, given the ones I kept from you for so long."

"Then what was the real reason?"

"It was because I..." He closed his eyes again. Took a deep breath. "I panicked."

"...Panicked? You?"

He hesitated, his eyes clenching tighter, as if trying to squeeze away an unwanted image in his mind. "It's been a long time since I've let myself really...care about anyone. I've failed to protect too many in the past. I've been too late, too many times. So I thought it would be easier if I..." He trailed off with a sigh.

Suddenly I knew what memory he was trying to squeeze away—the same one he'd recounted for me that day he took me to his siblings' memorials.

How many times had he relived the memory of his sister dying in his arms?

At least as many times as I'd relived the memory of finding my sister's blood in her bed, I imagined.

"I tried not to care about you, either," he continued, "but it still happened. And when things started to unravel—when I wasn't sure I could protect you any longer—I thought it would be easier to send you away."

The already small room felt smaller, suddenly, the world down once more to only me and him, to my hands working gently over his wounds, to the confessions tumbling softly but steadily from his lips.

"But as soon as you left, I only felt worse," he said. "Because there is no place that's safe for you, as you said earlier."

"No. There isn't," I agreed, voice thick with emotion. "But I feel safest here. And I know I said I don't care if you send me away, but that isn't true, I..."

"Sending you away once nearly broke me," he said, shaking his head. "I don't think I could do it a second time."

"So you're stuck with me until the end, it seems."

"There are worse fates, I'm sure."

Blushing, I returned my attention to his wound, finishing the work of dressing it. But thoughts of *the end* continued to eat away at me.

"I still can't see that ending clearly," I said.

He sighed again. "Nor can I."

"What are we going to do? The barrier between realms may be stable and relatively calm now, but it won't last. I saw the attack building on the other side. And I've witnessed the full depth of Andrel's delusion and plans, now—though I still don't know just how many weapons and allies he truly has at his disposal. I'm afraid to think about it."

I rose to my feet, suddenly overcome with a violent disdain for myself and all the problems I'd caused.

"I feel so stupid for trusting him."

"You are not stupid."

"And yet it feels like the world is crashing down because of the decisions I've made. I've given your enemies exactly what they need to hurt you. I was too slow to realize you were not the one I should have been fighting against all this time, and now..."

"It hasn't all come crashing down," he replied, calmly. "Not yet."

"It's only a matter of time."

He didn't argue against this.

"Can't the Moraki intervene? Won't they?" I had never truly put my faith in a higher power for anything, but I was suddenly desperate for such a power to swoop in and fix all of this, somehow.

But Dravyn shook his head. "The three of them have been arguing about this matter since it began—that's the reason for the signs of unrest we've witnessed. They don't typically involve themselves in mortal realm matters, though. They created us Marr, and granted us dominion over that realm, so that we could deal with these things on their behalf."

"But this could undo the entire structure of multiple

realms," I said. "It seems like they should make an exception and do something about it."

He shrugged. "And perhaps they will before the end—but I wouldn't count on it."

I went back to the desk and started to scribble notes and sketches, trying and failing to think of more solutions. Dravyn and I talked for the next half hour about all the different battles closing in around us, and I told him the things I'd learned about my sister, the veil, the weapons—all of it.

We weren't drawing any closer to any answers, though, and I was growing frustrated when the sound of a familiar voice drifted in from outside.

Mairu.

I stepped out of the room and spotted her speaking with Rieta at the end of the hallway. She caught sight of me, sighed in relief, hurried my direction and wrapped me in a light hug. There were tears shining in her golden eyes when she pulled away, I thought, but she averted her gaze and blinked them away before I could get a closer look.

"I'm so glad you're safe," she said.

"I'm fine," I assured her.

"And Valas?" Dravyn inquired, coming up behind me. "Zachar?"

"They're fine as well," Mairu said, "if restless. The three of us have come to a conclusion, however—that the encroaching threat cannot be dealt with by our court alone. We need to involve the others. And we don't trust Halar to communicate things clearly to his company; he's in no state."

Dravyn considered this, frowning, before he slowly agreed. "We can hold council here and decide what to do—all of us. Karys can share the same information she's shared with me and

Valas. It caught the Storm God's attention; hopefully the others will listen, too, and we can form a plan of some sort."

I stiffened, panicking a bit at the ludicrous image of myself standing before a room full of gods, briefing them for battle. But I quickly recovered and forced a confident nod.

"We'll make them listen," I said, just as I had told Valas we would.

"I'll go myself to summon them," Mairu offered.

Dravyn's concerned frown only deepened at this, but she was already heading for the door.

"I'll be fine," she said, waving a dismissive hand.

While Dravyn stayed behind to speak with Rieta about preparing for the other Marr's arrivals, I walked with the Goddess of Control out of the palace, standing in the courtyard with my arms wrapped tightly around myself as she prepared herself to travel to the other Marr territories.

"Well, you've managed it," she told me with a wry grin.

"Managed what?"

"To burn so brightly the gods could not ignore you."

I returned her grin despite the pit in my stomach. "For better or worse," I said.

Her smile disappeared. She held my gaze as her eyes flashed to a brighter gold and her body began to stretch into its serpentine shape. "I'll be back soon," she promised. "And let's hope it's for the better."

CHAPTER 52

Dravyn was still speaking with Rieta when I wandered back inside. She was inspecting his wound closer, despite his protests, and looked unimpressed by the job I'd done tending to it.

"It's in the blood," she was saying as I approached. "It needs soaking—drawing out—or it's going to fester."

He sighed. "Draw a bath, then."

She bowed and then disappeared up the nearby steps, and Dravyn motioned me closer. "The Storm Marr's magic...did it touch you while you were at the Edgelands?"

"Not directly, no." I shivered as I remembered the tingling static that had filled the air. "But I've been feeling strange pulses of electricity over my skin, even since leaving those lands."

"It has a lingering effect, much like what you experienced with the Star Goddess's magic. It will wear off on its own in time, but there are remedies to speed up the process. Remedies that Rieta is well-versed in, so I trust her opinion; she has a cure for everything, and a dogged determination to focus on healing, regardless of any other problems we might be facing."

I couldn't help the quiet laugh that bubbled out of me.

He gave me a curious look.

"You're far too calm and focused yourself, given the circumstances," I explained. "Agreeing to a bath is the last thing I would have thought of right now—even a practical, healing one."

He smiled. "If it's any comfort to your logical mind, I've been in a blind, fiery rage for the majority of the time you've been gone. Does that fit more with the sort of god you believe I should be?"

I started to say yes, but my smile faded a bit as I truly considered the question. "Not quite," I said. "Not as well as it used to."

"As long as you're close, I find it easier to think," he explained. "And I believe I'd rather face what lies ahead of us with a calm, clear mind, so I'm glad you're back." He said it so easily—so confidently—as if he'd never had any doubt that the two of us would be together, facing this battle ahead of us side-by-side.

The words I'd almost said to him at the Edgelands raced through my mind once more. Quieter, now. But just as bold. I'd thought I could dismiss them as a flickering desire, nothing more than a craving for something that wouldn't last, but now it felt as if my heart was truly rearranging itself, making a permanent home for them.

"We don't have much time before we'll need to be ready for the council meeting," he said. "You should prepare yourself while you can. Anything you need, Rieta can help you with."

It hit me all at once at his suggestion—how exhausted I

was. I wanted to go up and collapse in my bed, to sleep for as long as I could get away with.

But I could only think of one thing I *needed* just then.

"I think I should stay close to you," I said, "if I help you think more clearly."

His smile turned a bit mischievous. "You won't hear any arguments from me about that plan," he said, taking me by the hand.

THE WASHROOM WAS WARM, just shy of sweltering, and smelled of cedar, soap, and spice. The lights were dim, and the only sound came from our tired steps and quiet breaths—a welcome reprieve from the noisy wars on the other side of the door.

While Dravyn wasted no time undressing and slipping into the tub, I hesitated by the sink, studying my reflection.

The last few days had not been kind to it. Dark circles surrounded my eyes, while the rest of my face was sickly pale, almost gaunt, making the burn scars along the side of it seem darker and more pronounced than usual.

Yet there was strength in this reflection, too, I couldn't help but notice. A new kind of spark brightening my tired eyes and holding my chin up. Something even more powerful than the hatred that had fueled me for so many years—it was the same something that had made me jump back into this world, I think.

As I pulled my tunic off, I noticed for the first time just how much blood I'd drawn from my wrist. I thought I'd washed away most of it in my room earlier, but there was more hiding beneath my long sleeves than I would have guessed.

I started to wash the rest of it away in the sink, not wanting to soil the bathwater with it. I could feel Dravyn watching me as I worked, his gaze like a soft, intimate touch.

"The blood on your arm…" he said after a moment. "Who did that to you?"

"I did it to myself," I said, quietly. "When I was trying to get your attention near the mortal-side veil."

I could only see part of his face in the mirror, but it was enough; he looked clearly horrified at the thought of being even indirectly responsible for any of the marks on my skin.

It occurred to me then that I'd never actually shown him my claws—though I was certain I'd mentioned them at least once during all our time spent together. And I wanted to distract him from whatever horrible thoughts were rushing through his head, so I turned to him and held up my hand, letting my nails extend, flexing the sharp black tips for him to see.

He stared at them for a long moment, a bemused little smile on his lips. "Unpredictable," he mused.

"Like a wildfire," I finished.

"A more fitting nickname than *Sparrow*, I'm beginning to think."

All the ghosts of my past lifted their heads and snarled at this declaration, insisting he was wrong—that I would always be a sparrow, small and stuck in my sister's shadow.

I quieted the rebellious voices and took a step forward—toward this new name—despite all of the doubts and fears trying to hold me back.

Then I managed another step.

Another, another, another, until I was slipping out of the

rest of my bloody clothes, shaking off the dust of the world I'd walked away from and taking Dravyn's hand, letting him help me into the tub.

I sank down into the water with him, and he turned me around and pulled me back against his chest. We fit perfectly together, and for a few minutes I managed to relax against him, to forget about all the jagged pieces outside of this room that *didn't* fit into the future I had started to want, no matter how I tried to force them.

Dravyn wrapped one arm around my waist, his hand resting just above my navel. With his other hand, he took a cloth and ran it along the curve of my neck, up and down my arm, gently washing away what remained of the blood and dirt.

After a few minutes of absently trailing warm water over my skin and through my hair, his hands stilled near my right shoulder blade, just below the spot where I'd hit the corner of the table during my fight with Andrel.

"This bruise on your back...you didn't do that to yourself." It wasn't a question this time.

I didn't tell him who had done it.

I didn't have to.

"I never should have sent you away," he said, quietly, pressing his face into my hair and breathing deeply.

"You did what you had to do. The situation was unstable... and the gods of this realm are capable of far worse things than bruises." I knew Andrel was too, but I didn't say it. I wasn't ready to talk about that right now.

Dravyn didn't force any more details out of me. He only reclined more fully against the back of the tub, a deep sigh rumbling through him. "Damn all the gods of this realm, and all the demons of the mortal realm, too...all of them."

One of his arms remained loosely wrapped around my

waist. The other draped over the edge of the tub, and as he muttered and cursed the impossible battles pressing in all around us, his fingers clenched so tightly against the copper rim I was surprised they didn't sink into the metal.

The water heated around us, stopping just short of being uncomfortable. His skin burned against mine, occasionally flaring hotter—evidence of a darker, barely suppressed fire simmering just beneath the surface of him.

Because the calmness I'd witnessed earlier had only been an act, of course, and mostly for my benefit.

I took his hand and guided it away from the edge, pressed it against my cheek instead.

His fingers unclenched as soon as they touched my skin—from heated steel to softness in an instant.

He relaxed a little more as I sank closer to him, and I couldn't help marveling at the way he could shift so quickly, the way the layers of him were constantly rearranging themselves around me.

I'd once told him I didn't need him to burn the world down for me, but in that moment, I had no doubt that he would have done it—that he would have set fire to anything I asked, but never let the flames touch me. And it was a strange thing, to feel so safe in the arms of someone capable of such destruction.

After a few minutes of huddling against him, absently trailing my fingers over the muscles of his arm, I asked, "Has the pain from your injury stopped?"

"Yes."

I couldn't tell if he was being honest or just trying to comfort me.

His chest shook with a quiet laugh, as if he sensed my skepticism. "Relax, *miran-achth*. I'm fine."

"We're done with secrets between us, right?" I asked.

"I'm done with them," he agreed.

"Then you have to tell me what that means." I tilted my face so I could see his, and he smiled at the insistence in my gaze.

He tucked a damp strand of hair behind my ear. His smile turned sly for an instant, and I thought he was going to come up with a way to dodge the question once more.

Then he said, "There isn't an easy, direct translation into any other language...because it's more like an idea. A feeling. We have a story in my old kingdom, that when the one you're meant to be with enters the world, they steal a part of your soul with their first breath.

"And you exist, missing that part, until they find you and breathe it back into you. *Miran-achth* refers to the breath—the part that is missing. You can survive without it. Plenty do. But to have the missing piece is to breathe easier, more deeply. The first time the term left my lips, I wasn't thinking of that story, really; I was only thinking of how relieved I was to have you back with me. How you had survived the trial, so I could inhale again."

Slowly, I sat up. I was hyper-aware of the steaming water sliding off my skin. Of all the places where his body still pressed to mine. Of each beat of my heart, and his, and each breath we both took. Even now, without even meaning to, all those beats and breaths felt perfectly in sync with one another.

Maybe they always had been, and I'd just been too stubborn to see it.

Suddenly those three words I'd been struggling to say since our reunion felt inadequate.

"Are you all right?" he asked, after my silence had stretched on for nearly a full minute.

I shifted so we were facing one another; I needed to see him. I couldn't speak, so I simply nodded before leaning up to kiss him.

It felt like the first time I'd ever done it—softly at first, my lips just barely brushing his, my breaths spilling warm and slow into his mouth, his chest rising and falling with deep, deliberate inhales.

His hands gripped my hips, steadying me. His knees rose up, further pinning me in place before he took my face in his hands and pulled me deeper into the kiss.

The tub quickly felt too small, too confining, for the way I needed to kiss him, to touch him, to press myself against him.

He shared the same thoughts, apparently, because after a moment he stood and stepped out of the water, carrying me with him. He wrapped a towel around himself and grabbed a second one for me.

He placed me on the polished countertop—warming the stone with a touch of his hand—and trailed the plush towel over my damp skin while his lips and tongue continued to tangle with mine, drying me until only a few droplets of the bath still clung to my body.

He tossed the towel aside and drank these last beads of water away himself, his warm mouth pressing in and his tongue licking at the curve of my shoulder, the valley between my breasts, along the edge of my hip.

Soon the only dampness that remained was what was pooling between my legs; he drank of that too before straightening, planting an arm on either side of me on the countertop and leaning in to brush another kiss to my lips.

"Thirsty, are we?" I teased as he pulled away.

He smirked. "It turns out spending days away from you has a dehydrating effect on me."

I wrapped my arms around his neck and dragged him down into another kiss. Slow, deep, lingering—I didn't want it to end. I didn't want to leave this moment, even though I knew we had no choice, and even though I couldn't stop myself from mumbling, "I don't think we have time for this."

"Not to drink you fully in the way I want to, no," he admitted, his hands sliding underneath my thighs. "But I still intend to savor you for as long as I can. Unless you have any objections?"

I swallowed hard, my fingers brushing through his hair, curving along the strong line of his jaw. "It would be cruel to leave you completely thirsty."

"Yes," he agreed, lips quirking. "It would."

The towel fell from his waist as he lifted me and carried me into his bedroom, laying me back on the bed, trailing kisses from my stomach up to my mouth as he climbed on top of me. He lingered at my mouth for a moment, his tongue fully exploring it, while his hips sank toward mine and pressed his hard length between my legs.

One of his knees settled on the inside of my leg and pressed it outward, opening me to take him in more fully. He eased into me bit by bit, sinking the tip of his shaft inside only to draw teasingly back for a moment before returning, pushing deeper.

My lips formed a soft *oh*, which he mirrored with his own mouth, as he pushed fully inside, filling me so completely I couldn't help but cry out.

It was different from any other intimate encounter we'd shared in the past.

He'd used the word *savor* a moment ago, and he made good on that promise now; it was a slow, rhythmic, exquisite kind of torture, what he was doing with his hips, the way every rise and fall of them felt like a deliberate attempt to drag out every ounce of my pleasure.

My hands clenched the blankets on either side of me and my back arched, and he stopped rolling his hips for a moment and simply stared at me, his fingertips trailing thoughtful paths across my lower stomach and along the insides of my thighs.

The curtains were drawn. The light outside was fading into evening, casting him in shadows and splashes of warm, amber-toned light that highlighted every powerful muscle and line of his body. His skin still glistened from the steam that had clung to it in the washroom. His eyes were their normal silver shade, but aglow in the lighting in a way that made me think of smoke, thick and hiding a building fire underneath.

I couldn't look away from him.

And I couldn't help feeling...less than glowing, compared to his perfection—still ragged and raked thin as I was from my battles over the past few days—but the feeling soon subsided; it was difficult to feel inadequate while he was looking at me with eyes shining with wonder and lips softly parted, as if he'd never seen anything more beautiful, nor ever would again.

He leaned forward, pushing even deeper into me as he did, and he kissed me in the same slightly awestruck way. Little tastes of my neck, my jaw, the scars across my cheek. Kisses meant to memorize my skin rather than devour it.

I knew what it felt like to be so struck by a sight you needed to map it out, and this was what he was doing—committing me to memory, while he continued to move inside me, to lay claim to this territory he was discovering inch by inch, touch by touch.

My hands roamed over his body as his lips traveled mine, trying to trace him just as thoroughly, even though I was beginning to think I'd never manage to fully map him out.

His kisses trailed off and he sat upright again, reaching for a pillow and sliding it under my back as he did, creating a better angle for his thrusting. He smoothed a hand over my hips and brought it to rest between my legs, his fingers trailing through the dampness, circling and rubbing my sensitive bud of nerve endings while he penetrated deeper.

He continued this until I was writhing underneath him, practically begging for release, before he brought his lips crashing down on mine, pinning me fully underneath the weight of his strong body.

There was nothing but heat and sweat between us, and the occasional brush of plush blankets and silk sheets as we twisted and tangled ourselves among them.

We eventually ended up in a similar position to what we'd had in the tub—me in his lap, his arms wrapped around me in a warm, powerful embrace.

He guided his hard shaft into me once more. I sank slowly down against him, drawing a deep, rumbling growl of appreciation. His hands dug into my sides, power and heat rippling through his grip, and I thought for a moment he might lose control—but just as before, he slowed, deliberately relishing me instead.

His hands roamed over my body as he rocked against it, cupping my breasts and pinching their centers to hardened peaks before sliding down and continuing to map the points of pleasure between my thighs with precise, reverent touches.

We had no time to spare, yet it felt like he had never moved so slowly, never explored me more thoroughly.

I was entirely mesmerized by this patience—by all the sensations I could focus on when he moved slowly like this. Every throb inside of me, every twitch of his muscles, every heated touch of his fingertips against my skin.

And then his whispered command against my ear: "Arch your back for me again, love."

He groaned softly as I did so, head tipping back for a moment before he brought his mouth to the curve between my neck and shoulder. It was the last bit of torture I could take—the feel of his mouth latching onto this sensitive spot, sucking and kissing as I pressed back against him.

I no longer wanted to go slow.

I guided his hand to the warmth between my legs and held it there while I rocked against him with increasing speed and pressure.

His lips curved into a smile against my skin, and in between kisses and nips at my neck he murmured, "Do you have any idea how beautiful you look right now, fucking me like that?"

My answer was lost in a gasp as the first convulsion overtook me. He gripped my hips and held me in place, taking over the quicker pace I'd started, driving into me with a wild, relentless fervor until I came with a cry so loud they'd likely heard it in the heavens above.

He followed soon after, wrapping his arms tightly around my body, placing his hands on my shoulders and pulling me more fully down onto him. As he spilled into me, he buried his face against my back, muffling the roar of pleasure that tore from his mouth. The vibrations from the sound shivered down my spine, sending tingles shooting down my legs, curling the tips of my toes.

We stayed in this position for several moments afterward, his arms falling into a loose hold around my waist while he trailed kisses across my shoulders and continued to throb inside me.

I was still exhausted, but it was a different kind of spent—warm and heavy rather than cold and ragged. When he finally moved away from me, I simply slumped down into that heaviness, content to collapse and fall asleep in that exact position. He chuckled a bit at my sudden limpness, but only pulled the covers up over me.

Rest, I thought I heard him say, somewhere in the waves of ecstasy I was still swimming in. He kissed my shoulder again, went to grab a towel, and cleaned us both up before crawling back into bed beside me.

He wrapped me in a cocoon of hard muscle and soft covers, silent save for his deep, steady breathing and the occasional mumble I may or may not have imagined brushing against my ear.

Rest, miran-achth.

So I did, trying to hang on to the moments of perfect calm and clarity that I'd felt when I'd shattered against him minutes ago.

I don't know how long we lay there. I only knew it wasn't long enough before I felt him stir and sit up, and I could sense the change in his demeanor almost instantly.

His gaze was narrowed on the window.

I closed my eyes, wishing I could fall asleep and wake up to find everything somehow settled and safe. But when I opened them again, Dravyn was still frowning at the window.

"The first of our company has arrived?" I guessed.

"I'm afraid so." He disappeared into the bathroom for a minute before returning, partially dressed. On his way back to me, he stopped by his dresser and took something from the top drawer—a neatly folded set of my clothes.

It was a small, silly thing, but it sent another pleasurable flood of warmth through my body as he handed them to me—this proof that he'd been expecting me to end up in his room again. Or just hoping for it, maybe.

I dressed in a daze, too many competing emotions swirling through my mind for me to possibly pick one to focus on.

As I braided my damp hair with quick, nervous hands, I tried to mirror Dravyn's stoic expression as best I could. I thought I'd pulled it off until he caught sight of me and frowned, his brows pinching together in concern.

"After this business is dealt with," he said, adjusting the sleeves of his shirt as he closed the space between us, "we'll come back here. We'll rest easier. Together." His fingers brushed my cheek with the last word.

Together.

I tried to picture it.

But the last few days had put too many violent images in my head, and now I couldn't shake them or the fear they brought with them.

He started to turn toward the door, and suddenly terror rose up over all the other emotions tangled inside me—a loud, restless fear that I might not have another chance to say what I needed to say to him.

I grabbed his arm and pulled him back.

Our eyes met. The same spark that had struck me the day we'd first found one another shot through me again, and a feeling of fire coursed through my veins soon after—a fire that burned away the fear and made me brave enough to speak, if only for a moment.

"A truth for a truth?" I suggested.

He smiled at the familiar words. "Okay."

I took a deep breath and whispered, "I love you."

He went very still in my grip.

I let go of him, clutching a fist to my pounding, exposed and vulnerable heart. "And you..."

He caught my hand, brought it up to his lips, and answered before I even had an instant to doubt it.

"Yes," he whispered back, brushing a kiss across my knuckles, his eyes never leaving mine. "And there is the missing piece."

CHAPTER 53

Dravyn held my hand as we walked down the stairs together, and he didn't let go of it even as we entered the room filled with ill-tempered divine beings all bracing themselves for battle.

Several haughty looks turned our direction—more than one narrowing on his large hand eclipsing mine—but still he held on to me. A light, barely-there grip. Unconscious, almost.

But it felt like a statement being made: We were descending into whatever hell awaited us together, and that was how we intended to finish things.

I kept my head up and took in the faces all around me, refusing to cower no matter how hard they glared.

I recognized most of the gods by this point, though not the Miratar spirits who accompanied some of them; these spirits rarely left their Marr's respective territories, I'd come to realize —but apparently this meeting had been deemed important enough that they'd come along. I hoped this was a sign that the other courts were taking the threat we faced seriously.

Aside from Valas and Mairu, the God of Storms was also

here, as were the Star and Sky Goddesses who belonged to Halar's same court—though the Sun Court goddesses only loomed in the background, stoic and beautiful against the wall, watching me closely through narrowed eyes but not speaking.

Of the Stone Court, the Ocean Marr, Kelas, had come alongside Armaros, the God of Healing. They greeted me with cordial, if unfriendly, nods. The servant spirit at Armaros's side also greeted me. Her willowy body, and her hair made of white feathers, looked vaguely familiar—like perhaps I'd dreamed of her when the Marr she served had been treating my broken arm.

I felt something like peace as I stared into her pale pink eyes, and it was a long time before I managed to pry my gaze away and look back to the small army of gods surrounding me.

There had been more of these gods staring me down the last time I'd descended into this room—almost all of the middle-gods and goddesses had come to see me fail the Star Goddess's trial, but fewer seemed interested in helping to win this battle I'd come to warn them about.

Zachar was not here, either; he'd gone to seek an audience with the upper-god their court served, according to Valas, though he didn't elaborate on the reasons why; we were interrupted by prying eyes before he could.

The rest of the missing Marr, I chose not to focus on. There was already more than enough power in this room to be intimidated by, anyway.

Determined not to give myself a chance to feel that intimidation, I did what I always did when I needed to focus and keep moving forward—I broke the task into pieces, individual patterns and parts that I could lay out relatively plainly for my audience.

Dravyn had made sure to have paper and drawing utensils

on hand for me to use. Without any fanfare, I took these and went to work mapping out the realms as I'd seen them; the veil and the mortal areas surrounding it, the paths I'd walked between all these places. I told the gods everything I could about the threat approaching their realm. My theories, my fears—even, to some extent—my own mistakes.

It filled me with a strange combination of power and vulnerability, to speak so extensively before these terrifying beings.

Restless magical energy filled the air as I spoke, followed soon by mutterings and mumblings and more than one of the Marr acting as if they planned to leave. But I was not interrupted during my explanations or sketching—likely because of the way all three of the present Shade Court members had gathered around me, glaring daggers at anyone who became too intrusive.

It was the loyalty I'd developed toward that court that kept my hands drawing and my words flowing, determined as I was to protect this realm for their sake, even if the other courts never accepted me.

"We clearly need to investigate more thoroughly," Dravyn said, conclusively, as I laid down my drawing materials and took a step away from the center of attention. "But with caution. Until we can determine exactly how damaged the protective layers between our realms are, we don't know what scale of attack they might try to launch."

"Why so much concern about being *cautious*?" Halar sneered. "For all their posturing and rebellious warmongering, the Velkyn are mere mortals now, their powers diminished far beyond what they once were. Why should we—their new gods —fear them, whatever their numbers?"

"They don't see you as their new gods, I assure you,"

Dravyn said in a deadpan tone. "Have you not been paying attention? They've managed to drain all of Zachar's magic with their poisons already. You've already lost one servant to that same poison; are you suggesting we sacrifice more in the name of putting on an arrogant display of power?"

Halar scowled, the air turning electric with his displeasure.

The goddesses of his court shifted from their place against the wall, the Goddess of Sky lifting her hand and giving a slight flex of her fingers. The air all around the God of Storms flashed full of turquoise-colored symbols for an instant, and the uncomfortable static in the air lessened.

I stared at the goddess, at her sharp, intelligent eyes that were the same bright color as the magic she'd just summoned. I was not familiar with her power, beyond knowing that the humans prayed to her for protection, shields against all manner of disasters and ailments...but whatever she'd done, it seemed to irk the Storm God yet calm his irritated power at the same time.

The room fell silent for several long, tension-filled moments.

"We could simply wipe them out with a mass-scale attack of our own," the God of the Ocean suggested. "Hard and fast, like a wave breaking over them and dragging them off their feet. If we flex the full extent of our power, then their numbers will matter little. It will be over too quickly for them to counter, regardless of whatever tricks they've devised."

There were quiet mumbles of agreement from nearly everyone aside from the Marr of the Shade Court.

"The sort of attack you're suggesting would be catastrophic to more than just our targeted enemies," Dravyn said.

The Storm Marr—unsurprisingly—disagreed with this

concern. "Of the ones present, you know best about how effective wiping out entire cities worth of elves at a time can be, don't you? I seem to recall a story or two about you slaughtering them without hesitation in the past."

Dravyn didn't respond to the baiting commentary, though his eyes did flash briefly to a dark, fiery shade of red as he turned them on Halar.

"How unfortunate that you've turned squeamish about dealing with our threats now," Halar continued. "Because if you and your court had not exhibited such leniency toward them in the past, then we likely wouldn't be in this situation in the first place."

I shuffled my weight from foot to foot. I was sure the *them* he'd mentioned referred, at least partly, to my sister.

Dravyn blinked away the blaze in his eyes and turned, ignoring the God of Storms and speaking directly to the Ocean Marr instead. "It might silence them for a while," he said, evenly, "but it will only make our rule more difficult in the long run."

Halar *hmphed* at this, but said no more.

I was beginning to fear for our chances of winning any reasonable help from these foolishly prideful assholes when the God of Healing cleared his throat and said, "The Moraki have already spoken on that matter, anyhow. If they wanted the elves entirely wiped out, they would have done it themselves. But that is not their wish, so it shouldn't be ours, either."

"Yes, because mass murder is not the way to gain the adoration of those in the mortal realm. Go figure," said Mairu.

"Not all of us care if the mortals worship us," the God of the Ocean drawled.

The Healing God regarded his court member with a stern

look. "But some of us *do* take our obligations to the mortal realm seriously."

The Storm Marr looked ready to respond to this.

I interjected before he could; I was tired of listening to his mouth. "We don't know how many have been secretly preparing to rise up against you, or how powerful their weapons may be. If you won't think of sparing mortals, then think of sparing *yourselves*. You might go in with the intention of proving your might, but you could be walking into a much greater threat than expected...your enemy is more clever than you give them credit for."

Halar sneered again at this—likely because of the last remark, calling my kind 'clever'—and I started to launch another, more furious argument, but Dravyn placed a hand on my arm.

"She's right," he said. "Again: We all saw what happened to your servant, Halar."

Halar grew silent at this reminder, averting his eyes. The Star and Sky Goddesses bowed their heads.

I recalled Dravyn telling me how the Miratar were more than servants to the Marr they ascended to serve, and so I tried to dredge up sympathy toward the Storm God despite my annoyance toward him; his bitterness was at least partially fueled by grief, maybe. Anger was an excellent mask for such things.

He seemed prepared to drop the matter, at least, walking the length of the room with his eyes on the ground, as if deep in thought, for several minutes while the rest of us debated and discussed the matter more calmly.

But then he lifted his head, narrowed his eyes in my direction, and said, "Has it occurred to any of you that she might be leading us into a trap? She may have spent months in our realm, but she's still one of *them*. And inflating the numbers and skewing the details to try and prevent us from launching a proper offensive sounds exactly like the sort of thing a filthy elf would try to pull."

I tried, in vain, to focus on coming up with a logical reply despite the roaring in my ears.

"I suggest you watch your mouth," Valas replied for me, in a voice as cold as the magic he wielded. "And remember whose territory you're currently standing in."

Halar took a step toward the God of Winter, his fingers flexing, throwing off little sparks.

Valas stood from his place at the table—where he'd passed most of the meeting reclining with an impassive, almost bored look on his face—and the pale blue marks on his skin glowed to life as the God of Storms took another step toward him.

The air warmed in the same instant, and Dravyn's fingers dug deeper into my arm—holding himself back rather than me this time.

"That's enough from all of you," Mairu snapped, stepping between the Storm and Winter Gods, interrupting the deathly stares they were giving one another, and then turning to fix a deathly stare of her own on Dravyn. "Might I remind you all that we are on the same side of this battle?"

"Yes," the Healing Marr agreed. "And something will have to be done sooner rather than later—so could we kindly settle down and *do* it? The matter is exhausting enough without you all trying to tear one another's throats out."

Dravyn's hand slipped from my arm, his fingers clenching into a fist rather than into my skin, but the air cooled and he managed, once again, to turn away from the provocative Storm God.

I did the same.

"These developments are likely too complex to deal with in a single, hastily-called meeting." This was a new voice—one that was evenly measured, thoughtful, and that echoed in an ethereal sort of way. It belonged to the Sky Goddess, who now stepped fully away from the shadows and into the center of the room, her bright eyes flashing between us all. "My magic can reinforce the edges of our land for a time, at least. Or perhaps some combination of my magic and another's...Whatever it takes, I think we need to buy ourselves more time to plan a permanent solution."

No one immediately objected to this idea.

"So we drive them away from the veil, for now, and we reinforce the places they've damaged however we can," Mairu said in her quiet but confident, powerful tone. Between listening to her and the Sky Goddess, I found myself feeling more calm and confident myself; perhaps reason would win out after all.

The room fell silent as we all considered the task before us. A minute or two passed, and not even the Storm Marr managed to find an argument against this plan. "Simple enough," he said. "If we travel to the edges and—"

The sudden sound of feet scuffling up the stairs drew our attention toward the door to the lower floor, where a strange creature had just appeared; it was small, its movements quick and anxious like a rabbit's, its body relatively human-like save for its gossamer wings and the silvery, ribbon-like appendages it possessed rather than hair.

The Goddess of Stars stepped from her place against the wall and spoke for the first time since her arrival, moving to greet this creature. "My messenger," she explained. "Whom I sent to the Edgelands before I came here."

The creature bowed low as Cepheid approached it. It gazed up at the Goddess of Stars, blinking huge, dark eyes at her. One of its ribbon appendages stretched forward, its end opening like a quickly blooming flower.

Cepheid placed her hand to this bloom. They were silent, but clearly communicating; I watched the goddess's face for clues about what was being said.

After a few seconds, her eyes widened a bit and she jerked her hand away from the creature as though she'd just touched it to an unexpectedly hot surface. Her breaths became labored while the silvery-white swirls on her dark skin moved restlessly.

"Out with it," growled the God of Storms.

She regained her usual composure and narrowed her gaze on him. "There are mortals in the Edgelands," she said. "More than my messenger could easily count. *Velkyn*." She breathed in deep, and the starry spirals on her skin stopped moving but flared brighter. "The barrier has been fully breached."

CHAPTER 54

A SHORT TIME LATER, I STOOD IN THE MIDDLE OF what had once been the ocean of the Death Marr's magic, flanked on either side by a host of middle-gods and goddesses.

None of the Miratar had joined us, but the Storm, Ocean, and Healing Marr stood to my left. The Fire, Ice, and Serpent Marr to my right. The Goddess of Sky was traveling the parameters of the Edgelands—and was soon joined by the God of Death—seeking the spots where breaks had occurred, preparing to use magic to reinforce those places, as planned.

We had beasts on our side, too. Zachar's veilhounds roamed nearby, the pack of them like a bloom of silver-dark fog rolling this way and that against the drained landscape, seeking out the souls who did not belong within it.

The Star Goddess had also sent beasts on her behalf, great wolf-like creatures with piercing yellow eyes. They were larger and more powerful than the hounds, their bodies wrapped in black fur that glowed silver when they moved in certain ways, as though the long strands of it were concealing patches of starlight.

Cepheid had no taste for battles herself, apparently, but assured us that these creatures—the *rinx*, she called them—possessed something of her gift of foresight, and would be useful in spotting any impending disasters on the battlefield.

Several of the selakir—including Zell—galloped nearby as well. My loyal friend occasionally left his herd and darted closer, making certain I saw him, as if to tell me he was ready and eager for me to call him to my side.

The air teemed with the collective power of all these Marr and their creations, and for a moment I feared nothing as I strode through the wasteland.

What weapon could my kind possibly conjure up to contend with the power surrounding me now?

If I'd had a moment to stop and think, I might have wondered at the absurdity of it all, too.

Months ago, I'd wanted nothing more than to march into battle with the gods and their divine monsters...but *against* them, not alongside them.

There was no time to wonder, however, so I simply kept walking, shaking off the lingering dizziness from our travel as I went.

The instantaneous travel between the palace and here had not been as rough as normal—perhaps because I'd had three members of the Shade Court steadying me through it.

I felt sturdier than I had in some time, actually, and I was determined to help lead the way into this battle despite several of the Marr muttering about it, claiming I would only be in the way of them and their power.

I had no divine power, it was true—but I reasoned that this also meant I wouldn't have the same weaknesses to the weapons being used.

Some quiet, desperate part of me also hoped that I might

catch the attention of some of my kind if I was here. That I might be able to make them question what they were doing if they saw me on the other side. Maybe they would start to see things in shades of grey rather than black and white, as I had started to.

And maybe then I could start to untangle these violent threads that had been choking the life from both our sides for far too long.

A fool's hope, but I held to it just the same.

Either way, this was my fight, and I would not be left behind.

I'd made certain to carry plenty of weapons with me. Hydrus hung in its customary place at my side. I'd tucked the small flask containing the water of Melithra into the inner pocket of my coat, as well. I still had no idea what sort of powers the water held, but I'd gotten used to its weight, and for some reason I felt calmer when I carried it close to me.

Beyond my own collected weapons, Valas had gifted me a dagger of his own, which sent ice crawling over a target with even the most shallow of cuts; he'd performed a friendly demonstration of its power for me, using the Storm Marr as his target. Halar had been less than amused.

Dravyn had given me a bracelet similar to the one he'd sent me home with weeks ago, which would whisk me back to the relative safety of his palace even if he wasn't close by to take me —though he warned me it would be an unpleasant solo trip, especially if I couldn't clearly picture my destination.

Mairu had offered me the gift of disguise, prepared to use her magic to make certain none of my old allies could find me in the crowd.

This last offer, I'd refused.

I was done with disguises. I wanted to look like myself when I met Andrel and whoever else on this battlefield.

We didn't have far to march from our landing point; the Star Goddess's messenger had communicated the location of the breach well enough.

Our targets hadn't wandered far from the barrier itself; we merely had to land close to it, find the spot where the veil had torn—a place marked by a rushing wall of chaotic energy—and then we followed the obvious signs of where they'd traveled.

The veilhounds led the way, their long noses lifted to the air as they tracked, and we followed them as planned...but I could have tracked our enemies easily enough on my own, I thought.

They seemed to *want* us to find them.

Which struck me as strange. Wrong. Recklessly blood-thirsty, even by Andrel's standards—they couldn't possibly believe they could win a direct battle against the gods, and on divine territory at that.

Could they?

Before I could voice these concerns out loud, the first glimpse of our targets came into view. Only a small group of them—but there were more ahead, I guessed, disappearing over a hill that prevented us from seeing their true number.

Regardless of how many there were, once we caught sight of them, there was no quieting the restless energy of the gods alongside me. None of them made any sort of obvious show of power—not yet—but the air began to teem with their collective, rising energies.

The rinx drew to a stop well behind us, but the veilhounds raced ahead, a chorus of low howls rising up as they sighted their prey.

The last line of the elves stopped on the hilltop and turned to face the approaching creatures.

One by one, most of our party stopped, too, watching the Death Marr's beasts closing in. A few of the middle-gods laughed, no doubt expecting they were about to witness a slaughter, and I felt strange and hollow to be standing among that laughter, unsure of whether or not I should be eagerly anticipating such a thing along with them.

I had chosen my side, and I would have walked hand-in-hand with the God of Fire toward whatever battle lay ahead. But my heart was still raw from the battles behind me, the line between ally and enemy still painfully blurry and confusing.

All I knew was that I did not particularly want to witness *either* side being slaughtered.

For better or worse, the elves on the hilltop did not meet such an end.

Instead, they moved—in almost synchronized, planned fashion—to nock arrows and lift bows, which they quickly drew and aimed at the approaching beasts.

Arrow after arrow landed in the pack of hounds, scattering most of them and sending them off yelping in all directions. The ones who didn't scatter in time—who were struck by the arrows—let out a terrible symphony of growls and barks and whines as the arrows struck and unleashed plumes of grey smoke upon impact.

They fell, one after the other, as the darkening cloud of noxious energy swelled around them—a cloud similar to the ones I'd witnessed when I first returned to this dried-up ocean...only thicker. These puffs of poison didn't linger, however; once they'd consumed their targets, they were gone, leaving the air clear enough for us to see the damage they'd done.

Even from a distance I could see the way the hounds bodies had shriveled and curled into themselves, the heap of them like a pile of crumpled, discarded paper.

My heart dropped into my stomach.

The laughter around me had stopped.

The energy of the Marr's rising anger and magic twisted in the air all around me, a tangible weight that settled heavily over my shoulders and made it hard to breathe.

For the first time since I'd stepped into this dead ocean, my legs began to shake with fear of what we were truly walking into.

Dravyn moved to my side, his hand brushing mine as he took in the sight before us.

The elves on the hilltop were holding the line they'd formed. They'd been joined by others who had doubled back from the other side of the hill, so that now no less than thirty soldiers were watching our approach. Most of them held weapons—bows and blades and bombs that swirled and glistened with the same wisps of smoky poison they'd used to slay the hounds.

"I'd hoped it wouldn't come to this," Dravyn said, not taking his eyes off the enemy ahead even as his fingers briefly intertwined with mine and gave them a light squeeze.

"I had the same foolish hope," I breathed.

The elves were clad in dark colors that blended in so well with the cracked ground it made it difficult to count their true numbers, even as we drew closer. They wore masks as well, and hooded cloaks—all the protection they could get against the divine airs around us.

The God of Storms snorted at this display of armor. "They can't even breathe the air in here for long without succumbing to its power, can they? We could simply trap them, somehow—

let them die a slow, withering death while we watch from a distance."

"I'm sure they've accounted for the air of this realm in some way," I said.

He grumbled something incoherent in response.

"Regardless, let's make quick work of them and be done with it," said the God of the Ocean, lifting a hand and starting toward the elven soldiers. With a glance back at me, at the blade that had started to violently shake against my side, he added, "Mind that sword, Elf. My magic will call to it and draw it straight from your hands if you don't keep it under control."

I narrowed my eyes at him, clenching the grip of Hydrus tighter and pressing its sheath closer to my body, determined to prove that my earning it had not been a mistake—and that my standing here at the edge of this battle was not a fluke, either.

Before anyone could object, the Ocean Marr was striding forward, moving his hands alongside him in a scooping motion as though collecting magic, swiping it out of the air.

It didn't come from the air, ultimately, but from the ground—several great cracks soon zigzagged across the path before him, opening up to allow dark water to surge up from somewhere far below. He continued to move his hands, and the waters moved with them as though he held the swells on ropes that he could twist and sway at his will.

I couldn't help but take a step back as the awesome display of power rose higher—high enough to loom over the top of our enemies.

Hydrus bounced and rattled so hard against my side it was likely bruising my skin, but I fought the urge to draw it out, gripping it tighter and bracing my stance.

The God of the Ocean lifted his hands and dropped them with a flourish. His body lit with dark blue slashes and symbols, his eyes glowed like the moon on a midnight sea, and the waves in his command crashed down with a thunderous sound, submerging the hill.

By this point the elven soldiers had disappeared behind that hill, but I doubted they could have run far enough or fast enough to avoid the deluge coming for them.

The last of the waves crashed down, briefly turning the near-side of the hill into a raging waterfall.

We waited, assuming the other side of the hill looked the same.

Everything was silent save for the rushing of water and the anxious braying of the veilhounds far in the distance.

Then came a shout, followed by an arrow piercing the sky above the hilltop.

It struck nothing, yet somehow it still burst, unleashing a cloud that sank over the dark waters and made them flash with pale energy for a moment before causing the rush to slow. Then evaporate. Absorbing the magic making up those waters, presumably the same way it had absorbed the sea of the Death Marr's dark magic.

The line of soldiers climbed to the top of the hill once more, their numbers just as great—if not greater—than before.

The God of the Ocean gave a furious shout and swept once more at the air, sending more fissures through the ground. More currents of water surged up, less controlled than before, and roared toward the hill like rapids suddenly released from a dam.

Another cloud of countering poison fell like a net over the waves, calming the magic driving them, rapidly turning them into little more than a trickle.

The Storm Marr ran forward to join the assault in the next breath, slinging currents of electricity into what remained of the summoned water. The streams conducted the lightning swiftly and violently, sending a rush of power hurtling toward the feet of the elves.

It thundered across the hillside, crackling and booming, knocking several of our foes to the ground and sending others darting wildly out of the magic's path. For a moment it seemed the combined powers of Storm and Sea would be enough to overwhelm them and their tricks.

Then a thin, dark mist rolled over the hillside like a slow-moving sandstorm, stretching as far to the left and right as I could see. The gods' attacks were drawn into it, swirling up in a vortex of sparking and splashing energies only to scatter and dissipate as soon as they were fully within the toxic mist.

An odd sensation pinched and pulled at my skin as I watched—almost like I was being drawn into the mist along with the magic. I took a few steps backward—mostly to test that I still had control over my body.

In the distance, the Ocean Marr took a step back as well. The God of Storms was not so easily deterred, however; he strode forward instead, the edges of him turning electric and beginning to shift into his monstrous beast form.

But before he could finish changing, an arrow soared through the blanketing mist and struck the ground directly in front of him. As it hit, another explosion of a dark, hazy substance engulfed the god—the largest one yet.

His outline was hazy beneath the smog, but I could tell he had fallen back into his human form and dropped to one knee. A cage of lightning flashed to life around him as he knelt there, scattering some of the cloud, but not all of it.

The Healing Marr rushed to aid his fellow court member, his body blurred by swirling feathers and golden light as his power surged around him. That light bled more furiously from him as he reached Halar...

...but it was quickly eclipsed by the same darkness that had brought the God of Storms to his knees. It seemed to fare even worse than the magics before it, the light flickering out almost instantaneously—as though the pure element of his Healing power was particularly vulnerable to whatever this darkness was that the elves had conjured.

More arrows rained down all around them.

More clouds of fog erupted.

The misty storm of poison continued to drift continuously over us, creating a haze that made it difficult to see, to hear, to think.

It was all deteriorating even faster than we'd feared. There was no chance to truly strategize and little time to spare before the situation spiraled beyond controlled.

Sensing this, the rest of us exploded into action.

Dravyn and Valas took to the sky and into clearer air, embers and frozen crystals falling behind them as they went. Moments later, a rain of Fire and Ice poured down upon the battlefield, carving an uneven path through the haze, being absorbed by it in some spots, overwhelming it in others.

Mairu wove in and out of the cleared spaces, advancing on the enemy line and using her magic to control weapons and bodies alike, causing knees to crumple and arrows to misfire.

I called Zell to my side and leapt onto his back, racing for a better vantage point—for the edges of the battlefield and higher ground—in search of weaknesses we could exploit.

I soon made my way to a hill adjacent to the one our enemies had fanned out upon. Below me, the haze of magic and fog was thicker than ever, but after a moment I began to pick out patterns and potentially useful things.

The plumes of debilitating smoke stirred up from the strikes of the arrows dissipated relatively quickly.

But the thinner, constantly drifting mist lingered, and it seemed to be coming from some source other than the arrows. It also appeared to be the harder of the two types to overwhelm with divine power. The gods and their magic were slowing the longer they moved through it; a few more minutes of dwelling in that ever-thickening mist and this battlefield would become nearly impossible to even stand within.

While I was trying to puzzle out the source of it, I spotted Mairu nearby. She beckoned me to her side.

"Look there," she told me, pointing to a hilltop almost directly across from where we stood. It was difficult to see through the muddled air, but I counted three elves running along the length of it, occasionally kneeling to tend to some sort of apparatuses on the ground. "They're setting off some sort of weapons, I think—that's where all the constant fog is coming from."

I focused on one of the elves, and quickly saw that she was right; after he'd tended to one of the devices on the ground—fed something into it, it looked like—the mist pouring out of it billowed bigger and thicker before drifting over the battlefield.

As this elf rose back to his feet, Mairu narrowed her gaze and pointed at him. He stumbled and slowed under the control of her magic. But I could tell she was struggling to manage even that, which—given the sort of power I'd seen her wield in the past—sent a fresh tremor of concern through me.

"Even their armor seems to be resistant to magic," she said, her words faint and frustrated. Her fingers clenched and unclenched as though she was trying to determine whether or not to waste her energy on another spell. "I would normally be able to control dozens of these bastards all at once," she growled.

The situation seemed worse the longer I stared at it. The weapons, the armor, the different, strategic toxins…

They truly had been preparing for a full-scale war.

What other tricks did they have planned?

And what if more and more soldiers simply kept piling in through more and more breaks in the veil? What if they flooded this whole realm with that toxic mist?

Running a soothing hand along Zell's neck, my focus turned to the individual fog-dispensing weapons. There were at least a dozen of them, but only three soldiers tending them. They appeared small—built for ease of carry rather than for durability, I suspected. They didn't expect the gods to be able to get close enough to destroy them.

But *I* could get close to them.

Zell seemed to be less affected by the poison they were spewing, too, so if we could be quick enough…

I made up my mind in the next instant.

"I'm going to destroy those devices and help clear the air." Mairu looked ready to argue against this plan, but I kept going before she could: "I'm not divine, so their smoke won't affect me the way it affects all of you," I said, walking Zell in a circle to help calm his restlessness. "When the air begins to clear, you can all attack, all at once, with as much power as you can summon—overwhelm and overload their protections, their weapons, faster than they can absorb them or counter your attack."

I'd inwardly recoiled when the Ocean Marr had suggested such a show of force back at Dravyn's palace, but now it seemed the lesser of evils.

Mairu hesitantly agreed to my plan, and I galloped away without another wasted second.

The line of devices I was targeting stretched all the way across the hilltop. We paced at a safe distance until the soldiers tending them were all closer to the opposite end of the line. Then I urged Zell forward, running him straight at the first device.

I didn't withdraw any of my own weapons, afraid the fog being spewed would ruin their magic and potentially render them useless. Instead, I relied on physical force to destroy the devices, guiding Zell so that his fiery hooves stomped on the entire apparatus itself. We moved cautiously over the first one, making certain this strategy didn't cause an explosion or any other kind of blowback.

But the devices proved as fragile as I'd hoped, crushing relatively easily under Zell's weight.

The poisonous smoke nullified the divine fires his hooves set in the grass all around it—but not quickly enough to protect the body of the weapon itself. The flames melted and further destroyed the casing, and the mist spitting out of it came slower and slower before stopping altogether.

We managed five more destructive stomps without interruption.

But the seventh device we came to had just been reloaded; the fog pouring from it rushed out fast and thick, blinding me to everything around it—so I didn't see the elven soldier charging toward us until it was too late.

CHAPTER 55

THE SOLDIER BURST FROM THE MIST, HIS DARK armor blending so perfectly with it that I only caught sight of him by his bright blue eyes and the pale strip of skin around those eyes.

Zell reared wildly. I lost my hold on his mane and was forced to jump from his back, hitting the ground hard, twisting awkwardly to avoid falling on Hydrus.

The dagger Valas had given me was in my hand a moment later.

The elven soldier dove for me, and I didn't—couldn't—hesitate.

I plunged the blade into the only unarmored place I could see—that strip around his eyes.

Instantly, every inch of his visible skin froze. I heard the unsettling sound of cold magic spreading, crackling its way under the protective clothing he wore. The armor did indeed seem to resist the magic, as Mairu had said, creating a strange sight as the fabric rippled with the growth of ice only to fall back into place as that ice vanished.

But—like the devices I'd been destroying—the armor didn't resist it fast enough. The air filled with the nauseating scent of frost bitten and cracking flesh, followed soon after by oozing blood. The soldier squirmed and cried out in agony, tearing at his clothes, trying and failing to rake the ice away before it could damage him beyond repair.

He quickly exhausted himself. The scent of his destroyed flesh became overwhelming as he dropped to his knees and then crumpled the rest of the way to the ground.

I dropped as well, bracing a hand against the ground and trying to find balance. I needed to keep moving, but I couldn't take my gaze from him right away.

His skin was a horrible shade of reddish purple, his face swollen in a way that made his eyes look like they might bulge out of his head. His lips—also swollen, and covered in a trickle of blood—were moving. He didn't manage to push out any sound beyond a choking gasp, but I could read the word forming on those lips easily enough.

Traitor.

I got to my feet and stumbled back, whistling faintly for Zell.

I couldn't linger.

I couldn't think.

I had to finish what I'd set out to do.

We destroyed five more of the devices—what looked to be the majority of them—before two more soldiers tried to attack us. I kept Zell calmer this time, and I managed to stay upright and guide him out of harm's way.

The air was already beginning to clear, so the job was close enough to finished, I decided; we veered from the destroyed devices and raced away from the soldiers and everything else, not stopping until we were on the hill I'd originally stood on with Mairu.

Back at a relatively safe vantage point, I twisted Zell around and took in the scene unfolding before me with wide eyes.

My gaze was drawn first to fire, to the sight of Dravyn wrapped in ribbons of smoke and flame and moving across the field directly below me. The God of Storms was directly behind him, summoning violent gusts of wind that whipped away what remained of the toxic fog. Dravyn's magic burned brighter and bolder as the air continued to clear, and it was soon flanked on either side by more magic as the other Marr converged toward him.

It was a terrifying, awe-inspiring sight to see them all come together, all the different shades of their powers attacking at once, as planned.

Zell, sensing this gathering power, turned and bolted for safer ground. I didn't try to stop him. We ran hard, without ceasing, and I didn't look behind me for several minutes. My heart hurt, thinking of the destruction at my back—of what had already happened, what was happening now. Of another line drawn between myself and my old life, and the word on that elven soldier's lips...

Traitor.

I briefly considered just letting Zell keep running all the way back to Dravyn's palace.

But eventually, I pulled him to a stop and did an about-face.

The center of the battle was likely half a mile away by this point. I couldn't make out any real details, yet I was still overcome by a deep sense of awe and horror as the sky flashed, pulsing with different colors and energies, and the ground rattled even where I stood.

When it all finally began to settle, and I galloped back to the battlefield, I saw at least three dozen dead elves strewn across the ground. The ones who could still move were retreating, heading in the direction of the torn spot of the veil we'd first arrived at.

The God of Storms summoned another violent vortex of wind—one that crackled with sparks of electricity, this time—and pointed it in the direction of the retreating group.

I averted my eyes, bracing myself for the sight of more bodies littering the ground—but the God of Healing stepped in before Halar could launch his attack.

"Let them flee," he said. "It's over."

Dravyn agreed, stepping into Halar's path as well. "We should follow at a distance and make sure they're heading for the veil. They likely won't survive the journey back in their current state, and the ones who do won't be in any condition to inspire anyone to try and follow up their foolish attack, hopefully...let them crawl back as a warning to others."

Halar grumbled at the idea of leaving any survivors, but he was quickly overruled. Begrudgingly, he settled his magic and set off calmly in the direction of the retreating soldiers. The God of the Ocean followed, and then the God of Healing—the latter likely to make sure the first two adhered to the plan.

As they left, I slipped down from Zell's back and led him away from the worst of the carnage, keeping his body between me and the sight of the dead bodies, burying my face against his golden flank whenever the view became too much.

Dravyn soon followed us. "Karys...are you all right?"

I didn't want to lie and tell him *yes*, but I also didn't want to tell him how that elf's dead eyes and swollen skin were now seared into my mind. And the word on his lips...

Traitor.

I gave a noncommittal shrug and turned to rub Zell down, mumbling reassurances to him, promising him plenty of dried fruit as soon as we made it back to the palace.

And we *would* make it back. We were safe. We'd driven the intruders out, and it was over—at least for now. We had an opportunity to breathe and reassess...

But it didn't seem like a victory, for some reason.

And not only because of my torn, unsettled feelings about fighting against my own kind. I was starting to feel the same sort of anxiety I'd felt right before the battle had begun...like something wasn't adding up.

"This was too easy," I said as the other members of Dravyn's court joined us.

Dravyn and Mairu both gave me a curious, concerned look, but Valas only grinned.

"You underestimated our incredible power and abilities, didn't you?" the God of Winter asked, slinging an arm around my shoulders. "I've only begun to show you the extent of what I'm capable of, my little elvish friend."

I tried and failed to mirror his victorious good-humor.

I let him chatter on about the different facets of his power he planned to show me soon. But my uneasy feeling persisted, tightening the knots in my stomach and deepening my concerned frown until even he stopped trying to make light of the situation.

"I don't think this was an entirely planned attack, or at least not *all* of it," I said, ducking out of his embrace. "Andrel would not have missed this opportunity to be a part of it, if so —he would have been leading the charge. But I haven't seen him, nor any of the other leaders I expected to see."

Dravyn's jaw had clenched tight at the mere mention of Andrel's name. "Perhaps he made the wise decision not to show his face here, given the promise I made him the last time we saw one another."

My muscles tensed as I recalled their collision in the mortal realm. I had not forgotten the threats he'd made that night, and I doubted Andrel had, either.

But I *also* doubted any threat would be enough to keep Andrel from storming the gates of this realm as soon as the defenses were compromised.

So where was he?

"Something just doesn't feel right." I couldn't explain it beyond that.

Zell snorted, nudging me with his nose. I climbed onto his back once more, letting him carry me away from the others. I didn't have any real destination in mind; I simply let him lead while I kept my senses honed, searching for something—anything—to explain the feeling of impending doom that had burrowed into my gut.

It didn't take long before I spotted something strange: a flash of bluish-green energy lighting up the distant sky.

I drew Zell to a stop, watching closer.

We were soon overtaken by the rinx, who until this point had stayed far on the outskirts of our battle. They loped slowly in front of us, the silver streaks among their dark fur making them look like shooting stars beckoning me to follow them. Their movements were completely silent, and they stopped a short distance ahead of me and sat in a single horizontal line, still as statues.

All of them were facing the exact same direction—toward the strangely colored flash of energy I'd just seen.

Mairu caught up to me while I was still staring at them. "Something disastrous is soon to happen to the north, apparently?" She sounded skeptical of the beasts' disaster-sensing abilities. But before she could question them further, another flash of cerulean-colored energy caused her to gasp.

The rinx remained perfectly still.

Another flash, and the unease that rippled through me nearly sent me toppling from Zell's back.

Valas reached us, his gaze trained in the same direction as ours, all traces of humor gone from his expression.

"What lies to the north of here?" I asked.

We were silent for several breaths, all of us anxious and lost in thought.

Then, very quietly, Valas said, "They wouldn't dare."

I scanned our surroundings with fresh panic, searching for familiar things, way markers, trying to remember if I'd walked this way when I'd crashed through the veil earlier.

Slowly, I realized I had.

And I knew the answer to my own question—I knew what lay to the north. *A target.*

The attack we'd fended off had been nothing more than a diversion.

Another group of our enemies must have slipped in while we were distracted. One with stronger weapons aiming for the spot where they could do the most long-term damage to this realm—the spot where gods were made and their magic was shaped.

"Their real target was the Tower of Ascension," I whispered.

CHAPTER 56

It had been my idea, too, once upon a time— that I could put an end to the Marr if I could destroy the tower they originated from.

Maybe I'd even been the one to put it into the minds of my once allies.

Dravyn was at my side in the next instant. Knowing he could travel faster than Zell, I leapt from the Selakir's back and took Dravyn's hand. He wrapped his arm around my waist, I braced myself for movement, and it happened as quickly as that —in a flash of wind and fire we crossed through the Edgelands, landing on the stone pavilion that surrounded the base of the Tower of Ascension.

I'd prepared myself for another battle, for countless weapons to be aimed our way as soon as we touched down.

But what greeted us was...nothing.

The tower was still standing. No one seemed to be attacking it—though the air was filled with the foul, familiar-by-now stench of anti-divine magic.

Mairu and Valas appeared at our side an instant later.

"That's anticlimactic," said Valas, frowning as he scanned the eerily silent and empty pavilion.

"It still feels like something's wrong," I insisted, already moving toward the tower for a closer look. I doubted our attackers could have gotten inside—I personally knew what an ordeal that was—but the area around the tower was full of nooks and crannies, places where enemies could be hiding. Potential weak points.

At first, I found nothing.

But as I rounded a corner and came to the eastern face of the tower, I saw the first bodies.

My eyes were immediately drawn to the Goddess of Sky, who lay upon a marble inset in the pavilion. Her body was perfectly still, curled up at an odd angle, large patches of her ivory skin turned to a poisoned, festering black. The shiny marble she lay upon was splattered with blood.

That explained the turquoise flashes of energy—it had been her magic.

But what exactly had happened here?

There were several dead veilhounds scattered around the space as well, their bodies shriveled, their silver coats matted with still more blood.

Even more elves lay dead in between them, their bodies ripped by teeth and claws rather than destroyed or drained by magic; whatever divine protection their armor had granted them, it clearly hadn't stopped the veilhounds completely.

I rushed to the fallen goddess's side. Mairu was right behind me, while Dravyn and Valas searched the surrounding areas for any signs of our enemies.

Mairu knelt, placing a hand over the Sky Goddess's chest, feeling for signs of life.

I tried, desperately, to steady the rise and fall of my own breaths. "Is she...?"

The Serpent Goddess shook her head. "I'm not sure. I still sense her power, but it's very faint. And getting fainter."

"Will the reinforcements her magic made along the veil fade along with her?" I wondered, voice growing quiet at the thought. Was that why we'd seen the desperate flashes of her magic? Had she been trying to protect this tower—and now those protections had shattered along with her?

Mairu had no answers, either, but her expression reflected the deep, aching terror building in my own heart.

"The area is strangely clear," Dravyn said as he and Valas returned to us. His breath caught as he looked upon the fallen goddess again. Averting his gaze, he said, "We need to tell the others what's happened."

Valas agreed, and he disappeared in a flash of ice and snowy powder to see to the task.

I wrapped my arms around myself and stood, turning my back to the fallen goddess, unable to look at her any longer.

"It's still here," I thought aloud, looking the tower up and down, trying to make sense of it. "I thought for sure it would be under siege..."

What were we missing?

While Dravyn waited for Valas to return—preparing to help him calm the God of Storms, who was likely to fly into an entirely new kind of rage at the sight of his fallen court member —Mairu and I continued to search the area for clues.

I made my way to the opposite face of the tower, where a staircase wound its way up to a narrow landing jutting out over the pavilion—a potentially useful lookout point. I climbed as high as I could despite my fear of heights. Kneeling and clutching the edge of the landing tightly, I peered out over the desolate landscape below me.

And there, far in the distance, I saw what appeared to be a line of soldiers rapidly retreating.

Mairu joined me a few moments later, squinting and trying to follow my gaze. "Do you see something?"

"They're running away," I said, pointing.

"Running from what?" she wondered. "Us?"

We watched them for a moment, until a chilling explanation struck me, making my grip on the metal landing go numb. "Not from us."

Mairu gave me a curious look.

"They've likely planted something in the tower." I descended the steps even faster than I'd climbed them, ignoring the burning in my lungs and legs as I went. "A bomb of some sort," I further explained to Mairu, breathlessly, as we reached level ground again. "Something with a delayed fuse so they could escape before it ignited."

She still looked somewhat confused—such weapons were not exactly common—but I knew Andrel and the sort of tactics he used. I had helped him perfect those tactics over the years, after all, and it was the bombing of the temple in Cauldra that had set my life on the unexpected path I was now walking.

"We need to spread out and search," I ordered. "Tell the others. Hurry!"

Mai hesitated only a moment longer before nodding and bolting away.

I started looking, even though I didn't know exactly what I was looking for. I also didn't know what we would do with any bombing device if we found it—how we could defuse it, or how we could prevent it from doing catastrophic damage. I didn't know how much time we had before it went off, either.

I just kept searching, my mind flooded with flashes of all the foolish things I'd done to lead to this moment.

I'd told them about this place. About *all* the Towers of Creation. And maybe the divine things they'd collected from me had even been used to help construct their ultimate weapon. I'm sure my sister had contributed to their knowledge and materials, too—but I had been the one to finish things off, the last push they needed before they made the decision to attack.

So Savna and I had worked together to bring down the gods, just as we'd always wanted to.

Except, even when I'd been trying to follow in her footsteps, I don't think I'd ever pictured it like this—so many dead bodies, a bomb hidden in the dark while we ran away...

Was this really what she'd believed in?

Such violence and cowardice?

Tears stung my eyes, but I angrily wiped them away. I didn't need tears. I needed to think.

It had always been Cillian who focused on this sort of thing during our missions, but I had picked up at least some of his skills over the years. He would look for low spots, load-bearing spots, central spots...

I kept moving, kept searching.

In the distance, I heard the arrival of the other Marr. The *whoosh* of their magic carrying them in. The confused chatter. The horrifying roar of the Storm God as he saw what had happened to the Sky Goddess.

The sky filled with lightning. The air tingled with static—then with sweltering heat, as if Dravyn's magic was rising as well. Were they fighting one another again?

Desperation and fear pumped my legs even harder than before.

There was an answer here somewhere, a way to stop all the impending chaos and destruction.

I just had to find it.

Back and forth I went until finally I rounded a corner and flew down a small, narrow staircase to what appeared to be the lowest exposed point of the tower...and suddenly there it was, tucked against the bottom of the dark wall, nearly lost among the shadows.

It was larger than the hang-fire bombs Cillian had used in the Cauldra temple mission, but similar in its cylindrical shape, with strange markings on its face and a ring of gold in its center, circling around what appeared to be a button that had been pressed and locked into place.

I called out to the others, alerting them to my find before rushing down to inspect it closer.

Larger than the previous bombs I'd seen, maybe—but still relatively small and unassuming. A soft whirring sound hissed from the device, making it seem like it was alive, breathing, ready to go off at any moment.

We needed to move quickly; there was no time for another debate like the one we'd had in Dravyn's palace. Here was the target, and someone needed to do something about it before it ignited—simple as that.

I decided *I* would be that someone as long as no one else was here to do it, and I knelt, cautiously reaching to pick it up.

"Don't touch it," said a familiar, chillingly calm voice.

CHAPTER 57

I STOOD AND SPUN AROUND TO FIND ANDREL standing at the top of the steps, a bow in his hands.

"You're still here." I tried not to let my voice shake. Tried not to look at the tip of the arrow as he nocked it. Drew it back. "I...I thought you would have fled with the rest of them."

"Someone had to make sure our weapon went undisturbed until it had a chance to properly ignite."

"...And if you can't escape the fallout it causes? You're willing to die for the destruction?"

"If my dying is what it takes to start the fall of the Marr, then so be it. I'll consider the legacy of my house honored. Something that doesn't matter to you, I've noticed, so I don't expect you to understand."

The weapon made a terrible noise—a more violent hiss than before, followed by a *tick tick ticking* that seemed to grow faster as my heartbeats did.

I could barely breathe, but somehow I kept forcing words out. "This is madness."

Madness that was going to kill us both and do untold

damage to the structure at my back. And beyond destroying the tower itself, I couldn't imagine what sort of devastating, ruinous energy would be released when said tower came tumbling down.

My gaze darted about, searching for ways to neutralize the damage, for some path I could use to escape with the bomb.

But even if I could be quick enough to avoid his arrow, he was blocking the only exit to the little nook I'd found myself in. A placement that was by design, I suspected. He'd probably been watching from nearby, waiting and hoping to trap me along with his weapon.

"Don't do this, Andrel. Please." I didn't know what else to do but plead at this point. "It doesn't have to be this way. Tell me how to stop this bomb from going off."

"You can't. The fuse is already lit within it." His lips curved cold and cruel on his handsome face as he added, "And unlike the weak fire inside of you, this one won't be so easily put out."

I heard the sound of footsteps drawing closer.

Andrel readjusted the bow and arrow, fixing his aim more accurately onto my throat. "Shall I kill you now, so your dead body is the last thing your beloved gods see before the tower falls?"

The ticking grew even louder. Even faster.

"Or maybe I'll let you live, so they can hear your screams when it happens."

I didn't have to count the *ticks*, to listen for patterns among its noise; the mad gleam in Andrel's eyes told me I was out of time. He'd won. I couldn't stop this explosion from happening.

Tick, tick, ticktickticktick—

I snatched up the ticking, vibrating weapon and clutched it against my chest. Looked down at it. At the flame mark glowing on my skin, the scars I'd clawed into that same skin, the bracelet tied around my wrist...

An idea struck me.

My hand closed around that bracelet Dravyn had given me in the next breath, and I braced myself for traveling.

I didn't picture his palace as he'd told me to do.

Instead, I pictured the space between worlds, a specific spot in Eligas with rocky ground and a bright blue sky, where every sound and threat had been neutralized—the first place Dravyn had ever brought me to on the day he'd rescued me from the burning platform in Cauldra. He'd whisked me away from the chaos, and I'd been safe, able to breathe, able to decide what to do next.

I just had to believe this gift he'd given me could take me there again.

I clung to the bomb and the bracelet, and I silently pleaded for the magic to work.

Within seconds, fire and wind roared to life around me. The flames grew taller, folding over me, blocking most of my surroundings from view. What I could see in the narrow strips between the flaming threads was changing, the darkness around the tower brightening into entirely new scenery.

It was working.

I was so caught up in trying to *keep* the magic working that I didn't see Andrel diving toward me until he was already through the flames.

I didn't have time to gasp before he slammed into me, knocking me back against the tower. The flames kept going. Burning him. His armor protected much of him, but his hands and face were exposed, and the nauseating scent of seared flesh filled my nostrils.

He had been willing to bury himself in the rubble of his

planned destruction, and he seemed to think nothing of burning for his cause, either.

I bent, curling protectively around the weapon and the bracelet I held, and I didn't stop picturing Eligas.

The transportation spell kept going.

The flames roared faster and thicker and the wind did not stop swirling, even as Andrel's arms locked tightly around my waist and he pulled me off my feet.

As my feet slipped out from under me, I fell—and I *kept* falling.

He fell with me.

We passed through the realms together, tumbling and twisting between shades of light and darkness.

We didn't end up in the peaceful stretch of barren land I'd been aiming for. Andrel's attack had thrown me off course, and so instead we ended up lost in one of the strange rivers that crisscrossed the emptiness.

I ripped free of him and maneuvered as best I could in the murky water, cursing silently at him for dragging me into it.

But this was a better outcome anyway, I soon realized.

The bomb slipped from my hands, and I just barely caught it—but not before noticing that it had started to sink much, much faster than me.

So I simply...let go of it.

The key to my revenge, to the destruction I'd once wished for more than anything...I let it go, and it slipped through my fingers as easily as the water I was treading through. I watched it disappear into the depths, sinking like a stone while I fell slower than ever—almost buoyant, suddenly, the loss of its weight making me feel lighter in every sense of the word.

Floating off to my right, Andrel watched it sinking, too.

He started to dive after it.

I caught him by the sleeve and held tightly to him, pinning his arms behind his back, wrestling him as best I could in the strange water we were suspended within.

Finally, after the bomb had been well out of sight for several seconds, he stopped fighting and simply glared at me.

Then, somewhere far, far below us, the weapon ignited.

The light from the explosion was just a flicker at first, but rapidly grew and grew until it engulfed everything in a blinding glow, forcing me to clench my eyes shut. The waters churned to life around us, the current shifting this way and that, the magic within trying to orient itself in the wake of the debilitating power that had rushed through it.

A sudden pressure grabbed at my arms and legs and started to jerk me downward.

Then I was spinning, as if being pulled into a drain.

Everything was spinning violently out of control, but somehow Andrel's hand caught my wrist. His fingers dug in painfully hard, and we were pulled deeper into the depths together until suddenly we were not falling through water, but air, careening downward so quickly I couldn't breathe.

There was no sound. No light. Only the horrible sensation of falling away from everything into absolute emptiness.

We eventually hit water once more.

Breathtakingly cold, thick water.

Another river. One that led out of this realm, I prayed—one not damaged by the weapon I'd dropped, that could carry us somewhere, anywhere except into more emptiness.

Whether because of the magical bracelet I still wore, or by some stroke of luck, the water soon answered my prayers. The churning began again, spinning and pulling me along, and then the river expelled me like a living beast spitting out spoiled food.

I struck a rocky shoreline with violent force, my leg crumpling underneath me as I hit, bending at a sharp angle that no leg should ever be bent into.

Groaning, I rolled over and slowly tried to stagger back to my feet. No use—my crushed leg protested even the tiniest bit of weight I tried to put on it. I slumped and fell onto my back, throwing an arm over my eyes to protect them from the glaring sunlight.

I had no idea where I was. But judging by that sun—and the lighter feel of the air, and the countless familiar scents within it—I seemed to have crash landed somewhere in the mortal realm.

I heard the sound of someone else scrambling over mud and rocks, and I realized with a jolt of terror that Andrel had landed on the same shore as me, no less than twenty feet away. He had fared better than I had, too, and was already up on his feet and staggering toward me.

"Do you realize what you've *done*?" His voice was just above a whisper, yet it seemed to echo and rattle through me, like a horrible thud in the middle of a silent, pitch-dark night.

I sat up, shoving down a gasp of pain, trying to arrange myself into a formidable stance so he wouldn't realize the extent of my injury. "Ruined your plans," I growled. "That's what."

He stopped a few feet away from me, looking down at me. His body had gone as still as a beast crouching and waiting for the precise moment to pounce. Even his breathing seemed to have stopped.

I reached again for the bracelet Dravyn had given me, intending to disappear once more. I was dazed, overwhelmed, aching—but I could picture his face. Even through the pain and the fear, I could still find my way home to him. I'd done it before. I could do it again.

Wind swirled to life around me, flickers of fire appearing within it.

Just as before, Andrel dove through the building flames and tackled me.

But this time, the spell had not yet taken hold, because he *did* manage to stop it. The flames extinguished, turning to mere wisps of smoke, and my thoughts of escaping this realm turned to more immediate thoughts of escaping *him*.

I kicked free of his hold, swallowing down a scream of pain as I extended my injured leg. I dragged myself away, rising and balancing on only one foot and hobbling away as fast as I could.

But I knew I couldn't outrun him.

I would have to fight, somehow.

I'd lost Hydrus somewhere in the tumbling through realms, but the dagger Valas had given me was still against my back.

Before I could pull it out, Andrel tackled me again, tangling himself up and falling with me down the rocky shoreline.

I wriggled free again and rolled away, rising to a kneeled position, propped up on my one good leg. My claws were faster to unsheathe than any blade, so I unleashed them and braced myself. As Andrel dove for me, I drew back to strike, aiming for his throat.

I caught a flash of metal in his hand—a knife.

He swung forward too quickly for me to avoid it.

It sank into my chest, his wild strength surging after the tip was in, pushing it deeper and deeper, swiping it back and forth as it went all the way into my heart.

Our eyes met as the first flare of pain hit me. I made a sound—not a gasp, not a scream, but some horrifying cross between the two—before tumbling backward, my vision flickering.

Andrel caught me as I fell, cradling my body for a moment before laying me gently back against the pebbly ground.

I couldn't breathe.

I couldn't speak.

I couldn't move.

I was vaguely aware of the rocks jabbing into my back. Of the sunlight glaring into my eyes. Of Andrel kneeling beside me.

"I'm so sorry..." he said, smoothing sweat-soaked hair away from my face, "...that you chose the wrong side." He jerked the knife from my body, causing another white-hot flash of pain and a brief fountain of blood.

The sunlight above me seemed to dim.

I tried for a deep breath but ended up choking, coughing hard, the force of each exhale squeezing my blood out even faster.

My vision blacked out for a moment. When it returned, Andrel was still there, the knife twisting back and forth in his hands. "Your sister will be so disappointed when I tell her what's become of you," he said.

The meaning behind his words was lost somewhere beyond the agonizing pain and the disassociation I felt—like a cliff's edge just beyond the reach of my outstretched hand. I tried to hook my claws into it, but in the end my fingertips couldn't catch anything, and I fell once more into blackness.

When I managed to blink back into awareness one last time, he was gone.

I was alone, sprawled out, blood streaming over my chest.

My hand fumbled over my wound. I was feeling for the full extent of the damage, expecting my soft, foolish heart to be fully exposed and falling right out of my chest.

Instead, I found steel.

The metal flask containing the water of Melithra was still tucked into my coat's inner pocket, just below the spot I'd been stabbed. I took it out with a shaking hand and unscrewed its lid. I had no sensation left in my fingers, but I felt the lid falling, heard it hit the ground, *ting ting ting* against the rocks as it bounced away.

As the sound of it faded, so did all others.

I could think of almost nothing beyond my pain, but the Tower Keeper's words came back to me in a rush, somehow still perfectly clear in the silence.

Its waters have the power to completely transform you with merely a sip.

I gritted my teeth against the pain, the hopelessness. I had *already* transformed my heart and my mind, yet I had still met my end in a rush of blood and fury and vengeance, just as I'd always expected I would. Nothing had changed.

The sun seemed very far away.

I closed my eyes, letting it go—prepared to let *everything* go.

But then I somehow found the strength to lift the water to my lips, and I drank.

CHAPTER 58

THE SUN AND ITS WARMTH LEFT ME COMPLETELY, and the darkness that followed persisted for what felt like a lifetime.

I was certain I was dead. That my punishment for my mistakes, for all the destruction I'd caused, was an eternity of this void I'd landed in.

But then, little by little, I became aware of sounds—the trickle of water. The whisper of breaths. The flutter of wings.

Then came scents. Stone, and mud, and something bitter-sweet that I couldn't place.

I felt my hand move. As before, it was reflexively searching, feeling for the gaping wound on my chest. I no longer felt blood—dried or otherwise—on my clothing or skin. But the evidence of Andrel's knife stretched across my heart in the form of a large scar.

"Yes, it's still there," said a quiet but powerful male voice.

My fingers reached next for the burn scars on my face.

"So are they."

I wasn't certain I was dead any longer.

"You will find that this tower and its waters do not erase the marks of the mortal life you lived," said the voice. "And for good reason."

I startled further into awareness at the mention of a *tower*.

"Though the bone in your leg has been healed," said the powerful voice. "Belegor's doing."

"Consider it a gift," said a new voice, low and strong and somewhat indifferent compared to the first. "So that you might stand to properly face the end of your final trial."

The end?

I wasn't aware I'd even started a trial. Unless...

Curiosity finally gave me the strength to open my eyes.

I was lying on a floor composed of stone and glowing crystal, next to a familiar pool of turquoise water—the same water I'd drank from while dying on the shores of the mortal realm.

And just as when I'd first entered this chamber, days ago, a figure stood on the other side of the pool.

He was not the one who had greeted me last time, but I thought I'd seen him once before, through the window of Dravyn's palace. His figure had been eclipsed by shadows that night, but his dark hair and darker, feathered wings were familiar, as was the sword at his hip.

Malaphar.

The God of the Shade.

As soon as he realized I was looking at him, his smile curved in an intrigued sort of way, and he began to change. His hair turned silver, his pale blue eyes became glowing white orbs with unsettling black centers...and he still looked familiar.

The Tower Keeper.

They were the same being.

He was not alone, either. There were two other ethereal creatures standing on either side of him.

A female stood to his left—a goddess—with dark skin swirled through with golden patterns. Ivory wings fluttered at her back. Her eyes and hair both shone like still more gold, and her entire body shimmered as if holding in a powerful source of light, as though a piece of the very sun somehow dwelled within her chest.

She was Solatis, the goddess associated with the gift of life. She must have been.

On Malaphar's right was the one who I assumed had healed my leg, and spoken in that low, strong voice a moment ago—Belegor. The one who had given form to the worlds. His rugged, muscular appearance suggested exactly the sort of being capable of shaping entire realms with his bare hands. But despite his obvious strength, he was the most human-looking of the three, with no wings nor strange glow about him— though there was something in the crease of his brow and the depths of his dark eyes that suggested an ancientness beyond mortal comprehension.

Slowly, it dawned on me that I was still on the ground, sprawled out before the most powerful beings in existence in a rather undignified manner. I wondered if I should stand, or bow, or even grovel—but I only found the strength to make it into a kneeling position.

They spoke as if I wasn't right in front of them, either way.

Belegor cast an indifferent glance toward the God of the Shade, and with a yawn he asked, "You truly think her worthy of ascension?"

"I gifted her the water of this pool," said Malaphar, dipping his hand into the pool in question and letting its waters drip through his long, elegant fingers. Fingers that had claws like mine, I couldn't help but notice. "And I fully expected her to hand them over to the war-hungry beasts among her kind. But though she took them to the mortal realm, she ultimately brought them back. Protected them. Drank of them."

The Sun Goddess frowned at him. "A risky bit of betting you were doing, potentially putting that water in the hands of the corrupted Fallen. Don't you think?"

He smirked at this.

Chaosbringer, my kind often called him, and I suddenly understood why.

"Nevertheless," he said, "this is the trial I devised for her, and she has passed it. And then some. Not only did she protect the waters of this tower, she protected the tower itself. Make an argument against *that* if you care to. I'm waiting to hear it."

The goddess rolled her eyes at the clever smile he fixed on her.

I slowly fought my way to my feet. The combined power rolling off them was effortless yet overwhelming, making me want to sink right back to the ground. But somehow, I stayed upright.

The God of Stone appraised me for a moment, then looked once more to Malaphar and said, "And the one she intended to ascend on behalf of, the God of Fire and Forging..."

"Has offered up an unprecedented amount of his power to her for the transition."

My heart clenched at the mention of Dravyn.

"Her kind were cast out of such power for a reason," the Goddess of the Sun reminded the other two. "We take a great risk, allowing *any* of it to transfer to her—much less such a large amount."

"Yes, but with what he offers, she will be as much a goddess as an elf—and perhaps her two halves might help make the worlds she has walked between more whole," said the God of the Shade. "Consider the poetry of it, my dear Solatis. There is more beneath the surface of all these beings than we give them credit for."

The Goddess of the Sun sighed. "You and your foolish poetry."

He smiled that clever smile again, and she responded in a language beyond my comprehension—one that all three of them were soon speaking in, presumably arguing even more furiously over my fate.

I still did not know what that fate might look like, but there were a few things I needed to know regardless of what happened to me.

"The God of Fire you mentioned..." I began, loudly, the sound of my sudden voice startling them into silence. "Is he safe? And the middle-heavens outside of this tower? What became of them? Are they okay?"

They all turned to look at me. I met the eyes of the Goddess of the Sun, first, and found I couldn't look away from her.

Her fiercely powerful gaze softened a bit the longer we stared at one another, until finally she said, "The God of Fire waits at the tower's exit. We pulled him into the tower along with you, as we had need of his magic for what potentially comes next."

"And yes," said the God of Stone. "Nerithyl stands untouched. Damage has occurred in Eligas, but the magic of that realm withstood the weapons of your kind better than the middle-heavens could have. It can be repaired easily enough."

"What cannot be repaired so easily is you," said the God of the Shade. "You were dying on the shore of the mortal lake known as Irithyl. I had my servant—you know him as Zachar, I believe—stall your soul's passing long enough to transport it here. But that death is imminent, and cannot be reversed unless we were to break the very laws we created. You cannot go back to what you were."

He seemed to be questioning me—testing me—with the last sentence, but I didn't have to think hard about my response.

Not anymore.

"I don't want to go back to what I was," I said.

The upper-god nodded, pale eyes shining as though he understood the very depths of all my painful thoughts and questions that had led to this decision.

"The other option is to allow your soul to ascend to its final resting place," Solatis said. "For your service to the divine, we would, of course, offer you a place in the most brilliant of mortal afterlives."

It was tempting, if only for a moment, to think of an eternity spent in peace and paradise without any more worrying about the wars between my kind and the gods.

But there would be one very obvious thing missing from that eternal paradise.

And I still had questions to answer, besides.

Things I needed to fix.

"I want to stay," I said, quietly but firmly. "There's more I'm meant to do, I think."

The God of the Shade looked pleased. "Then so be it," he said.

The other two looked more solemn than him, but they didn't object to my decision.

Quietly, they took a step back as Malaphar stepped toward me, and we all watched the God of the Shade lift his clawed hand and summon a small, dark orb. It floated above his outstretched palm for a moment, threads of shadowy energy pulling toward it from out of thin air.

The threads circled it for a minute before slowly shifting to a reddish-gold shade.

"Inhale," said the upper-god, "and breathe in this power that I offer you now."

I stared at the fiery-colored energy. My thoughts raced for an instant of panic, realizing what I was about to do...but in the end it was as easy as breathing, the decision to step forward and do as the god had commanded.

A deep breath in, and suddenly I no longer ached, or feared, or doubted.

Everything was bright and warm. I was brightness and warmth myself—and then there were flames peeling from my skin, forming rippling, beautiful ribbons that wrapped around my body. I felt a moment of pure peace as they cocooned me, as I thought of all the times the God of Fire had wrapped his arms around me in a similar way.

Whatever happened now, I didn't care, so long as I could face it with him at my side. He had started to heal parts of me that I didn't even realize were broken, and now I would return to him, and together we could forge something new.

The fires around me became so intense I had to shut my eyes. I could still see the glow of them from behind my eyelids, and I drifted in the warmth and the muted brightness for several minutes, soaking it all in.

When I opened my eyes again, the Moraki were gone.

My body trembled with so much power that it took me a moment to remember to breathe, and then several more moments after that to remember how any other part of my body worked. My senses were as newly powerful as the rest of me, and I was so overwhelmed by the sudden onslaught of details that I couldn't pick out any individual sights or sounds or smells at first.

After several deep breaths and lots of effort, I finally managed it, and I started to sort my surroundings into something I could make sense of.

I was standing on the first floor of the Tower of Ascension —a place I remembered as dark, even to my elvish vision—but now it appeared to be cast in the brightest daylight, all the ancient symbols upon its obsidian walls alight. I could have spent hours studying and taking notes on those symbols, had my eyes not been drawn to the figure standing by the front door.

Dravyn.

A soft gasp fell from my lips.

He turned to face me, and I saw him as I never had before. He was in his familiar, mortal-like form, yet all the edges of him seemed to glow. I felt as though my elven eyes had not been capable of seeing him for what he truly was—a being that was somehow even more breathtakingly beautiful than I remembered.

I managed a few steps toward him before I slowed, overwhelmed and in disbelief over what was happening.

He closed the rest of the distance between us with long, confident strides, reaching for my hand as he approached. I took it, and as our palms touched, a warmth unlike anything I'd ever felt flared in the depths of my very soul.

A warmth that felt like home.

"Hello, Wildfire," he said with a smile.

THANK you so much for reading this first half of Karys and Dravyn's story! The second part of the duology will be coming in Spring 2024—be sure to follow me on Amazon or elsewhere for updates.

Instagram: @authorsmgaither

Tiktok: @authorsmgaither

You can also join my reader group on Facebook here: https://www.facebook.com/groups/852408648935331

And/or sign-up for my mailing list using this link: https://shorturl.at/eFQY6

Last but not least, if you enjoyed this story, please consider taking a moment to leave a quick rating or review. Thank you!